LIFE BOAT

A NOVEL

LUKE ECKLEY

All Rights Reserved

Life Boat © 2023 by Anatolian Press

This is a work of fiction. Names, characters, businesses, places, events, locales, and incidents are either the product of the author's imagination or used fictitiously. Any resemblance to actual persons, living or dead, or actual events is purely coincidental. No part of this book may be reproduced or used in any manner without the written permission of the copyright owner except for the use of quotations in a book review. For more information, email micah@anatolianpressllc.com

Cover design and art by Sadie Butterworth-Jones

Cover redesign by Miblart

Editing by A. Vogel and Andrea Couture

First paperback edition May 2023

Paperback ISBN: 978-1-959396-13-0

eBook ISBN: 978-1-959396-15-4

Hardcover ISBN: 978-1-959396-14-7

Please visit us at

www.anatolianpressllc.com

Dedication

    This book was written with the three most important females in my life at the forefront of my thoughts. Listed in the order in which I met them, I dedicate Life Boat to my mother, my wife, and my daughter. Karen, Valerie, and Brooke, thank you so much for the encouragement, love, and inspiration you've given me every day of my existence. Your presence in my life motivates me to be a better son, husband, and father. In essence, a better man.

when death is the water
and love is the raft,
grief is the oar
let it move you through.
- Alix Klingenberg

Chapters

Dedication iv

Chapter 1 – Illuminated (Day 282) 1

Chapter 2 - Light Extinguished (Day 1) 4

Chapter 3 – Wrecked 8

Chapter 4 – End Of The Song.. 14

Chapter 5 – Impactful 20

Chapter 6 – ITS 29

Chapter 7 - Shrink Rap (Day 118) 33

Chapter 8 – Memory Lane... 40

Chapter 9 – *Career Day* 46

Chapter 10 – Company 51

Chapter 11 – Not Good Company 60

Chapter 12 – Bad Company 64

Chapter 13 – Prescription for Peace 72

Chapter 14 - Shark Night 76

Chapter 15 – Shark Day 87

Chapter 16 – Shark & Shark... 105

Chapter 17 – Mood Sweetener 111

Chapter 18 – Flow of Life 117

Chapter 19 – *Luce Plan*.. 126

Chapter 20 – Feer Not 135

Chapter 21 – Biggest Feer 144

Chapter 22 – July 4th 150

Chapter 23 – Independence Day 153

Chapter 24 – Good Company 161

Chapter 25 – Follow Up 173

Chapter 26 – Thad's Hope 177

Chapter 27 – Negotiation 180

Chapter 28 - "Research" 186

Chapter 29 – Feedback 192

Chapter 30 – Renegotiated 197

Chapter 31 – Less Than Transparent 201

Chapter 32 – Deal Seal 203

Chapter 33 – Loose Ends 208

Chapter 34 – Tying Ends 211

Chapter 35 – Insurance Policy 217

Chapter 36 – Lucie 220

Chapter 37 – Minor Detail 224

Chapter 38 – Lifeboat 229

Chapter 39 – Ends Tied 233

Chapter 40 – Shrunk 237

Chapter 41 – Lyrics 241

Chapter 42 – Group Session 244

Chapter 43 – Apprehension 249

Chapter 44 – Separation 254

Chapter 45 – Connection 258

Chapter 46 – Say Cheers 264

Chapter 47 – Lifeboat? 270

Chapter 48 – Come Sail Away 276

Chapter 49 - Sesame Noodles 281

Chapter 50 – All In The Legs (Day 282) 285

Chapter 51 – Water 294

Chapter 52 – Weather Report 299

Chapter 53 – No Mas 306

Chapter 54 – Shooting Star 310

Chapter 55 – The Past and the Passed 316

Chapter 56 – Lifeboat 325

Chapter 58 - Wake Up Call 330

Chapter 59 - Storm of the Eye 336

Chapter 60 –Air 343

Chapter 61 – Warmer Air 348

Chapter 62 – Aired Out 351

Chapter 63 - Carcharodon Carcharias 362

Chapter 64 - Horror Movie 366

Chapter 65 - The Jaws of Death 372

Chapter 66 - Solace 378

Epilogue (Day 851) 382

Acknowledgments i

Luke Eckley

Chapter 1 – Illuminated (Day 282)

It was undeniably beautiful. The bluish-green neon glow passed below at five knots, as the catamaran cut through the otherwise black ocean. Even in his sickened and depressed state of mind, Cort was able to appreciate the phenomenon of the bioluminescent algae. The tiny particles flashing an alien-like light as the surface water was parted by the smooth fiberglass hull. Even now, engulfed in a misery catalyzed by the rolling waves, the ocean fascinated him. Fighting the nausea, he pulled up a memory of the waters off of Cabo San Lucas, with Celeste standing in it waist deep and framed by the brilliant turquoise bay. Cort knew that if she could only be here now, she'd appreciate the light show below him as much as he did.

The churning in his gut paused, long enough to form a series of thoughts. He wondered about the chemistry of the algae. The miniscule plant-life, masked in darkness, floating invisible through its existence, until some random event interfered unexpectedly. That disturbance releasing an energy and transforming it to a brightly lit beacon. Cort desperately wanted the chemistry of the human brain to work similarly. This unlikely course of action that he and Lucie had concocted was supposed to lighten their darkened lives - act as a resurrection and replace the bleak existence and lack of purpose they'd felt for the best part of the past nine months. It was the theory that brought him to where he lay now, but presently that theory was in serious jeopardy.

The thought only lasted seconds - his stomach demanded attention again. A dry heave, then another, followed by the scarce contents of his stomach being pushed up the esophagus and hurled out through his mouth and nose. Despite the nagging anxiety caused by his condition, Cort reassured himself.

Stay calm, you'll be fine.

The malaise had ignited a small flame of fear in the bowels of his mind, a fear that the seasickness would threaten their plan. It wasn't time to panic yet, but the muted alarm tucked down deep in his brain was increasing in volume with each passing hour. Spitting bile and thick saliva, he wiped his mouth with the damp paper towel and clung tight to the stainless-steel rail post with his other hand. The remains of the mucus felt cool on the rim of his nostril. It didn't disgust him - he was simply relieved that it was out. Maybe now, with his stomach emptied, the intense nausea would subside.

"You okay?"

Cort turned to the now familiar voice coming from behind him and reached for the fresh paper towel being extended.

"Yeah, I'm fantastic," a sarcastic smirk formed across his lips before slowly morphing into a pained smile. "Thanks, Thad."

"No problem, bud. You're clipped in, right?"

"Yes." Cort rolled over halfway and showed him the cable and clip that was attached to his life vest.

"Good deal. Just shout if you need anything."

"Will do."

"It's neat, right?" Thad lingered a second, enjoying the light show off the aft deck.

"Really cool, yeah. I've only seen it a few times in my whole life. I'm thinking this will be the last time." Cort smiled another sarcastic grin and gave a thumbs up to reassure Thad that he wouldn't actually be dying of seasickness.

"Hang in there, Cort. It'll get better, just takes time."

Thad turned and headed back through the slider and into the cabin, as Cort turned to the rear again feeling another wave of nausea coming on.

Staring back into the fluorescent phenomenon of nature below, Cort's unstable brain drifted back to February and the events that led him to where he now lay. As it always did, the replay started with visualizing the exit ramp itself. He'd analyzed that quarter-mile stretch of road hundreds of times now, dwelling on the speed limit, the grade, the signage, the angles and curves, the road surface, and every other physical feature that a highway exit ramp can have. After the clips of the road faded from his thoughts, they transitioned with great lucidity to other particulars of that day. He recalled the weather, what he'd eaten for breakfast, the email he was working on, and the exact time of the phone call. More times than he could count, those details had crossed his mind in agonizing clarity.

The past day had been worse than most. As he spat away more thick saliva and suffered this unexpected new hell, the events of that fateful day played through his mind again. The positive healing effects of the recent therapy sessions had seemingly been hurled out of his body with the sesame noodles, leaving his current brain activity in a sea of negativity. He thought about Lucie, hoping the image of her face would temper the gloom, but instead, the fear of failing her only increased. This sail was supposed to be the key to salvaging their future and mark the beginning-of-the-end to his guilt and sadness. Instead, his despair was growing increasingly stronger with each passing nautical mile.

Chapter 2 - Light Extinguished (Day 1)

There wasn't any real panic in Celeste's voice.

"Hey, it's me, I need your help."

They'd been married for sixteen years, and by now he knew the difference between his wife's worried voice and her annoyed voice. She was a little concerned, but more frustrated than anything.

"Everything okay, what's up?"

"I'm fine, but the tire's flat. The front right, and it's *really* flat. Should I call Triple-A?"

"Um, maybe. Where are you?"

"I just left yoga about 5 minutes ago. I'm on the exit ramp. The Evans City exit."

Cort listened as he stared at his computer screen, trying to analyze the last sentence he'd typed in the email, simultaneously deciding on her question about calling for road service.

"Yeah, go ahead and call them, but it might take a while. I'll head over there too and bring my plug kit and a can of fix-a-flat. Maybe I can take care of it before they come."

"Okay, I'll call. Where's Lucie?" Celeste's voice was apologetic.

"She's next door. I'll text Jen and see if she can stay there for a little while."

"Sorry, I know you're working."

Cort cringed. He'd tried to keep his voice calm, but Celeste had sensed his frustration.

"No biggie, it's just the UPMC deal," he sarcastically referred to the very large contract he'd been working to secure for over eighteen months, chuckling to let her know he wasn't upset. This, like most every other challenge in life, was minor in comparison to losing a pregnancy. The reminder zipped through his brain and his next words carried a nonchalant tone. "If I can't fix it, we'll just wait for triple A and have them change it. Where on the ramp are you?"

"I'm kind of in the middle, just to the right of where it splits to go south or north. Know where I mean?"

"Yeah, I do." Cort hesitated as he pictured the location. "Are you far enough off the shoulder?

She interpreted the question quickly. "As far as I can go, yes. Do you think I'm okay here?"

"Yep, you're fine Celeste. Just stay in the car and lock the doors until the Triple A guy or I get there."

"Sure. Sorry. Hey, if it helps, I have a little surprise for you."

He sensed the smile in her last words, further softening his frustration. Still slightly annoyed, he wondered when she'd noticed the low tire. *Why get on the highway?* There was a sensor on the dash that signified when the tire was low, and it was impossible to miss. Cort decided not to voice that curiosity, knowing she'd interpret the question as his annoyance.

Minor details, who cares Cort.

"Don't worry about it, I'll be there in twenty minutes. Better be a good surprise. Bye."

She giggled, and he smiled back through the phone before tapping the red circular END button on his screen.

The phone remained in his right hand as he pressed his right foot down. Cort pondered the situation. A minute passed as scenarios crossed his mind, and he considered the fastest way to her. There was little choice other than to enter I-79 going north from Rt 19, which would have him pass by her location on the other side of the highway. He'd need to drive three miles north to the next exit, take the off ramp to the bottom, turn left and back under the highway, then enter 79 south via the on-ramp. Driving the three miles southbound again to the Evans City exit would get him to her without issue, but the loop around would take almost ten minutes. Counter-productive. There was one other possibility; a route that would shave off the ten-minute loop. He could stay north on Rt. 19 and drive just past the off ramp from 79 where she was parked, then back up the shoulder of the ramp until he reached her. That route was surely breaking some traffic law, and a bit dangerous, but maybe worth the gamble. The chance a cop would pass him was slim to none, and given the situation, there was as decent chance he could talk his way out of a citation anyway. Cort weighed the risk and pondered one last variable.

He glanced at his phone screen and slid his finger to the "recent calls" icon. Tapping Celeste's number, he moved his finger to the bluetooth option, and sent the call to the car's audio system.

"Cort?"

He heard the slightest hint of a question in her voice - an expectation of a change to the plan they'd just discussed.

"Hi. Just passing the Sunoco station now. Hey, about how far is 19 from where you're sitting?" Cort made an extra effort to sound indifferent.

"It depends on which way you're talking about?"

More question in her voice now. She knew him well enough that when he led with a question, an idea often followed that she'd be skeptical about.

"Uh, to your right, as if you were going towards Zelienople." He clarified and knew her wheels were spinning.

"I don't know, maybe a hundred yards or so." The answer hung in space for a split second before she continued. "It's cold out. You don't want me to walk down the ramp, do you?"

"No, no, don't do that. I was just thinking about something. I'll be there soon."

In painful retrospect, he should have hung up in that second. But he'd hesitated for safety purposes as he passed a car and prepared to get back into the right lane. Hitting the *End Call* button was delayed by his acute attention to the road, and the delay was just long enough for Celeste to decipher his question about the length of the ramp.

"Cort? Cort?"

"I'm here." He answered reluctantly and knew from her tone what was coming next.

"Don't you dare back up this exit ramp. That's illegal, and dangerous."

"Celeste, it's not dangerous if I stay on the shoulder. If I get back on 79 it's like a 10-minute loop around before I get back to you."

"No hagas eso, you'll get a ticket."

He didn't respond immediately. Celeste tended to speak Spanish if she was especially angry or concerned. He wasn't as fluent as her, but he deciphered her insistence that he should not do what he was contemplating. She was right, of course, but his way was more practical. After a lengthy pause, he reluctantly complied.

He pondered the situation another second or two before ending the call.

Should I tell her to drive down the ramp with the flat tire and pull off into the first parking lot or side road?

Picturing that stretch of 19, he tried to recall how far she'd need to drive before she reached one of those options. His concern was the tire rim, and the potential damage that might occur if she drove any further on it. Unable to remember, he decided against the suggestion and kept the thought to himself. Calmly, he finished the call.

"Just stay where you are. I'll be there soon."

Chapter 3 – Wrecked

Cort's mind wandered as his car merged onto the interstate. Her SUV was literally a couple hundred yards away, across the highway and down the bended exit ramp. Still a little miffed that it would take him ten minutes and an 8-mile loop around to reach her, he took a deep breath and clicked the turn signal off. A glance at the dash – 5:42 - it had been completely dark for more than fifteen minutes. That would change, Cort knew without a doubt, and he took some relief knowing the winter solstice was six weeks in their wake. Just this morning, the groundhog had emerged from its den in Punxsutawney, marking the mid-point of the darkest season. It wouldn't be long now. In a couple months, there'd be plenty of daylight left at 5:42 P.M., and the days of being outdoors with Celeste and Lucie were approaching.

Accelerating, he pictured himself on a hike near the creek alongside his two favorite people. Thank goodness Celeste was a nature lover. She'd swept him off his feet with her natural beauty and kind heart, and it would have been impossible not to fall hard for her. But if she'd been uncomfortable in the wild outdoors, specifically around water, it would have likely been a deal breaker sooner or later. Likewise, Lucie's love of nature was well beyond what he could have hoped for in a daughter. Other than himself of course, she gravitated to the water more than anyone else he knew. The more water the better, and Lucie always jumped at the opportunity to be somewhere she could get wet. He'd scored the 2-for-1 deal of a lifetime with his wife and little girl. Picturing them both as he drove north on the cold dark interstate, their images bathed his soul in warm sunlight.

His daydream was interrupted by the shrill scream of the siren, racing south on the opposite side of I-79. *Somebody's busted. Probably a lead foot.* The thought was fleeting as the flashing red and blue lights of a police cruiser faded from his peripheral vision. He let off the gas pedal some and checked his speedometer. A mile further up the highway, he watched an ambulance, also in full emergency mode, bolt down the south bound lane too. As it passed in a flash through his driver side window, a twinge of worry entered his mind. He hoped there wasn't an accident between him and the Evans City exit, hindering access to the ramp where Celeste was waiting for him.

The first real wave of concern rolled through Cort's brain as he crested the last hill prior to the exit. It was at that point the lights from the emergency vehicles could be seen in the distance, and the faint noise of their siren blares became audible. The Evans City exit ramp, only a half mile further, was still blocked from view by the hilly terrain. He didn't need to see the scene - Cort had no doubt the issue, whatever it might be, was in proximity to his destination.

Shit!

The ensuing waves, seconds later, pulsed through his mind and crested with considerably more panic. As he passed the third flare, the police car came into view on the shoulder. Cort picked up his phone and held it, deciding not to dial until he was pulled over and stopped. Fighting panic, he managed to slide his vehicle off the side of the highway just behind the cruiser. With his pulse rate increasing by the second, the rear-view mirror was hardly checked as he shot out of his car. Running down the shoulder, he managed to open his phone and tap the *Recents* button. The back of the fire engine came into view just around the bend on the exit ramp as he hit Celeste's number. One ring, then straight to voicemail. Hitting the *End Call* button as he moved faster, Cort wasn't willing to stop for even a few seconds to leave a voicemail.

"Hey, you can't go through here!"

Cort heard the volunteer fireman's voice, but the warning didn't process. The pace of his heartbeat elevated with the sound of the sirens, which were approaching from all directions now. The flashing lights blinded him as he strained his eyes to see beyond the fire engine to what was further down the ramp. His legs were getting increasingly heavy, like he was running from the sand into the shallows and about to battle surf. While it wasn't visible yet, Cort sensed the presence of a tsunami that was just out of sight, about to crash on his world.

"Sir!" The fireman shouted forcefully this time as Cort took a wide berth and skirted around the man waving a light-wand at him.

Another fireman, smaller and nimbler, stepped out of the engine and came in pursuit. Cort could see the ambulance now, then another police cruiser in front of it. Another hundred feet beyond, the accident was coming into view – the stench of burning plastic already thick in the air. He couldn't quite make out details of the jumbled heap of wreckage, but there was a hint of recognition in what remained of a taillight. Turning his head back to see both firemen in pursuit, he saw their lips moving but their words weren't registering in his brain. As he cocked his head forward again, Cort ran smack into the dark form of a state trooper, whose hat toppled backwards as Cort collided with him head on. The man's large arms snapped around Cort like a bear trap, forcefully catching him in motion and keeping them both from tumbling to the asphalt.

"Stop now! That's as far as you're going!" The officer's voice was way beyond a polite business tone, and the look in his eyes left no room for misinterpretation.

"Sir, officer, I need to get down there. My wife! She's... I need to... please!"

The officer freed Cort from his grasp and backed up a few steps.

"Calm down, sir." The trooper's voice was a few decibels lower, but still carried authority. "I need you to stay here. I'll go check. What's your wife's name?"

"Celeste! Celeste Palmerton! She's in a white SUV. Please go find her right now!"

Despite the fact Cort was nearly yelling, the officer's eyes softened. He turned away uncomfortably, as if to check on the status of the crash, and Cort's heart sank as the trooper's gaze returned to meet his. The lines around the trooper's dark eyes were telling.

"I'll see what I can do, but I need you to wait here, inside my car."

Staying in front of Cort, the trooper directed him into the back seat of his cruiser and promised he'd be right back. Before the trooper closed the car door, Cort blinked his watery eyes and was able to make out the name on the officer's breast plate.

"Officer Leonard, please, make sure my wife is okay." As the words left his mouth, the door closed, and he heard the click of the lock.

Breathing heavily, Cort tried to slow his pulse by focusing on the radio in the front seat and the intermittent chatter being emitted. He pictured the black and gray Ford Expedition he'd just watched rocket past him in the southbound lane. He knew there was a good chance he was sitting in that same vehicle now, and as beads of sweat dripped from his forehead, Cort wondered about what had been transmitted over that radio just a few minutes ago.

***

"Unit 12 from station, I have a two vehicle 10-45 involving a tractor trailer and a car. Witness on scene reporting a 10-7. Evans City exit ramp from I-79 south. Please respond."

The dispatcher's request hung in the stale air of the cruiser, and State Trooper Josh Leonard sighed before responding. Having patrolled the western PA highway system for 17 years as an officer, in addition to the years of driving the area as a teen growing up in the North Hills of Pittsburgh, he knew the location well.

The exit was close, maybe five miles tops, and he could reach it in a matter of minutes, but it was behind him. Josh was headed east on 68 towards the Butler barracks, where he was expecting to sit at his desk for fifteen minutes with the last cup of coffee of the day, complete some paperwork, and finish out his shift. Instead, he reached his left hand around the wheel, pulled the turn signal lever down, and responded to the dispatcher's robotic request.

"Unit 12 to station. 10-4, I'm en route."

Officer Leonard wasn't so much disappointed about the timing of the call. They didn't have any plans this evening. Shay would feed the boys. Later he and she would eat their reheated dinners together. She would wait for him; she always did. There would be no complaints. Shay was used to him being late by now, understanding it was part of the job. He wasn't especially bothered by the fact that this call would involve a crash investigation either. In his 17 years, he'd handled more 10-45's than he could count - well into the hundreds. There would be a good chunk of time and paperwork involved. The interviews, the official reports, the insurance company correspondence. He'd take the time to document the details. The report would be professional; Leonard was always thorough and professional. This was only a two-vehicle crash; relatively easy compared to a multi-vehicle crash. The worst was a 13-vehicle pile-up on the turnpike a few years back, requiring the most heavily traveled throughway in the state to be closed for twenty-six hours. He'd been filing documents for that accident more than two years after it happened.

None of those were the reasons he swallowed hard. What had his gut churning as he spun the cruiser around in an empty lot was the second two-number code the dispatcher had monotonously uttered. A 10-7 was rare, but he'd responded to it now a dozen or so times in his tenure with the force. It never got easier, and in fact, each one had progressively evolved to be more onerous than the last. The two numbers echoed in his head again as he applied a little more pressure with his right foot. The black and gray Ford Expedition accelerated and Josh flicked a switch to turn on the sirens. He pictured the exit ramp in his mind. There would be evidence to preserve, so he turned his focus to closing off the roadway and pushed his thoughts away from what he was about to witness at the scene. He made quick calls over the two-way for additional patrol units and another to the local volunteer fire department. They, in turn, would reach the nearest EMT's and direct them to the scene. Before putting the receiver back, he made one more outgoing call asking for the accident reconstruction unit. Turning hard onto the entrance ramp, the cruiser rocketed south towards the crash site. With no more than 120 seconds between himself and the scene, Josh exhaled deeply and began to mentally prepare himself for an accident that had earned the 10-7 code for "fatality."

Chapter 4 – End Of The Song

After that 2nd day of February, every aspect of daily life had changed. Some things were more significant than others, affecting Cort and Lucie's existence on a daily and even hourly basis. Many of those were obvious, even to an outsider, and could be observed with little or no insight; for example, getting Lucie on and off the school bus each day.

Making meals was another change. Twice a day, most days of the week, Cort found himself cooking eggs, chicken, soup, oatmeal, casseroles, mac-n-cheese, and the like. Mixing tuna salad, slapping together various sandwiches, and the cutting up of fruit and vegetables became part of the new routine. There were also take-out orders and fast food, or on the rare occasion, he and Lucie would sit down and eat in a restaurant. But mostly, Cort prepared and cooked their food, and Lucie assisted when she could. He'd read the recipes, mix the ingredients, and make the meal as instructed.

It wasn't that he was a total novice, it was just that Celeste had done 90% of the cooking in the past. Back then he'd just help with some portion of the process, like washing and slicing the potatoes; it was a fine arrangement. Now he was performing just about every aspect of their dietary consumption. While time consuming, and sometimes done in a robotic state of mind, Cort didn't hate it. In an odd way, it was a task he found to be therapeutic. Preparing a meal provided some purpose in a world that was losing its ability to motivate him. It also helped pass many of the agonizingly long minutes that occurred each day. Furthermore, cooking was a small but significant connection to Celeste. He channeled her through the recipes that she'd unintentionally left behind in a three-ring binder. Maybe most importantly, cooking had offered a unique portal to connect with Lucie.

Most days Lucie offered to help her dad, and usually he took her up on the offer. For a ten-year-old, she followed instructions well. Despite her mental state being volatile like his, she took great pride in her assistant role and typically did so with a smile. Pancakes had evolved into the single favorite food item for both, and they'd fallen into a routine of making them together on most Saturday mornings. Ironically, "pancake" accurately represented his mental state. His whole being had been flattened, more like crushed, by the loss of Celeste. Before February 2nd, he was a ball of hope and happiness, excited about life and fully content to exist in the world that they'd built together. Those days were over. Her death had pulled the plug, releasing the positivity from his soul, and those feelings of optimism had been replaced with fear and depression. The woeful thoughts of death weighed down his psyche, pushing down and deflating him into a pancake of sorrow.

Preparing and eating meals with his daughter had become one of the few positive parts of Cort's week, but even that came with a degree of pain. Lucie sat across from him at the distressed gray-wash wooden table just off the kitchen. There were four chairs, but they always chose the same two; neither had even considered the one "Mom" used to sit in. Much of the mealtime passed in silence, but some small talk was managed.

"How do you like the sweet potatoes, Luce?"

"They're fine."

"Good, thanks. They're good for your brain function and eye health."

Not exactly what 10-year-old girls were interested in. He realized Lucie didn't quite relate, but nonetheless appreciated her smiles and the occasional giggle at his commentary. He'd try to reciprocate with a forced smile or laugh, wondering if he was fooling her into thinking they were genuine.

Lucie's facial features and personality served as a stark reminder that part of her mother's beauty and spirit would live on, but Cort had no misconceptions about seeing Celeste again. He knew the best-case scenario was that they'd meet again when he died, and even that belief had been challenged as of late. His doubts about God and Heaven were starting to grow stronger, his faith seemingly drifting out to sea. He was hanging on, praying intermittently, asking for the strength to persevere through the pain and remain a good father. Cort's current perception, however, was that God hadn't answered him, and the requests to his divine maker were beginning to carry a slight tone of anger.

Work continued to be less and less productive after the accident. Several times a day, he'd find himself staring into the computer screen. The email at hand could be read six or more times before it was comprehended. It wasn't uncommon that he'd drift away in thought, and Celeste would occupy his mind with some memory of a vacation, or simply a talk that they'd had.

"Where do you want to renew our vows on our 20th, Celeste? Maybe back in Cabo?"

"Ooooh, good question. How about Hawaii?"

In a quick jerk of his head, he'd snap out of the daze and find that 15 minutes had passed, sometimes more. In that first six weeks after the crash, nobody from corporate had spoken to him about it. There were the emails reminding him of the various benefits that came with his health plan, with hints towards the psychiatric related ones. By April, however, management was getting concerned with his lack of activity and their need to field customer issues he should be handling. Cort certainly sensed management's discontent but was also keenly aware he was barely giving a fuck.

Other aspects of his life were touched less directly, but no facet of his daily routine was left unscathed. The month of April, historically one of his favorites of the twelve, had come and gone quietly. The budding of nature's spring in Western Pennsylvania had passed by and he'd barely noticed. While the days grew longer, birds chirped more frequently, and the lawns turned greener behind the flowering azaleas, Cort's mind stayed focused on death. Thoughts lingered on those who had passed, primarily his parents and Celeste, but also notions of his own death became more frequent, and the pit in his gut continued to grow. At times he wondered if the sensation he was feeling might be some variation of cancer feeding on his despair. It was a reoccurring theory, and one that didn't scare him as much as it was almost a welcomed thought. Only the consequential suffering Lucie would endure kept his mind in check, but the aspect of dying sooner, rather than later, was growing in strength.

    The happy beats and rhythms of daily life had faded, both figuratively and literally. Music had always brought Cort a sense of peace, providing a way to lose stress and find inspiration. The lyrics of the past several decades were part of his vocabulary, and he peppered the rhymes and prose into his daily conversations. It wasn't only the lyrics that soothed him. The sounds of instruments were engrained into his mind and his soul; he picked them out of music as if it were part of his own personal game show contest. The guitars, drums, and synthesized tones were easy. When he was alone, and could really focus, he'd listen for the sound of a solo trumpet, or cello, or that background tambourine. Even the occasional bagpipe or harmonica would tickle his eardrum like a feather. He liked them all as individual sounds but was mesmerized by the way they came together in harmony. In a different life, he'd have taken more music lessons as a kid, trying every instrument he could and becoming skilled at all of them. Maybe he'd join a band, or teach music, or do something where he was surrounded by the tones and melodies of song.

    That was all prior to February.

    Since that day, he hadn't been able to hear tones, chords, or notes. Music became dull, monotone noise that scraped at his eardrums and barely got deciphered. Not only was listening no longer enjoyable; it wasn't even tolerable. Every song was a reminder of Celeste. He'd tried many times to turn on the radio or pull up a playlist on his phone. If he could get past the song title without making a connection with her, it was only a few seconds into the song before a lyric would do the same thing. A simple facet of life that had brought him so much joy had become a catalyst for pain and sorrow. The furthest he'd made it through a song in three months was the forty-three second intro of a Foo Fighters jam. As soon as the lyrics began, that was it - those first seven words were all he could take.

Hello, I've waited here for you

Everlong

Dave Grohl's voice incited a quick tap to the power button on the dash, and then a swift and angry swat to the side of his steering wheel. It was hopeless. He was hopeless.

***

At least a few times each week, Lucie would exchange a glance with her father between bites, and she'd see the deep pain in his eyes. She knew the same faraway look was in her own expression too sometimes, and when he'd catch her blank stare, they'd both turn away uncomfortably. After such an exchange, Lucie would watch in her peripheral vision - the flutter of his lids, that's how she knew it was coming. Within five seconds, a tear would roll down his cheek. Most of the time he'd attempt to hide it, either dabbing his face with the napkin or getting up and pretending his water glass needed filling. Other times, he just didn't react at all, and the tear would run down and drop right down onto his plate.

"Dad, it's gonna be okay."

"Huh? I know, Lucie… we'll be okay… I just miss her… I know you do too."

He always said that. Lucie knew the response by heart. Seconds later he'd sit up a little straighter and force another smile, followed by a brief apology. She wanted to cry with him, but something inside begged her to remain strong. Her thoughts were sad too, but she refused to show him the deepest of her pain. Instead, she'd silently take another bite of food and wonder if either of them would ever be happy again. Her doctor said that her 10-year-old brain still hadn't completely 'processed the death,' and she wasn't quite accepting her mom was gone. She knew the doctor was right, because sometimes, in random places, Lucie still expected to see her mother. Just last week, in the grocery store, she'd had the strongest feeling that her mom would be standing there waiting for them, as she and her dad turned the corner into the cereal aisle. Further away, in the dark parts of her brain, she understood it was just her and Dad now. She'd follow him wherever he might go from here, making sure he was safe. In one of her worst recurring dreams, he was drowning in the ocean. She was there with him, trying so hard to pull him above the surface, but his weight was too much. As he sunk further, Lucie had to make the choice of letting his hand go to save herself or joining him forever in the underwater grave. She always held on, not willing to watch him sink into the darkness and disappear from her view. The idea of death was less scary than walking through life alone, but Lucie would wake from her dreams more frustrated than anything else. She was determined to avoid both death and loneliness for her dad and herself, but hadn't quite figured out how to save them yet.

Chapter 5 — Impactful

Cort placed his right hand on the back of the russet toned oak bench, supporting himself under what felt like an especially heavy mass of anger, pain, and remorse. The burden had been present every day for the past three and a half months, loading down his mind and body with the unshakable weight. Deep down, he knew he should be grateful today. The fact that this trial was taking place less than four months after the accident was the equivalent of a judicial-process miracle. Today, however, was the third and final day of the proceedings. Today was the day the truck driver would be taking the stand, the anticipation of which had seemingly increased earth's gravitational pull on Cort's physical and mental being.

He lowered himself into the seat next to Celeste's parents, Manny and Gabby, taking in a deep breath of the anxiety-ridden courtroom air before morosely sliding into his sitting position. Following their prior 2-day courtroom tradition, he offered his open palm to Celeste's parents, and the three of them held each other's hands. Watching their expressions, Cort focused on their facial features, picking out those traits that had combined to shape Celeste's beauty. His in-laws closed their eyes, and Cort knew they were praying silently to themselves. His eyes remained open, and he decided yet again to refrain from prayer. For the first time, as he looked around the room, he made the connection between the courtroom and a church. The rich features of the warm wood and elaborate paintings donning the walls evoked a similar sense of importance - a higher power at hand. The benches and the gallery mimicked the pews and the congregation. His gaze moved to the front of the room and stopped at the witness stand, which immediately reminded him of the confession box. He was thankful nobody could hear the sinful thoughts of violent vengeance flooding his brain and threatening to drown any sense of moral goodness that remained.

Fuck you God, you failed me.

Cort's eyes clenched closed, and his face contorted into an apologetic cringe as the horrific thought raced through his mind. A miniscule shard of relief interrupted his awful notions, as he opened his eyes and watched the man in the black robe sit down behind the "altar." Cort inhaled a deep breath, and hoped the judge wouldn't also fail to do his job.

The murmur of the gallery ceased as the honorable authority figure settled into the black leather chair behind the bench and called for order within his house of justice. The judge was a large man, magnified because his black robe blended in with the chair back. Cort estimated him to be in his late 60's or early 70's, evidenced by his white hair and pale skin. The combination left a distinct lack of color within the judge's appearance, his image almost entirely black and white. The analogy Cort drew in his mind seemed fitting, and he hoped the trial itself would lack any gray areas.

At the advice of his attorney, the defendant had waived his right to a jury trial and given the judge sole authority to determine his fate. Cort half-listened as his honor explained the order of the day's proceedings to the audience, then reviewed several minutes of procedural bullshit. Finally, the defense was instructed to call their defendant to the stand.

Twenty-four minutes passed as the defense attorney questioned Aaron Stevens. Their goal was to establish two key concepts. First, that Mr. Stevens was an experienced driver with a clean driving record. That was easy, based on his spotless motor vehicle report, and seven accident-free years of employment between two trucking companies. The second concept, that the highway itself was to blame for the accident, was more of a circumstantial stretch. The defense suggested that the sharpness of the curve where the ramp split to go right, was too extreme. More warning signs were needed, and the speed limit on the ramp should have been lower. They submitted overhead images of the ramp, and photos of two other truck rollovers that had occurred within the past decade in the same location. Based on the subtle reactions of the judge, attorneys, and gallery, the defense had done their job in providing a degree of vindication for the defendant.

Cort had known the truck driver's testimony would be difficult to hear but hadn't quite expected the growing feelings of fury within his chest. This was as close as he'd ever been to the defendant, Aaron Stevens. Even at the scene of the crash, Cort had been restrained by an especially strong state trooper, preventing him from getting within a hundred feet of the truck driver. Now, from a distance half the length of an 18-wheeler, Cort watched Stevens, clad in a new suit and tie, fresh haircut, and clean-shaven face, answer the defense attorney's final question. Inhaling several deep breaths, Cort attempted to temper his vexation. Turning to his right, he looked to his in-laws, and the three of them exchanged supportive nods while the prosecuting attorney and her team prepared for the cross examination.

From discussions with the team over the past several weeks, Cort knew their plan and looked forward to watching the defendant squirm on the stand. The prosecution would be making use of an animated video that simulated the path of the tractor-trailer. The video would be played on a large screen television, set up near the front of the prosecution's table. The screen was in a position along the front left wall of the courtroom where the defendant and judge could view it, as could the attorneys from both sides and most of the gallery. The prosecutor would control the video remotely, playing it in segments and pausing at intervals, at which point she'd ask the defendant questions about his thoughts and actions at key points in the timeline.

Aaron Stevens had already stated his name for the record and sworn to tell the truth, so the prosecutor, in her charcoal pantsuit, was able to dive right in. Cort listened as she established Mr. Stevens employment history with Bravo Trucking, then subsequently focused on a key policy that pertained to all company drivers. She plucked a 3-ring binder from her table, held it up high to show the defense team, and presented it to the courtroom as 'exhibit A.' Swiftly carrying it to the stand, she handed the binder to the defendant, and asked her first question.

"Mr. Stevens, do you recognize this document?"

"I think so." His voice was immediately sullen and an octave lower.

"You think so? Please read the title of the document on the front of the binder, Mr. Stevens."

"Bravo Transport Corporation Personnel M-m-manual."

Cort stewed as Aaron read the words, his stutter apparent for the first time since taking the stand. The prosecutor asked Mr. Stevens to turn his head toward the microphone and read it again. The defendant turned to the judge, who simply nodded, instructing Aaron to repeat his answer. After Aaron complied, the prosecutor continued.

"Thank you, Mr. Stevens. And did you read this manual after being hired at Bravo?"

"Um, yeah, I read m-most of it."

Cort clenched his teeth, sure that the answer was purposely vague.

"You read *most* of it, Mr. Stevens?" The prosecutor walked back to her table and picked up a laminated sheet of paper and presented it as 'exhibit B.' "This is page 27 of that personnel manual Mr. Stevens. It states that the manual has been read and understood in its entirety. It's signed and dated at the bottom." She handed the defendant the laminated page. "Can you tell me whose signature that is, Mr. Stevens?"

Aaron answered slowly, inhaling then sighing before his response, "It's m-m-mine."

Successfully establishing that the defendant had read and understood the manual, the prosecutor next cited the specific section of the document that addressed the electronic device policy. Without objection from the defense, she further established that the defendant was aware that the use of any electronic device (aside from the onboard routing system) was not permitted while the truck was being operated. She was clear and concise, and kept the defendant on point. Despite a few stuttered answers, she was able to curtail any significant distraction from the facts by asking mostly 'yes' and 'no' questions.

The most damning evidence was presented in tandem with the video simulation. The events in question were displayed within the very-well-constructed, high-quality animated video. The video was only two minutes and twenty seconds in total length, depicting the six-and-a-half minutes prior to the point of impact. It took much longer to watch, because the attorney paused it at least eight times, hammering the defendant with questions during the intervals. Her voice was passionate, and Cort detected a muted tone of disgusted anger in her questions. Cort's own rage was building as the testimony was given. The thoughts pinballing through his head were disturbing, and he wondered if he'd be able to remain present without erupting.

Cort, Celeste's parents, and the rest of the gallery watched the video showing the truck's path as it approached the exit ramp. The tractor trailer itself was large in scale and dark in color, purposely exaggerated to portray a menacing and evil character. Contrastly, Celeste's SUV was white, and small in comparison to the 18-wheeler. Over the ensuing forty-two minutes, as each segment of video was intermittently played between testimony, Cort watched the behemoth truck get closer and closer to his wife's disabled vehicle. In several clips, the animated three-mile stretch of highway was shown from a distant overhead view. The highway itself was marked by a red line, while every area surrounding the roadway was a light blue color. Cort drew the comparison of the tractor trailer to that of a shark, a Megladon in this case. Celeste's SUV was the apparent helpless victim, innocent and unaware that the killer shark was approaching from behind. The red highway, seemingly a trail of blood leading predator to prey, fit the bill perfectly. He hadn't discussed the details of the video with the team, but Cort wondered if the prosecution had intended the exact comparison that he was making.

If only it were a shark, she'd have been fine.

Cort knew that in reality, a shark would have come upon the human and likely veered sharply left or right to avoid contact, or even more probable, turned around and retreated. Sharks were focused and in control, not irresponsible pieces of shit who didn't pay attention to the road.

Fucking Humans!

The insult towards humanity darted through Cort's mind, and it took a concerted effort to keep it internal. A bead of sweat formed on his brow as the urge to blurt it out loud grew stronger. Apparently noticing the wrath in Cort's expression, Manny patted his shoulder in a gesture of both support and concern.

"You okay?" Celeste's father whispered the question in Cort's right ear.

"Yeah, sorry." Cort whispered back a bit too loudly, prompting a warning scowl from the judge.

Cort hadn't felt such bitter hate for any single person before, let alone disgust for the whole human race. While he'd been prepared to experience more than the usual feelings of ill-will during the trial, this degree of loathing was beyond his expectations. He closed his eyes, desperate for help, and tried to will away his rage with happy images. *Lucie.* Covertly reaching to his left breast pocket, he pulled the photo out. His daughter's wallet-sized 4th grade school picture immediately calmed his nerves.

The prosecution continued questioning the truck driver and the truth was pulled out slowly, stuttered with trepidation. Aaron's testimony told of an over-the-phone argument with his girlfriend, Brittney, that began roughly ten minutes prior to the crash. The call lasted seven minutes and was followed by three disparaging texts from Aaron, all occurring while he barreled down the highway at

77 miles per hour. The attorney cited data recovered by a tech-forensic specialist from both the truck's on-board routing system and Aaron's cell phone. The data showed that the phone and text correspondence ended less than a quarter mile prior to the Zelienople exit, which had been part of the pre-determined delivery route. Aaron reluctantly admitted that he'd missed the intended exit because of the phone distractions. The next exit, Evans City, where Celeste Palmerton's car sat disabled on the side of the ramp, was never part of Aaron's original route.

Cort knew about the general circumstances leading up to the crash. The prosecution had shared pieces of Aaron's deposition weeks ago. Now, as he listened to the truck driver's testimony in real time, the words stung more than he could ever have imagined. Anger, regret, and pure anguish consumed him.

The prosecution continued the questioning, disclosing more facts in the process. After the call and texts to the girlfriend, the cell phone data showed that Mr. Stevens had gone to his browser. There were links to two different x-rated sites, viewed just seventy-four seconds prior to the time of impact. The phone records were undeniable hard evidence. It became crystal clear that Aaron Stevens had violated the trucking company's electronic device policy, and was without a doubt, grossly negligent in his actions.

"No more questions, your honor." The prosecution concluded.

The ill-effect on Cort, however, was far from over. As Aaron Stevens stepped down from the stand, Cort could barely suppress the urge to scream at the man who'd killed his wife.

I'll execute you myself you fucking...

The venomous words sat at the end of his tongue, ready to be spat from behind his clenched teeth. His heart thumped wildly, threatening to explode with rage - he grasped at his chest to prevent it from detonating. As the accused passed by on the way back to his seat, Cort glared at the truck driver and stood. When he rose from his seat, the gallery gasped, sensing that an attack from the widower was about to transpire. The judge shot a look to the bailiff and motioned for him to move into a defensive position.

"Mr. Palmerton, are you okay!?" The judge bellowed from behind his bench, ready himself to jump down and restrain Cort if need be.

Cort's palm, still planted on his left pectoral, felt the rectangular outline of the photo in his breast pocket. The image of Lucie came back, and not a microsecond too soon. His head lowered for a brief second, before raising again and meeting the judge's eyes.

"I'm, uh, I'll be alright your honor. Sorry."

"I understand you're upset, Mr. Palmerton, but if you do that again I'll hold you in contempt. Understand me?"

"Yes, I understand. I can't stay here. I need to leave."

With that, everyone in the room watched in silence as Cort shuffled down the bench past three members of the gallery, made his way down the aisle, and exited the courtroom.

He didn't return, simply unable to witness Aaron Steven's sentencing. He'd missed the truck driver's solemn plea to the judge before it was handed out. Cort didn't get to hear the defendant's sincere and heartfelt apology to Celeste's parents, and to Cort himself. Aaron's tears were genuine as he choked and stuttered the words out, asking for forgiveness from Celeste's entire family first, and then from God.

The convictions for one count of felony reckless endangerment and one count of 2nd degree manslaughter were read out loud by the judge. Cort would hear those convictions, and the penalty, second-hand from his mother-in-law. Aaron was sentenced to 8 years in prison, with parole on the table only after the 4th full year. He'd serve his time in the Erie County Prison, a correctional facility located a mere twelve miles from the house where his girlfriend Brittney and their three-year-old son lived.

Furthermore, the conviction and sentencing were part of a compelling presentation in the civil suit, filed against Bravo Trucking Corporation shortly after the criminal trial was over. While the civil case was still pending, all indications were pointing towards a swift settlement in favor of the plaintiffs, Cort and Lucie Palmerton.

Chapter 6 – ITS

Sitting at the kitchen island, he sipped his coffee and tried to forget the dream, but the images wouldn't leave his head. He'd awoken at 4:14 A.M. lathered in a full sweat, unable to go back to sleep. In his nightmare, it was prior to the crash, and he was at a neighborhood barbecue with Celeste and Lucie. As he was biting into a cheeseburger, he caught a glimpse of a man in the corner the yard, standing by himself. The man looked familiar, but Cort couldn't place his face at first. Unable to recall where he'd seen him, Cort had the sense the man was not an invited guest. As he swallowed back a sip of beer, it came to him. The man was Aaron Stevens, the driver of the tractor trailer, somehow in their presence before Cort even knew of his existence. In the dream, Cort somehow understood what was going to happen on February 2nd and could only come up with one solution to prevent it. He dropped his beer and plate of potato salad and slammed his burger into the ground. Walking swiftly past the grill, Cort grabbed the 10-inch-long meat fork out of the grill-master's hand and trotted toward the truck driver. There was no defensive posture by Stevens, even as Cort thrust the two-pronged utensil deep into the man's chest. When the stainless steel pierced his heart, it was almost as if Stevens had known it was coming, and fully welcomed his pre-crime punishment. Laying there in the grass exhaling his final breaths, Aaron smiled up at Cort, signifying proper justice had been served. Cort had smiled back, then woke sitting straight up in his bed, drenched in perspiration.

Despite the less pronounced sliver of justice the judge had handed out, Cort's emotions after the trial were increasingly desperate and further removed from the sense of happiness that he once felt. He endured the weekends because

Lucie was home and could keep his mind occupied. Weekdays were nearly unbearable. He'd sit at his desk and attempt to be productive, only to lose his train of thought repeatedly, checking the clock every 20 minutes until it was time to pick Lucie up at the bus stop.

By the end of May, production at work slowed to a crawl, and upper-management was growing impatient. He still hadn't visited with a client in-person since the accident. Cort managed to keep in touch with the UPMC (University of Pittsburgh Medical Center) guys, and a few other key clients, but the communication was sporadic and less thorough than it needed to be. The COVID-19 virus era had ended three years ago, but his weeks were reminiscent of those many months of social distancing and remote correspondence. He wished that the virus, or some vengeful mutant strain, would return now. It would be the perfect cover for his desire to stay in a hole and avoid his clients, neighbors, and even family and friends. Solitude would also prevent his growing urges to lash out at other people from becoming a reality.

At first, his circle of support was most appreciated. People came out of the woodwork to show him compassion and help in any way they could. The initial outcry of help was acceptable and tolerated. Meals came from all over the community; everyone reaching out to him with their sympathy and condolences. After a month of the commiseration, however, Cort grew weary of the gestures, and by the end of March he wanted them to stop. The hugs, the tears, the empathy - it was all beginning to smell like bullshit to him. These people had no idea what he was dealing with, no matter how hard they tried to pretend they did. He couldn't see anyone, let alone talk to a person, without the subject being broached. He'd leave the conversation wondering why they didn't realize that every time her name was mentioned, it equated to hours of torturous memories. It was enough already.

As winter faded into spring, the showing of support was increasingly having an ill effect on his psyche, the most interesting and troubling of which was something he self-diagnosed as ITS (**I**nternal **T**urrets **S**yndrome). Concerning words and phrases had been entering his thoughts; some were downright disturbing. They were always negative, many times even violent, and the worst part was he couldn't control them. The most serious incident had occurred right there in the courtroom, and nearly transgressed into an assault. The odd mental condition had started soon after the accident. Cort couldn't quite pin down exactly when, but thought the first bout had been as early as the funeral. Celeste's father, Manuel, had stayed quiet for the most part, somberly making small talk with the guests. He was sullen and still somewhat in a state of shock, just as Cort was. Amid his own deep and dark despair, Cort felt very sorry for his father-in-law Manuel, or "Manny," as he preferred. Towards the end of the viewing, Manny approached Cort at a strategic point, when Lucie was elsewhere and very few people were left in the funeral parlor.

"Cort," he said, "you let Gabby and I know if you and Lucie need anything."

If he'd ended it with that, the two men would have left each other on a peaceful note, both able to mourn a woman who'd defined so many aspects of their separate lives. But Manny didn't, he added another sentence, and it resonated with Cort long after it was uttered.

"And you try to take care of that little girl now, you hear me?"

Cort recalled staring into Manny's dark eyes for four full seconds, unable to react at first. He'd clenched his teeth together as his brain begged for the words to be released, "*TRY to take care? What's that supposed to mean Manny, you fuck! Of course I'll take care of Lucie. What? You think it was my fault that a truck rolled onto your daughter's car? You think I could've prevented Celeste's death, you stupid asshole! How about I take care of you? How about I break that precious Yonex racket over your goddamn skull, huh, how about that!?*"

The thoughts had pinballed through his brain as he strained to keep them from reaching his tongue. His eyes closed as he pleaded with himself to excuse the remark. He knew her father's thoughts were extremely dark that day, just like his own. Manny wasn't truly blaming Cort for his daughter's death, but that realization was not helping Cort contain the urge to respond with his twisted feelings. Instead, he exhaled a deep breath, and the words came out slowly.

"I will. Thanks for coming. Bye Manny."

As the weeks ensued, the internal turrets had surfaced sporadically, but they were becoming more common and there'd been numerous times in recent weeks. It would happen in odd places, with unlikely people. And strangely it wasn't just happening out of anger, or in response to a negative comment. He was experiencing the ITS when someone was offering sympathy for his loss, or some gesture of forced optimism. Verbally he'd respond with something like, "Thanks, I appreciate it." But the thoughts that would cross his mind in the moment were more like, *"Piss off,"* or *"Don't pretend you understand, Ass-Face."*

What was worse, the thoughts would sometimes come with the urge to physically harm the person on the other end. There had been more than one occasion now, when he'd envision responding to someone's consoling efforts by punching the person in the face. He could see it clearly in his mind, his fist reaching out and catching them on the bridge of their nose, cracking cartilage and making a bloody mess. That would certainly shut them up and teach them not to comfort him again. He would picture these actions in his mind, but so far had managed to refrain from acting them out. At least there was self-awareness with the urges; he knew they were extremely unhealthy and that he was beginning to lose his mind. The realization, however, did not stop the thoughts and urges from coming. Furthermore, Cort began to wonder if he'd ever be himself again. Maybe his old self had died with his wife, and he was destined to a life of a miserable monster, and possibly a danger to others. Maybe even dangerous to his daughter. It was ten days after the trial ended – that's when Cort decided he would get help. He owed it to Lucie to make an attempt. If that didn't work, there were other ways to end his suffering and keep her safe.

Chapter 7 - Shrink Rap (Day 118)

Dr. Galley, his recently prescribed psychiatrist, had squinted when Cort leaned back into the couch and described the ITS to him. Cort read into his expression, which seemed to convey, *"That's not totally out of the ordinary Cort, but you're definitely f'd up in the head."*

Instead, the doctor nodded introspectively, and chose to delve into the subject of Cort's father-in-law, Manny.

"What's a Yonex racket?" he'd asked, as if that was the most important part of what Cort had divulged.

Cort realized long after the appointment was over, that the doctor had cleverly segued into the subject. In the moment, he found himself giving a background history of Manny's life, and the doctor let him talk without interruption.

At $217 per billable hour, the guy is a fantastic listener.

"Celeste's dad grew up poor," Cort began. "He never really knew his father, and his mother raised him by herself in Mexico. She was a maid at some high-end resort in Cabo San Lucas back in the 60's, way before it was the mega-tourist-attraction that it is now."

Cort spoke from experience, having visited the area with Celeste seventeen years ago, and again 2 years ago. The area had really blown up.

"Anyway, Manny's mom was forced to take him to work a lot when he was a young kid. Apparently, she'd keep him hidden and out of sight, but one particular day he'd wandered off. Before she even realized he was gone, he returned to the room she was cleaning, escorted by the resort tennis pro, James. James was a good-looking white guy, and had a thing for young Mexican señoritas. Now, James didn't report the incident to management because Manny's mother was very attractive. You can guess where this story goes, right?"

Cort glanced up at the psychiatrist who stopped writing on his pad, peeked over the top of his glasses, and returned a knowing grin and a single nod. Dr. Galley was probably early to mid-fifties, with thinning reddish-brown hair that was showing some gray and doing its best to cover the scalp. His mustache and beard matched perfectly, connecting at the edge of his lips into a well-groomed goatee.

"In fact, doc, Manny has a sister who's about 8 years younger than him. She's half Hispanic, half White. Beautiful lady, Aunt Hillary. Celeste and I really like her and her husband, and her daughters - Celeste's cousins."

Cort paused and thought about Aunt Hillary momentarily, wondering when he'd even see her again. She was at the funeral, of course, but flew back to California afterwards.

"Sorry, I'm getting off track. So, this tennis pro takes a liking to young Manny, I guess. Or maybe he was just pretending in an effort to get into the mom's pants. Not sure. I've only heard this second-hand. But the pro starts working with Manny a little bit after hours, showing him some technique and hitting some balls around the courts. Well, this continues off and on for a couple years, Manny grows into a teenager, and before you know it, he becomes a good tennis player... of all things, right? Eventually the pro hires Manny as his assistant, and he works there at the resort all through high school. The guy never married Manny's mom, but I know they stay in touch. Manny's sister visits him two or three times a year. I mean, it's her father after all. Odd situation, but whatever. That's another story that I literally can't afford to tell you."

Smirking for a second, Cort got back to the explanation at hand after seeing that the doctor didn't appreciate his joke.

"Anyway, Manny ends up getting so good at tennis that he gets a full ride to Baylor U, which is where he met Gabby - Celeste's mom. She was on the women's tennis team, and those two married a year after they graduated from Baylor."

Realizing he was rambling again, Cort glanced over to Dr. Galley, and thought he was looking a bit sleepy.

"Long story short, doc; Manny played on the pro-circuit for a few years after college, and Yonex, a brand of tennis racket, gave him a sponsor contract. He swears to this day that they make the best racket on the market. I have one too, but only because he gave it to me as a birthday gift one year. So that's it. When I said I had the thought about cracking the 'Yonex' over his skull, that's the backstory."

Cort grinned at the idea, and thought he caught a slight smile on Dr. Galley's lips too. He wasn't quite sure if the doc was humored by the story, or by the fact that Cort had this disturbing mental condition that would guarantee many more hours of therapy.

During Cort's very next couch-session, he and the Dr. did a role-play exercise to address the ITS. Dr. Galley played the role of the person trying to offer condolences to Cort, and Cort was supposed to respond out loud with the thought he might have.

"Okay, Cort, let's pretend I'm one of the other dads at Lucie's soccer game, and I come up to you afterwards in the parking lot."

"Alright." Cort replied hesitantly, not sure he was comfortable with role playing.

"Hey there, Cort," Galley spoke with a slight alteration in his voice. "Just wanted to say how sorry I am about Celeste. You know if there's anything we can do, just say the word." He paused, then instructed in his actual voice, "Now you respond with what might be going through your mind."

"Well," Cort started, "my actual response might be something like, 'Thanks Jim, I appreciate it. Great game, right?' But what's going through my head is more like, 'You know what, Jim, yeah, you can do something for me. How about you take care of your perfect little family and don't worry about me and Lucie, otherwise I'm gonna break that big fucking nose of yours!"

Cort glanced over to Dr. Galley before continuing, "You know, uh, something like that."

Dr. Galley stared at Cort for a few seconds, seemingly trying to swallow the information but having a bit of indigestion.

"Alright, okay. That's good, thanks for being so honest there. I'm sensing that maybe you resent some of these people because their families are generally well." He nodded and paused. "Is there something about the man's nose that has significance, Mr. Palmerton."

"Yeah, I'm sorry about that Doc. I have nothing against big noses, honestly. I sometimes get caught up in people's facial features - the eyes more than anything else. They tell a lot about people - where they're from, or how their life has been, you know? Sometimes it's the nose, or some other feature, but mostly it's in the eyes. The eyes tell way more than people realize. So that's all - I was just picturing one of the dads on Lucie's soccer team. He has a decent sized honker. Very nice guy though, I must say."

Cort stopped rambling, his face a bit flush. He looked back at the doctor, who he was almost certain was Irish or Scottish. The blue eyes and reddish-brown hair and beard were big tells, not to mention the last name 'Galley' fit the bill. He was tempted to ask, if only to prove his theory to his psychiatrist.

"That's fine, Cort." Dr. Galley sighed and snuck a peak at the large clock on the wall. The face had black hands and black roman numerals, with a faded background of crackled creams and browns, purposely colored that way to make it look aged and authentic. "We can end on that note and pick it up next session."

"Sure, sounds good."

Cort snatched the light jacket he'd laid across the end of the couch and stood up. He walked to the door, and thanked Dr. Galley in passing, just as he did at the end of every previous session. Twisting the brass knob of the door, he turned back to the doctor before pulling it open.

"Doc, you're Irish, right?"

The doctor looked at Cort and pondered the question before answering very matter-of-factly, "50% Irish, 25% Scottish, and a mix of English and French on the other 25%. I'll see you next week, Cort."

Cort was perfectly satisfied with the answer, which confirmed he was basically correct. Closing the door behind him, he stepped into the small lobby of the office and moved to the desk of Dr. Galley's assistant, Trina. The room was the entry foyer of the 98-year-old Victorian House. Trina, seated at her small desk in the corner, raised her head and smiled, but Cort's eyes wandered around the oak paneled wall and ornately beautiful staircase behind her.

Returning his focus to Trina quite suddenly, he thought he saw her eyes move up from his torso in a flash. Cort felt flush and self-conscious. Celeste had always told him she liked the way his chest and arms formed attractive outlines in the fabric of a soft t-shirt. He was wearing one such t-shirt now, but his lack of weightlifting and cardio had negatively changed his body over the past few months. Even his face was different. The thick eyebrows, dark hair, and strong jaw line that Celeste had always complimented him on, were now overshadowed by the dark circles under his eyes. The dimple on his left cheek, another feature his wife had adored, only showed when he smiled. Very few people had seen it since February 2nd. It didn't matter. He felt the need to impress nobody, and only returned Trina's smile to be polite. Robotically, he offered a hello, and she responded in her usual pleasant demeanor.

"Hi, Mr. Palmerton, how are you?"

She'd been on the phone when he arrived, and Cort was relieved he'd been able to avoid small talk with her. Trina was nice enough; petite and attractive with a friendly disposition. Despite the smile she offered, he focused on her eyes and noted the lines around the brows and forehead. They unveiled the fatigue and guilt of a woman who'd been through a nasty divorce less than eight months ago. She hadn't divulged the information to Cort directly, but enough people around town knew, including the friend that had recommended Dr. Galley to him. As Cort was now painfully aware, small-town gossip travels fast. The rumor was that she'd shacked up with Dr. Galley after working in the office for less than a year. Joseph Galley was 12 years her senior and had also recently been divorced. Not a coincidence. Cort fought off a reply that popped into his brain, and instead smiled politely and replied.

"I'm okay, how are you, Trina?"

"Good, Cort, I'm fine. I hope you and Lucie are doing well?"

Ugh. The ITS beckoned a quick and nasty response – something in reference to her and the doc and the couch in his office. He desperately pushed the thought away as the words tried to escape. Though he was able to suppress the zinger before it left his mouth, there was an uncertain fear that he was beginning a horrific phase in his mental health.

"Mr. Palmerton?"

Her voice brought his brain back into focus, and he shifted his eyes to meet hers again.

"Oh, um, yeah, sorry Trina, that's been happening to me lately, where I get lost in a thought. I was starting to say that we're doing better, and I'll tell Lucie you said hi."

He watched the confused expression as she paused, trying to fully process his response. He realized that she'd never met Lucie, and hadn't asked him to tell her hello. It didn't matter and he didn't care. He simply offered a brief smile as her head bobbed hesitantly.

"Good. That's good. Thank you, Cort."

Cort turned to the door and mumbled as he walked through it.

"Have a good day, Trina."

Her reply was barely heard as he pulled the door shut and walked down the steps to the sidewalk.

Chapter 8 – Memory Lane

Relieved to be done with the therapy session, and vowing to never return, Cort headed west towards Main Street. Whatever his psychological struggles would be going forward, he'd deal with them himself, in his own way, for better or for worse. The only thing he liked about the office anyway was its location in the heart of Beaver, PA, a beautiful historic town full of old homes and storefronts, as well as old money. Like many county seats, Beaver was the showcase town of the area, and the resident government officials made sure it stayed that way.

He and Celeste had journeyed the twenty five-minute drive here on many occasions, taking walks through town and frequenting the colorful patchwork of boutiques and restaurants. Those memories popped into his mind now, playing brief snippets, then fading away just as quickly with each passing footstep. Lost in thought, he decided not to return to his car. It was a warm day and he needed air. Turning right on Main Street, he shuffled through the crosswalk and drifted past a few storefronts. Reaching Mario's, a quaint Italian bistro that had been one of his and Celeste's favorites, he paused. There'd been the hope of bringing Lucie here one day, but as he peered through the large window, he couldn't imagine ever walking through the doors again. Staring into the glass, past his own reflection, he focused on a table where he and Celeste had shared many bottles of wine and discussed their life plans over salad and wood-fired pizza. Envisioning her sitting across the table from him, a wave of sadness forced his gaze back to the sidewalk, but her image stayed ingrained in his thoughts; the beautiful face framed perfectly by the dark hair. Her eyes were easy to read, and he'd stared into them a thousand times over the past two decades. They were brown like her father's, pleasantly complementing the warm hue of her half-Mexican skin. Her eyes told of a mostly happy existence, secure in both her beauty and place in life. The lines that ran horizontally away from the corner of her lids were subtle, however, and unveiled a deep-seated desire for something more. Cort had always thought those lines would fade away with the birth of another baby, but that next child was not to be.

He moved past the restaurant window, recalling their conversation about children. Both he and Celeste had always agreed that three kids would be the right number, never imagining that Lucie would be their only one. Their second pregnancy came three years after Lucie was born. They'd timed it that way, wanting to enjoy those early years with her, but hoping to keep the age gap between Lucie and her first sibling within a four-year window. Thirteen days after that positive pregnancy test, Celeste miscarried. The following weeks were so difficult, especially for Celeste. He'd downplayed the situation, telling his wife it was a fluke, and they'd be pregnant again before she knew it. She'd taken it much harder, and it was nearly four months before her head was straight. Eventually she was able to put the loss behind her, and a few months later they'd resumed their efforts.

Cort sighed at the thought, looked up from the sidewalk, and shook his head a little as if answering a question from someone, but nobody was there.

He remembered the third pregnancy more clearly; it was a month before Lucie's 4th birthday when Celeste found out. She'd just bought the test at the pharmacy and gone straight into the store's bathroom. She called him while still perched on the toilet seat.

"Cort, I'm at Walgreens."

Her voice was different, and he sensed excitement or panic, but couldn't quite tell which.

"What are you doing there? Is everything okay?"

"It's fine, it's fine. I couldn't wait until I got home to tell you. I was shopping and felt this little wave of nausea, so I drove straight here."

Cort knew before she finished, and he could hear her getting choked up with joy as the last few words came through the phone. It was a memorable day for him, but for her it was beyond fantastic, like a magical switch had been turned on in her brain. She'd gone to her gynecologist the next day and pleaded for a walk-in appointment. Despite the doctor being booked for the next several weeks, he relented and squeezed her in. The positive test was confirmed, and the estimation was that she was 6 weeks into the term. Cort had convinced her not to tell anyone until at least 12 weeks, reminding her they weren't really in the safe zone until week 14. She'd agreed but buckled in the 10th week and let it slip out to her mother. Gabby in turn had told Manny, and so Cort felt it was only fair to tell his parents that same week. The grandparents were in the loop.

It happened that next weekend, early Saturday morning as she sipped a half-cup of coffee and watched channel 4 news by herself, waiting for Cort and Lucie to wake up. The pain and fear in her eyes terrified him when she shook him awake and began describing the cramping. They both knew, but still came up with at least four other reasons for why she was having them. Thirty-eight minutes later she came out of the bathroom and sunk into his arms, sobbing in anguish. That second miscarriage had hurt physically, but emotionally it was excruciating. The loss was felt much longer than the first. For over a year, there were changes in their relationship, most notably in the intimacy category. She'd made him wear a condom if she suspected her cycle was even close to the ovulation. Cort didn't like it but said absolutely nothing to protest. He just listened and tried to comfort her about the emotions he could not quite relate to.

Neither of them could fathom going through another miscarriage, so they were careful. Again, the disconnect and sadness faded with time, and by the time Lucie was five years old, they were back to having regular and reckless sex. Whatever happened would happen, they agreed, and they'd deal with it like a supportive couple who were grateful to have even one child.

Cort stepped over a scoop of ice cream that lay melting on the sidewalk and thought back to those days. It was early in 2020, just before COVID-19 was unleashed upon the world. His mom and dad had cut their vacation in Italy short to get back stateside, then tested positive three days after landing in the U.S. Both ended up on respirators and suffered for three weeks in intensive care. His dad died first, his mom passing three days later. They'd barely made it to their 70's, and it was another devastating emotional setback for the Palmerton family. The pandemic prohibited a funeral and any kind of proper good-bye, preventing total closure and causing another level of mourning. But he, Celeste, and Lucie shared their grief and supported each other, bringing their small family of three closer together. Another year passed, and like it does without exception, time marched on.

Celeste hadn't even confirmed she was pregnant when she miscarried that third and final time. She'd missed her period, but unwilling to get her hopes up, she'd decided not to take a test until there was another sign. It happened on a rainy Thursday afternoon. She called her OBGYN and described the remains - the doctor estimated the embryo was six to seven weeks old.

There was a numbness to that last one, and both she and Cort threw in the psychological towel. There would be no testing to see what the problem was. Both agreed it wasn't worth the time, money, and mental pain, and then very likely still not learn any definitive reason behind the miscarriages. She obviously wasn't infertile, and he wasn't sterile. Lucie was biological proof their parts worked. Instead of all that rigmarole, they'd reluctantly accepted that Lucie would be an only child. By that time, she'd asked on several occasions about having a little sister or brother, so they told white lies to settle her curiosity and spare her the disappointment. She was very astute for a girl who hadn't even turned seven yet. Lucie had an uncanny perception of the world around her, and very little went unnoticed by her big bright hazel eyes. Cort and Celeste knew the questions would keep coming, and eventually they'd explain the truth to her. But not yet, for now they'd tell her fibs and make excuses, hoping some additional years of maturity would help her better accept the reality. Their own acceptance, however, had an ill effect on the relationship, and Cort remembered the not-so-subtle disconnect in Celeste's touch.

They struggled for many months, and there were very low points where they had doubts about their marriage surviving. Celeste battled depression, and her eating habits changed. She'd lost nearly eleven pounds over the following year, and with her slender frame, she didn't have any to spare. If it weren't for having Lucie during that grueling year and a half, divorce could have easily been the result. But they stayed the course, focused on raising their daughter, peppered in some couple's therapy sessions, and over the next two and a half years, emotions healed again. At the turning point, Celeste said something to him one evening in bed as she laid her head on his chest.

"Cort?"

When he didn't answer, she turned her head up to meet his eyes, and placed her hand gently over his. In a soft and comforting voice, she continued with three simple words.

"Life goes on."

Right then and there, they decided her words would be their mantra going forward, no matter what. During the healing process, Cort and Celeste threw around the prospect of adoption, or maybe even a surrogate. At first it was just wishful fantasizing, but the conversations had turned more serious that Fall. Those options became a regular topic of conversation, and a fair amount of research was invested in both. On Lucie's tenth birthday in early November, they'd sat her down and talked about the notion of having a sibling. To say the least, she was extremely excited, and to her parent's surprise, she had no preference for a sister or brother. Either would be "really awesome," as she'd put it.

They made a plan, to get through the holidays, do some more research over the next few months, then start narrowing down some surrogate candidates and/or adoption agencies by springtime. The plan had put a spark back into their marriage, energy back into their lives, and Cort felt their connection returning. Intimacy picked up over the next couple of months, and there was excitement in the Palmerton household again. Celeste's appetite came back, and she gained the weight she'd lost, even adding a little more. He welcomed the extra pounds. She needed them, and he liked the feel of her curves; they were a sign of health, both physically and mentally.

Now, as his feet traded turns taking the lead on the gray cement sidewalk, he thought back to late December. They'd taken Lucie to Austin to visit Manny and Gabby, and during breakfast on Christmas, she'd announced their plans to have another child. Cort could see Celeste clearly in his mind's eye, sitting there on a stool at the kitchen island, downright giddy talking about the possibilities. She was literally like a kid on Christmas morning. Everything that had capsized in their world was turning upward, slowly and surely righting the ship again. And then, like a massive tidal wave, February 2.

Chapter 9 – *Career Day*

Cort snuck a peek at the dashboard clock as the engine sparked to life. It was more out of habit, and less because he was worried about being on time. Normally he'd have been a little anxious before meeting with a prospective client of this size, but that was then; he could barely relate to that mindset these days. Today he was numb, just like most of the past 136 days. His emotional state was worsening by the week, and his will to be productive was diminishing steadily.

Management at Comstart had placed him on an "action plan," which was a precursor to an eventual termination if performance didn't improve. Despite his decreasing desire to do his job, he focused on closing what would be his biggest deal since taking the position. Landing the UPMC account would equate to 125% of his annual goal, get corporate off his ass, and pay a commission that would be the largest in his employment tenure.

Merging from the exit ramp onto 79 south towards Pittsburgh, Cort tried to mentally prepare and rally himself for the meeting. Today was the day to finalize the deal, the day to wrap up nearly two years of massaging Richey and John, his UPMC contacts. Over the past 24 months, he'd entertained these guys with meals, rounds of golf, and various sporting events, probably totaling 150 hours or so of his time. He'd be in the upscale town of Sewickley in twenty minutes, where they'd meet for lunch. The three of them would eat a fantastic meal, summarize the highlights of the proposal, and discuss any loose ends.

He checked each side view mirror and the rearview twice before he eased into traffic. He'd reviewed the specs of the contract last night to get refamiliarized. Richey and John knew the product, and more importantly, they knew his expertise.

For a decade and a half now, Cort had been promoting ComStart's passive and wireless network infrastructure products to a variety of vertical markets; corporate offices, government buildings, and other healthcare complexes like UPMC's. Nobody in his industry knew them, or the pending project, better than he did. UPMC was Pennsylvania's largest health care provider, becoming a world renowned $23 billion entity that was still expanding their network of state-of-the-art hospitals and health care facilities. His primary focus was on their latest project, a new ten-story vision care facility on the existing Mercy Hospital campus downtown. The facility was only the first phase of a plan to build seven more complexes over the next five years, all of which would need superior cellular coverage for patients, staff, and visitors. This pow-wow was really a formality to ensure both sides were on the same page. Barring any major hiccups, the contract should be bound before lunch ended.

There was only one problem; none of those factors had Cort convinced he could close the deal. His self-confidence was at an all-time low, and his enthusiasm was even lower.

Pushing the gloom to the rear of his mind, Cort tried to focus on his two contacts, both of whom he liked a lot. Richey Kristan, UPMC's Vice President of Technical Service, was critical to having the deal approved. John Mastley, their Manager of Wireless Communication was an equally important decision maker in the final order. Richey and John were nice men, extremely intelligent, and typically talked on a level that was over Cort's head. They were nonetheless fond of Cort, and the three had formed a good friendship over the past couple of years. Cort liked to believe they admired his golf game, in addition to his vast knowledge of communication technology. Deep down, however, he knew what had really piqued their interest in ComStart's products had nothing to do with golf, or him for that matter.

As he pushed the turn signal lever up and merged right off the exit, his mind drifted back to that pivotal dinner with Richey, John, and their wives. Cort wanted them to meet his wife, so he and Celeste met them at an open-air brew pub in a trendy section of town. Celeste looked even more stunning than usual that night, and it was a little uncomfortable when she was first introduced. Richey and John had that nervous look men get when they don't want to stare too long. The introductions were a bit awkward, but Celeste handled it gracefully, and had charmed all four of them by the second round of cocktails. She ordered premium tequila shots for the table and told funny tales about her Mexican grandmother and growing up in Texas. Cort interjected here and there, but Celeste was certainly the headliner that night and their four guests took a genuine liking to her.

He recalled her reaction to one of John's jokes; an eye-roll followed by the flash of a beguiling smile that could soften the heart of a demon. He'd seen the reaction many times. It was followed by a crinkle in her nose and a subtle giggle, letting the joke-teller know that she'd gotten the humor. She'd done it twice that evening, and John and Richey had been totally taken in by her. After that night, communications were noticeably different between Cort and the UPMC guys. Their interest level had literally increased five-fold, and from there it was a slow and steady path that led them to this day. The memory of that dinner troubled him now as he turned the wheel onto the Sewickley Exit ramp,

Until a few months ago, Cort had been ambitiously driven by the pending deal between ComStart and UPMC. The significant financial win and the prestige he'd gain within his division had once been very motivating. The circumstances were so different now, and those motivations were all but gone.

Drifting through a stop sign, a twinge of anxiety began to fester in his gut. The thought of seeing Richey and John was nearly overwhelming, and Cort knew it had little to do with the lack of motivation to close the deal. He admitted to himself that his confidence was gone, perishing alongside Celeste more than four months ago.

Four minutes later he parked in the restaurant lot but did not exit the car. No matter how much he willed himself, Cort simply couldn't open the door. He'd have to answer their questions, talk about the details, and lie about how he was living now. He reached his right hand to the gear shift lever and pulled it into reverse. After checking the three mirrors and the back-up camera image, he let off the brake. It felt like the point of no return, but that feeling didn't cause a change in his course. As the vehicle backed into the center of the lot, he pulled the shifter down again and applied pressure to the gas pedal. Before turning right out of the lot, he picked up his phone, tapped in the contact, and dialed Richey.

"This is Richey."

"Hey, Richey, it's Cort."

"Yeah, hi, Cort. You running a little late?"

Cort paused and swallowed. "I just pulled in, Richey. I have to cancel."

"What do you mean? Are you alright?" Richey's tone was of genuine disappointment.

"I'm fine, but Lucie, she's sick," he lied, "I just got a call from her friend's mom. Really sorry, Richey. Please give my apologies to John too. We'll need to re-schedule."

"Well shoot, that stinks. I'm sorry to hear it, Cort. Hope she feels better soon."

Cort sensed a bit of doubt in Richey's cadence, but he didn't care. This meeting wasn't happening today, and it was becoming more and more plausible that it never would.

"Thanks, Richey, and sorry again. I'll touch base with you guys soon."

"Sure thing, Cort, take care."

"Bye."

The call ended; Cort put the car in drive and headed back the way he'd just come. As he drove in the opposite direction through the poshly quaint town, he admitted to himself that this day would likely mark the end of his career. Deep down, the thought materialized into the realization that this just might be the beginning of the end of everything.

***

Soccer practice hadn't exactly gone well today, and Lucie was in no mood to listen to the post-practice pep talk. Her thoughts wandered as she blankly stared at Coach Liam - his words going in one ear and out the other. Her only focus was her father.

Dad looked so stressed out today.

Maybe it was the important meeting he'd mentioned, but she was almost sure it was the sadness. It just seemed worse this morning. She stared at the coach's moving lips, pretending to be interested, but not caring at all. Coach Liam's strategy for their game this weekend just couldn't compete with her fear of Dad not getting better. What if, instead, he continued to get worse? Would he leave her behind, and search for happiness somewhere else? As she sat in the grass next to her teammates, the questions pecked at her and sent little waves of anxiety through her already hurting heart. She needed to come up with a plan, some sort of distraction to change his focus. That was it, she decided, if he didn't look any better by this afternoon, she'd do something. What that would be, she had no idea, but she would figure out a way.

Chapter 10 – Company

As the exit for Cranberry approached on his right, Cort pushed the gas pedal down and increased his speed, rapidly moving past the ramp that would have led him home. The decision was made; today would be the day that he'd confront one of the many plaguing demons in his head. With one hand on the wheel, he reached over to the glove box and pulled out the small, gift-wrapped box. He'd gathered it from the coroner's office, along with a pair of pearl earrings and her wedding band. Apparently, everything else on her person was unsalvageable - blood stained and torn - and the coroner's office manager had mercifully made the decision to discard most of it. He'd put the jewelry in her closet organizer, tucking it away until the time came to give those pieces to Lucie. The wrapped gift, however, he'd put in his glove box, with the plan to open it once he was emotionally stable. That was close to five months ago and he'd all but given up on that plan. The new plan was to open it when he was in an especially dark place, hoping the gift itself would bring him some sliver of happiness. Today seemed appropriate, as his life and emotions were sliding dangerously out of control, in the direction of rock bottom and even beyond. The pit in his stomach was deepening, and the thoughts in his head were getting darker. He couldn't imagine feeling worse, so the gamble was minimal. He'd go to the spot and open the box, and maybe, just maybe, Celeste's final gift to him would be a sign of how to proceed... how to move on and away from his guilt and pain.

Traveling the same route as he had that February day, Cort drove north past the exit, and made the round-about loop until the Evans City exit came into view. He slowed and pulled his vehicle to the shoulder before he reached the exit and stopped just at the point where the main highway and the ramp connected. The deja-vu was thick, and laden with despair. Pressing the 4-way flasher button on his dash, he turned the engine off and checked his side mirror before exiting the vehicle. Cars and trucks whizzed by at 75 miles per hour, with the occasional vehicle slowing down to take the exit. The sound of air brakes startled him as an 18-wheeler approached from behind him. His heart jumped and then sank, as he turned to see the grille of the tractor-trailer speeding past him. Cort moved closer to the side of the road and continued down the right shoulder of the ramp. Within thirty seconds, he could see ahead to the curve, where the ramp split, and the location of the collision came into view. Another vehicle raced by him on the exit ramp, and the beep-beep of the horn being tapped startled him again. Moving further right onto the disappearing shoulder, he trudged as close as he could get to the guard rail, just at the edge of the asphalt. With the box in one hand, Cort reached over the rail with his other to a cluster of wildflowers, tearing a bunch from their stems. Each blossom had six yellow petals.

Maybe buttercups...she'll like these.

The memory of that February night flooded his thoughts, as the scene became all too vivid. He'd raced down this same shoulder after ignoring the roadblock of emergency vehicles and firemen. It was a state trooper that eventually came between him and the mangled, smoking mass of debris. The officer had literally stopped Cort in his tracks, physically restraining him from moving any closer.

Glancing at the yellow flowers, he focused on their color and design and pushed the images of the scene away. Continuing down the shoulder, he glanced backwards regularly to make sure he knew what was approaching from behind. Part of him worried about being hit by a vehicle, while another dark part of his mind welcomed what could be a quick death. Another check of the road was made to verify it was clear before dashing across it to where the ramp split. A few more yards ahead, and he knew he was now standing on the spot. Examining the area, he noticed small shards of glass, both clear and colored, still scattered into the shoulder where the gravel and grass meshed together. A section of metal trim finished in chrome, lay a few yards further down into the landscape, and while the grass and weeds had mostly recovered by now, there was still evidence of tire ruts and damaged turf. He knelt into a soft area of grass, directly in the middle of the presumed collision location. Wind from a passing car blew the flower petals in rhythm. Cort didn't turn around. The world surrounding him turned quiet, as he lay the flowers in the grass before him.

    He looked up, focusing further down the ramp. There was a spot up the road about two hundred feet, where she could have pulled the car over. Had he told her to drive further, and not been as worried about the tire rim, she'd have ended up there and avoided the accident. The deep guilt pulsed through him as he confirmed what he'd feared was possible.

    "I'm sorry, Celeste. I miss you so much."

    Her memory crushed him like a giant wave, taking away his air and choking his lungs with grief. Tears rolled down both cheeks as he brought the gift-wrapped box over his thigh and began tearing the paper away. The box itself was mostly plain and white, with a muted imprint of a pattern on the lid. It could easily pass as a woman's watch or jewelry box, peaking his curiosity as he contemplated opening it. There wasn't enough weight to be a watch, but maybe a ring or bracelet of some kind. Instinctively he knew that wasn't it; he'd never asked for any kind of jewelry, and she'd never bought him anything of the sorts. Slowly, reluctantly, Cort pulled one side of the lid up, and then the other, until it cleared the lip and easily fell to the side. A piece of paper lay on top, folded once into a square, nearly matching the inner perimeter of the box perfectly. It was propped up, resting upon the object that lay directly beneath it. Presuming the paper to be a handwritten note, Cort flipped up one side without lifting it from the box and read the short two-word message.

Ten Weeks!

The confusion only lasted a half-second, before he removed the note to reveal the hard piece of plastic underneath. Several more tears fell as he picked the self-pregnancy test from the box and turned it in his hand. Two faded colored lines were revealed in the viewing window, and there was no question as to what they meant. The revelation washed over him like an enormous second wave that hits just after recovering from the first one. His body sunk down, head into his chest, as Cort knelt and sobbed on the side of the exit ramp. He was drowning now, and the concept of dying was less of a threat, and more of a welcomed ending to his pain.

Time passed by unnoticed as the world around him continued in silence. It could have been a minute or an hour. The sorrow overwhelmed him, precluding any real cognitive thought. He simply wanted to hold her again, and the weight of her loss was crushing his shoulders down. Sinking further into himself, Cort's head was nearly touching his knees when the blare of the siren shocked him back into reality.

"Jesus F'ing Christ!"

Cort turned and shouted in surprised anger at the police car that had pulled onto the shoulder fifty feet behind him. As he stood, he used the sleeve of his shirt to wipe the liquid trails, still wet on both cheeks.

The trooper stepped out of the cruiser with the roof lights still flashing and Cort felt a twinge of regret about his reaction. He'd shouted at a police officer, who'd surely stopped to ensure Cort was okay. The sense of regret grew as the officer closed the cruiser door and his frame was revealed. The man was built well; there was no mistaking that the lines in his shirt were the loose outlines of biceps and pectorals. His dark skin and uniform carried a look of intensity, and as an added factor of intimidation, his gait was both strong and deliberate. The expression on the man's face was mostly of concern, but Cort picked up a subtle hint of agitation along the trooper's brow. As the cop approached, however, his face softened a bit.

There was an acknowledgement of sorts. Maybe he'd seen Cort wipe the streaks of pain and regret from his face, but it seemed to be something more. Cort recognized him, and the look in the trooper's eye conveyed a reciprocal recognition.

Standing and simultaneously pushing the plastic pregnancy test into his back pocket, Cort raised both hands to his sides. He gave a double wave to the officer, both as a friendly gesture and to show that his palms were empty. As the cop approached to within ten feet, Cort remembered his face; the **[J.Leonard]** name plate on his chest confirmed Cort's initial suspicion. He was the same trooper that had arrived at the accident scene a few minutes before Cort himself.

"Hey, officer," Cort spoke loudly as a tractor trailer passed by on 79 South just a hundred yards away.

"Cort Palmerton?" Officer Leonard asked matter-of-factly, but not harshly. There was a tone of compassion in the question. Cort nodded back and J. Leonard gave a solemn nod in return.

"I recognize you. You were the trooper on the scene here back in February, right?"

"Yes, that was me. Tough day." Leonard paused, lacking words. "Damn tough day. I never really got the chance to talk to you before Officer Simms took you home."

"Yeah, no, but that's fine. I think you left me a couple voice messages maybe?" Cort swallowed hard, still trying to suppress the images and emotions connected with the pregnancy test that he could feel against his upper right butt cheek.

"I did." Leonard gave another quick nod.

Cort sensed just a bit of awkwardness in the trooper's voice, likely uncomfortable with the subject at hand too.

"Yeah, that's right. I remember." Cort half-uttered the confirmation to himself, sensing the odd tension as well. There was another pause that lasted much too long, as both men thought back to that horrific day and recalled the scene.

"I'm not in trouble, am I?" Cort broke the silence, in the hopes of curtailing the memory and ending what already seemed like a very odd traffic stop.

"No, you aren't." The cop answered abruptly. "And you can call me Josh."

Josh Leonard, Josh Leonard?

The name was familiar to Cort, and not just from those follow up voice messages the trooper had left for him.

"Oh good. Well then, if I'm not in trouble Josh, what can I do for you."

"How about you jump in the cruiser with me? I need to get you off the side of this exit ramp." The question came off as more of a strong suggestion than it did a request, and Cort paused before he answered.

"Sir, Josh, I can just walk back up to my car. It's just off the shoulder up around the bend there." Cort pointed up the ramp.

"You mean the silver Ford, with the four-way flashers on?" The question held enough sarcasm that Cort understood it wasn't truly a question.

A forced grin crossed Cort's lips, followed by a half-hearted nod. "Yeah, I guess you just passed it. But anyway, I can just walk back. No need to trouble yourself.

The officer looked back at Cort, and shook his head from side to side before speaking again.

"You know what, I'd feel a lot better if you just got in my car. I'll take you back up around and bring you down 79 to your car. Don't want you walking up the side of this ramp…"

His sentence ended awkwardly, as if he'd nearly added something else but caught himself. Cort wondered if Leonard was going to follow with "it's dangerous," but then realized Cort was the last person that needed to be told.

"Yeah, I get it. That's fine. Gimme a minute." Cort turned his back to the officer and returned his gaze to the grass just off the shoulder.

He picked up the box and lid and pushed them together into his front pocket. Reaching into his back pocket where he'd stuffed the hard piece of plastic, he grasped the pregnancy test, closed his eyes, and made a silent and solemn plea. *Celeste, please help me. I'm lost in all of this, and I don't think I can be the father Lucie needs right now. I want to be with you there, and my gut is telling me that Lucie will be better off without me here. If you could just give me a sign, any kind of sign, guiding me down the right path. Please Celeste.*

A minute later he was still lost in thought, staring out the passenger side window of the cruiser. Officer Leonard had said something to him, but the words didn't register.

"I'm sorry, Josh, what did you say?"

"I asked if you still lived in Cranberry."

"Oh, yeah, we do. Lucie and I… Lucie's my daughter, we've talked about moving, but just hypothetically. The problem is we don't know where we'd go."

"Mmm Hmm." Josh acknowledged the answer.

Thirty seconds of silence followed, and the cruiser made a couple u-turns that were surely illegal to the everyday commuter. Cort sensed that Leonard, like himself, wanted this to be as short of a car ride as possible. As they entered the highway ramp and merged onto 79 north, Cort felt powerful acceleration as the cruiser gained speed. A glance at the speedometer showed that they were approaching 80 MPH.

"I'm not too far from you then, Cort. We're down in Wexford."

Cort surmised that the "we're" referenced Josh and his family.

"So yeah, you're probably within 20 minutes or so from me. I'm assuming you have a family?"

"Yes, married. We have three boys." Josh kept his voice steady.

"Oh, nice."

J. Leonard just nodded twice and continued driving in silence. It wasn't until they'd exited 79 north, driven under the highway, and entered the ramp back onto 79 south before Josh spoke again.

"You know, Cort, if I could stop by sometime, I do have a few follow-up questions for you. Just some loose ends I need to tie up before I close my file."

Cort's chest muscles tightened. The last thing he wanted to do was answer questions about that day again. There was nothing left to tell. He'd given his statement, more than once, describing the events prior to the crash exactly as they'd unfolded. It was all recorded. What could this cop possibly need from him? Negative thoughts began to materialize in his head, and Cort sensed the ITS emerging at the edge of his brain waves. He took a deep breath and prematurely replied with the first thing he could think of.

"Sure, officer, I mean Josh. Just let me know. You have my number in your files, right? Never mind, of course you do. You've already left me messages, duh."

Inside his head, he cringed at the fact that he'd agreed to do something so dreaded. His ITS was unleashed, only this time he cursed silently at himself.

Dammit Cort, you jackass!

***

As he watched Cort walk back to his own vehicle, Officer Leonard thought back to that February evening. He'd bear-hugged Cort, using most of his leverage to prevent the frantic man from reaching the accident, and that was the easy part. The image ingrained in his head now, was the one of Cort sitting in the back of the cruiser, as he'd returned from the wreckage with Celeste Palmerton's driver's license. Josh remembered Cort Parlmerton's face clearly, staring out the window of the cruiser, already realizing what news he was about to receive. Josh opened the door, handed the driver's license to him, and remorsefully moved his head from side to side. He'd placed his hand on Palmerton's shoulder, as the man's chin dropped to his chest. No details were exchanged – none needed to be. As Cort's head and shoulders shook in a silent sob, Leonard had simply told him that he was very, very, sorry. Josh related to him all too well. The pain, the guilt, the loss – all emotions that Leonard understood. Maybe he could help Cort Palmerton. It was worth a shot. Leonard got the impression that Cort would reject his efforts, but that didn't matter, it wouldn't stop him from trying.

Chapter 11 – Not Good Company

Hearing the click of his seatbelt, Cort pressed the start button then peered in the rearview mirror. Within seconds, the sirens of the cruiser behind him went dark, just as the cop had promised they would. Checking the mirrors multiple times, he pulled the car off the shoulder and accelerated down the ramp and onto Rt 19 south.

The feeling of hopelessness returned as he was alone again with his thoughts, fresh off the discovery that his unborn child was also lost in the accident. The timing could not have been worse. Just a week ago, he'd made a promise to himself to think more positively, in an effort to subdue the influx of suicidal thoughts. He'd hoped they would have slowed once the school year ended and Lucie was home more, but it was over two weeks into summer break now, and the morbid scenarios he'd been considering were still on the uptick. As he changed lanes rapidly, those thoughts were forefront and center. Cort accepted he was not a human other people wanted to be around. Suggesting "he was not good company" was nothing less than a gross understatement; like saying the devil wasn't the best guest to invite to a baptism. Lucie seemed to be the one person who wasn't completely uncomfortable around him, and he was sure that would change soon.

At the top of the hill, he turned right into the lot of the Sunoco gas station and parked in an empty stall. He searched his pockets for her photo, the wallet-sized one he'd been loosely carrying around with him the past several weeks. To see Lucie's face was instant therapy, her image reminding him of the one part of his life that mattered. Finding nothing except empty pockets and an empty soul, Cort sat and stared blankly out the front window, his eyes blurring with tears. He wiped his face with his sleeve and reached for the phone. Opening the Google app, the Butler County Coroner's Office was searched, and the phone icon next to the phone number tapped. Seconds later, he heard the ringing of the phone through his car speaker system.

"Butler County Coroner's office," The woman's voice on the other end was surprisingly pleasant.

"Yes, hello. I need to speak with the coroner." Cort gulped and cleared his throat.

"The Chief or the Deputy sir?"

"Uh, well I'm not sure. Whoever performed the autopsy on Celeste Palmerton."

"Alright sir, and who am I speaking with?"

"This is Cort Palmerton, the deceased's widow. Sorry, widower."

"Just a second, Mr. Palmerton." There was a 10-second pause before she responded again. "Okay, it was Deputy Coroner Bill King. Let me see if he's available to talk."

Placed on hold, Cort wiped moisture from under his eyes and drank from his water container. When the phone clicked back on a minute later, a male's voice came through the speakers.

"Mr. Palmerton." The voice was deep, possibly a result of smoking.

"Yes sir, this is Cort Palmerton. I was hoping to ask you some questions about an autopsy you performed on my wife back in February. Her name is... was, Celeste Palmerton."

"I have it pulled up here. What is it I can tell you?"

Cort detected a slight hint of apprehension in the deputy coroner's voice.

"Well, I'm not sure what you remember or what information is contained in the report, but if you could just summarize the findings for me." Cort could hear his own voice shaking and hoped the coroner didn't detect it on the other end.

"Well, let me see here. In brief, it looks like the autopsy was ordered due to your wife's death being ruled a homicide. It's standard procedure in that case."

King paused a second, and Cort assumed he was trying to remember back to February.

"Um." Another pause. "Quite honestly, Mr. Palmerton, it wouldn't have been necessary otherwise. The cause of death was very apparent in your wife's case."

"And that was blunt force trauma to the head and torso, correct?" Cort swallowed hard. He remembered what was listed on the death certificate clearly.

"Well, yes, that was the primary cause. Secondary cause was, um, critical volume of blood loss."

Cort was aware that his wife had nearly been decapitated, and appreciated Bill King softening the secondary cause, but he could feel his gut begin to churn with nausea.

"I can tell you this if it means anything, Mr. Palmerton, your wife's death was probably instantaneous - she did not suffer."

The heavy sigh Cort heard was his own. Five long seconds passed before he was able to speak again.

"Thank you, Mr. King, I appreciate that." Another pause, before Cort continued. "Sir, can you tell me if there was anything in the report suggesting my wife was pregnant?"

Cort could nearly hear Deputy Coroner Bill King's heart skip a beat as the question registered.

"Mr. Palmerton, there was no indication of a...." He stopped mid-sentence and his tone turned a bit defensive. "Mr. Palmerton, I'm not sure I'll be able to answer all of your questions in this case."

"Mr. King," Cort replied in a softened tone, "I'm not asking you in a legal sense or anything here. This is all off the record, I promise you. I recently learned… I have reason to believe Celeste was pregnant at the time of her death."

"I'm so sorry about that, Mr. Palmerton. There was no indication of pregnancy from anyone in the family, or anyone else for that matter, so there'd be no real reason for us to test for it. From my recollection, there also wasn't any visual indication she was pregnant. As I'm sure you know, many women don't even begin to show until late into the first trimester, or even early second trimester sometimes."

"She would have been about 10 weeks." Cort offered the information.

"Again, I'm very sorry, Mr. Palmerton." The coroner paused in consideration, then resumed with a hesitant tone. "Uh, there's only one way to, um, confirm pregnancy at this point."

"Exhuming the body?" The words came out of Cort's mouth with a crack in his voice, and another wave of nausea hit him."

"Correct. That would have to come via court order at the request of the DA."

Cort inhaled and exhaled deeply to strengthen his voice. "I understand. Thank you, Mr. King. I don't have any other questions... appreciate your help." He was losing his ability to speak.

"Certainly, Mr. Palmerton, please let me know if there's anything else I can help you with. And uh, well, I'm... I'm very sorry for your loss."

Cort detected the heavy sigh from the other end of the line this time. He made an unsuccessful attempt to thank the coroner for his sympathy. Struggling to breath, let alone talk, Cort tapped the button to end the call, tossed his phone into the seat next to him, and wept.

Chapter 12 – Bad Company

Swallowing back a long drink of water, Cort finally put the car in reverse but kept his foot on the brake. He'd sat in the gas station lot for nearly ten minutes, unable to settle his stomach and completely process the information he'd learned. He almost dialed his attorney's number. Surely the legal team would use the pregnancy to open the criminal case again and add to the civil suit. The truck driver would possibly be charged with another homicide, and likely have time added to his sentence. And with the civil case, the damages would most certainly be increased, quite possibly doubled. Cort put the phone down, picturing the court room, each side making their case as to whether a ten-week-old fetus constituted a life, or not. He couldn't be part of a trial - not another one. It would be unbearably painful. Though he realized his physical presence would not be necessary in the courtroom, it wouldn't change the fact that Celeste's body would need to be exhumed. He couldn't fathom it, and the image of it made him more nauseous. He threw the car back into park, opened his car door and vomited into the gas station parking lot. The pregnancy would be information that only he would know for now, and quite possibly forever.

Pulling out of the lot and back onto Rt 19, the suicidal thoughts returning. He wanted it all to end sooner than later. The pain of missing Celeste was searing, and the guilt of failing to prevent her death was unbearable. None of Celeste's future dreams would come true. She wouldn't see Lucie graduate, or get married, or hold her grandchild. And poor Lucie wouldn't have her mother by her side through any of it. It was his fault, and he shouldn't get to be part of his daughter's life. More than ever, Cort welcomed death, and more importantly, he believed he deserved it.

Desperate for it all to end, he drove mindlessly, considering the different options for ending his life. The car could be a solution, driving head on into a stationary object without his seatbelt buckled. It should work, he considered, but it wasn't a guarantee by any means. The airbag would deploy, and likely prevent death. He might become maimed or dismembered, but that was not the goal.

A gun shot? He didn't own a gun, but he presumed it wouldn't be too difficult to get his hands on one. Maybe he could borrow one, but from whom?

Damn it Cort, think simpler!

The toaster in the bathtub method would be easy, and he had both a bathtub and a toaster. But, he considered, whoever found him fried and naked in the tub would be emotionally scarred forever. There would be considerable planning involved; he'd have to make sure it wouldn't be Lucie who discovered him. The idea was abandoned, though the water element of it was somewhat appealing, and incited the best idea he'd come up with so far.

Drowning. Death by water, the substance which had brought him so many joyful experiences over the past 40 years. Somewhere in his twisted thoughts, he theorized it would be fitting to spend his last minutes of life surrounded by the thing that had made him the happiest.

Or is that just morbidly psychotic?

Confused at his own reasoning, he tried to focus elsewhere, reminding himself of the silent request he'd made to Celeste not more than an hour ago. That request repeated in his thoughts again.

Send me a sign, Celeste, please send me a sign.

Slowly reaching for the button on the dash, he contemplated whether the radio should be turned on. It hadn't been possible to listen to music since February 2nd, and there was no reason to think today would be any different. There was the fact, however, that he desperately needed an immediate distraction. Otherwise, the impulse to drive into an electrical pole going 70 mph might just get the best of him.

The right song could take his mind somewhere else; a different reality far from his own. Maybe he'd find another inspiration in the music; an idea for how to move forward, or on the other hand, end his life.

His pointer finger felt the cool plastic of the power button. Before pushing it, he moved it once in a circle around the button's circumference. Cort decided it was worth the gamble for the chance at some sort of therapeutic benefit.

Worth a shot. Not much left to lose.

Two-second intervals of music filled his car for the first time in a long time as Cort flipped through the six preset stations using the button on his steering wheel. The Pop station came on first. Click. No way he could tolerate some upbeat song about young love. Another click, passing on the Country station - way too risky. He paused after a couple more taps, settling on the city's classic rock station. It was his best chance for a non-sappy song, and that assumption was confirmed immediately. He instantly recognized the familiar piano and slide-guitar rift as the ending of *Layla,* by Derek and the Dominos. It was a love song, but the Eric Clapton sung lyrics were over, leaving the long instrumental ending that triggered a shift in his brain function. His thoughts were immediately taken to the movie *Goodfellas,* a mob-flick he'd watched a dozen times over the years. This song always brought his thoughts to that scene; the bodies of the characters connected with the Lufthansa heist being discovered all over the city. The clips played through his head to the soundtrack, as he pictured the corpses of Johnny Roastbeef and his wife in the pink Cadillac, Frenchy in the garbage truck, and of course Frankie Carbone frozen in the back of the meat truck. The distraction was briefly successful, but it took less than a minute for the images of death to weigh heavy on his psyche. Wisely, Cort fast-forwarded his brain past the scene in the movie. The dead bodies were replaced by an image of Henry Hill, the only principal character who didn't end up dead or in prison. The piano interlude played on as Cort thought of Henry, standing in his doorway at the end of the movie. Having had his former life crumble down around him, Hill was destined to live out his years as an average Joe in an average suburbia. Seeing the scene in his mind, Cort couldn't help but connect Henry Hill's future to that of his and Lucie's. Would they be destined, like Henry, to a life of solitude, frustration, and bitterness, about a past that could never exist again? The thoughts struck him like bullets, piercing his heart and brain with shots of emotional torment.

Before more tears materialized, the song's ending faded away, and there was radio silence for what seemed way too long. Seconds passed and Cort's finger moved to the scan button again as he prepared to change the channel. The station seemed to be experiencing technical difficulty, but just before he pressed the button, another song began. He immediately recognized the soft guitar and drums, connecting the melody and chords to a memory well before the vocals of Paul Rodgers even began. The song was from an album that his Uncle Burke had given him many years ago, back in the mid 90's when Cort was entering his teens. Uncle Burke was cool, and by simple default, Cort respected his taste in music. It was one of several CD's his uncle had gifted to him over the years. The album title, *10 from 6,* was a compilation of 10 songs from the bands 6 prior albums. Cort had scarcely heard of the band, Bad Company, prior to the day his uncle gifted him the cd, but he soon became a fan after just a few listens. Most of the ten songs were very good; catchy rock rifts that captured the 70's and early 80's era. The single that was Cort's favorite by far was now playing through his car speaker, and instead of turning off the radio, he touched the button on his steering wheel to turn the volume up a notch.

"Shooting Star" was also a song about love - the love for music. It told of a young boy who was inspired one day to pick up a guitar, and his consequential rise to rock stardom.

> *Johnny was a schoolboy*
> *When he heard his first Beatles song,*
> *Love me do, I think it was*

From there it didn't take him long

He listened as images from his childhood bedroom flooded his thoughts, scenes of himself laying on his bed with his stereo system turned up. The lyrics went on to tell how Johnny bought a guitar and practiced playing it every night, eventually joining a band and hitting it big. The song title, "Shooting Star," referenced Johnny's fast rise to musical fame. As the electric guitars came in after the second verse, Cort tapped his fingers on the steering wheel to the rhythm. He was distracted from the suicidal thoughts, no longer interpreting each passing stationary object as a potential means to end his suffering. Just what the doctor ordered.

As the guitar interlude between the second and third verse played, Cort took a deep breath and got lost in the music, wondering if music could be a positive experience for him again. Just as he was about to accept that theory, he remembered the ending of the song. Up until right before the third verse started, he'd forgotten about Johnny's fate.

Johnny died one night, died in his bed.
Bottle of whiskey, sleeping tablets by his head.
Johnny's life passed him by like a warm summer day
If you listen to the wind, ...

Cort hit the power button and cut Paul Rodgers off mid-sentence. His shoulders slumped and his vision blurred. He barely had the wherewithal to pull over but managed to get his car onto the shoulder and into the lot of a Dodge dealership. Thoughts were scrambled as he threw the car into park and buried his face in his hands. He was overwhelmed by the last words he'd heard, and their interpreted meaning was of shock and relief simultaneously. *Whiskey and sleeping pills, of course!* Why hadn't he thought of it before. So simple, so clean, and so painless. Cort pulled his hands down to his lap and tilted his head back as far as it would go. Staring upwards, projecting his vision through the roof of his vehicle, Cort remembered the solemn prayer for help he'd made to Celeste earlier. His eyes closed, and he softly whispered his appreciation to the heavens.

"Celeste, thank you."

Eyes shut tight, Cort processed the lyrics. Johnny had lived a fast-paced dream-come-true existence. The price, however, was a short lifespan with an apparent not-so-pleasant ending. Something had driven Johnny to pills and alcohol, and he'd ended whatever pain it was that had plagued him. Rock-star Johnny had burned bright and fast, just as the object of the song title. Cort made the connection to his own life as a tear of painful enlightenment leaked from his left eyelid. He'd lived in a muted state of euphoria for the years he'd been together with Celeste. There were speed bumps, as in any marriage, but for the most part they were the happiest people he knew. Blessed with Lucie at the halfway point in the fairytale, their lives had been full of love and satisfaction through it all. He'd lived like a shooting star in his own right, and February marked the instant in time when his light began the process of burning out. He was convinced that by some miraculous answer, Celeste had been responsible for the song coming on at that moment. She was calling him back to her, and now he knew the path to get there.

"Can I help you?"

The voice through the closed window was muffled but discernible, and most definitely not Celeste's. The question was followed by a rapid tap on the glass.

Cort's head jerked forward and his eyes shot open as he turned toward the rat-tat-tat from the passenger side window. He made a quick wipe of his face for what seemed like the twentieth time today, eliminating any evidence of crying, then hit the power-window button. As the glass descended into the door, the man wearing a shirt and tie offered a brief smile and spoke again.

"Are you waiting for somebody, or maybe I can help you find a vehicle?"

Cort detected some confusion in the man's voice, but there was also a slight hint of annoyance.

"No, I'm not waiting for anyone. Just pulled in to get my bearings." Cort tipped his head and pursed his lips in a non-apologetic gesture. The man reciprocated Cort's frosty demeanor.

"Yeah well, I can't have you parked here in front of the aisle." The man pointed at two rows of cars on the other side of Cort.

Cort turned his head in the direction of the man's pointer finger. Suggesting he was blocking access to the aisle was beyond an exaggeration. The ITS immediately kicked in as he looked back at the man with his own exaggerated expression of annoyed confusion.

"If you don't mind," the man paused and barely softened his tone, "maybe you could get your bearings somewhere down the road."

Simply nodding and shifting his car into drive, Cort closed his lips and sent a brief smile to the man before calmly responding.

"Yeah, sure. And hey, if you don't mind, maybe you can go fuck yourself?"

With that, Cort made a 360 degree turn in the lot and passed by the man who simply stood with his arms crossed, seemingly trying to decide whether he should yell after the car or not. Cort hit the brakes and waited, hoping to some degree that the man would yell something nasty back. He was certainly open to a physical altercation with the car-guy. Cort hadn't been in a fist fight since he was nineteen, and that one hadn't ended well. He'd suffered a fractured jaw and permanent damage to his left eardrum. His opponent was banged up too, and in the end, their attorneys convinced both to drop the assault charges against each other. The last thing Cort needed was another layer of negative attention in his life right now, and yet he put his right hand on the gear shift, ready to jerk it into park and jump out of the car. Ultimately, the man in the shirt and tie wisely chose the high road and turned back towards the showroom. He'd just about reached the glass door when Cort tapped his horn twice, sending a final gesture of saltiness.

    Nearly in unison, both men uttered the same word to themselves.

    "Asshole."

Chapter 13 – Prescription for Peace

Shooting another glance at the dash mounted clock, Cort realized he had over an hour before he was due to pick Lucie up at her friend's house. He was expecting the deal-closing lunch to be a long one - certainly longer than the time it took to pull into the restaurant's lot and abruptly turn around to leave. Instead, he'd spent his time learning information that deepened his pain and depression to an all-time low. He'd struggled to get out of bed this morning, now wishing he'd stayed there. He admitted to himself if it hadn't been for Lucie, he'd still be wrapped in the sheets and balled up in his misery. Convincing himself his new path was the correct one, he apologized internally to his daughter.

I'm no good for you anymore, Lucie. Trust me, this is best for both of us. I'm sorry.

He had until 3:00 before Lucie was expecting him, which gave him enough time to gather some supplies. Driving and searching his contact records simultaneously, he found Dr. Galley's number and hit the phone icon. Trina's familiar voice came through his speaker system after the third ring.

"Good afternoon, Dr. Joseph Galley's office."

"Hi, Trina, this is Cort Palmerton. Is Dr. Galley available?"

"Oh, hi, Cort." Her voice remained cheery. "I think he might be between sessions but let me check for you."

Cort sighed as she placed him on hold. Her desk was just outside of the doctor's office door. He was either *in* a session or *not in* a session - did she really not know. He decided she knew either way but had played the *unsure* card just in case Galley didn't want to talk. Fair enough. When the phone clicked back, it was the doc that answered.

"Hey, Cort, how are you?" His voice was dry, and Cort detected forced concern.

"Oh, you know, just peachy, Dr. Galley." Cort chuckled sarcastically. "I'm actually really tired doc," he lied. "It's been a few weeks since I got a solid night sleep, which is why I'm calling. Is there something you can prescribe to help me catch some Z's?"

There was a pause as Dr. Joseph Galley considered the request. "Have you tried melatonin, Cort?"

"Yeah, I gave it a shot. I think it helps me fall asleep, but I don't stay asleep." Cort fibbed again.

"Mmm Hmph." Galley feigned a higher degree of concern.

"Doc, it's getting to the point that I'm not functioning well during the day. I'm driving home right now and feeling like I want to drift off - it's getting bad." Cort stretched the truth, though part of him did want to 'drift off' the road, and it had nothing to do with fatigue.

"That's not good. Hmph."

"No, it's not good," Cort agreed and played the part convincingly. "I think it's actually getting a little dangerous."

There were a few seconds of silence, and Cort could almost hear Galley pondering. He knew doctors didn't like to prescribe anything without a visit first. Patients were known to lie about symptoms to satisfy prescription drug addictions, but the doc should know Cort wasn't that kind of case. He'd verbalized his anti-prescription stance once or twice and rejected the previous depression and anxiety drugs Galley had prescribed.

"Listen, Cort, I'm going to call you in a prescription. It's the Rite Aid in Cranberry, correct?"

"Yes, the one on 19."

"I'll call it in when we hang up, but here's the deal. You need to promise you'll come in for a session within the next couple of weeks, okay?" The doc's conditional offer hung in the air.

"That's fair, I'll do that." Cort made the promise assuming it wouldn't need to be kept.

"Good. Now listen, Cort. This script I'm calling in is nothing to mess around with, alright? You never take more than one pill. In fact, I'd recommend starting with half a tablet, and see how that works first. If you still have trouble sleeping, go to a full pill, but never more than that. If one pill doesn't do the trick, we can always try a different prescription."

Cort hesitated in his response, still considering the fact the doctor had used the word 'tablet,' just like in the song. He decided it was in sync with Celeste's sign, confirming his planned path.

"Okay?" Dr. Galley added, patiently waiting for Cort to agree to terms.

"Sure, yes, absolutely. Thank you, doctor."

"Give it twenty minutes or so and you should be able to pick up the prescription. I'm going to switch you over to Trina now so you can set up a session."

"Perfect. Thanks again. And hey, doc, I know I'm not the best patient. I'm sure you can tell psychiatry isn't really my thing. But hey, I uh, I appreciate you trying to help me through this. Thank you."

Another brief pause. Cort clenched his fist, hoping Galley would interpret Cort's gratitude as a small breakthrough in emotion, and not as a subtle good-bye.

"You're welcome. Get some sleep and I'll see you soon. Here's Trina."

Several seconds passed as Cort waited on hold, giving him time to contemplate what was happening. Half of him was disgusted by the course he was considering, and the other half of him anticipated the promise of peace. Trina's bubbly voice came through his speaker again, breaking his mental tug-of-war. He accepted the first possible date and time that Trina offered, hollowly agreeing to come in for a session next week. The call ended with a guilty sense of satisfaction that he'd be getting his sleeping tablets; the end of the pain and suffering was within reach. He checked the digital clock on the dash and decided there was plenty of time to stop by the liquor store. Unable to remember if there was whiskey in the house, he wasn't taking any chances.

***

As the door opened, the view of her dad's face caught her off guard. She expected to see him there when the doorbell rang, but his expression was noticeably different, almost shockingly so. At first, she'd thought that maybe the sunlight was causing the effect on his facial features. Minutes later, however, as they entered their own house and her dad turned to her, Lucie was positive there'd been a change. She could see it more clearly now - the puffiness around his eyes and the deepened lines in his face. An intense wave of fear washed over her young mind as she stared at her father's eyes. Her instincts were telling her she was on the verge of losing both parents in the same year.

She'd already resolved to tell the doctor about the concern for her father, but her next session wasn't until Tuesday. Five days away. Something needed to be done sooner, and Lucie's mind raced for an idea; some sort of temporary band-aid to treat the deep and painful wounds in his expression. Pushing aside her own mental pain for the moment, she focused on a plan to help her father.

Chapter 14 - Shark Night

Cort absently thanked Lilly's mom for having Lucie over and spun away after a brief wave good-bye. A few minutes later they entered their own house. Cort set his phone on the counter and turned to his daughter. As she stared at his face, Cort detected an unsettled concern in her eyes. Fairly sure he was the cause of any consternation she might be having, a fist of guilt jabbed him in the gut and added credence to the plan he'd laid earlier.

"Did you have a fun time with your friend Lilly today?"

His daughter nodded silently.

"Good, that's good. Lucie, what would you think about spending some time with Manny and Gabby? I mean Pappy and Grammy?"

"Okay, yeah. When are we going?"

"I don't know. Soon though. I need to talk to them and figure it out."

Cort pondered the loose plan in his head, and his heart ached at the thought of leaving his daughter. Her life uprooted to be raised until adulthood by her maternal grandparents.

She'll be better off.

The voice in his head was convincing. He and Celeste had talked about moving away from the bubble community they'd lived in now for too many years. Austin had been one of their choices for relocation. Even though they'd never taken any significant steps, the move had been discussed more than once. He and Celeste agreed the diversity in Texas would be good for Lucie - good for all of them. And to be close to her parents just made sense for several reasons. The plan had always included the three of them, and now, as Cort stared at his daughter, the thought of

Lucie being in Texas without her parents put a painful lump in his throat. He stood from his crouched position before the gloss in his eyes had a chance to materialize.

Jesus, I'm a freaking basket case!

He feared Lucie had already picked up on his sense of despair and was about to ask about his appearance. Instead, she asked a question that completely surprised him.

"Dad, can you watch Jaws with me tonight?"

Cort hesitated at the question, his mouth hanging open briefly. Lucie's request seemed like a desperate change of subject, and the randomness of the question caught him off guard. Raising an eyebrow, the dismal thoughts in his head cleared and he snapped back to reality. Cort felt his face contort into a confused expression as his daughter's mouth shifted into a subtle grin.

Why is she smiling?

"Jaws?" Still processing, he managed the single word response.

"Yeah Dad, Jaws. The movie about a Carcharodon Carcharias."

More confused, he slowly repeated what he thought she'd said. "Car-care-o-don... car-carry-us? Lucie, my Spanish isn't what it used to be. You know Jaws is a shark movie, right?"

"That's Latin, and it means Great White." She informed her father very matter-of-factly, with no demeaning tone nor any hint of boasting.

He continued staring at her, a little annoyed, but mostly impressed with her choice of words. Most people, especially a kid her age, would simply have used the word 'shark' to describe the movie's main character. Not only had Lucie described Jaws as a Great White, but she'd used the Latin species name of all things. It was a very cerebral description, and while he already knew she was intelligent, this vocabulary surprised him.

She must have googled that.

Cort knew his daughter, like himself, was very interested in the animal kingdom, especially ocean life, and most intrigued by the shark species. There was a sense of respect in her choice of words, and had he not been so depressed, he'd have smiled.

"Yes, I know what the movie is about, Lucie, I've seen it no less than 20 times."

"Then it must be a good movie, Dad. Nobody watches a bad movie 20 times."

"It is a good movie, one of my favorites. But it's, I don't know, I'm not sure if it's something you should watch. You know?"

"No, I don't know. Why not?" She pressed on.

He didn't want to insult his 10-year-old daughter by insinuating that she was immature, but he knew the violence in Jaws was scary and intense in at least a few parts.

"Lucie?" He stalled.

"What?" She immediately pushed again, "you said once summer started, I could stay up later, and we could watch more movies."

"Right, yeah, I did say that. But Jaws, well, it's just kind of violent. It might scare you, and I don't want you to have nightmares."

Cort recalled seeing Jaws when he was about her age. While he loved the water more than anyone he knew, it had changed his approach to swimming for a short stint. If memory served, there was a brief period-of-time after seeing the movie, that he was a little tentative about jumping into a lake or a river, let alone the ocean.

"C'mon Dad, seriously? You think a movie about a shark is really what'll give me nightmares these days?"

Cort stared at her another second, or maybe four, considering her comment. He knew exactly what she was referencing and did not appreciate her tactic at all; it was insensitive, and conniving. It was also quite smart.

Damn this girl!

"Hold on a second, Lucie," he spoke as he picked up his phone.

He googled "Jaws" to see if it was appropriate for her age. He was sure it was rated R, which would be his defense to decline his daughter's request. But there it was, to his surprise, with a PG-13 rating. The rating still should have been enough to decline the 10-year-old's request, but deep down he knew her intelligence and maturity level might just be right up there at a 13-year-old level.

"What time is it on?"

Lucie grinned victoriously and responded, "I recorded it, Dad, we can watch it whenever we want."

Cort had other plans for tonight, namely talking to his in-laws about a visit and commencing to plan out his exit strategy. While Lucie's movie-night suggestion would delay that plan, he appreciated the fact that it had distracted him from his dark thoughts. He contemplated her offer, scratching his chin as he did so.

"We'll start it around 8:00. I'll make popcorn."

Hours later, after they'd eaten dinner and taken a short stroll around the park, Cort found himself deep in thought again. Staring at the corn kernels as they heated in a layer of vegetable oil, the notion of Lucie's future had him struggling. He saw himself as a burden to his daughter, and a barrier to her healing process. Would it be completely selfish of him to take his own life and leave her parentless, or was it more selfish to stick around and impede her path to a happy future? The pop of the first kernel startled him, mercifully pushing the morbid choice aside.

He finished drizzling on the melted butter and filled two oversized plastic bowls. Lucie was in charge of the drinks, and they'd agreed it was a special occasion and warranted a full can of Coke each. Father and daughter met on the sofa, put their treats on separate tray tables in front of them, and Cort clicked the remote to pull up the recordings. While his psyche remained grim, tonight was the first instance of anticipation for anything since the accident. Deep down he knew this movie probably wasn't the best parenting move, nor would the violence necessarily be good for his own mental health. Still, he welcomed the next couple of hours of distraction with Lucie.

Positioning himself on the couch in a diagonal trajectory, he situated himself so he could easily shift his eyes from the TV to his daughter without her noticing. Cort watched carefully during the opening scene. The brief nudity of the skinny-dipping woman wasn't graphic by any means, and Lucie didn't appear to flinch at the sight of the barely visible breasts. A minute later, he stole several more glances at his daughter, as the swimmer on the screen was tugged below the surface. His eyes were on Lucie more than the television during the terrifying scene. As victim #1 was pulled beneath the moonlit water for the last time, Cort noticed a slight squirm in Lucie's position. He returned his focus to the TV for a few seconds, hit the pause button, then turned his whole head in her direction and smiled. The grin she returned seemed to hold a bit of discomfort, or maybe slight annoyance, or possibly both. Maybe she'd noticed the glances he'd shot in her direction.

"Hey, Lucie," he offered, "at any point we can turn this off you know. Don't feel like we need to keep watching if you don't like it."

"I'm not scared. I like that beginning, but I just hope they show the shark soon."

"Yeah, okay, that's fine. I'm sure they'll show the shark soon."

He returned a sarcastic grin to his daughter and laughed a little. Cort was nervous about continuing, thinking ahead to some scenes that were considerably more gruesome. On the other hand, this was the first time in a long time he could remember not focusing on his own misery. There was something very cathartic about getting lost in a horror movie with his daughter; something about focusing on the dilemma of the character's lives, and not thinking about the shit-show that was his and Lucie's. A sliver of optimism was embedded into the depths of his mind. Cort wondered - if he could avoid killing himself, somehow move forward with life and find a degree of peace again, maybe he and Lucie would someday think back to this evening as a memorable experience they'd shared together.

He snuck several little peeks toward Lucie at pivotal attack scenes, cautiously reading her expression. They paused to get a popcorn refill after Chief Brody got slapped by Mrs. Kintner, the mother of the boy whose bloody raft washed up on the beach.

"That was sad," she offered.

"Yes, that *was* sad, Lucie."

Cort took some solace in hearing his daughter express her emotion, but hesitated before continuing, concerned that the repeated subject matter of death might be too harsh for either of them. Lucie waited anxiously for his next words; her eyes relaying the eagerness to hear her father's thoughts.

"Most movies don't have kids die in them. The guy who wrote the book, and the director who made this movie - they both realized the impact it would have. I know it's sad, but it's also part of why this movie is so horrifying and so memorable."

"Yeah, I guess so." She leaned back into her spot on the couch and got situated with her new bowl of popcorn. "Okay, hit play."

Cort pressed play and again pondered his decision to let her watch the movie. The last movie he'd watched with her was animated. Frozen II maybe, he couldn't quite remember. The material on the screen now was a huge departure from singing snowmen, but Lucie was invested now, and it would be a fight if he decided to terminate the experience at this point. They watched together as the residents of Amity Beach put together hunting parties with the intent of finding and killing the shark. Jaws was now public enemy number one, hated by everyone in town.

Maybe that's what I'm becoming? Cort watched silently and drew the unwelcomed comparison of the shark to himself. *How long before I've made enemies of everyone around me? How long before Lucie hates me?*

Reluctantly, Cort pushed the dismal thought aside and let the movie play on, continuing to glance Lucie's way intermittently. The two didn't speak for nearly the whole second half. One of the only comments was made by Lucie, as Chief Brody was sloshing chum into the water from the back of Quint's boat, *Orca*. As Brody spoke and smoked a cigarette simultaneously, Lucie turned to her father. Cort paused the movie so he could hear whatever remark she was about to make.

"Dad, there's a way better chance that Chief Brody will die of lung cancer than he will by shark attack."

Cort grinned, then laughed, and Lucie laughed with him. They enjoyed the moment of levity together before Cort finally stopped and replied with a smirk and a bit of a dramatic tone.

"Hey, maybe you should watch the rest before you make that prediction?"

He shrugged his shoulders, conveying that he himself didn't know exactly what Brody's fate would be.

"Dad, there's no way the Chief is gonna die. He's the main character, and he's a good guy. I'll bet you ten dollars he won't die."

Cort laughed again nervously. He needed to respond without serving up a spoiler, and she put him in a precarious position with her confident wager.

"Listen, just watch the movie. I'm not betting you anything, because I know what happens, and that wouldn't be fair."

"Whatever." She grinned and turned back to the TV, then nodded her head in a gesture that Cort understood to mean "continue."

He shook his head. He wanted to call her a brat, but this was easily the most fun he'd had in months. He refrained and turned back to the TV. Five seconds later, Jaws emerged from the water just feet from the back of the boat, sending Brody into a horrified trance as he backed into the cabin, cigarette frozen between his lips.

Lucie was certainly interested now, intrigued as more and more scenes included views of the shark. This was not the high-tech CGI that she'd become used to in the current cinema, but from Cort's vantage point, she appeared to be enjoying the classic effects. Forty minutes later, they nervously watched the closing scenes. Cort saw his daughter cringe as Quint's torso was pierced by the massive teeth. She moved a little closer to her father. As the *Orca* sank down and Brody climbed out onto the mast, now hovering inches above the calm sea, Cort reached out and put his hand on Lucie's. He was sure that his daughter was wondering if she might lose the pseudo-wager about the chief's fate.

"*Smile you son-of-a!*" Brody peered down the barrel to the sight and squeezed the trigger.

While the pieces of the shark floated down through the cloud of red ocean, Lucie straightened her posture some, and sighed a heavy breath. Cort presumed it was a sigh of relief but sensed there was something more to it. They watched as Hooper resurfaced, asked about Quint, and the two heroes were left to kick their way back to shore. As the credits scrolled up the screen, Lucie turned to her father's nervously smiling face.

"I didn't really like the ending."

"That's okay. I'm sorry if it was scary. That last scene when Quint, you know? It's always hard to watch, no matter how many times I've seen it. You won't have bad dreams, will you?"

Lucie shook her head in frustration. "Yeah, I guess it was a little scary at the end, but that's not why I didn't like it."

"Oh, no?"

"No, Dad. I don't like that they had to kill the shark."

Cort crinkled his brow and glared at his daughter, waiting to see if she was pulling his leg. She stared back with a serious expression, then continued.

"I mean, it was eating to live. That's what sharks do. The people were stupid for going in the water all the time, weren't they?"

She stared back as he wagged his head a bit, an incredulous expression forming across his face. Lucie ignored the gesture and finished her critique just as she'd started it.

"I just didn't like that they killed Jaws."

Cort paused another second, now convinced that his daughter had not been disturbed by all the blood, violence, and death left in the wake of the most notorious shark in movie history.

"You're serious, aren't you, Lucie?"

Not wanting to spoil the experience with a lecture, he remained silent as Lucie nodded back at him, confirming her feelings, then got up to take her empty popcorn bowl and Coke can into the kitchen.

Cort was left wondering about the mindset of his daughter. Of all the great characters in Jaws, his 10-year-old little girl had sympathized with the blood-thirsty serial killer. He scratched his chin, unable to decide whether he should laugh or call Lucie's psychiatrist. Her comments had been startling, but also interesting and even enlightening. Cort knew he'd never view the characters in the same light, especially the main antagonist for whom the movie was named.

Still awake over an hour later, laying his head on the pillow, Cort allowed himself to grin. He was relieved that she'd interpreted the movie as she had. Lucie was right – the shark, after all, was innocent of murder, only acting instinctively to feed its hunger. Benchley and Spielberg had done a fine job of convincing readers and viewers that the great white killer had a conscience. Their intent of the story and film was certainly meant to evoke feelings quite the opposite of Lucie's. In reflection,

Cort felt an odd sense of pride in her analysis. He chastised himself some for not feeling that way about the shark sooner. He knew better and should have been the one lecturing Lucie about the absurd behavior of the shark terrorizing the fictitious beach town of Amity Island. He knew sharks weren't vindictive in real life, and he appreciated the fact that Lucie wasn't swayed from the facts either. Up until now, he'd always felt some sense of satisfaction when Jaws met his demise at the end of the movie. Not anymore. Moreover, the whole shift in his attitude towards Jaws had an interesting effect on his psyche too. Just a small bit of burden was lifted from his self-deprecation, as he considered the chance that maybe he wasn't quite the monster he saw himself as. It was a glimmer of silver in the dark cloud that he was immersed in, and he was reminded to make a stronger effort to survive the darkness.

***

As annoyed as Lucie had been, she'd remained silent and let him do his visual checks throughout the movie. The only real fear she'd experienced was connected to his state of mind. Staying quiet, she hoped she was reading his expression correctly. It seemed different now, and she was almost certain he was focused on her and the movie more than anything else.

When he asked her about the ending, she told him the truth even though she knew it would probably surprise him. She tried to conceal her grin at his reaction, completely satisfied because the look in his eyes had shifted. Lucie was sure her sympathy for the shark had caused the change. She could see that her compassion for Jaws had surprised him, but she hoped it hadn't disappointed him. She'd watched at least a hundred shark videos, from YouTube clips to episodes of Shark Week on the Discovery channel. Sharks weren't the vicious man-eaters the movie portrayed. Certainly, her father, a smart man and also very compassionate towards the animal kingdom, must realize that too.

It didn't matter. The only thing she really cared about was that the concern across Dad's brow was for her. Lucie was satisfied that for a change, it wasn't related to her mother's death. She needed to continue the distraction, and her band-aid plan, until real help was available. Laying her head on the pillow, she offered a silent prayer to her mother.

I'm taking care of him Mom, I promise.

Chapter 15 — Shark Day

He glanced at his phone to see the time. 11:34 PM. It would be at least an hour before he'd drift off; probably more like two. But he'd put the sleeping pills in the nightstand drawer, and for now they'd stay there next to the bottle of top-shelf whiskey. Images of Jaws still floundered around in his head, which sparked a memory he hadn't thought about in several years. The recollection had always been crystal-clear in his mind, it was just that he hadn't had the opportunity to reminisce about it with her. The experience was his and his mother's, the only two people present, and since she'd passed away three years ago, the memory hadn't come up. Over 26 years later, laying wide awake in bed, he thought back to that morning. He could see the multi-million-dollar homes they'd passed, cruising through the river towards open water. The many years gone by had faded some of those residual images into blurry recollections. Of the week they'd spent in Florida, ninety percent of his visual memories were comprised of that one single hour. Watching Jaws tonight had served as a stark reminder, and the events of that April day in 1995 were clear and present in his thoughts now.

***

As an overly adventurous 13-year-old, strong swimmer, and owner of plenty of snorkeling experience, Cort agreed with his mom without hesitation. Admittedly, the slightly crooked post protruding from the reef's edge did look a bit far; maybe a quarter mile from their boat. Beyond it, there was a good mile or two of ocean between the reef and the shoreline. If they couldn't swim back against the current, continuing forward until they reached land was a possibility, but not a viable option; assistance would surely be required to get back to the sailboat. There wasn't any real doubt, however, that he and his mom could make the swim there and back. Their flippers, of course, would do a significant part of the work.

They'd flown into Ft. Lauderdale three days prior, as part of an extremely rare Mother/Son excursion. Cort's two older siblings were in high school and had other interests besides visiting their grandfather in Florida, and they really couldn't afford to miss four days of school anyway. His mom, however, hadn't seen her father in over a year. Booking the flights was triggered by a combination of daughter-guilt and a sense of cabin-fever during the Western Pennsylvania winter.

Gramps, as Cort affectionately called his mother's father, picked them up at the airport in a borrowed car. He didn't own a vehicle or a house; his 36-foot trimaran sailboat counted as both his home and his primary mode of transportation. The boat would be their living quarters during the week-long stay in Florida and Cort couldn't be more excited about it. Thanks to Gramps, he had more experience on a boat than just about every kid his age, always jumping at the opportunity to feel the one-of-a-kind exhilaration of sailing.

He woke Wednesday morning with anxious anticipation. Gramps had told them the plan during dinner the evening before. They'd leave their mooring in Stuart after breakfast, motor through the St. Lucie River for a couple miles until they reached the Atlantic, and then a couple more to clear the shallows. Once the sandbars and reefs were behind them, they'd put the main sail up and head due south using only the wind as their fuel.

Supposedly there was a shipwreck in the waters roughly 5 miles south of the St. Lucie Inlet, partially visible during low tide. The ship had been out there for over two decades now, having gone aground on the bordering reef back in the early 70's. A shipwreck was always an attraction for fish, and therefore offered a fantastic location for snorkeling. Gramps predicted they'd be able to get close enough to the reef for him to anchor, allowing Cort and his mom to swim out to the wreck for a couple of hours.

Holding their masks tight to their faces, mother and son slid off the aft deck seconds apart, plunging into the mild Atlantic water. They cleared their snorkels, spat away the salty water, and swam towards the front of the boat. Per Gramps' instructions, they needed to confirm the anchor was holding. Cort found the chain attached at the bow of the boat and followed it with his eyes to the sandy bottom. He watched as his mom inhaled a deep breath and pulled herself below the surface using the anchor chain, diving fifteen feet until she reached the halfway point to the bottom. She was able to see that the two flukes of the anchor had dug themselves in and were buried in the sand nearly all the way to the crown. Secure. He watched as she came back up, surfaced, and simply gave her dad a thumbs up. Gramps nodded back and responded with even simpler instructions. "Have fun!"

Both waved in confirmation, then lowered their heads into the water and swam with the waves in the direction of the reef. Low tide had peaked about an hour prior. As the earth turned and Florida moved closer to the moon, the ocean was beginning to rise slowly again. Staying a few arm lengths apart, Cort and his mom moved their legs up and down in slow motion, propelling through the water at an easy pace. There wouldn't be much to see for the first two to three hundred meters, other than small clouds of sand on the ocean's bottom, sparse clusters of sea grass, and the occasional fish. Every hundred feet or so, they paused to clear their snorkels and scan the surface for their target. Adjusting their heading a few degrees ensured they were still moving in the direction of the exposed post. No words were exchanged; they'd simply nod to each other and proceed in anticipation. If it were indeed the mast of the ship that they were moving towards, there would soon be an abundance of sea life to gaze upon and excitedly point out to each other.

Thanks to his grandfather's position in life, and his family's adventurous spirit, Cort had snorkeled at least a couple dozen times over the years. It became one of his favorite activities, and he was in his glory now as the rays of the late morning sun warmed his back. The most pronounced sound was that of his own breathing; each inhale and exhale passing through the snorkel next to his right ear as he took in the sights of the world beneath the surface. Even without much sea life to focus on, it was easy to lose oneself in wonder and forget about everything else happening. The ocean was having its effect on Cort, as he blocked out the rest of the world and absorbed the scenery. Moving rhythmically with the rolling surface, the faint sound of waves breaking in the distance became audible. Looking forward, he could see the dark outline of the reef as they approached from 100 meters out. Even from that distance, the uptick in fish quantity increased. Another five minutes of relaxed floating, and they'd be on top of the coral heads. Seeing his mom lower her legs and poke her head up out of the water, Cort followed suit to check bearings again. A visual check of the boat revealed they'd covered most of the quarter mile that separated the sailboat from their target. They spectated for a couple seconds as Gramps busied himself on the deck, unaware he was being watched. Mom waved briefly to her dad but stopped abruptly when he absently turned his back to them. She turned to Cort.

"We're not too far now, Cort. That post doesn't look as much like a masthead from here, but let's keep going."

Cort silently agreed that the object they were swimming towards appeared to be more of a set post, possibly an older stake that had supported a warning beacon. Given the shallow water, it would make sense. Even from their distance, it was evident the barnacle-coated pole was not likely being used for anything anymore. Without discussing it, they held out hope. Beacon posts were usually straight up and down in the water. Given the fact this one was not perfectly vertical, the two maintained a degree of faith that it was the only part of the sunken ship not submerged. Nodding to his mother, he acknowledged he wanted to keep going. It was too soon to abandon the mission, and no matter what they'd find beneath the exposed pole, they'd surely see plenty of ocean life along the way.

The incoming tide was becoming more evident, and the current had pushed them off course more than they'd realized. A more pronounced adjustment was made directionally, as they took a diagonal angle with the approaching reef line. The water slid over their bodies more from the side now. The wave-size was increasing, requiring additional exertion and more frequent checks to stay on course.

Closing the distance between themselves and the reef by another 50 meters, the line of dead coral was much clearer and evident now, and the subtle breakwater was more audible as well. Experience told them that swimming over the deepest parts of the reef would be safest. Shallow areas where coral heads protruded further upward would be potential contact points and should be avoided.

Cort watched his mom point under water to an area of the shelf that appeared to be especially deep. Confirming with a nod, they adjusted their heading. He lifted his head alongside hers and they found the target again. Satisfied, Cort lowered his mask below the water and began moving forward past his mother, whose head remained above the surface. Just as her flippers left his peripheral vision, he felt the tug at his swim-trunks. Knowing his mom wanted his attention, there was a brief jolt of excitement. He assumed she'd discovered something new - possibly more evidence of the shipwreck. He did an abrupt about-face and joined her above the waves. Her mask was raised to her forehead, and the expression on his mother's face was **not** one of confidence. It was just the opposite, in fact, and if he was reading the crinkle in her brow correctly, there was a hint of concern being advertised.

"Cort," she put her left hand around his forearm and pulled him slightly closer to herself. "I think I can see a part of the ship sticking up, just to the right of the post."

Following the direction her right pointer finger was aimed in, Cort found the post again and scanned the area to the right of it. It took only a split-second to find the object she was referring to. His heart skipped more than one beat as his eyes sent the message to his brain; the message that the dark triangular shaped object was not stationary, but in fact was moving.

"Mom, that's a fin, and it's moving toward the post… in this direction." His voice remained steady and calm despite a golf-ball sized lump in his esophagus.

"Okay, I thought maybe it was too."

She followed with another less than realistic inference, and Cort knew she was trying to keep them both calm.

"It's probably a dolphin, Cort, let's not panic."

Cort had always been adept in most facets of math, but especially excelled in geometric and spacial-relationship problems. He was able to quickly judge the size and distance of an object by using the surrounding objects as reference points. His eyes darted, making calculations based on the post, waves, and everything else he could see in the distance. It took only seconds to conclude the body of the fish beneath the fin was of significant size.

Turning around fast, they looked back at the sailboat, rolling gently in the swells. The deck was empty. He knew his grandfather must be below.

"*Shit!*"

It was a long swim back into the current, through deep water and against the waves. Cort tugged at his mother's shoulder. Her gaze was still aimed at the boat, but he'd turned his attention back to the fin.

"Mom."

"What?"

Cort didn't answer… he didn't need to. The alarm in his voice told her it had gotten worse, and she found the second fin almost immediately. Even from fifty meters, it was evident that they were both dorsal fins, belonging to two separate fish.

"TWO fins?" She sounded frustrated, but the underlying fear was apparent too.

"Yeah, Mom, and they aren't going under water. Dolphins only come up for a second and go back under. Those are sharks."

His mother knew that he was right. She nodded her head in silence, acknowledging that what he'd deduced was correct.

"We need to get to a shallow area… the highest point of the reef we can find." He didn't disagree with her plan. Trying to swim for the boat was too risky, and they both inherently knew it.

"Yes, let's go now." Cort anxiously agreed.

Pulling their masks down with haste, they scissored their legs with purpose, making a bee-line for the edge of the reef. Swimming towards what looked like the highest line of coral, they could already see bubbles from small breaking waves. Son and mother shared a real sense of hesitation as they swam towards a point that the fins were also converging on. The hope was that the high point in the reef would be shallow enough to prevent the sharks from approaching. He held fast to the knowledge that most shark species were not aggressive, at least towards humans, and that the sharks would need to be very large to consider them as a potential food source. He also silently hoped just maybe they'd mistaken a single shark's tail fin as the dorsal fin of a second shark. Two predatory fish were significantly worse than one. It was worth taking another quick peek, and he couldn't fight the urge to find their location again anyway. Picking his head up, he found the fins immediately, his stare lingering in a state of increasing panic.

"Mom!" He yelled loud enough that she'd heard his voice from her submerged position.

As she stopped and adjusted into a vertical posture again, she glanced at Cort to find him pointing in the direction of their fear.

"Damn!"

It was the only word she uttered in response to seeing the four fins he was pointing towards. They were multiplying, and closer now by at least fifteen meters, closing the distance much too fast. Taking a rapid glance at the boat's still empty deck, he watch her pull her mask back on.

"Let's go, Cortland, now."

She'd used his full first name. He heard and felt the uptick of panic in her voice and decided not to delay their swim by asking questions or pointing out the obvious. Submerging again, he took more solace in the proximity of the reef. They'd reach it in another forty seconds, and he could see a plateau now on the coral head not more than three feet deep. The feeling of security in the shallow depth was being challenged by a nagging counter-realization. *The tide is coming in.*

A minute later, Cort and his mom pulled their flippers underneath them and stood up on a large round coral shelf, approximately ten feet across. His mother struggled some, but eventually gained her balance and stood beside him. With the initial break of the waves behind them, they'd reached a calmer position in the surf that was thirty feet inside the shelf. His mother was still taller than him, and the water reached the mid-point of her thigh. The rippling saltwater lapped a little higher on Cort, covering most of his legs and submerging his swim trunks to the crotch.

Both turning their heads while getting situated, the dorsal fins were spotted again immediately. Another wave of panic hit them as they witnessed seven fins in total now. The triangular forms were well past the post, nary thirty meters and closing, and headed in a trajectory that would miss the mother and son pair by no more than twenty-five feet.

Cort stared at the scene, waiting for direction from the woman who'd protected him every day of his life thus far. She would know what to do, and his mind told him to remain calm until she figured it out. Before speaking, Mom reached her right hand out and placed it firmly on Cort's shoulder. When she leaned into him a little, he realized she needed him for support. She pulled her right leg upward and out of the water, grasping her right ankle with her left hand. Lifting her leg up higher, she held it above the water.

"Oh man!"

Her words needed no explanation, as they both watched blood trickle out from a scrape just below her knee. In her rush to stand on the reef, she'd caught her right flipper on the coral and dragged her leg. The cut itself was minor, and the blood flow was barely enough to warrant a band-aid. But it was blood, and they both knew the repercussions of what it could bring. Both cringed internally as she reluctantly lowered her leg back into the water and let go of his shoulder. It was an unbelievable development in their already precarious situation.

"Cortland, we'll be fine. Hear me?"

"Yes." His one-word reply was shaky, as he'd detected an ever-so-slight tone of doubt in his mother's statement.

"Listen to me. They're headed far enough in front of us that they might not even see us. Once they pass, we can swim through the shallows to the post, and climb it. Just until we can get the attention of my dad or another boat."

She sounded unsure and looked at him for confirmation.

"Mom, the sharks… they'll see us swimming. And even if we make it to the post, it's covered in barnacles. We'll get sliced up."

"Okay." Releasing a breath, she nodded, seemingly in agreement that her plan was not a great one.

"Mom." Cort pointed again in the direction of the fins. I'm counting nine now."

She stared and squinted, and Cort could tell fear was beginning to get the better of her. He watched her count in silence before reluctantly confirming the number.

"God, there **are** nine."

Mother and son stood in silence, temporarily speechless as their minds scrambled for another option. Mom glanced to the boat again and saw her father on the deck. She desperately waved with both arms and Cort followed suit. Gramps was not looking in their direction at first, but after an agonizing ten seconds, he turned and miraculously made visual contact. He appeared small to them, and they would certainly look small to him. It was too far away to tell if he was wearing his glasses, but if he wasn't, they'd be no more than two small blurry shapes above the water line. There was an instant of relief as he waved back to them. Unfortunately, his gesture was in reciprocation for what he interpreted as a friendly wave. Their assurance ended succinctly as he turned his back again and continued whatever it was that he was doing. A few seconds later he abruptly disappeared below deck.

"Shit! DAAAAAD!"

She only screamed it once, and they both knew he was way too far to hear their cries for help.

Turning back to the sharks, Cort and his mother watched in terror as the forms altered their course by a few degrees in the wrong direction. Had they heard her scream? The school was now moving in a trajectory that would nearly put them on a collision course with the two humans. As the fins moved methodically closer, Cort's overwhelming fear held an ever-so-slight sense of awe. He'd never seen sharks this close before, and something deep down told him an attack was unlikely. They were in shallow waters, and from what he knew, it was unlikely the sharks would leave the safety of the deeper ocean. He scanned the water in front of him. The reef stayed shallow for maybe twenty feet, before dropping off dramatically to a lower shelf he guessed to be ten or fifteen feet deep. Surely they'd stay in the deeper waters. He repeated those thoughts again and tried desperately to convince himself they'd be safe.

Please stay in the deeper waters.

"Stay perfectly still."

He'd heard his mother's whisper but certainly didn't need to. His plan was to do exactly that, equipped with the knowledge that sharks were attracted to movement and sound.

As their forms moved closer, the shadows of their bodies became clearer beneath the surface. They were larger than either of them expected them to be. Cort estimated eight to nine feet - way out of his comfort zone. He was familiar with sharks, more so than most kids his age. He'd been fascinated with them for as long as he could remember and studied them on his own via books and nature programs. Like most, he could identify a Great White or a Tiger shark immediately but could also accurately identify at least a dozen other species. He knew which ones to be cautious around, and which ones were virtually no threat at all. Not quite recognizing the shape of the dorsal fin, or the stark white coloration on the last few inches of their tip, he made the assumption they were likely Bull or Reef sharks. Regardless of their species, he was certain there were nine of them. And the fact troubling him most, was that just about any species of shark could be dangerous in a frenzy situation.

Both mother and son watched intently, and completely stiff in their posture, as the dark forms swam slowly closer. The sharks appeared to be traveling in pairs, a bit staggered, except for the last one, which hung back roughly twenty feet or so behind the group. Cort had seen a few sharks in the ocean, but never more than one or two at a time. He'd never heard of them traveling in groups. The morbid notion zipped through his mind - they could be swimming together as some sort of hunting party. The thought sent a chill up his back, and he struggled to control his bladder.

The hoarse whisper from beside him broke his dismal thought, "Cort."

"What?"

"Don't move right now, but if it looks like they're going to, uh… come too close, I want you to climb up on my shoulders."

Cort nodded his head and answered in a soft and shaky whisper. "Okay."

The reason for his mother's request was understood, and Cort took comfort in the fact that she wanted to keep him safe from an attack. But he also deduced his safety would be temporary at best. If his mother was bitten in the leg, she'd certainly fall. The pair would make a large splash into the bloody water - he didn't want to imagine what would happen after that. This was not an ideal time to be arguing with his mother. Instead, he agreed to her request out loud, with the mindset of doing no such thing.

While Cort remained motionless, his eyes shifted from the fins to his mother, who was slowly crouching down and reaching into the water with both hands. When she stood again, she was holding a chunk of dead coral, nearly the size of a cantaloupe. Returning gradually to her standing position, she cradled the gray hunk of limestone in her hands. There was no question to ask. Cort knew why she'd grabbed it, and although he was convinced it would do little to alter whatever course of action the sharks decided to take, he took a small degree of solace in her having the makeshift weapon.

A quick glance downward was taken to check the water level. It hadn't raised, or had it? With eyes locking back on the menacing shadows moving towards them, he did some mental math. Their bodies were long, and large. While each foot in length offered an additional level of fear, their large size offered an ironic advantage to him and his mother. The depth from the bottom of the pectoral fins to the top of the back was probably two and a half, maybe three feet. Even with their dorsals completely exposed to the air, these sharks would need at least thirty inches or more of depth to swim unabated. Cort estimated he was standing in roughly forty inches of water, maybe a little less. The shallow reef would give the sharks a tight swimming lane if they were so inclined to make contact. His comfort in the calculation was balanced by the dread in the fact that the tide was steadily rising. It was possible for contact to be made and would likely depend on how hungry and aggressive the sharks were.

Mom shifted the coral to her left hand and reached out her right hand slowly in the direction of Cort. He instinctively offered his left hand back. She grabbed it and squeezed it, relaying a false, but much appreciated, sense of security to him.

The sharks had reached them, fortunately staying in the expected path of the deeper water, twenty feet away. He silently wondering if their legs were being watched as the fins moved by in staggered pairs. Their bright blue flippers were surely not going unnoticed, and Cort silently cursed the people, whoever they were, that had decided to make them that color. Two by two, with approximately ten feet separating each pair, the fins and dark forms moved in a caravan from their right to their left. The ripples and waves of the ocean altered their perception of everything below the surface, but the sharks were close enough for Cort and his mother to make out details of these enormous fish. The eyes, gills, pectoral fins, long torso, and eventually the tails. Completely paralyzed with fear, Cort and his mother stood like statues. As each pair of fins passed by, their sense of hope grew exponentially.

Keep going, please keep going.

The thirty seconds it took for the four pairs of fins and tails to move past them lasted an eternity. The final shark, however, lingered, giving considerably more distance between itself and the pair in front of it. It was swimming in the same direction, and finally got to a point where it appeared to be moving past them. But it didn't.

The ninth and final shark stopped, hovering in a position perfectly perpendicular to their location. The pit in Cort's gut doubled in size and his sphincter muscles tightened simultaneously. Was it the unusual shape of he and his mother, the color of their flippers, the scent of blood? Maybe all three? The shark remained stationary, and there was no doubt as to what its eyes were fixed on.

Oh no. Please no.

Their grip on each other's hands closed harder. The shark's tail moved to their left as the head circled around to the right, until it was positioned like a missile and pointed straight at them. Like an ever so cautious predator about to make the final attack move, the shark inched closer to them in the water just barely deep enough to contain its massive body. This shark was larger than the others; easily nine feet if not ten. The distance between human and shark became smaller with each movement. Twenty feet became fifteen, as its tail swayed ever-so-slowly from side to side, propelling all 1400 pounds of its body through the rippled ocean.

His mother's grip on his hand tightened again. He was sure he heard her whimper, though it could have also been himself releasing the vocalized fear through clenched teeth. The dark mass drew closer, until it was ten feet from their legs. One more length of its own body, and there would be no distance separating it from them. Cort pondered his mom's earlier request again, reconsidering the piggy-back offer. The problem with the offer now was that he was frozen in place, petrified and unable to flinch, let alone move a body part.

He scarcely moved his lips and whispered, "Mom?" The trepidation in the single word was thick.

"Don't move!" She whispered back.

The shark stopped. There was a visible recognition in its posture. The world around them halted, and no sound was audible. Their sense of time was lost, and neither could quite tell how long the shark remained still. In retrospect, Cort wondered how he hadn't fainted. He knew his consciousness was necessary not only to his own safety, but for the support of his mother. Finally, after what seemed like an eternity, the two-foot-wide head of the shark turned slightly to one side. Was it trying to turn around, or simply gaining a more direct view with one eye? Silent prayers were whispered internally, as the pair asked God for assistance. *Keep turning, keep turning.* Cort visualized that the head would continue its semi-circular direction, willing it to retreat. It did not, and in fact, moved back to the position of pointing straight at their legs. But something remarkable occurred in those seconds, something both he and his mother would discuss and marvel over years later.

Keeping its head aimed at the four trembling legs, it began to move backwards. As if it were equipped with some magical reverse mechanism, the body of the shark drifted away from them with the incoming tide. Cort exhaled for the first time in what seemed like minutes, watching in relief as the shark backed up with barely a hint of movement in the tail or dorsal fin. As the enormous dark body increased its distance from them, his mother's grip relented and the blood flow in his hand resumed. Drifting slowly and silently back to the deeper shelf, the shark ventured one more curious look, and with a swift swoosh of the tail sending a splash of sea water upward, the shark darted towards its awaiting shiver.

 Mother and son were beyond belief as the intense fear of death dissipated into the rolling waves. The pair continued to stare in the direction of the shrinking fins, watching as they moved further and further from the shallows. Eventually the fins began to disappear below the surface a couple at a time, just as they'd first appeared.

 As they squinted into the distance, Mom inched closer to her son, dropped the coral, and turned to accept his waiting embrace. They hugged hard for a few seconds, while Cort watched over her shoulder. She let go and turned her gaze again to the same spot, where now only one lonely fin remained. Beyond the fin, they noticed movement in the distance, simultaneously identifying it as a boat. It was moving fast and coming closer to them by the second. They waited with hands raised high, refraining from shouting just yet. Without discussing it, they were both afraid that their yells would be heard beneath the surface. As the boat grew larger and larger, the pair waved their hands back and forth frantically, reaching further skyward to make their forms bigger. Another sense of relief raced through their veins as the boat slowed down and altered its direction, signifying visual contact and recognizing the need for assistance. Slowing to a crawl, the boat inched its way toward the breaking waves, knowing the coral heads beneath the breakwater would be devastating to their craft. Cort and his mother offered a part "friendly" part "thank you for coming" wave to the three men in the fifteen-foot fishing boat and waited patiently for them to get closer.

The man at the bow of the vessel, nearest to them, made the first verbal communication, "You two okay?"

Cort waited for his mother's reply, but she could not speak. Her head nodded affirmatively, but he knew emotion had overtaken her vocal cords. He spoke for them.

"We're okay. There's a school of sharks!" Cort pointed southwards to where they'd last seen them, and all three men looked in the direction.

"Sharks?" One of the other two men yelled back over the 50 feet of ocean separating them, unsure that he'd heard the boy correctly.

"Yeah, sharks!" Cort raised his voice a few octaves.

All three men looked in the direction simultaneously, not spotting anything resembling a fin. It was apparent, however, that the men did not doubt their claim.

The driver of the boat came to the front and examined the ocean in front of them. After a brief analysis, he spoke.

"Is it just the two of you?"

Both nodded back in unison.

"The reef is shallow where you are, but I can back up and get a little closer. Looks like it stays deep up until around there." His finger pointing at the drop off in the coral heads.

Returning to the wheel, he threw a lever and the boat slowly backed up. Shifting again, the craft swung around as if it were leaving. While Cort and his mother were confident they weren't being abandoned, a shot of anxiety pinged in their guts. A few seconds later, the rear of the boat was moving in their direction and stopped with about 25 feet of water separating it from the pair.

"You'll need to swim a little bit." The largest of the men instructed them.

No answer was given, as Cort's mom simply looked into her son's eyes and motioned for him to go first. He understood she wasn't treating him as a guinea pig, but was rather ensuring he would be the one to reach the boat first. There was no argument, and he did as instructed. Mom lowered herself forward with a few feet of clearance between them, and they both churned through the twenty-five feet of ocean faster than either had ever swam before. Within seconds, the men had pulled them both up and over the starboard transom, and they sat for a moment catching their breath.

"You two hurt at all?" One man noticed the tint of red on his mom's leg where she'd nicked herself on the coral.

"We're fine," escaped from both of their mouths, and Cort breathed a heavy sigh. As he turned to give his mother a hug, she lowered her head to her knees and sobbed heavily. The three men shuffled away towards the cockpit, giving the woman and boy time to themselves. Cort swallowed hard, not willing to cry in front of the men. For his mother, however, no amount of shame or embarrassment could douse the uncontainable solace in the fact her son was still alive; the acceptance abruptly materializing into large tears and soft whimpers. Cort hugged her anyway and assured her he was fine. And he certainly was. While the shock and terror of what had just occurred was still front and center, the fear had subsided to a manageable degree, and Cort was focused on the fact they were alive and safe.

***

More than two and a half decades later, Cort lay with his head on the pillow and reflected on the ordeal. He could almost feel the wave of profound relief that had washed over him when the fishing boat returned them to Gramps. It seemed so long ago, and yet the brief experience was still so vivid in his mind. It didn't deter him from the water, nor did it embed any fear of sharks in his psyche. In fact, the encounter had done just the opposite, and only weeks after it had happened, he began to appreciate the experience more as a rare encounter with nature than anything else.

Adjusting the pillow, Cort inhaled and exhaled deeply, trying to dispel the frustration the memory brought about. His mother had survived the shark experience, as well as many other ominous situations over her 70 years of life, only to be taken by an invisible virus. Now two of the three most important females in his life were gone. Lucie was the remaining one, and he consciously focused on her now rather than his late mother and wife. Lucie was such an interesting person; intelligent, pretty, full of life, and impossibly resilient.

Would she really be better off without me?

The thought of her being alone was so painful, and yet the concept of her being drained by his depression was equally hard to swallow. Cort got out of bed and quietly shuffled into the hallway and up to her bedroom door. It was opened a crack, making it feasible to open it wider without creating much sound. Pushing his way through the threshold slowly, the faint illumination from a night-light enabled him to navigate to the side of her bed. Her angelic face in the soft light brought him a sense of peace and hope, mixed with an odd sense of fear. Leaning down slowly he placed a soft kiss on her forehead, then smiled as he watched her stir slightly. The confirmation she was breathing enabled him to turn and walk back to his bed. He laid down, got comfortable, and for the first time in a long time, found his own deep, deep, sleep.

Chapter 16 – Shark & Shark

Friday morning. They'd both slept later than usual. Cort rose and stretched, then dropped to the floor and struggled to do twenty-five push-ups. They were his first in several weeks, and the struggle he felt was a dismal reminder he was way out of shape. Six months ago he could've knocked out fifty push-ups without a problem. His hands went to his mid-section, confirming that an additional ten pounds had materialized since February.

Pulling on sweatpants and a t-shirt, Cort rubbed his rough facial hair and left his room, still a little out of breath. Lucie happened to be leaving her room at the same time, and they met in the hall. She was already dressed, hair brushed, and wide awake.

"Morning, Luce," choosing the shortened version of her name. "How long have you been up?"

"I got up at 7:30 I think. That's later than usual, huh?"

"Yeah, it is, but you'll start sleeping a little later every day... you're probably still adjusting to the summer schedule."

"Right." She nodded and agreed, then continued, "so, what are we doing this weekend, Dad?"

"Well, I'm not sure, but I'm starting it with coffee." He smiled, realizing she wouldn't quite find the humor he intended, "Your last soccer game of the season is tomorrow."

Neither of them were overly excited about the game, both soccered-out and ready for the season to be over. He continued.

"Let's think about that and see if we can come up with something fun to do, okay. It's only Friday, so technically I'm supposed to work today." He watched as her lips moved into an exaggerated frown. "I need to talk to the lawyer this morning, and then maybe I'll just do a few emails and we can start the weekend early. Cool?"

Her smile returned, "Cool." Cort watched her turn and walk toward the kitchen, then stop abruptly and spin back around. "Pancakes tomorrow, right?"

"Absolutely." Cort nodded and grinned, genuinely excited about the notion.

Lucie nodded back in thoughtful pause, and her eyes widened a bit, like she'd just discovered something important. "And this is Shark Week on TV. I already recorded a bunch of good episodes, including *Air Jaws*."

She was referring to a program that examined the feeding habits of great white sharks. It focused on the way they attack from below and get some serious airtime as they breach the water's surface, simultaneously biting their prey. It was an older program, originally airing several years ago, but they'd seen it more than a couple times now. It was always fascinating to watch.

"Awesome!" Cort exaggerated his excitement slightly. "We can watch some shark shows too then."

"Yeah," she snapped back, "and we can see some *reeeaaal* shark behavior."

He laughed a second with his daughter and responded with raised eyebrows. "You think that was bad, Luce... they made a fourth Jaws movie. It was called *Jaws Revenge*, I think. In that one, Jaws follows Chief Brody's wife and son to the Bahamas and goes after them there."

"Wait, what?" Lucie's tone was incredulous.

"I know, right?" Cort laughed again whole-heartedly, as his daughter processed the information.

"First-of-all, Dad, Great Whites don't live in the Bahamas. I think they migrate to warmer waters to have babies, but not that warm. Second-of-all, how did he know they were in the Bahamas? And third, I thought Jaws was dead?!"

Cort just shook his head and grinned, impressed with her knowledge and confirming her questions were good ones. He also knew the premise of the movie was completely ridiculous.

"Dad," she continued, "does that mean there was a Jaws 2 and a Jaws 3?"

"Uh huh, there was," he nodded with a disappointed smirk. "Jaws 3 sucked as bad as number 4. But you know what, Jaws 2 was actually pretty good. Maybe we should watch that one sometime."

"Really?" Lucie replied hesitantly and paused before continuing. "If Jaws dies at the end of that one too, I'm not interested."

"Yeah, well, never mind then I guess." Cort smiled and looked at his daughter, who simply shook her head back and forth with a disappointed realization. Cort changed his expression to serious, and continued, "Maybe someone should make a movie where the shark eats all the town's people, then just swims off into the sunset at the end?" He offered the outlandish suggestion and tried to keep a straight face.

"Yeah, I'd watch it, Dad!"

Lucie's serious reply brought another smile to Cort's face. "I bet you would, Lucie. I bet you would." They laughed together before Cort finally ended the conversation. "Go get yourself some breakfast. I'll keep my day in the office short, and then we'll start the weekend early."

"Okay." She smiled in satisfaction.

It didn't take long for Cort's somber state-of-mind to return, as he opened his computer systems and began reading the first few messages in what had become an overwhelming inbox. The prospect of addressing them, even one of them, seemed impossible. He stared out his office window for at least a few minutes, watching the sun shed light on what was forecasted to be a beautiful summer Day. He wanted to be anywhere but in his office. Mostly, he wanted to be with Lucie, outside somewhere, with his mind occupied by his daughter and the weather. After reading and staring blankly at a few of the email messages designated with "Important" in the heading, Cort decided to ignore all of them and begrudgingly make the call to his attorney, Donald Chark. The lawyer had texted him the day before, saying they needed to discuss the settlement. Within a few seconds of dialing, the receptionist answered the same way she always did.

"Chark & Chark, Attorneys at Law."

It was the only thing about the firm that made Cort smile; impossible not to connect the name with the word shark, at least in his mind, and he thought it was ironically odd they were lawyers. Brothers, Donald Chark Jr and Eric Chark were equal partners in the firm they'd started over twenty years ago. They ran one of the largest law firms in Pittsburgh and had a reputation for winning big settlements in wrongful death suits. Cort hadn't really cared about any of that, but the prosecutor in the criminal case had referred him to the firm.

Within a minute of dialing the phone number, he was patched through by the receptionist, and Don Chark Jr. picked up the call.

"Hey Cort, how are ya buddy?"

I'm freak'n fantastic. He bit back the sarcasm and went with a non-ITS response.

"I'm fine, Don, hanging in there," Cort softened his true emotions.

"Good, that's good. And Lucie, how's she doing?"

Spare me the goddamned niceties, Chark!

"She's doing better, thanks." At least this time, Cort believed his answer was truthful.

"Good, great, give her my best. Well, hey, Cort, I won't beat around the bush. Got some real good news for you."

"Alright." Cort heard some rustling of papers on the other end before the attorney answered.

"The settlement is official. Bravo Transport agreed to the sum of $5.5 million, just like we were expecting."

"Okay." This time Cort tried to add a little enthusiasm into his voice, but it fell flat.

The attorney paused, expecting more to come, but finally gave up and continued.

"So, after the firm's 30% cut, and some processing fees, you'll net $3,848,000, and some change."

As the attorney waited patiently for a response, Cort punched some numbers into the calculator and did some quick math.

Two grand in processing fees. What the hell?

He decided not to ask. Not only would he sound disappointed, which he was, but it would also come across as greedy.

"Well Don, that's great, I guess." Cort finally sighed out the reply.

"Yes sir, it certainly is. That amount will be deposited middle of next week, into the account you provided us, and the funds will likely be available by Thursday or Friday I'd guess." The attorney struggled to add something more profound but could only offer some generic advice. "You know Cort, you might want to think about putting the majority of it into an estate, or maybe an offshore account. I don't know, just a thought."

Thanks Don. And you might want to think about putting your $1.65 million straight up your ass! Oh, and don't forget about the other $2,000 processing fee. Stick that up where the sun doesn't shine too.

Cort pushed the ITS thought away and began speaking before he could put a proper response together.

"Don, hey...." Cort paused, then paused longer. The hesitation lasted too long. The lawyer sensed it and tried to help.

"Yeah, Cort?" He finally asked.

"Um, just, you know, thanks." It was the only polite offering that Cort could muster, as the sacrifice that had been made for the monetary gain was front and center in his head. He sensed the lawyer getting ready to respond and nipped it in the bud.

"Bye Don, have a good day." Without waiting for a reply, Cort hit the End Call button on his phone, and placed it on his desk. He clicked his mouse a few times and put his "out of office" setting on his email for what seemed liked the hundredth time in the last several months. *Screw it.* He decided today, and the majority of the days going forward, regardless of how many or how few there would be, would be spent with his daughter.

Chapter 17 – Mood Sweetener

Joining Lucie at the kitchen table, Cort unplugged the toaster, poured a second cup of coffee, and sat down as she finished a bagel and some apple slices. The faint scent of cinnamon lingered in the air.

"Do you want the rest of this, Dad? I'm getting full."

Cort checked her plate and pondered the question. He wasn't really interested in the last quarter of the bagel or the two remaining slices of apple. He was even less interested, however, in wasting food.

"How about I eat the bagel and an apple slice, and you eat the other slice?"

"Deal."

Picking up the last section of bagel from her plate, he put the whole thing in his mouth. The cold dough was a little tougher to chew, so he washed it down with the apple before speaking again.

"Hey, Lucie, I'm done working. I think we should take advantage of this beautiful June day and spend it outside."

"That sounds good. Where are we going?"

"I was thinking maybe a hike? We could go up to Moraine or McConnells Mill." Cort was referring to two different state parks within a twenty-five-minute drive. Both had great trails with a variety of terrains to choose from. Lucie knew both very well, as he, she, and Celeste had frequented both parks a half-dozen times in the past couple of years. Secretly he hoped she would choose McConnells Mill, which had less elevation change. Plus, the trail followed Slippery Rock Creek, a beautiful body of gushing water.

"Definitely McConnells Mill." She answered immediately as if reading his thoughts.

"Awesome! I'll pack us a lunch and we'll make a day of it."

Lucie grinned large and showed all her teeth, "When are we leaving?"

Cort glanced at the digital clock on the oven. 10:15 already. He could change, pack lunches, and be ready inside of the hour.

"Let's shoot for 11:00. Can you be ready in 45 minutes, Luce?" He raised his eyebrows in expectation of her response.

"I'm ready now, Dad. Well, I'll change, and brush my teeth and fix my hair, then get my water bottle filled. Okay, 11:00 sounds good."

Lucie darted out of the kitchen and up to her room, while Cort remained behind in the kitchen. He haphazardly ate a banana, sipped at his lukewarm coffee, and made chicken sandwiches for their lunch. For the second time this week, he felt genuine excitement for what was coming. It wasn't that the nagging despair was gone, but it had a slice of anticipation mixed into it - just enough to stave off the depression and the suicidal thoughts. He focused on his tasks and hustled through preparations, checking his phone twenty-eight minutes later. 10:43 A.M., and he had the backpack next to the door; they were ready to ditch suburbia.

"Luce, I'm ready when you are." Cort hollered, projecting his voice through the family room and up the stairs to her bedroom.

"Dad, I'm right here." The slightly annoyed voice came from behind him, and he twitched in startlement.

"Oh shit! Sorry, where'd you come from?"

Lucie laughed, both because she'd scared him and at his choice of words.

"I was sitting right here," she managed through her chuckling.

Cort smiled and offered his daughter a fist bump, which she reciprocated.

"Don't scare me like that," he pseudo-scolded her, and they shared another giggle.

Two minutes later, the garage door went down and they backed out of the driveway. The day was gorgeous already; seventy-four degrees on the dash thermometer. The forecast predicted close to eighty for a high today, but down in the valley near the water, it wouldn't get much higher than mid-seventies. Perfect for the t-shirt and shorts they were both sporting. Lucie took a strategic seat in the back, caddy-corner to the driver, which made conversation easier - Cort could safely make direct eye contact with her sporadically. She was maybe a year and ten pounds shy of being able to sit up front, but both knew it wasn't a safety law they'd stretch the boundaries on.

There was a rare air of enthusiasm in the car as they drove north on Rt. 19. They talked about positive subjects like the sunshine, flowers, and the hopes of seeing some animals on their hike. It was one of the character traits she'd picked up from her father, despite ninety percent or more of her personality coming from Celeste. Both loved nature, and when it came to outdoor adventure, he'd always clicked with Lucie. They discussed the general plan, which was to start at the covered bridge next to the old mill and hike downstream past Eckert's Bridge for a mile or so. After turning around, they'd hike back upstream, cross Eckert's Bridge, then continue up the opposite side of Slippery Rock Creek back to their starting point. Round trip would only be around 4 miles, but they'd take their time and go off trail a little bit too. There'd be some great boulders to choose from for a lunch spot, which was always a nice way to break up the walking. Lucie asked if she could pick the boulder, and Cort agreed without hesitation.

They were caught up in their conversation and excitement, so much that Cort didn't even realize their location it until it was there. The exit ramp - two hundred feet ahead on their right, and he couldn't avoid passing the spot where she died. It was completely visible from their angle. Cort realized he was taking the exact route he'd suggested to Celeste on the phone. He could plainly see the oncoming ramp that he'd wanted to stop and back up to her location. If he'd ignored her instructions warning him against it, she'd likely be sitting next to him in the passenger seat right now. He stopped breathing, and nearly choked on the knot in his throat. Turning his head, he gazed out his driver side window so his peripheral vision couldn't pick up the other side of the highway. The car grew silent, but Cort kept his line of sight to the left and hoped Lucie hadn't noticed the abrupt change in his demeanor. A glance in his rearview mirror showed Lucie scanning the passenger side windows, instinctively looking in the opposite direction of his gaze, trying to figure out what he'd seen or heard. Cort kept his stare to the left for ten seconds as they passed the area. After they'd moved beyond it, he turned his head slowly to the front and center position that it belonged in, hoping she hadn't been watching him closely. He thought he'd succeeded, until she spoke.

"Dad, was that the… was that where…?"

Cort inhaled through his nose, so his anxiety was less obvious. He tried to focus on something other than the images racing through his brain.

"Dad?" Lucie interrupted his trance for the second time.

"Yes Lucie, that was the spot." He swallowed hard and desperately held back tears. He'd cried so much in the past few days, weeks, and months. Today he decided he wouldn't, not right now in front of his daughter.

"I want to go there sometime, Dad."

Cort simply nodded his head in understanding. He'd felt that same urge up until yesterday, and if it hadn't been for the "gift" Celeste had left for him, it very well could have been a therapeutic visit to the place she'd breathed her last air.

"I'll take you, Luce. Not today though, okay, just not today."

They drove in silence for a minute - Cort feeling guilty for not being able to hide his sorrow and inadvertently spoiling their jovial mood. A mile later, on a whim, Cort made an abrupt right turn into the parking lot of Baldingers. He'd nearly forgotten it was there, as he hadn't driven this stretch of road since before February. He turned his head to Lucie and winked, and she smiled back. It was perfect timing to snap them out of their sullen state of mind. He parked and both got out in eager anticipation. Cort held the front door open for his daughter and followed her into Baldingers, a candy store that had first opened for business over 50 years ago. The current location wasn't the original store, but a good bit of the décor, including a couple antique cash registers and scales had made the transition, bringing some of the nostalgic feel to the present space. It was laid out in sections, each one with several tables that held large jars of candy. The sweets were organized by price-per-pound, and there were no less than 200 different selections. That didn't include all the full-size bars, boxes of candy, and other sweet treats that adorned the perimeter shelves of the store. Lucie led Cort to the right, knowing exactly where they'd start. It was the same spot they always began, where the faint smell of cocoa wafted above the glass jars, beckoning patrons to indulge - the table with the chocolate malt balls. An oversized jar of them sat among a dozen other large glass containers, filled with items like chocolate covered peanuts, chocolate caramels, peanut butter cups, and chocolate dipped raisins. As they lifted each lid and self-served using scoopers, the sweet smell teased their salivary glands. Filling one bag, very heavy on the malt balls, they moved around the store methodically and made four more goodie bags, trading turns picking out which candy would get scooped up next. Twenty-one minutes later, they got back into the car equipped with 3 ½ pounds of sweet diversions.

"We may have overdone it, Luce."

"Let's eat some right now." She ignored his ridiculous notion.

"Oh, you know we are!" Cort winked in the rear-view mirror at his daughter, and they chowed on various items of chocolate, gummies, licorice, and Swedish fish. Finally, Cort sealed the bag back up with the twist tie and pushed it away as far as he could to the other side of the passenger seat.

"We'll have some more after lunch, alright Lucie?"

He turned his head to the rear when she didn't answer. She immediately nodded her head and smiled, showing him the orange gumdrop remnants stuck between just about every one of her teeth. Cort simply smiled back and turned around, thankful for the sugar-rush distraction that had quite possibly saved their day.

Chapter 18 – Flow of Life

The small lot next to the covered bridge was expectedly full, so they drove across the bridge and up the mountain road a few hundred yards, parked, and the pair traversed back down to the valley's floor. The weather simply could not have been more perfect. As the sun crept towards its highest point in the sky, father and daughter entered the trail-head full of anticipation. The air above the creek was cooled as it floated over the rushing water, partnering with the shade to move a comfortable breeze across their skin. Solar rays filtered through the leaves, piercing the canopy with long swords of light and bouncing off the water to create thousands of tiny white flashes on Slippery Rock Creek.

Cort and Lucie chatted intermittently, stopping every few minutes to point out unique features of their surrounding; a lichen covered log, a tiny waterfall within a small tributary stream, an insect being spotlighted in one of the sun beams. The pair took turns taking the lead, traversing small obstacles that were just off the beaten path. It was a game of sorts, where the follower had to successfully accomplish the same feat as the leader. Cort kept his mini-obstacles short and relatively easy, while Lucie tried to achieve balancing acts on boulders and logs that she didn't think he could manage. Feigning surprise, Cort acted tentative to attempt some of her stunts. The shape of her smile told him that she knew he was acting, but seeing her smile was worth all his dramatics.

After hiking and trading order for an hour or so, they came to a small deviation in the path. Going right would take them up an incline, where they'd traverse a section of the trail that led halfway up the mountain, eventually making its decline back to the edge of the water again a half mile later. There were more than a couple great views from the higher elevation, and probably 90% of hikers chose that scenic route along the well beaten path. To the left was a path less groomed that stayed low and nearer the creek. There would be more fallen trees, unbridged side streams, and sections of muddy trail and slick rocks to go over or around. The lower path would also be much less crowded, and it offered the white noise of flowing water. Both agreed that the tranquil gurgle of moving water was possibly the most peaceful sound in existence.

There was little hesitation as they turned to each other and pointed to the left fork simultaneously, then slowly made their way down some natural stone steps and approached the edge of the creek. Without discussion, they ended the follow-the-leader game, and gave more attention to each footstep. While the level ground was a bit less physically demanding, the terrain demanded a greater deal of attention and caution. They relished the heightened challenge, both subconsciously aware that for now their brains weren't focused on the negative aspects of their lives.

After ten minutes of silent walking, Cort paused and surveyed the area.

"Hey, Luce, start looking for a good boulder. I'm getting hungry and could use a little breather too."

"Okay, I'll find us a good one."

Minutes later, Cort helped Lucie over a small inflowing stream, lifting her as she simultaneously jumped from the last dry rock she could reach by herself. As he put her down on the other side, movement in his peripheral vision drew his attention. Cort stopped to watch the unmistakable back and forth s-motions of an eight-inch-long snake. Cort adjusted his feet slowly and stretched his right foot onto a stable rock. Bending down he swiftly but gently grabbed the snake around the midpoint in its body, cradling the beautiful creature softly between three fingers.

Swinging his feet over the stream and joining his daughter, "Lucie, check this out."

"Awwwww, he's so cute."

Cort stroked the snake's gray skin lightly, showing Lucie that it was completely harmless.

"It's a ringneck, Luce. See the yellow band there around its neck?"

"Yeah, that's cool. We've seen these before, right? They aren't venomous."

"No, they aren't. Completely harmless."

She reached out her hand. "Can I hold it?"

"Oh yeah, absolutely."

Cort gently put the snake in Lucie's hand, instructing her to keep just enough pressure with her fingers so it didn't slither out and fall to the ground. She listened and complied and smiled large as the snake's smooth body weaved itself around her thumb and pointer finger. A second later they watched as a small drop of discolored liquid ran down the back of Lucie's hand.

"Daaaad?"

He couldn't help but laugh a bit before answering her. "It's alright, Lucie. It's just a little pee."

"Awww daaad, that's gross!" Her grin transitioned into a frown as she squinted her eyes and crimped her nose.

"It's fine, Lucie, that's just the way snakes tell you that they love you."

"Daaaad." She let out a half-disgusted, half-amused sigh, "C'mon, you take it now."

Cort was well aware that the waste product of snakes had a highly putrid smell and didn't exactly care to get the scent on his hand.

"Just put it down right over there, next to the creek. I think that's his house over there by that rock." Cort mused and she did as he asked. "Now just wash your hands in the water there, and we can go eat some lunch."

Lucie vigorously rubbed her hands together in a small pool of water before finally standing and drying them on her shorts. They'd only walked another two hundred feet when she paused and pointed towards the water.

"Right there, Dad, that boulder. Let's climb up onto it and have our lunch on top."

She'd pointed to an especially large boulder surrounded half by land and half by water. The top had a large circular surface that was mostly flat. It was indeed a beautiful rock, surely left behind in that exact spot some 25,000 years ago as a glacier melted away. Cort noted the several smaller boulder's surrounding it, which would act as makeshift steps and enable a fairly easy climb to the top. Before proceeding, he hesitated, silently scoping out the form of the rock again and glancing around the perimeter. Initially he couldn't identify the sense of familiarity he was experiencing, but as they proceeded forward and approached their lunch destination, the location hit Cort like an uppercut. He'd been here before, in this exact same spot. It was probably more than six years ago now; a wave of memories washed through his mind. He and Celeste had left Lucie home with a babysitter and gone hiking. It was a few months after that second miscarriage, and the goal was to remove themselves, if even just for a few hours, from the bitter reality they'd been suffering. Along their hike, they'd planned to have a heart-to-heart and find a spot where Mother Nature could offer a bit of mental health. Cort shook the brief sense of sadness away, remembering what had been a healing conversation on top of the boulder.

"It's amazing that you picked this exact one, Luce." Cort muttered the thought under his breath.

"What, Dad?"

"Uh, never mind. I was just saying this is an amazing spot you picked.

"Should we eat our candy first?" Lucie suggested it with a straight face.

"Ha ha, you wish." Cort shook his head, not convinced that his 10-year-old daughter was even kidding.

The pair sat and chewed chicken sandwiches, mostly in quiet, occasionally pointing to a bird or floating leaf. Cort and Lucie appreciated the absence of human-based sound and basked in the music of Mother Nature. The soft song of the water flowing past them and the whisper of the wind through the trees providing the perfect soundtrack for their lunch date. Before he realized it was happening, Cort became mesmerized by the water, like he often did, and sat staring in a trance at the creek some ten feet below them. Thoughts of Celeste swirled around his head like the ripples below the rocks, and he nodded in silent serenity to himself. Finally, Lucie's voice broke his daydream, and he jerked his head in her direction.

"Dad, why do you always stare at the water?"

"Huh. Oh, sorry Lucie, was I staring?"

"Yeah, you do that every time we're around a river, or a creek. One time when we were at the beach I watched you stare at the waves for like fifteen minutes straight."

Cort released a little chuckle, knowing that her observation was accurate.

"I'm not sure. I know a lot of people like to watch water. But I'm probably an extreme case. It's always fascinated me, and I'm not really sure why. But you're right, I like to watch it."

His daughter just nodded and watched the stream flowing below them, and he could almost see her wheels spinning, making the connection that he was referring to. Cort was remembering part of the conversation that he'd had with Celeste in this exact spot several years back, and he decided to try a similar analogy to talk to Lucie now.

"Lucie, see the section of stream, starting up there at that large boulder, and then all the way down there, to where that fallen log is." He moved his hand from left to right, panning the two-hundred-foot section of water.

She listened, and scanned the stream as instructed, twice, before pausing and meeting her father's eyes again. "Yes."

"If you look back up to that deeper pool there next to that boulder. See how the water is mostly flat and calm?"

"Mmm hmmm." She followed his finger and nodded in confirmation.

"Well, that's kind of how life was for a while for you, Mom, and me. We were sort of just moving along in a steady flow, without any major turbulence." He watched her nod again before continuing. "Then we sort of hit some rough spots, just like there, where the creek narrows a little. See that part right there?"

"Yeah, I see where you mean." She replied with a nod.

"So," Cort continued, "there were a few years that got a little rocky for us, but we survived it and things were beginning to calm again. And then… well… you know. February 2nd." He exhaled and willed himself to keep it together. "February was like that part of the creek right there, as the elevation drops and the water has nowhere to go except over the submerged rocks. That's what causes that waterfall and the rapids, and all the white foamy water down below it. I feel like maybe that's where we've been for a few months now Lucie… you and I. And it's hard. I know it's hard for both of us. And we have to be strong to keep our heads above the churning water. But if we don't fight that current, and help each other, we can get pulled below and things could be bad. Does that make sense?"

A single tear leaked from Lucie's eye, and she nodded again to confirm that she understood his analogy. Cort moved closer and wrapped his right arm around her in an endearing hug, holding her for a long moment before releasing her again.

"Here's the important thing, Lucie, and it's the part that I think I've been struggling to remember the most. See further downstream there, past that bus-shaped boulder and closer to that big Sycamore tree?"

"Yes." Lucie wiped away the moisture from beneath her eye and smiled at the notion that she was expecting to come next.

"That calmer part there, where the green color gets darker." He pointed downstream and waved his hand to span the view of a larger, deeper section of quiet water. "We're going to make it there, Lucie. Even if it's just you and I, we're going to make it to that place of calm and happiness again, I promise you that."

Lucie tilted her head up at her dad, nodding a smile to acknowledge that she agreed. The lines around her smile concealed the feelings of apprehension and highlighted a roadmap of hope. They both knew that there would be more rough water along the way, but there was a confidence in the notion that they had each other to manage it.

"Dad?"

"Yeah, Luce?"

"I understand your comparison. And you know what else?"

"What's that, Lucie?"

"Even when we get to that dark green water where it's calm, we still need to swim, or we'll drown. You know what I mean?'

Cort sighed and swallowed the enormous lump in his throat as he processed what she was saying. It took everything he could do to keep his eyes dry, and he spoke to stave off the tears.

"Yeah, Luce, you're 100% right. You're also a very smart little girl, do you know that?"

She smiled coyly at him, and he returned a heartfelt grin before she leaned on his shoulder. Cort continued his thoughts silently, furthering the analogy into the future. He pictured the creek's eventual merger with a river. In that larger body of water, there would be threats to the bond between him and Lucie; other interests to gain her attention. Soon enough he'd be dealing with teenage girl issues, and he had no idea how he'd handle the challenges normally resolved by a mother. More troubling in his mind, was that he knew the river would eventually empty into an ocean. That's likely where'd he'd part ways with his daughter, as she explored the opportunities and other facets of life; the parts that excluded him. Of course, they'd still see each other on occasion, visiting their respective corners of that ocean. By then she'd have her own life, and if all worked out in the bitter irony of parenthood, he would be replaced by another person; one that she'd love and cherish even more than him. The thoughts incited both sadness and joy simultaneously, but there was also a fear that came with the predictions of what lay ahead. He needed to ensure that she'd make it to that point in life's path, happy and secure along the journey, so that her future could be eagerly anticipated. While the realization was always there in the depths of his mind, it was now that Cort accepted his ultimate duty as her father. He could only fulfill his obligations by treading water beside her, existing physically and mentally as her guidance and protection. He'd find a way to handle the pain and suffering of Celeste's death. Manny's statement at Celeste's funeral zipped through his mind. *Try to take care of that little girl*. He knew now it had been warranted, and he issued a thought of forgiveness to his father-in-law. It was time to be a man, and more importantly, be a father. Whatever needed to happen, he'd figure it out, but one thing was for sure; his own death was no longer an option.

"Hey, Lucie." Cort broke the silence that had grown long.

"What?" She turned back to the water and leaned her head deeper into his shoulder.

"No matter how rough the water gets along the way, I just want you to know that I'll always be here for you."

Lucie nodded, hugged his arm, and buried half of her face into his chest. There was a pause in the conversation, and he sensed that her mind was racing for a response. Finally, she turned her face back to the water, and he heard the four words that she'd uttered to him every day for as long as he could remember.

"I love you, Dad."

Cort clenched his eyes closed, wanting so much to reciprocate immediately, but his vocal cords were stuck in a sea of emotions. Seconds ticked and he swallowed hard twice, trying to free his voice from the choking waters. Finally, he turned his head into the top of hers, and was able to say the words she was waiting for.

"I love you too, Lucie."

***

    Her mind dwelled on his words, and the promise he'd made about being there for her. It warmed her soul. She completely understood his promise, and wondered if he knew how much comfort, love, and security his words gave her. As the wave of feelings washed over her like bath water, she told him she loved him with more emphasis than usual. His promise gave her a boost of confidence that her strategy was working, and she exhaled when he finally told her that he loved her too.

    It seemed that there'd been a change in him today, but it was too soon to be sure. She'd push harder with her distractions, and come up with something bigger, something to get him excited about life again - maybe even something to get them both excited about life again.

Chapter 19 – *Luce Plan*

The ride home was more upbeat than any forty-five-minute span they'd had in the past five months. Cort drove a longer, less direct way home, keeping the route to the two-lane country roads with better scenery. Mostly, the alternate route was to avoid the area that they'd inadvertently passed on the way in, and it worked. There wasn't a negative remark during the entire drive. Even the question he'd asked Lucie about how her visits with Dr. Burns were going had been responded to positively.

"We talk mostly about the good memories." She said it without hesitation, and he believed her statement.

They gazed at the cattle on the sprawling farms, even pulling over next to a herd of dairy cows at one point. Silly variations of 'mooooo' sounds were bellowed out their windows until a few cows stopped chewing cud and raised their heads. Cort then started to tell her the best cow joke he knew.

"Hey, Luce, why do cows wear bells around their neck?"

She answered in an exaggerated impression of her father, "Uhhhh, because their horns don't work."

Cort chuckled, slightly embarrassed. "Sorry, I guess I told you that one?"

"Only like three times Dad," Lucie laughed at her father's short memory.

"Oh geez, now I'm *udderly* embarrassed." Cort hoped she'd catch the pun.

"What?" Lucie's brows were furrowed.

"Never mind, if I have to explain the joke, it was probably dumb."

Cort pulled away and decided it was a good opportunity to unveil his tentative idea of moving. He laid out his proposed relocation in no uncertain terms and asked his daughter's input with every aspect of the plan. She was surprisingly agreeable with almost everything. By the time they'd pulled into the garage, they had a loose plan laid out including a 60 to 90-day timeline for enacting it.

They both agreed that the general area around Austin, Texas would be the location that made the most sense. Lucie loved Manny and Gabby, and she'd been in Austin a half-dozen times over the past several years. The familiarity of the area helped, and her grandparents had always doted over her when she was in town. There were so many other facets of moving but he decided Lucie didn't need to hear them. Selling their house, packing everything, and then actually moving it all. He also considered it would be best for Lucie to start the new school year in Texas on day one, rather than bring her into a mix of new classmates a month or so into the Fall. His timeline was probably closer to the sixty days than it was ninety, but he considered she could get started in Austin with Manny and Gabby, while he remained behind for a few weeks to work out loose ends. He felt unsettled, especially with his job, and felt a true sense of guilt with the way he was handling his position.

"Hey, Dad." Lucie interrupted his troubled considerations.

"Yeah, Luce?"

"We should watch some of our Shark Week shows tonight."

Cort glanced in the rearview mirror at his daughter, whose eyebrows were raised and beckoning his agreement with the idea.

"Sure, that sounds good. But hey, big soccer game tomorrow morning, so we can't stay up too late, alright?"

"That's fine. I'll be glad when this season is over."

"Yeah, well, I've really enjoyed watching your games this year, Lucie, but I'll sort of be glad it's over too. You play that team with the nasty goalie tomorrow, don't you?"

"Arsenal, yes. Her name is Maggie. She scares me."

"Yeah, I get it. I wouldn't want her to be mad at me." Cort turned and winked at his daughter, evoking a brief smile.

"Coach Liam tells us not to get too close to her… he knows she's nasty too."

"Well then listen to coach, right? Avoid her. Take your shots before you get inside the box or pass it if you need to."

Cort contemplated the advice he'd just given, wondering if it was good or not. He didn't understand the game nearly as well as Lucie, and they both knew when he offered strategic suggestions, it had the potential to be completely wrong. He'd grown up playing American football. When he was a kid, soccer was something only foreigners played. A talented goalie was not what he thought of when the word "defense" was mentioned. Instead, images of Steelers greats like Jack Lambert, Mean Joe Greene, and Troy Polamalu came to mind. He, Lucie, and Celeste had watched a couple NFL games together the past Fall, and he was tickled that his daughter had shown some interest. Football was as foreign a concept to her as soccer was to him, but she asked questions and was genuinely intrigued by the rules of the game. He smiled as he thought back to how shocked Lucie was by the degree of physical contact. After watching one especially egregious tackle, she'd asked how the two players could even walk afterwards. After laughing out loud, he explained how the pads and helmets protected the most important body parts, but it still hurt sometimes. Then he'd shown Lucie how to make a proper football tackle, as if she needed to know for her future career as a linebacker. After he wrapped her up and picked her off her feet, he tossed her down onto the sofa next to Celeste, then bear-hugged his wife and daughter simultaneously. Six months ago, now seemed like an eternity. He dismissed the thought and focused back to the present.

"So anyway, Luce, let's pick up a few groceries before we go home. I was thinking we could maybe make some homemade pizza tonight for dinner?"

"Oh yeah! Let's do that."

"When we get home, I need to call Pappy and Grammy. We'll see if we can get down to Austin a couple times this summer and find a place to live. Then we'll make some pizzas, and after dinner we'll watch some shark shows. Deal?"

"Deal."

Cort grinned at his daughter and Lucie smiled back at him in the rearview mirror.

Three hours later, they were rolling out dough, spreading sauce, and adding cheese and toppings. There was excitement in the process, not just with the anticipation of eating homemade pizza, but in the conversation. Cort told Lucie everything he and her grandparents had just discussed on their fifty-minute-long phone call. He went over some of the tentative plans with her again, which included flying to Austin the week of July 4th to do some preliminary house-hunting. He and Lucie would spend most of the nights in a hotel downtown, but Cort had agreed to stay at his in-laws over the 4th weekend. They'd have a barbeque with Manny and Gabby before watching fireworks from their back deck. Cort also told her that based on Pappy and Grammy's suggestion, they'd be visiting the Museum of Ice Cream too.

After gorging on a small salad and what turned out to be decent pizza, the two changed into pajamas and reconvened on the couch. First up was the highly anticipated *Air Jaws* program, which still held excitement despite this being their 3rd or 4th watch. Normally they'd have saved that show until last, to ensure they ended the evening of shark watching with a bang. But Lucie decided that she wanted to save another program for the final watch. An episode she claimed was new, and that she'd never seen. Cort cued up the program and read the description before hitting play. "Great White Bite" was an episode about the feeding habits of the most deadly shark in the ocean. The show was hosted by a married couple that lived on the ocean and studied the sharks from their home/lab/sailboat. Most of the episode took place off the coast of South Africa, where the charming couple was from. Cort always enjoyed that South African accent, which he interpreted as some hybrid between Australian and English. The husband and wife were attractive, appearing to be in their early forties, and they had a son that was maybe 12 or 13. The boy was shown intermittently, helping his parents with various boat related tasks. Cort wondered if Lucie thought the boy was cute but decided not to ask.

The couple discussed interesting facts about the attack and bite strategy of Great White, and there was plenty of good video to accompany the narration. The hulls of their sailboat were a beautiful light-blue and the deck was primarily the warm amber hue of teak wood. Across the stern was an emblem of the South African flag, with a nicely hand-painted rendition of a shark next to it. The name of the boat was printed underneath it in bright red Calibri font; "BITE ME." Cort and Lucie watched enthusiastically. Within the jarring images of sharks chewing the heads of real tuna fish and seal replicas, the couple educated the viewers about the true nature of sharks. At no point in the program did the man and woman say that Great Whites routinely attack person after person, in small island communities off the coast of Massachusetts. Cort and Lucie enjoyed the program thoroughly, quite satisfied with its content. He checked his phone as the credits began to pop up on the screen. 9:52 P.M.

"Hey, Lucie, what do you think? Probably need to start thinking about bed?"

She nodded in agreement, but Cort sensed her mind was elsewhere. Before leaving the sofa, she voiced her thoughts very matter-of-factly.

"Dad, we should do that."

"Do what?" Cort shrugged.

"We should live on a boat like that. We could go anywhere we wanted to."

He hesitated before processing her words. "Oh, you mean like that couple in the show?"

"Yeah, Dad, like them."

Cort paused and watched her, waiting for a sarcastic smile to crack, but it never did.

"Seriously, Luce?"

"Yeah, that would be the best house ever."

Cort stood, glancing up at the blank TV and envisioning the already fading images of the sailboat. It was a novel, if not unusually attractive notion, that Lucie had thrown out there. She'd proposed it as if the idea should be a forgone conclusion. He pondered it briefly before realizing how preposterous it sounded, and then shook his head before responding.

"Yeah, that would be cool, Lucie. If only it were that easy, right?" He baited his response to see if she truly understood how unrealistic her suggestion was.

"I don't know. I guess if you say so, but it wouldn't be hard for me. I could do homeschooling and some cyber-learning, just like that boy on the show did."

"What about all your friends? You wouldn't see them at all if we lived on a boat." Cort pressed, knowing there was no way she'd considered all the consequences.

"What about them? I could still text and Snap with them."

Cort realized he wasn't getting through to her sensible side and decided to end the defense case that he was rapidly losing.

"Let's talk about this later little girl. It's time to hit the sack and rest those legs for tomorrow. Okay?"

"Whatever." Her response held more than a hint of disappointment.

Cort processed her reply but decided not to engage further. Instead, he took the strategy of distracting her away from the conversation.

"Now, pretend the floor is the ocean, and it's filled with hungry sharks. You need to get from the sofa to the steps without getting your feet in the water."

She smiled at the challenge and nodded a quick acceptance. Looking around the room, she strategized her potential path to the stairs. She could use the ottoman for her first traverse, then lay some pillows down as imaginary floating pads to make her way across the remaining "waters." Cort watched in awe as her mind worked to solve the problem at hand. He silently admired her agility as she leaped from the ottoman to a cushion she'd tossed out onto the hardwood floor. She hesitated before jumping to the next one, which she'd tossed quite a bit further than she'd intended. Lucie was in a bit of a pickle now, too separated from the ottoman to leap back, and a couple feet too far away from the second pillow. Cort watched anxiously at her dilemma. Finally, after she searched the room for an option, she aimed her finger at him.

"I see a whale swimming towards me," pointing at Cort with a smile, "I'm gonna jump on its back and get a ride to the other side."

Cort laughed in admiration at her creativeness, then processed the whole notion.

"Wait, are you saying I'm as fat as a whale?" He raised his brow and gave Lucie an exaggerated look of disdain. She shook her head in denial and genuinely laughed hard, not able to speak for a few seconds. Finally, she gathered her breath and tried to cover her tracks.

"C'mon Dad, I didn't mean it like that. Now get over here and give me a piggy-back."

"Oh, I see, now I'm a piggy! I think I like whale better. Get on the back of this fat whale." They laughed again together as she jumped up onto her father, now squatting in front of her, back turned.

As they approached the top of the stairs, Lucie struck again.

"Hey, dad, remember that snake we picked up today."

Having no idea why she was asking the question, he confirmed immediately, anxious to find out why she'd brought it up. "Yeah, I sure do."

Lucie's reply was immediate, "Well, if I pee on your back, it's just my way of telling you that I love you." She burst into laughter as soon as the last word left her mouth.

Cort doubled over in laughter with her, nearly dropping his passenger as he pushed through her bedroom door with his head. Dumping her off onto her bed, he pointed his finger at her, still trying to contain his chortling.

"You are a wise-ass, Lucie Palmerton." He smiled a large mouth of teeth at his daughter, who was still calming herself.

"Yeah, Mom used to tell me the same thing, and she'd always say I got it from my dad."

Cort and Lucie curtailed their laughter succinctly, both shifting their thoughts to Celeste. Cort kept his smile visible, not wanting to advertise the sudden flood of memories that had just entered his head. He replied quickly to keep the mood positive.

"Well, your mother always told the truth, so I guess I'll admit that she was right about that." He paused and grinned at his daughter who appeared to be content. "Okay, Lucie, let's get some sleep and get ready to kick some butt tomorrow morning."

"Good night, Dad. Love ya." Lucie wrapped her arms around his neck, lifted her head, and kissed Cort on his scruffy cheek.

"Love you too. Good night, Luce." Reciprocating a peck on her forehead, he turned and left the room.

After a quick shower and a check of his phone for potentially important texts or emails, Cort tucked himself into the king-sized bed and laid the phone on the nightstand. Turning towards the other side of the wide berth, he stared at the empty pillow and undisturbed section of the duvet. There was an intense emptiness within the view, and the feeling of loneliness couldn't have been greater if he were floating solo through an endless ocean. His mind conjured up an image of Celeste laying in the spot next to him where she should be. He could see the curves of her form and the warm tawny hue of her skin. Imagining her there, he pictured Celeste reading a book in the dim light, wearing the tortoise shell reading glasses that she always did. Rolling over to her side of the mattress, he put his head into her pillow, and desperately inhaled through his nose. There was still a faint whisper of her scent. Cort inhaled again even deeper, and let his tears absorb into her pillowcase. A somber minute passed. Before returning to his own side, he opened the drawer on her nightstand, and found them. They were there as he'd expected they would be, and he laid them on her pillow. The glasses brought him just a sliver of comfort, knowing they were something she'd worn just about every evening.

I'll be okay Celeste, I promise. But I miss you more than I ever thought I could miss anyone.

He lay awake in thought for a few minutes, shifting his musings from Celeste to Lucie, reflecting on what had been the best day he'd had since before Celeste had left their world. As he put his head into the pillow and adjusted his body into a comfortable posture, Cort had a profound realization. He admitted to himself that Lucie needed him, and if there was never any other reason, she'd be enough to sustain his purpose on the earth. Curtailing the drop of liquid desperately trying to escape from his tear duct, Cort thought about the Bad Company song he'd perceived to be a sign from Celeste.

Sorry Celeste, I misunderstood. I know now you were not answering my request in that moment, and my death is not the solution.

As he took solace in the notion of turning a corner today, he reached over and grabbed his phone. Opening the Google app, he tapped in the search box and typed a simple query:

🔍 sailboats for sale

Chapter 20 – Feer Not

The heavy weight of the conversation on the boulder with Lucie still pressed on his psyche, and he was most definitely dragging from a short night of sleep. By 1:00 AM, Cort had perused over seventy sailboats on a dozen-or-so broker or marina sites. He dwelled on everything from the engine capacity to the upholstery of the cabin cushions, reviewing all details with the goal of narrowing down some of the most desired features. There was so much to take in, and now, as he sipped a strong cup of coffee, some of the favorite vessels he'd looked at were still imprinted on his gray matter. More overwhelming was he'd spent all that time on what was a pipedream, and he was angry with himself for hoping it could become reality. Still, as he swallowed back the liquid caffeine, he thought about the boats.

Those catamarans were so damn sweet!

It was time to head to the field, and Cort was happy to have the game as a distraction. For the next hour or so, he'd focus on Lucie's soccer skills, trying to analyze her moves, her skills, her understanding of the game. He knew the basics, comprehended the rules for the most part, and certainly got the athleticism involved. It was her fourth year, and Lucie was becoming quite good for her age. She had a considerably better grasp on the sport than he did. Nevertheless, he'd lose himself in the game, and more specifically, her game.

Twenty minutes later, he set the legs of the folding chair on the grass and opened them. It was one of the processes that had been oddly difficult to get used to. Setting up one chair instead of two; some of the simplest routines were the most painful. This season, the spots he picked to sit in were always further down the field, away from the midline, strategically placed with a significant amount of distance from the area where most spectators congregated. In seasons past, he and his wife would be in the thick of the crowd, setting up near the middle and conversing with the other parents. Not anymore.

Already quite warm for 9:30 A.M., the humidity made it slightly uncomfortable. The sun was visible but dull, subdued by a haze that promised to bring worse weather with it by the afternoon. Cort plopped into the wobbly canvas chair with a sense of frustrated anxiety. He stuck his water container into the makeshift cup holder, keeping his line of sight on the field. Making eye-contact with another spectator was a gamble, potentially bringing unwanted company and conversation. Deep down, Cort knew these were good people, genuinely concerned, at least on the surface. He took their condolences politely, and while the ITS thoughts begged to differ, he returned their gestures with a "thank you" or a handshake, and even the occasional hug. Still, he was looking forward to the season being over, thereby ending the potential for those interactions.

He watched Lucie take her position as forward and turn to coach Liam for confirmation of her spot. The players for Arsenal Lady Force also moved into position and waited for the first whistle. Arsenal was a good team, and one that they'd played twice already this season. Their strength was their defense, and more specifically, the net tending. Cort glanced in the opposing goalie's direction; the girl was standing comfortably at the far end of the field. Even from this distance, the goalie commanded a presence. Her name was Maggie, and she carried an intimidating reputation. Maggie was bigger than any other girl on either team, both in height and width. She stood a good four inches taller than Lucie and Cort estimated she had an additional 25 pounds on his daughter. Maggie was nimble for her size, however, and played with sound goalkeeper skills. As for her reputation of being a bit nasty, Cort and Lucie both knew she lived up to the infamy. Maggie didn't take kindly to players getting anywhere near the box, making her physical presence known if an opposing player got within twenty feet. While she kept most of her play within the rules, it was rumored that Maggie was the most penalized player in the league - nobody doubted the rumor.

Cort returned his focus to the opposing forward, just across the midline from Lucie, noting the name SIMMONS across her back. He remembered that Lucie was envious of the Arsenal uniforms, as her own team jerseys only displayed their numbers – no names.

The man with the black and white striped shirt blew the whistle, and for the next thirty minutes, the teams battled back and forth defensively. Cort focused on his daughter, watching her take three shots during her minutes in the first half. Maggie saved them all, including a diving hand-save to her right, just barely preventing the ball from getting inside the post. He watched the goalie jump back up and sneer at Lucie, silently taunting his daughter and provoking some ITS-worthy choice words, but he wisely bit his tongue and watched Lucie turn away. If she could ignore the poor sportsmanship, he could too. With less than a minute left in the half, Maggie punted the ball hard out of her end, sailing it over Lucie's head and clearing nearly two thirds of the field. Lucie maintained her forward position and stayed patient. One of Cranberry's midfielders suddenly emerged from a scrum of four players who'd met at the ball simultaneously. Instinctively, Lucie took off for the opponent's end of the field and called with a shout.

"AVA!"

Ava hadn't needed the prompt. She'd seen Lucie bee-line in the direction of Arsenal's end. A sweeping leg kick struck the ball with force, sending it back over the midline and into enemy territory. On it in a heartbeat, Lucie settled and controlled the ball, slowing only briefly to ensure she stayed on-sides. Cort stood in his spot as Lucie juked around the last defender and sprinted into a breakaway opportunity. He glanced at the goalie, who bounced slowly from her left knee to her right, then he looked back to Lucie. Sprinting with the ball towards the corner, Lucie took a less direct angle to the goalkeeper. Most of the spectators watching were surprised by the direction change, but Cort could see what his daughter saw. The other Cranberry forward had moved into space and was streaking unnoticed toward the goal too. Lucie stayed right, sucking Maggie with her towards the near post. When the goalie was confident that she had the angle of the shot covered, Lucie made a cross field pass, perfectly positioning her teammate for what became an easy goal. Cort saw the subtle smile form across Lucie's lips as he clapped and yelled from the sideline.

"Nice play, Lucie! Great job!"

She shot him an appreciative glance, then jogged to the middle of the field, where her fellow forward was waiting to exchange a high five with her. With her back to the opposing netminder, Lucie couldn't see the utter expression of disdain on Maggie's face. The goalie's glare was fixed on the girl who'd just strategically taken her out of position. Cort anxiously noted the promise of revenge in Maggie's eyes and was relieved when the whistle blew. Halftime.

The second half started ideally, with Lucie scoring three minutes in. The goal came easily on a rebound after the ball fortuitously ricocheted off the goal post; a lucky bounce, and not the goalie's fault. Nonetheless, a frustrated Maggie took a whistle and a warning, after she kicked the ball hard out of the net and away from the waiting referee. The look on her face was borderline hatred.

"Do that again and you're out of the game." The referee pointed his finger at her with a stern warning.

"Whatever." Maggie uttered the rebuttal just low enough that the ref didn't hear her clearly, but Cort read her lips. The ref turned towards the sound of her voice and only gave her a look of disapproval.

Up two to zero, the coach took Lucie out of the game and gave additional minutes to other players. She didn't return until late in the second half with her team leading 3-1. It wasn't long before Lucie found herself on another breakaway opportunity with at least ten steps in front of the nearest opponent. Cort watched nervously as his daughter streaked towards the opponent's net, focusing more on Maggie, who was hunched in a position of anger and determination. Her body language told that she would bitterly defend against her nemesis at any cost. And she did. As Lucie got close and made a final move to the left, Maggie suddenly rushed from the goal box on a collision course, haphazardly leaving the net unattended. Cort knew the move surprised Lucie, evident as she stutter-stepped, regained control, and positioned her body to take the shot with her left leg. The brief hesitation was exactly what Maggie had been counting on, and before the shot could be taken, the goalie launched herself feet first at the body of the smaller girl. Lucie couldn't react, and unable to avoid the contact, Maggie's cleats struck her upper-right thigh and kicked Lucie's lower body out from under her. Both girls landed in a heap, Lucie's body taking the full brunt of the fall and slamming the turf with a thud. Cort could almost feel the pain in his own leg as his daughter's face contorted. Even from 150 feet away, it was evident that she was biting her lip to avoid tears. Cort stood, ready to erupt at the goalie in a barrage of expletives. He bit on his tongue as Lucie sat up and rubbed her thigh with both hands. Maggie walked two steps closer to her fallen opponent, and Cort could see the goalie say something to Lucie, but she was too far away to make out words. There was a whistle followed by the referee shouting something to the opposite sideline, but Cort was too focused on his daughter to comprehend what he'd said. Unable to stay put, Cort trotted halfway out onto the field, stopping only when she looked in his direction.

"Lucie!" Her eyes met his, causing him to choke out a call of concern. "Are you okay?"

***

Lucie turned her face away from the spectators, massaging the pain away from her upper leg and trying desperately not to cry. Her ears picked up the sound of footsteps behind her before she heard the mocking voice of the goalie.

"What's the matter? Mommy not around anymore to pick up her little baby?" Maggie nearly spat the words out before turning around and trotting back towards the net.

Lucie's stomach tightened and her eyes became glossy as she processed the words. There was already an awareness that most people in her school district, and a few neighboring districts, knew of her mother's death. It had been on every local news channel and the Palmerton tragedy was in the media around the greater Pittsburgh area for most of the month of February. But the fact that somebody she barely knew, even a mean-girl, could utter those words; they cut straight to her heart. The pain in her thigh was suddenly overshadowed by the rip to her soul. The piercing shrill cry of the whistle broke her dark thoughts, as the referee rushed to her side holding up a yellow card.

"PK against green!"

The ref's voice was followed closely by her father's, who had run halfway out onto the field.

"Lucie!" She winced at his voice, and then turned towards it. The look on his face was painful to see. It was if he'd suffered the blow to his leg. Once she made eye contact with him, he continued. "Are you okay?"

Lucie stood on a shaky set of legs and nodded to her dad. Inhaling deeply to suppress the pain, she limped back towards her coach who had also come onto the field.

"Lucie, you sure you're okay?" Coach Liam rubbed her shoulder softly as he stooped down to read her eyes.

Lucie nodded back to her coach, stifling the urge to leave the field and cry by herself in some dark shadow of the park. Her leg certainly did hurt, but not nearly as bad as her pride. Turning her head to the sidelines, she watched her father pacing. He looked like he was either going to cry himself, or rip somebody's head off in rage. As the negative emotions flooded her thoughts and threatened to drown her resolve, her dad's expression somehow gave her the strength to overcome them. She knew he needed help, and in the moment, his pain took hers away. She straightened her posture and looked back to the field where Maggie stood next to the net. The grass was a green sea of negativity, churning with fear and anxiety and threatening to pull her under. But it also held an opportunity – the chance to show her father that she was a strong swimmer, and that she could overcome the fear and survive the dark waters.

"I think I'm alright coach."

"Do you want to take the penalty kick, Luce? If not it's alright, I'm allowed to sub for you in this situation."

"No. Let me take it." Lucie replied without hesitation and looked up with an expression erasing any doubts her coach had. A sudden urge took control of her, and she decided there was only one course of action that would salvage her pain and embarrassment. She had to take the kick herself and show Maggie she hadn't won.

Gingerly making her way back towards the goalie box, she passed her teammates who were lined up closer to the right sideline. This would be a one-on-one kick, just Lucie against Maggie. The players from both teams could watch from a distance, but there could be no interference from anyone but the netminder.

"You got this, Lucie!"

"Do it, Luce!"

A few of her teammates were able to shout their support before the referee put his hand in the air, signifying everyone to stay quiet. He walked past Lucie, over to one of the lines outside the goalie box, set the ball down in a precise spot, then walked backwards to where he came from. As he passed Lucie with his back to the other team's sideline, he bent down slightly and whispered.

"Good luck, number twelve."

Lucie nodded subtly without looking at the ref. His quiet vote of confidence was appreciated, and further stoked the fire that was now roaring inside her. Taking a position roughly twenty feet back from the ball, she surveyed the net. Her eyes moved back and forth, as she internally determined her placement. Her team was up two goals, with less than two minutes left in the game. It was well in hand, and if she didn't score, it wouldn't be a critical miss. She took comfort in that fact as she closed her eyes and awaited the ref's whistle. Under her breath she whispered five words at a decibel that only she could hear.

"This one's for you Mom."

The screaming whistle broke the silence once more, and Lucie opened her eyes. She took two slow steps before increasing her speed to a trot, then increased it a bit more for the final eight feet. Her right leg moved behind her into position as she stared Maggie straight in the eyes for a split second before looking down. As the right foot swung forward like a heavy pendulum, Lucie controlled its motion abruptly, nearly stopping her foot just before it struck the ball. The inner portion of her cleat contacted the ball with scarcely enough force to roll it slowly in the direction of the far post. To everyone watching, it appeared that she'd forgotten how to kick. The spectators watched in stunned silence as the ball made its way to Maggie's right side, with a speed and trajectory that barely required the netminder to exert herself. Maggie turned toward the ball in a slow jog, poised to intercept it easily before it got anywhere near the goal line; it hardly had enough inertia to reach the net. The goalie was as surprised as the crowd, so much so she gazed toward the row of players and parents on her sideline. She threw her hands in the air, in a gesture that said, *What the hell was that?*

Everyone around the field was so focused on the ball, only a few people even realized Lucie's foot had only slowed to tap the ball forward, but her legs and body moved into a full sprint towards the girl wearing the Arsenal jersey. Lucie timed it perfectly, and just as Maggie turned away and raised her hands in confusion, Lucie lowered her shoulders and flexed every muscle in her upper body. She launched her whole self into a horizontal dive, enabling her left shoulder to strike just under the armpit, crushing against the goalie's ribs and lifting the entire 122-pound body off the turf. It was audible to anyone within 100 feet; the sound of air being forced from Maggie's lungs, up through her esophagus, and out of her mouth in a muffled bellow. They landed together with the full weight of Lucie's body pushing the other one into the turf. After sliding a few feet, Lucie rolled away and popped up like a dandelion on steroids. Before walking back to the sidelines, she turned to the goalie's fallen body. She looked down at Maggie, who was still curled up on her side and holding her ribs with both hands, wincing in discomfort, attempting to regain her breath. Waiting until Maggie made eye contact, Lucie shook her head from side to side before speaking.

"Maybe your mommy should teach you how to tackle."

It was the best Lucie could come up with on the spot, but by the change in expression on Maggie's face, Lucie was almost sure the words had hit their mark. The girl laying on the ground had no rebuttal, and as the tears welled up in her eyes, she attempted to hide her face and slowly roll away from Lucie. Before leaving the wounded girl, Lucie glanced at the back of the goalie's jersey. She'd forgotten Maggie's last name until now, and only now appreciated the irony as she read the four letters printed across her back – F E E R.

Chapter 21 – Biggest Feer

Every player, coach, and spectator on both sidelines watched Lucie trot off the field, past her teammates, and into the waiting arms of her father. Eventually the upset Arsenal spectators calmed down, the game clock started again, and the ref blew the final whistle less than 100 seconds later.

Cort had already folded up his chair and was walking with Lucie toward the car. His daughter had summarized what had happened, namely the remark Maggie had made about Celeste. Furious as he was, Cort knew the best course of action was to simply get Lucie and himself out of there. She was still visibly upset by the ordeal, and he knew if he stuck around, it would not be a good scene. While Lucie had certainly left a lasting impression on everyone who'd witnessed the "football" tackle, neither she nor her father wanted to be present for the after party. Cort had curtly explained to coach Liam that Lucie would be skipping the post-game team meeting, which usually only lasted a few minutes anyway. Lucie waved a somber good-bye to her teammates and took her dad's hand as they scurried towards the car. Cort whisked his daughter away from the field, highly upset and afraid the goalie's words would have a lasting impression on Lucie. His biggest fear, however, was that the ITS thoughts inside his head were about to transition to *External* Turrets Syndrome.

They'd made it all the way to the parking lot; Cort was just pulling the key fob out of his pocket to hit the unlock button, when the voice from behind him beckoned.

"Hey,... Palmerton."

Without turning around to answer the prompt, Cort squatted to Lucie's eye level, gave her the key, and told her to wait for him in the car. He could see the nervous energy in her eyes as she stared back.

"Dad?" She briefly protested but was cut off abruptly.

"Lucie, wait in the car. I'll just be a minute." Cort's words were softer and more controlled, and despite a look of hesitation across her face, Lucie abided.

Turning around matter-of-factly, Cort found himself staring at a man much larger than himself – literally, the biggest Feer. He had already assumed that the voice behind him was that of the goalie's father. The man's six-foot, five-inch, 307-pound frame only further evidenced Cort's guess. Under normal circumstances, Cort would have been intimidated... even afraid of a physical altercation. Instead, he sized the man up in two seconds, with the mindset of *the bigger they are the harder they fall.*

"I'm Cort Palmerton."

The immense human male, who was scowling with his arms crossed, stood just in front of a woman who was pushing around a considerable amount of weight herself. Next to the woman was the girl who'd played goalie for Arsenal and had made the verbal strike at Lucie. Maggie was holding an ice-packet against her rib cage and was sneering with an exaggerated expression of pain.

"You want to tell me what the hell that was out there on the field?"

"What was what?" Cort kept his voice steady with an ever-so-slight tone of annoyed sarcasm.

"You know exactly what! Your daughter putting an illegal tackle on my little girl. Don't play dumb with me."

Cort nodded and clenched his teeth in a pained grin, feigning that he was indeed remembering now. His ITS beckoned for a reply like, *"she's not that little."* Even deeper down, he was trying to extinguish his inner David Banner, who right about now would surely begin the process of turning into a large green hulking monster. *Don't make me angry Mr. Feer. You wouldn't like me when I'm angry.*

"Oh yeah, that tackle." Cort paused for effect, further pretending his memory was returning. "Yeah, that tackle was simple retaliation."

"Retaliation my ass!" Mr. Feer removed one arm from its folder position and was now aiming his meaty pointer finger in the direction of Cort's head. "Maggie was defending her goal. Her tackle was a little rough, and she took the penalty for it, but that BS your daughter pulled was way uncalled for!"

By now a few parents and other players had gathered in a semi-circle behind the Feer family, and a couple of the assistant coaches from both sides had made their way to the growing crowd. Cort glanced beyond Mr. Feer's large frame and then scanned around his own perimeter. He noted that a couple dozen other adults and children were watching him. Despite the inner voice pleading with him to remain calm, he knew the ITS was dangerously close to becoming vocal. For a mini-second, he decided to turn and walk away, but his feet would not move. His lips, however, did not remain still.

"Listen here, Jack," he ended the fictitious name just before adding the word 'ass' to the end of it, "maybe you need to ask your little girl what she said to my daughter after kicking her legs out." He tried to stifle any additional words, but two quick ones escaped, quite loudly and completely unaltered. "Little bitch."

An audible gasp ascended from the growing number of people that had gathered, and one spectator uttered the word 'Jesus.' Two other adults and one teen pulled their phones out, tapped into video mode, and pointed them at the only two men talking.

"What the hell did you just say!?" Mr. Feer took a half step closer to Cort.

Responding with a half-step forward of his own, Cort replied to divert from his previous slander, and more importantly, to shame the man and his daughter.

"I said maybe you need to ask your daughter what she said ABOUT MY DECEASED WIFE!"

The watchful heads, waiting nervously for the progression of the situation, abruptly shifted their eyes at Mr. Feer. Another phone began videoing, as the crowd suddenly realized the father of the girl who'd plowed over the goalie was more justified in his stance. Both of Maggie's parents turned to see their daughter shrug her shoulders and raise her eyebrows in denial. Maggie made a brief statement in a tone meant to convince everyone she was innocent of the accusation.

"I didn't say anything to her." She looked from her dad to her mom, then back to her dad.

Mr. Feer turned back to face Cort, only half-believing his daughter, but still fully angered at the prick who'd just called his daughter a bitch.

"Just so you know, Palmerton," the finger was back pointing at Cort, "I'm taking my daughter in for some x-rays right now. I have your name and address from your team manager, and I'll be sending any medical bills straight to you."

Walk away Cort. Just turn around and walk away.

The impossibility of the internal request to himself nearly made him laugh out loud.

"I'll tell you what, Feer. You go ahead and send me your medical bills. When I get them, I'm going to do three things."

The mammoth-of-a-man suddenly sensed the rising anger in Cort's tone, but it didn't prevent him from asking the question.

"Oh yeah, what's that?"

"Well first, I'll gather up the paperwork you send my way and put it in a Tupperware container. I'm gonna piss all over them until they're nice and saturated, and then I'm going to bring them to your house and put them in your mailbox."

More gasps escaped from several of the onlookers, and the phones were raised a bit higher. It only fueled Cort to continue.

"Second, I'm going to find myself a reaaallllly good team of defense attorneys and put them on retainer. And third...." Cort hesitated and looked down at the sidewalk below Mr. Feer's feet, then slowly stared back into his eyes. "Well, the third thing... you can just use your imagination. You understand me?"

Mr. Feer's expression changed from anger to one of shock, and he took a half-step backwards and glanced at his wife. She wore an equally shocked expression, which succinctly morphed into a scowl that resembled her daughter's. Mr. Feer spoke again a little louder so everyone gathered around could hear.

"Are you threatening me?"

"I don't know, am I?" Cort's open hands clenched into fists.

"It sounds like a threat to me." Feer scanned the crowd, beckoning their heads to nod in confirmation with him.

Cort needed to end this war-dance and leave the facility before he totally lost all control and something drastic materialized. Despite that need, he simply could not part ways without another response. Contrastingly, he took another half-step toward the man.

"You can call it whatever you want asshole. A threat, a warning, a promise. I don't give a shit! I'll make you one guarantee right now though. If you don't get out of my face within the next three seconds, I'll just skip those first two steps and go straight to number three." Cort lowered his brow and shifted his feet, just enough to let the man in front of him know that he wasn't fucking around.

With the unleashing of what was certainly a physical threat, and language that was deteriorating by the sentence, the crowd suddenly stepped away from the men and began to disperse as if Cort had been addressing all of them. Mr. Feer, silently beginning a three count in his head, turned to his wife and daughter before quietly uttering,

"Let's go." He turned away but Cort heard him mutter, "this guy's a little crazy."

Cort lingered a few seconds, letting the man and his family shuffle away in muted shame, before turning around and walking to his own car. As he approached the driver side door, he noted the ignition was on and the window of the rear driver-side door was down. He slid into his seat and buckled his belt, taking a quick glance in his rearview to see the expression on Lucie's face. It was one of surprise and satisfaction, all wrapped into a hesitant grin.

"Dad, did you call that goalie the B-word?"

Cort pulled the car into reverse and ignored the question verbally but turned his head to the rear. He shot a quick nod of confirmation to his daughter and pursed his lips to give the impression of embarrassment.

"I'm not proud of what I said, Lucie, but I'll be honest, I feel so much better. How's your leg?"

Lucie assured her dad the leg was fine, and they both remained quiet until the park was in the rearview mirror. Finally, Cort broke the silence.

"Hey Lucie, you remember yesterday how we talked about moving?"

"Yeah, of course I remember."

"Right, of course you do. Well, I'm thinking, maybe we should get out of town sooner than later."

Cort picked her eyes up in the rearview mirror again, and they exchanged knowing grins that morphed into full-fledged smiles.

"Hey Dad?"

"Yeah?"

"I think we should just get some ice cream."

Chapter 22 – July 4th

The Kaleidoscope of colors exploded into the night sky, illuminating the dark land below in muted blankets of reds, whites, and blues. They sparked memories of years past on the day marking the peak of the Summer Season. It wasn't the first July 4th he'd spent on the back deck at his in-law's house, but it was the first time the holiday was without Celeste in fifteen years. He couldn't help but think about her as the random flowers of fire blossomed into the atmosphere. They'd most definitely made some memorable fireworks themselves, proof of which sat next to him in a wicker rocker.

"That one was cool." He leaned to his right and repeated the phrase to Lucie for the second time. Lucie simply glanced in his direction and nodded this time, confirming the last firework was indeed one of the best so far. Cort knew her emotions must be mixed tonight. She was aware July 4th was her mother's favorite holiday.

Cort shifted his head forward and shoved the last bite of cake into his mouth. Returning his fork to the paper plate, he scraped up remnants of the whipped cream and stabbed at a blueberry that had made an unsuccessful attempt to escape. Gabby glanced in his direction, and he threw a smile her way; a silent gesture to convey his approval of her delicious dessert. His mother-in-law flanked Lucie to their right, and Manny sat to his immediate left. The feeling was strange at best, their presence no longer holding the same essence as it had when Celeste was here.

Taking another glance back to Lucie, he was in a relatively positive frame of mind about their situation. The last few weeks had been tough, but markedly better. Since the soccer field incident, Cort's ITS has subsided substantially. Apparently, the outburst towards the extra-large soccer-dad had released a lot of his inner anger. While there were still some lingering foul thoughts from time to time, Cort felt he'd mostly turned a corner with the Tourette's issue. As he snuck another peek at Lucie's profile, he silently thanked her for his improvement. In an odd way, he attributed his mental upswing to the pain she'd suffered at the hands of the goalie. There was also a subconscious awareness that she'd somehow managed to shift his focus away from death at the most critical point in his suicidal depression.

Thanks, Luce.

The three days in Austin had been just okay. They'd seen several very nice areas of the surrounding suburbs, checked out a few schools, and got the lay of the land. Manny and Gabby had steered them towards mostly bubble communities, not unlike the neighborhood they resided in now. The homes they toured were newer, with open floor plans and in-style finishes. The surrounding areas were chock full of amenities, including parks, walking trails, and athletic fields. All but one of the schools were private, and the public one was an upscale 42-acre campus, littered with children of yuppy-parents, resembling a small college. In a nutshell, they were boring communities, with a lack of diversity, and none of them were of any appeal to him. He sensed it in Lucie too, and he wondered if her thoughts, like his, had remained fixated on a house shaped exactly like a sailboat.

***

Lucie had hoped the trip to Austin would be more exciting. They did have one day left to see a few more homes, and she was a little excited about the ice cream museum. Still, as she brushed her teeth, there was a feeling of disappointment she couldn't shake. It wasn't so much an issue with moving. She was just as interested in a new environment as her dad was, but she feared that Texas was not the right fit. While the homes and schools they'd looked at were beautiful, it felt like there was a disconnect between her father and the Austin suburbs. She'd felt it too but couldn't quite put her finger on it. Rinsing the toothpaste from her mouth, Lucie wondered if the disappointment had something to do with Mom not being here. Her dad seemed uneasy about the idea of calling this area home. Maybe, she wondered, it was because there wasn't much water. The only time he'd seemed a little excited about a house was for the one that had a partial view of a river, or lake, or whatever it was.

I'll pick that house if he asks me about my favorite.

Chapter 23 – Independence Day

They spent July 5th in Austin and toured three more houses over the course of the morning. The results were the same. Both his and Lucie's moods deteriorated throughout the first half of the day. Thankfully the afternoon was salvaged with a visit to the Museum of Ice Cream. Their last full day in Texas ended on a high note, as they sampled more flavors than could be counted. Several brain-freezes later, they trudged out of the museum with sweet tooths overly satisfied. The frozen treats, however, had barely cooled the flame of adventure that had been ignited inside him.

Their flight back to Pittsburgh on the 6th was an uneventful one-stop-hop, descending into Western Pennsylvania through a slight bit of turbulence and touching down on a rain-soaked runway. After driving thirty minutes through intermittent showers, the pair pulled into their garage just before 4:30 PM, drained of energy from a combination of the travel and the unhealthy diet they'd had over the past five days. Cort suggested they unpack, make a salad, eat, then relax. Lucie concurred.

By 6:00, they were crunching greens and sliced vegetables under a scattered layer of grilled chicken. He made small talk with Lucie, but Cort's thoughts were elsewhere. Hundreds of images and discussions from the past week circling through his mind made it difficult to focus on the present. Finally, he pushed his empty plate away from the tables edge, and decided it was time to have an important conversation with his daughter.

"So, Luce, tell me again which neighborhood was your favorite, and which houses you liked the best too?"

Lucie thought a second before answering, "Definitely the house that we could see the lake from... was it Lake Travis, or was that the Colorado River?"

"I think technically the lake and the river are the same body of water." Cort scratched his chin trying to remember what the real estate agent had told them. "That was my favorite too, Luce." He paused and his thought strayed. If he was totally honest with himself, none of the houses they'd seen this week even came close to those sailboats he'd looked at. Snapping back to the conversation, he continued. "And that school was nice, right? I remember the lady telling us they had a good soccer team there."

Lucie hesitated, "Yeah, that one wasn't bad. Was that one of the schools that I'd have to wear a uniform?"

"I think it was, yes. You don't like that idea?" Cort had wondered about the uniform requirement earlier but hadn't asked until now.

"Not really, I don't want to wear the same thing every day. And, um, the soccer," she paused hesitantly again, nearly refraining from continuing the thought, "I was thinking of trying a different sport once we move." She looked into her dad's eyes now, waiting for his case against quitting the sport she'd played for nearly five years.

"Sure, that's fine with me." He watched a gleam of delighted surprise fill her eyes as he agreed with her sentiment. "So, what other sport were you thinking?"

"Maybe swimming?"

"Oh yeah, duh, of course. That makes total sense."

"I really like to swim, but I'm just afraid that if I *have* to do it all the time, then maybe I wouldn't like it as much. I don't know, what else do you think I should try?"

He balked at her question, trying to think through the psychology of his response. She was nearing the age that she could be contrary to his advice, but at the same time he sensed she really had no idea what another alternate activity might be.

"Hmmmm, I'm not sure, how about running Cross Country?"

"Running?" Lucie wasn't convinced.

"Yeah running. It's a great sport, and you can do it your whole life. But hey, maybe you don't even want to do a sport. Maybe another activity, like learning an instrument?"

Cort watched her eyes grow a bit wider as she considered the possibilities.

"Oh yeah, an instrument would be cool. How about the guitar?"

"That's fine with me, Lucie, anything you want to try, you should. We'll get you guitar lessons, and any other instrument you're interested in too. Heck, maybe I'll take lessons with you."

Lucie's mouth transitioned into a wide grin, "How cool would that be!" She turned away, seemingly in thought. "And I want to start running too. I think Cross Country is a good idea."

"Awesome, I think that would be a good sport to try. You're already fast... you'll just need to get your endurance up, which I'm sure won't be a problem." He paused a second as she considered his analysis, then needled in a light jab. "Now, Luce," his face morphed into a reflection of serious concern, "you realize that you can't tackle anyone in Cross Country, right?"

They both laughed out loud before Lucie finally shook her head and got serious again.

"Hey Dad, how about you and I start running this summer together, and you can help me train?"

Cort watched his daughter, whose grin was still there, but had changed into one with a bit of a different feel. He couldn't quite tell if her suggestion was a return punch or was maybe aimed at his well-being. Possibly both.

"I'm up for that, Luce. I guess it wouldn't hurt for me to start running again anyway, right?"

"You used to run all the time, Dad - maybe it's time to start again?"

Cort grinned back at her and nodded, but his mind shifted away from the current conversation to what was really eating at his thoughts. He silently wondered how irresponsible it would be to broach the subject, and possibly give Lucie hope for something that may simply be impossible to achieve. He himself still had serious doubts about the plausibility of the alternate plan, but the more he thought about moving to Austin, the more his gut was telling him to continue exploring the sailboat possibility. Before he could stop himself, the words escaped his mouth.

"Hey, Lucie, I want to show you something after dinner?"

"Oh yeah, okay. What is it?"

The curiosity in her voice was thick.

"Um, just something I was thinking about buying for us. I just wanted to get your opinion on a couple things." Cort remained guarded, allowing himself an escape route in case he changed his mind over the course of the next twenty minutes.

"Like what?"

She'd be hard pressed to wait that long, but he deflected like a pro.

"Uh, well, it's something related to trying activities other than soccer. It'll make more sense when I show you. Let's clean up our plates and we'll check it out in a little bit."

The wait time was condensed into twelve minutes, as Lucie's expression grew more eager with each passing one. Cort pulled the power cord out of the laptop and carried it with him to the family room sofa. He opened Google and tapped in the search box. Several recent searches popped up below the box; *Sailboats for sale* was near the top. As Lucie sat down beside him, he tapped and chose the same link as he had a few weeks ago. He'd picked it specifically because it only encompassed boats available in the United States. She was just beginning to focus on the screen when the page opened, showing a cache of 1,354 based results.

"Dad?"

"Yeah?"

"Are you seriously thinking about buying a boat?"

"I don't know. Let's look at a few and talk about it, alright?"

"O-M-G, uhhh, yeah okay!"

Cort turned to see his daughter's wide smile. She watched as he placed three filters on the results. The search was condensed to catamaran's that were a maximum of 15 years old, and no more than 46 feet long. As the filters were applied, the list was condensed to 21 results.

Manageable.

For the next two hours, he and Lucie went over each of the 21 catamarans, perusing the features the same way Cort had done himself that night in bed. He explained what some of the styles and amenities were and why they were important, and they'd narrowed the field down to five favorites. Not surprisingly, Lucie agreed with most of what he proclaimed to be important, sensing which ones he preferred and concurring when he pointed out a candidate that should move up on their list. Their top five were all beautiful, and all expensive. The lowest-priced one of the favorites was $450,000. The highest was $800,000.

"Dad, isn't that a lot of money? How would we even have enough to buy one?" Lucie asked the question carefully.

Cort knew she was expecting the shoe to drop on the fairy-tale-boat-search. He pondered the question briefly, considering how to explain their recent windfall.

"Lucie, remember a couple months ago, I told you that the company the truck driver worked for would have to pay us for mom's… accident… you know?"

"Yeah, I think so."

"Well, basically they've paid us now, and if we want to buy a boat, we have enough money."

Lucie sat silent, considering the apparent trade.

"Dad, do you think Mom would want us to use the money to buy a boat? I'm not sure she would like that?"

"You know what I think, Lucie?" He looked down and met Lucie's watery eyes. "I think Mom would want us to use the money for whatever would make us happy. What do you think?"

Lucie simply nodded as a tear ran down her cheek. Cort gently wiped it away and gave his daughter a sideways hug while fighting hard to keep his own cheeks dry. He began talking to distract himself from the sadness.

"The more I think about it, Lucie, the more I'm not sure we'd like it in Austin. We need a change of scenery, but also change of pace, and I think we need to go on an adventure together if we're going to heal from mom's… passing. I think her spirit will guide us too."

Lucie nodded again and laid the side of her head into her father's arm.

"If you think so dad, then I think so too. Do you think Grammy and Pappy will be mad if we don't move to Austin."

"Hmmmm, well, yeah. I think they might be a little disappointed. And that's why I'll tell them this was all your idea."

She looked up from his arm to find a wide sarcastic grin across his face. Shaking her head, Lucie punched his leg lightly in retaliation for the teasing. After a pause, she made an apologetic admission that was coated in sarcasm and carried a slight tone of satisfaction.

"It actually was kind of my idea, wasn't it?"

"Well, yes, I think it was your idea, Luce. And you know what, it was maybe the best idea I've ever heard."

Lucie smiled again and Cort knew her wheels were already turning.

"Dad, when will we buy the boat and when will we start sailing it? We'll live on it like that family in *Great White Bite,* right?"

"Yes, just like on that show. That would be the plan. But hey, Lucie, I have no idea when we'll sell our house and leave town. There's a lot of details to work out still, and honestly, there's a chance it could all fall through, so I don't want you to get your hopes up too much. And listen, don't tell Pappy and Grammy about this. Don't tell anybody. Not yet. Got it?"

"Got it."

"Good. This is going to be our secret for now. I'm gonna check out some of the boats we have on our top five and see about learning how to sail. We can't buy a boat if we don't know how to sail it, right?"

"Right." Despite nodding in agreement, Cort could see from her expression that she was less than thrilled about the doubtful tone in his question.

Cort noted the time on the laptop. 9:14 P.M. He folded the screen down to the keyboard and turned to his daughter again.

"Well Luce, I'm kind of exhausted. What do you say we get a good night's sleep, and maybe start tomorrow with a run through the park?"

"Deal." She reached over and shook his hand, sealing the agreement.

They both got up from the couch and began turning lights off. Minutes later Cort lay in bed, thinking about the mammoth endeavor they'd just discussed. He stayed awake for a long time, contemplating whether he'd made the right decision to share everything with Lucie. He considered the real possibility that this scheme was simply an attempt to run away from the guilt and despair, and he was justifying it because Lucie had brought the idea to light. If the plan failed, Lucie would end up being collateral damage. He further wondered if Celeste would really be on board with the decision to trade safety and security for the chance to experience an adventure like no other. He reminded himself that this plan was not a total departure from a reality he and Celeste had once fantasized about. Her image filled his mind now, as he thought back to that second trip they'd made to Cabo. He could see her, sitting across the table from him with the ocean in the background, her long dark hair slow dancing in the breeze. They'd talked about buying property one day, right there in Cabo, and a sailboat too. It could be docked at one of the local marinas and taken out on occasion when seas were calm, and the weather was perfect. The plan he and Lucie were talking about was markedly different, however, and he couldn't help but feel somewhat irresponsible for planting the very large seed in her head. Still, as he lay there considering the possibilities boat-life would offer, he couldn't help but be excited. If everything came to fruition, the discussion he'd just had with Lucie would be remembered as their declaration of independence.

***

She imagined all the different lands they would sail to, envisioning the wild animals of Africa and Australia. Even more vivid in her mind was the endless miles of water, varying in color from brilliant turquoise to the deepest of Navy blue. The vision of the water calmed her and gave her a sense of tranquility. More importantly, she could see her father standing on the front of the boat smiling at her, at peace with himself. It would be nearly an hour before she settled her mind and became drowsy. Before drifting off, Lucie talked to her mother and told her about their plans.

Don't worry Mom, everything will be okay.

Chapter 24 – Good Company

It was never easy to go back to work following a holiday weekend. Wednesday, July 7th was more difficult than most, given everything that had happened over the past few days, weeks, and months. Cort and Lucie started their day with an inaugural run. She made it just over a mile without stopping, and Cort was thankful when she finally decided to walk. As he stepped into the shower, he took note of an improved mental state. He'd nearly forgotten what the runner's high felt like, remembering now that it was well worth the soreness in his legs. Life had been progressing at the pace of a glacier, keeping him frozen in place and unable to move forward. The past few weeks had brought a considerable thaw to their lives, and while there were still many large chunks of painful ice to manage, Cort was thankful for the noticeable flow that had returned to their existence.

After a long, hot, cleanse, he resolved to spend a solid morning in his office. Lucie made herself breakfast and busied herself around the house for the next couple of hours, preparing for the noon hour when she'd cross the street and swim at her friend's house. Cort intended to do some non-work research once she left, but until then he diligently answered emails and made several phone calls. Two of the calls went to John and Richey at UPMC. Comparing schedules with both men, he promised to make good on their previously cancelled lunch meeting within the next few weeks. Before 11:00 A.M. rolled around, he'd even participated in an online meeting for the first time in months. Though he stayed quiet and refrained from adding any questions or comments about the subject matter, the meeting went relatively well.

By 11:30, he'd logged his most productive morning of work since late January, and while he was far from getting caught up, it was a step in the right direction. After ensuring Lucie was slathered in sunblock and ready to swim, he watched her cross the street from the front stoop and went back to his desk. Eagerly opening his personal laptop, he navigated back to the sailboat search that'd been saved from the prior night. For each of the sailboats that had made their "Top 5" list, he printed the information under their respective links then stapled the pages of each one together as its own candidate. Methodically, he began calling the number for each of the listing brokers. Unsuccessful in reaching a human in all five cases, messages were left requesting a call back as soon as possible.

It was after 12:30 when Cort decided he should eat something. After munching on vegetables and humus, he moved from the kitchen to the back deck for some air and sunshine. Immediately after plopping into one of the two Adirondack chairs, he fantasized that Celeste was in the empty one.

"We always loved sitting here together?" Cort spoke out loud to the summer air then turned his head, visualizing Celeste sitting there and reaching for his hand. Her image was so clear in his mind - it was those simple moments he fiercely missed.

"I'm so sorry you aren't here." He quietly apologized into a light breeze passing silently across the deck like a funeral procession. There was no escaping the thoughts filling his head, the events of February 2nd playing yet again. The wave of sorrow was countered by the vision of Celeste, sitting next to him with a kind and affectionate smile.

The sad yet somehow comforting fantasy was interrupted by the buzz of his phone, evaporating her image into the light wind. It was a local number, but not familiar. He let it go, and the buzzing eventually stopped. Eight seconds later it started again - same number. He contemplated ignoring it again, but his already guilty conscience got the better of him. He reluctantly tapped the green button on his screen.

"Hello, this is Cort," his voice abrupt.

"Hey there, Cort, this is Officer Josh Leonard."

"Oh, hey officer. Sorry, I mean Josh. How are things?" Cort was already regretting taking the call but softened his tone and stayed polite.

"Good here, Cort. What are you up to?"

"Oh, just um, you know, trying to stay busy. Sitting outside not doing much of anything right now." Cort second-guessed his words immediately, realizing he'd left the door open for a longer conversation.

"Uh huh. What do you have going on this evening? Would you be open to a visit?"

Cort flashed back to his ride in the cruiser, remembering Josh had wanted to ask more questions about the accident. He thought on his feet, not ready to have the trooper cajole him into an uncomfortable follow-up interview.

"Well, actually," Cort fibbed, "Lucie and I are leaving here around 4:00 this afternoon to grab an early dinner, then we plan to catch a movie. I won't really be around this evening at all." He clenched his teeth slightly, satisfied that he'd momentarily evaded the police.

"So, you're not busy now, and aren't leaving until 4:00, which is perfect. I'm on my way to your house, only a mile away. I'll see you in a few minutes?"

Cort barely processed what had just transpired before stammering an answer.

"Uh, um, okay. That works, I guess." After Officer Leonard thanked him and hung up, Cort rushed up the stairs to brush his teeth, cursing out loud for being outsmarted.

Four minutes later the pestering chime of the doorbell sounded. Internally thankful he'd showered after his run with Lucie, Cort turned the deadbolt and pulled open the front door.

"Surprise." Josh's lips moved into a wry grin.

Cort couldn't hide the shock in his face, and he knew a seasoned cop like Leonard would read his expression easily. Startled to see the trooper in plain clothes, Cort was even more shocked to see a beautiful woman standing next to Leonard. Dressed in white shorts and a lavender blouse, both garments popped brilliantly against her dark skin. The other detail catching Cort's attention was the disposable aluminum pan she was holding with both hands. He surmised the woman was not a fellow trooper as his brain tried to process the unexpected scene in front of him. In the confusion, his mouth could only manage one word.

"Hi."

"Hey Cort. This is my wife, Shay. She made you a meatloaf." Josh unnecessarily pointed at the pan.

"Hello, Cort, it's nice to meet you." She greeted him with a nod, unable to offer her hand.

Cort returned her greeting and noted what sounded like a slight accent, not southern U.S., but maybe Caribbean.

"Nice to meet you, Shay. C'mon in." He stepped aside and waved them both through the door. "And thank you for the meatloaf."

As the couple walked into the front foyer, Cort felt a peck of guilt for wishing he'd been able to avoid their visit. Shay interrupted the thought.

"You look like a healthy eater, Cort, so you'll appreciate the meatloaf is made from ground turkey. Much leaner. And there's lots of good vegetables chopped up in there, but you'll barely taste them." Shay's accent was pleasant, and her voice genuine.

"Thank you, Shay. My daughter will really appreciate that." Cort grinned and both Shay and Josh let out a small laugh. "You shouldn't have gone to the trouble. Come on in and sit down. Can I get either of you something, coffee maybe?"

"No thank you, I'm fine." Shay replied first.

"Coffee would be good, thanks."

Josh accepted and the couple let Cort pass, then followed him to the kitchen.

"Absolutely. Have a seat, and I'll put a pot on. You can start with the questions whenever you're ready, Josh. I don't want to hold you two up this afternoon."

Cort had his back turned but could see a blurred reflection of the couple in the stainless-steel coffee maker. In the obscured image, he was able to make out Josh's head turn towards Shay, but his expression was muddled beyond recognition. Cort hoped the cop read into the psychology of Cort's apparent gesture of courtesy, taking it as a signal that time was short. As Cort grabbed the coffee from the refrigerator, Josh spoke.

"Well, Cort, my first question is, did you realize that we went to high school together?"

"You went to Butler?" Cort acted more surprised than he was. "You know, I thought I knew you, Josh, but I couldn't quite place your face the last time... well, you know. I mean, the past couple of times I saw you, I wasn't exactly," Cort paused and bowed his head for a second, "but yeah, anyway."

"Of course, sure. I wasn't positive either, until after I dropped you off back at your car that day. I did a little research and confirmed my suspicion. You graduated a couple years after I did."

"Right, yes, that makes sense. I was thinking maybe you were in the class or two before me. Did you play baseball?" Cort's memory of Josh was faint, but as he scooped coffee from the can into the filter, he faintly recalled Josh from the athletic fields of Butler High School.

"Yeah, I sure did. And that's really where I remember you from. You came up from JV and played a couple games with varsity my senior year. You were a good player." Josh nodded at Cort, acknowledging his ability on the diamond.

"Thanks. We, well *you*, had a great team that year, right? Didn't you guys go to states? I guess it would have been 02?"

Josh smiled and nodded again. "That's right. We lost in the semifinal by one run. Good memory Cort."

"We'll spare you the details of our glory years Shay." Cort cut their trip into the past very short, still feeling a bit guilty for not being more upbeat about their visit.

"Thanks, but I'm sure I've heard most of them already anyway." Shay giggled, having no idea what thoughts were circling through Cort's head.

He joined the couple at the kitchen table and tried to ignore the fact that Shay was sitting in the seat that Celeste always had. Nobody had occupied it in over six months. He caught himself chewing the inside of his lip and tried to focus on anything else. Mercifully, Josh spoke and ended what seemed to be a long silence.

"Cort, I'm obviously not here to relive high school days with you, and honestly, I don't have any follow up interview questions for you. There weren't really any unclear details of the accident, and now that the criminal and civil suits are over, I wouldn't be interested in changing anything in the report anyway."

Josh's demeanor and tone was more serious, and Cort sensed slight discomfort in his voice. From the corner of his eye, Cort saw Shay's arm move slightly in Josh's direction, and assumed she was reaching for her husband's hand under the table.

"That's fine. But?" Cort ended his sentence with the question, now more skeptical than before.

"Well," Josh paused, "Shay and I just wanted to check in and see how you're holding up?"

"I'm doing better, thanks." Cort reluctantly talked about himself and Lucie for a minute, awkwardly offering some details of their summer activities so far. Mercifully, the coffee pot beeped, and Cort rose from the table. Still annoyed at the question, Cort managed to stay even in his response. Taking two mugs from the cupboard, he pushed away an ITS response and turned back to Josh.

"Cream and sugar?"

"Just sugar. Two please."

"No problem." *Sorry I don't have any donuts.* Keeping his back turned to his guests, Cort clenched his teeth as the words threatened to leave his tongue. *Jesus Cort, don't!*

He cringed to himself, willing away the cop-targeted-jab. Shifting thoughts, Cort pivoted back to the question of his well-being, paranoid the cop at his kitchen table had somehow read his mind.

"And I've had some sessions with a shrrr... a psychiatrist." Cort balked at himself, realizing now he was being too careful. He turned back to the table, thinking he'd recovered until Josh replied.

"You can say shrink."

Josh smirked another wry grin, concealing brilliant white teeth behind his closed lips. Cort felt his face get a little flush through a forced laugh.

"Okay then, a shrink." He placed the cup of coffee in front of Josh, more paranoid now than before. "Are you sure I can't get you something Shay?"

Cort noticed Shay glancing at her husband, with a scolding look in her eye. She then replied with a smile.

"I'm okay, thank you."

Cort focused on her smile and the lines in her face, searching for some revealing sign of her past. Her complexion was nearly flawless, its beauty concealing any sign of potential distress.

"Your accent, Shay – is that Caribbean maybe?" He posed the question hesitantly.

"Nice call, you have a good ear. I was born and raised in Trinidad, then moved to the states with my family at the age of 14. Most of my island dialect has disappeared over the past 25 years, but there's obviously still a hint of it in there."

Josh interrupted the niceties, apparently eager to push his agenda before Cort cut the visit short.

"So, Cort," he interjected in a softened voice, "have you considered any grief counseling? Maybe through a group setting?"

Cort pondered the question a second, shifting back into defensive mode.

"Well, no. But again, I'm seeing a psychiatrist."

"With all due respect," Josh countered, "has your psychiatrist lost his wife?"

Cort understood exactly the point of the question but wasn't willing to concede it just yet. He chose humor to cover his discomfort.

"Yes, actually, he did lose his wife, but that was by choice." Cort grinned, softening the joke he thought might be in bad taste as soon as it left his mouth.

Josh paused a second, returned the grin, and let the play on words slide by.

"I'm sure there's a story there," he chuckled. "But you know what I mean, Cort."

"Yes, I do know what you mean, and I get your point. That said, I'm not sure I think group grief therapy would be any different. I assume you're suggesting the people in the group have also lost their wife, or husband, or a loved one, so maybe they can relate to me better."

Cort could feel himself getting a little uncomfortable, shifting into defensive mode now as Josh began to respond.

"Yes, that's exactly what…"

Cort interrupted and cut Josh's response short.

"Let me stop you there, Josh," keeping his voice calm and respectful, "I understand you're trying to be helpful, but with all due respect, you don't know what I'm going through." Cort paused and took a deep breath, "I mean, look at you and Shay. Happily married I assume?" He watched as both Josh and Shay nodded quietly. "And you have three boys? Isn't that what you told me in the police cruiser that day?" He watched the couple nod again before continuing. "So, you have this beautiful family, and everything is relatively well. You're going to pretend you know how I'm suffering and what remedy I need? I'm sorry, and again with all due respect, but you can't possibly get my pain."

Cort watched the expression become sullen on both Josh and Shay's faces. He detected slight movement from Josh's arm this time and assumed the couple's hands were together under the table again.

"Cort," Josh began but paused in reflection.

"Yes?" Cort beckoned.

"Shay is my second wife. I'm her second husband. Two of our boys are from my first marriage, the other is from hers."

Cort's irritation changed to confusion as Josh finished his sentence then turned to Shay. She continued her husband's thoughts.

"My first husband died almost four years ago. COVID." Shay glanced back to Josh, signaling him to add his own portion of the explanation.

"My first wife died almost five years ago Cort." Josh's voice remained steady, but his eyes became shiny. "Drunk driver crossed the center line. Head-on collision. She died almost instantly."

Cort's face contorted into an uncomfortable grimace. With his elbows resting on the table, he put his face into his hands and tried to conceal the painful embarrassment.

"Oh God, I'm sorry. I'm so sorry."

"It's okay Cort, you didn't know," Josh offered the reprieve immediately, "Shay and I met in grief therapy. It's, uh, I guess it's been about three and a half years now, right Shay?" He looked to his wife for confirmation, which she acknowledged with a nod and a smile and then turned back to Cort.

"Before we met there, Josh was going to therapy for about four months, and I had gone to several sessions myself. It was good to share our pain with people who had gone through something similar. We'll both tell you the grief therapy helped us heal. The fact that we met there and eventually fell in love was wonderful, uh, what's the word… happenstance?"

Cort felt more shame and shook his head apologetically.

"I'm happy for both of you, and sorry about your losses at the same time. Thanks for sharing that with me, I appreciate it."

"Of course," Shay nearly whispered the words.

"How about I tell you that I'll try it. In fact, if you give me the information for the program you two used, I'll promise to check it out within the next month or so?"

"No obligation, Cort," Josh spoke as he reached into the pocket on his shirt breast and handed him a card, "but this is the place if you decide to try it. Just go online and you can sign up and schedule a session that works for you."

"Thank you, Josh. Thank you both." Cort reached out and shook both of their hands, still unsure about their suggestion but trying desperately to break the awkwardness.

The three talked a few minutes longer, mostly about their respective kids. Josh swooshed back his last sip of coffee before turning to Shay, "We better go honey, the boys will be home soon."

His guests stood simultaneously, and Cort followed. Thoughts zipped through his brain as he walked behind them towards the front door. He thanked Shay again for the meatloaf as they opened the door.

The couple walked onto the porch, then turned back to Cort. Shay hugged him and Josh shook his hand firmly.

"Take care of yourself and let us know if you need anything, alright?" Josh offered the gesture genuinely and Shay smiled in agreement.

"I will, and thanks again for coming. I'll let you know how therapy goes."

"Yes, do that."

As his guests walked down to the sidewalk in the direction of their car, Cort's conscience reached a breaking point.

"Hey, Josh," he called to him just before he was out of view.

Josh released Shay's hand and turned around, walking a few steps back towards the front porch as Shay continued slowly to the driveway.

"Yes sir?" Josh walked to within ten feet of Cort.

"Josh," Cort began awkwardly, washing his hands together, "sorry for trying to avoid you. Lucie and I aren't really going to dinner and a movie. I just didn't want to talk to anyone about, well, you know. But I'm glad you came."

"It's not a problem, Cort. I figured as much anyway. Something in your voice told me you were lying earlier." Josh offered his signature wry grin at first, but this time it transitioned into a hearty laugh.

"Busted by the police." Cort offered the admission and laughed back.

They laughed together for a few seconds longer before Shay's voice came from the driveway.

"Let's go officer Leonard. That's enough harassment for one day."

Josh waved bye and turned away, now chuckling at his wife's sarcastic jab. Cort laughed too, shook his head, and went inside. He walked back to the kitchen, emptied the coffee pot, and put the mugs in the dishwasher, all the while replaying the conversation with Josh and Shay. As his guest's humorous departure subsided, Cort was left with a lingering sense of guilt and sadness, having prematurely judged their family dynamic and their intentions for visiting. At the same time, Cort felt a bit of relief, and even some comradery, knowing the couple could relate to his pain. Another notion crossed his mind, and his gut tightened.

God, I hope Josh wasn't one of the officers called to the scene of his own wife's accident.

As he pulled the business card from his pocket and read the title, "Grief Therapy," he thought about the promise he'd made, and accepted the fact he'd be attending a session in the future. Further contemplating his first houseguests since becoming a widower, he decided that despite what felt like an overly tense visit, Josh and Shay were most certainly good company.

Chapter 25 – Follow Up

A full week had passed since the visit from Trooper Josh Leonard and his wife Shay. While Cort and Lucie had stayed busy, running, cooking, and getting outside as much as possible, both were growing impatient. She'd asked about the boat options several times, and Cort's responses were getting increasingly concerning. He'd followed up with each of the five boat brokers late last week. All but one had returned his call the following day and listened to Cort's loose proposal outlining a variation of a traditional purchase - a lease period that allowed Cort to "test-drive" the sailboat for a year, with the option to buy the boat at the end of the 12-month term. Those four brokers relayed the information to their seller, and the next day he was declined on three of them. The fourth broker took a little longer but had left him a message just yesterday. His client had also declined the offer.

The last of the five remaining boats was named "Sea Sleigh." She was one of the top two on Cort and Lucie's list. Their hope for a deal on it was fading fast, as the broker for Sea Sleigh hadn't even called back. With Lucie's prodding, Cort agreed to call the number for Atlantic Coast Yacht Brokers one more time. If there was no response, they agreed to go back online and start over. He knew the deal he was proposing was a long shot, but at the same time he wasn't ready to spend a half a million dollars or more on a sailboat he wasn't sure he could sail. Lucie followed her dad into his office and sat on the floor next to the window. He didn't object, and simply asked her to stay quiet during the call.

Just after the fourth ring, a British accented male's voice was heard on the other end.

"Atlantic Coast Yachts, can I help you."

"Yes, hello, my name is Cort Palmerton. I'm interested in one of the boats you have listed online."

"Sure, I can help you with that. Name?"

Cort hesitated briefly, pondering the fact that he just told the man his name. A second went by before he realized the man was asking for the name of the boat.

"Oh, yeah, sorry. It's called Sea Sleigh."

"Righty then, let me pull that up." More seconds ticked by. Cort thought he heard a slurping sound on the other end, like the British guy was drinking something. Finally, the man spoke again. "Sir, I have it up here… still available. What would you like to know?"

Cort hesitated, gathering his thoughts to be concise with his inquiry. His first inkling was to ask why the hell nobody had returned his initial call, but he refrained and stayed polite.

"Well, Mr?" he phrased it as a question and waited, buying time as the man spoke.

"Oh, sorry. This is Mr. Marcus. Simon Marcus. I am the selling agent for Sea Sleigh. You have the right person."

"Great. Mr. Marcus, I'm very interested in Sea Sleigh, but I have a proposal for its purchase that's a little out of the ordinary."

"Alrighty, and what would that be?" Simon sounded apprehensive already, but willing to listen.

Cort glanced at Lucie and held up his left hand, showing her his crossed fingers.

"So, Mr. Marcus, basically I want to offer the seller full asking price, $675,000, but I'd like to lease the boat for a year first. I'd pay a monthly lease amount he's comfortable with, and then if I'm satisfied with the boat, I'd make the purchase after the year is over. The seller keeps all of the monthly lease fees regardless."

"Mmmmm-Hmmmm. Okaaaay." The hesitancy in Simon's voice was thick. Cort heard him take a sip of something before continuing.

"Honestly, Mr. Palmerton, I highly doubt my client would be interested. He's looking for a quick sale. I know he'd appreciate the full asking price, but I'm just not sure… well, I don't know."

"I understand it's an unorthodox proposal, but could you at least run it by your client. Tell him I'm open to a five-figure monthly lease fee, and I'd also pick up the cost of maintenance and insurance." Cort pleaded, not willing to give up yet.

"Well now, that is a very generous offer indeed. Maybe we could roll those expenses into the final sale price. Cheeky."

Cort interpreted 'cheeky' as a positive term, and sensed the man was silently thinking about the additional commission he could make if the sale price increased.

"Sir, let me do this; I'm going to give you my email address when you're ready. Send me the specific details of your offer, and I'll forward it to Mr. St. Maaa… excuse me…to my client."

"Absolutely, go ahead with that email address." Cort responded with enthusiasm in his voice. Twenty seconds later, he'd written the email address down, thanked Mr. Marcus for his time, and ended the call. He looked over to Lucie again - the anxiety in her expression was telling.

"Worth a shot Lucie…let's give it a shot."

***

Lucie watched with an eager smile as her father tapped an email into his computer. She had a positive feeling about this boat that was named Sea Sleigh, remembering the pictures of it from the internet. There were so many they'd looked at, but something about the boat in question had stood out to her. She thought maybe it was because many of the pictures of Sea Sleigh were taken while it was under sail. Recalling more clearly now, she remembered being able to picture her and dad on the deck, heading out to sea on a beautiful sunny day, just like the one in the photos. She inhaled a deep breath of hope and exhaled a bit of worry, and as her dad finished sending the email, she spoke silently to her mom.

This boat will be the one.

Chapter 26 – Thad's Hope

Thad glanced at the text from a number he didn't recognize, but after checking the (772) area code a second time, he surmised it was from the Stuart, Florida based brokerage firm selling *Sea Sleigh*. Realizing he'd never made a contact record for Simon Marcus, he tapped one into the phone and added *Atlantic Coast Yacht Brokers* into the space designated "Company." The text from Simon was a good sign; most likely there was an interested party. But the short message only referenced that he'd sent Thad an email, and that the email contained an interesting proposal from a guy named Cortland Palmerton.

Despite it being a buyer's market the past 18 months, the sailboat shouldn't be overly difficult to sell. *Sea Sleigh* was in great condition, and Leopard catamarans were a quality craft with a great reputation. In a normal market, it would likely be sold inside of 90 days, but there hadn't been any interest since the first offer fell through nearly two months ago. While the text brought a bit of excitement at the prospect of a potential buyer, it was also a stark reminder of the fact that he and his family would be ending a phase of life they'd enjoyed for the past seven years. The next few years promised to be some of the toughest. Selling *Sea Sleigh* was the first step, a necessary step, and Thad opened his email icon with hope that the context of "interesting" in Simon's text would be something good.

He read the email with the subject "Palmerton Proposal," then started from the beginning and read it again to make sure he was understanding it correctly. Apparently, this Palmerton person was interested in purchasing the catamaran for the full asking price of $675,000 but wanted to do some sort of lease-to-own deal prior to the purchase. He was proposing a one-year lease period, during which he'd pay the owner $10,000/month over and above the sale price, plus all the costs to insure and maintain the yacht during those twelve months. At the end of that year, assuming Mr. Palmerton was satisfied with the boat, he'd sign the purchase docs and close the deal. As another incentive, there was an offer to the owner of *Sea Sleigh*, promising very generous compensation for sailing lessons.

While the offer was highly unorthodox, Thad didn't immediately dismiss it. After all, it would get him the full asking price for his beloved sailboat, plus the potential of another $120,000, and there would be no ownership costs incurred during the lease term. At the end of one year, he'd essentially earn $795,000 for a boat that was being sold for $675,000. Still, it was not without risk, and if Thad understood the email correctly, the buyer could nix the deal if he wasn't satisfied with the boat at the end of the twelve months. While Thad would still walk away with $120K and keep his boat if that happened, he would have lost twelve months of potential buyers. In Thad's world, twelve months of time simply couldn't be sacrificed. The conditions of the Palmerton Proposal were both intriguing and disappointing all at the same time. While the purchase offer for Sea Sleigh was very lucrative, even beyond his expectations, the timeline simply wasn't doable. His wife and mom were the only other people who knew why the money was needed, but only Thad knew why they could not wait a year for the boat to sell. Against his instincts, Thad decided not to dismiss the offer right away. Instead, he emailed Simon Marcus back, instructing him to relay a message to the potential buyer, letting him know Thad would call him directly in a day or two.

He would listen to what Mr. Palmerton had to say and see if there wasn't some flexibility in his initial offer.

Maybe this guy will compromise.

At the very least, he decided, he'd call this Cortland Palmerton, hoping the man could speed up his timeline. Thad clenched his teeth, pursed his lips, and nodded his head slowly; a gesture to himself, signifying a bit of hope for his dire situation.

Chapter 27 – Negotiation

By the fourth ring, Thad prepared for the voice mailbox and gathered his thoughts to leave a message. After the fifth ring, the sound of the call being received caught him off guard.

"This is Cort."

"Hi, is this Cortland Palmerton?" Thad asked the obvious question, buying himself a couple more seconds as he pushed his fingers through the long, thick waves of his sand-colored hair.

"Yes, this is Cortland Palmerton."

The sarcasm and frustration in the man's voice was evident, and Thad was sure he heard a sigh of annoyance come through his receiver.

"Yes, sorry. Hi. This is Thad St. Marie. I was calling… you had expressed interest in my sailboat. It's a catamaran named Sea Sleigh."

The voice on the other end immediately changed to an apologetic tone of interest.

"Oh jeez, yes, sorry! I thought you were about to tell me my car's warranty had expired… blah, blah, blah. Thanks very much for calling, Mr. St. Marie."

"Yeah, no problem." Thad accepted the apology and got to his point. "The broker at Atlantic Coast Yachts sent me an email outlining your very unusual purchase offer." Thad moved to the bay window as he spoke, lifting one of his bare feet up onto the cushion-covered foot-deep sill.

"Yes, my offer, Mr. St. Marie. Full asking price of $675,000, plus the other incentives. What'd you think about it?"

Mr. Palmerton's tone changed yet again, this time carrying a note of cautious optimism. Thad sensed the potential buyer was hoping he'd accept the offer on the spot.

"Well, yeah, it's a generous offer, Mr. Palmerton."

"Please, call me Cort."

"Okay, and you can call me Thad. It's a good… it's a great offer, Cort. The only issue I have with it is the timeline. This twelve-month lease deal is way longer than I can wait." As Thad spoke, he stared out the window beyond the gentle sloping yard of manicured grass, and out to the long gray dock. Sea Sleigh bobbed gently in the bay water just beyond, where it would remain until November - unless he found a buyer first. July was more than half gone, and they'd only pulled her anchor once since the season started nearly four months ago. Inhaling deeply, then sighing softly through his nose, he still couldn't quite come to grips with the aspect of selling her. The voice on the other end of the phone broke the woeful thought.

"Oh, well, um, you know I'd be paying you $10,000 a month during that period, right?"

Thad completely understood the offer, which had been spelled out quite clearly in Palmerton's email, but he remained polite and answered appreciatively.

"Yes, I do understand that part, Cort. But, well, I'll be blunt. I'm just not in position to hold onto the boat for a full year, especially with no guarantee that you'll do the final purchase after that year. If you changed your mind, I'd be back to square one."

There was a pause, giving Thad some hope that maybe some kind of flexible negotiation was about to begin.

"Well, I understand that. But you might also not sell the boat for a year anyway… or maybe longer. At least with my offer, you're 120 thousand in the green after a year, no matter what."

He's holding firm, damn it!

Thad was about to speak and stop wasting both of their time, but Cort Palmerton pushed another thought through the phone before he could reply.

"Mr. St. Marie, Thad, I'm very interested in your boat. It's not a matter of whether I like it or not, it's just a matter of whether I can handle a boat of that size. If I'm comfortable sailing it after a year, which by the way, you can help guarantee that I am, then I'll absolutely make the purchase. My only hesitation is that I've never sailed a boat on my own, so I just don't want to make a $675,000 purchase and then find out I can't operate it."

"I can appreciate that," Thad pretended to be sympathetic, "but twelve months is just not a timeline I'm able to entertain at this point. And quite honestly, I don't expect the boat to be on the market more than three or four months. If your offer was a four-month lease period, I'd probably consider it."

Despite not wanting to let this bird-in-the-hand fly away, Thad knew he didn't have the kind of flexibility this buyer assumed was available. Turning away from the window and walking back towards the opposite side of his office, he stopped in front of the hand-carved teak-wood desk. He slid his free hand over its smooth surface, remembering the birthday that Amelia had given him the custom-made work of art. He lifted his head and focused on the wall behind it, a prominent reminder of those glory years. Each medal was framed in a gray wood shadowbox. One silver, one gold, both popping brilliantly against the red-velvet material it rested against. He stared from one to the other, waiting for a response from the man named Cort.

Finally, the reply came, and there was a little ground given up in the response.

"Well, can you think about it at least? I'll consider a shorter lease term too, maybe there's a compromise in there somewhere."

There was a brief pause before Cort spoke again with an attempt to strengthen the offer.

"Thad, I'm sure you're very busy, but if you could give me sailing lessons, which I'll pay you for, maybe I could learn the boat and how to sail it sooner than I'm expecting."

"I can certainly think about it." Thad agreed to consider Cort's suggestion, but in his own mind he knew the money simply couldn't wait. There'd soon be some extremely rough waters he'd have to navigate, and time was of the essence. Giving this guy private sailing lessons sounded feasible on the surface, but in a few more months, it might prove to be impossible.

"I appreciate that. Let me know if there's anything else I can do to help you say yes." Palmerton offered the final sales push.

Scratching the back of his head, Thad responded hesitantly. "Well, Cort, if you want me to keep your offer in consideration, a pre-approval letter from your financial institution would be appreciated."

"Actually, Thad, I should have mentioned this, but the offer is an all-cash one."

Somewhat expecting a punchline to follow, Thad waited a second before responding.

"You're serious?"

"Yes, I'm serious."

"Okay, well, that definitely strengthens the offer." Thad tried to hide his shock and enthusiasm by keeping the positive reaction as low-key as he could. "Cort, would you mind giving me your full name and address, and I'll promise to take your offer into consideration."

The stranger on the other end gave Thad the requested information after a brief hesitation, likely realizing he planned do a background check. As Thad finished writing the city, state, and zip, a final thought was offered by Cort.

"Thad, the money is from a settlement I recently received. I won't go into details right now, but it's all legit. I'm not into drug dealing or any other funky profession. Do as much checking as you want, but you have no reason to be concerned."

"Cort, I appreciate that. Give me some time to digest all of this, and I'll reach out to you again as soon as I can."

"Sounds fair, thank you."

"Thank you, Cort and enjoy the rest of your day."

Thad pushed the end call button on his phone, thinking a deal in the future was possible. He stared at his phone for a long fifteen seconds. The screen-saver photo of him with his arms around Amelia and Gracie always brought a smile to his face. The smile came again easily, but now it also carried a degree of pain. He immediately got choked up, remembering back to early February when they'd posed for the picture on Sea Sleigh's bow. Mom had snapped the shot as he'd stood with his wife and daughter, all four of them having flown to Florida for a break from the Rhode Island cold.

Damn that was a good day!

Pushing the thought and the tears away, he tapped the screen again, and pulled up his Google app. Some research needed to be done before he could get his hopes up any higher.

***

Cort hit the button and ended the call, pondering the conversation more. He was hesitant to take the counteroffer that Thad had presented, which negated two thirds of the time to learn how to sail. There were many boats on the market to choose from. He'd barely scratched the surface. And while he was ultra-focused on Sea Sleigh, drawn to it for reasons he wasn't even sure of, Cort reminded himself there were others like it available. Plus, there was something uncomfortable about the man's rush. The seller seemed to need the money sooner than later, and that part left a twinge of anxiety lingering in Cort's gut. Then again, it was becoming apparent that his 1-year lease idea wasn't exactly popular with any of the other seller's either. He stood staring out the kitchen windows, watching Lucie on the swing. She looked lonely. She needed change, maybe more so than he did, and maybe sooner than later was a good thing. Visualizing the fun adventures they'd embark on while sailing around the world, Cort made a decision. He'd give Mr. St. Marie a few days to counteroffer, and if he hadn't heard anything by early next week, he and Lucie would start their sailboat search again.

Chapter 28 - "Research"

Yesterday's google search of Cortland Palmerton had been nothing short of enlightening. At first, he'd clicked on the typical links to a Facebook or Instagram page. Thad had perused them both a bit, pausing on several of the photos. They appeared to reflect the happy family life of a man, his wife, and daughter - seemingly an only-child. Mr. and Mrs. Palmerton were certainly a handsome couple, and the little girl reflected both of their best features.

It was a family dynamic Thad related to, and the pics were in many ways reminiscent of those happy times he, Amelia, and Gracie had captured in photos. As he'd scrolled down the screen on his office computer, however, a small pit of anxiety formed in his gut. There were several articles and news clips from various Pittsburgh based media outlets. All of them summarized the same event, a devastating highway accident that left one woman dead and another man seriously injured. The deceased woman shared Cort Palmerton's last name, and every article explained the same accident with a slightly different angle. They reported the events that began with the woman stranded on the Evans City exit ramp of I-79, waiting for road-side assistance. Names were cited, both the truck driver's and his employer, and the name of the thirty-eight-year-old wife and mother of one, who had not survived the crash. Cort and Lucie Palmerton were highlighted as members of the woman's immediate family. In one article, Thad found a link to Celeste Palmerton's obituary. He read the brief history of her life and scanned through the rest of the half-page death notice. Most of it centered around the love she'd given and received during her marriage and motherhood. It was difficult to read, and Thad couldn't help but relate it to his own wife and daughter as he absorbed the words. He turned to the barn-wood framed photo of Amelia and Gracie that rested contently in the left corner of his desk, then pushed the thought away.

Scrolling through a few older articles and an outdated LinkedIn profile, Thad learned some limited information about Cort Palmerton's career with a tech company. After thirty minutes or so, he shrunk the screen on his monitor, and leaned back in his chair. He'd been hopeful yesterday, forming a loose plan in his head to foster the man's purchase offer. A plan that would include Mr. Palmerton as a crewmember aboard Sea Sleigh for a week or so. The information he'd just uncovered could be an issue, however, and Thad wondered if there might be reason for concern. Mr. Palmerton had sounded so confident and collected on the phone, but according to the articles, the accident had occurred in February, just under six months ago. Emotional stability would be paramount during the sail, and Thad wondered how much trauma Palmerton might still be dealing with. He and Mom would need their second mate to be mentally strong, especially when alone at the helm for hours on end.

As he considered squandering his loose plan, an idea struck him, bringing hope back to his psyche. He thought about his mother, and her position with the church. She'd been on a mission for nearly two years now, to save as many souls as she could through prayer and emotional support. She'd joined him on each of the past three trips from Rhode Island to Florida, and he was sure she'd be up for the sail again in November. Bringing along a man who could probably benefit from some spiritual healing right now, might just turn out to be the perfect third member of their sailing party. It was a conditional assumption, and Thad would need to ensure that his and his mother's safety were paramount. Deciding to run the plan by her immediately, he picked up his cell phone with an edge of excitement and punched a few icons until he heard the outgoing call ring.

"This is Marilyn."

"Mom, it's me, Thad. Can't you see that on your caller i.d.?"

"Hi Thad, I thought so, but I wasn't sure... I don't have my glasses on and couldn't quite make out the name. How are you son?"

A short chuckle escaped before Thad spoke again. "I'm fine. Mom, I told you I can attach a photo to some of your contact records, so you'd see the person's picture pop up when they call."

"Don't laugh at your mother, young man." She returned an affectionate giggle. "What's up?"

They talked for twenty minutes as Thad explained the situation, reiterating his and Amelia's plan to sell the boat. His mom was already aware of his intentions, but he knew she didn't quite believe he'd go through with the sale of Sea Sleigh. She probably assumed he'd simply sell off a few of their real-estate holdings to pay for the medical procedures. It had been almost two years since Mom relinquished all day-to-day operational duties of their partnership, and while she was still the 51% majority owner, he knew it didn't matter. He was her son, and he, Amelia, and Gracie meant everything to her. She'd given him the blessing to sell off whatever was needed to gain funds. He knew she was concerned, but her faith that God would take care of everything was unflappable. Thad and Amelia were not as confident and hadn't even told their 8-year-old daughter Gracie just yet. They justified that the less time she had to comprehend and be concerned about the condition, the better off she'd be.

Thad knew that much of his worry and guilt was a result of the fire. He'd veiled the true dilemma from everyone, even his wife and mother.

Maybe I'll just tell Mom the fire was uninsured.

As she droned on about how God would be their savior, not fully comprehending the dire nature of her son's predicament, his guilt grew stronger. The financial position he'd put his family in, on top of the critical health crisis, would be too stressful for Mom or Amelia to handle. The insurance "issue" was easy enough to conceal, because his mother's full attention had completely shifted to her congregation over the past couple of years. Her deep focus of saving troubled humans kept her in what Thad perceived to be a haze of altered reality, rendering her somewhat oblivious to the trials and tribulations of the broader world around her. And Amelia simply didn't ask much about the fire. She'd been sympathetic about the loss of the property but would never have imagined it wasn't insured - he'd never given her any reason to believe that it wasn't.

This is my burden, not theirs.

Thad continued reviewing his plan for moving the boat to Florida, and his mom mostly listened. It would be just as they'd done every year for the past four, basically repeating the same agenda, in the same month of November when hurricane season was just about over. The only difference would be their third crew member.

For the past two years, Thad's youngest cousin Katie had been that third. She was a seasoned boater and knew her way around Sea Sleigh well. But Katie wouldn't be available, having just accepted a new job with a rigorous 4-month training program. While it wasn't even August yet, Thad knew now was the time to secure another sailor. He'd been delaying, with the hopes that his catamaran would already be sold before it needed to be moved south. Now he had a plan that could satisfy both issues at once.

He told his mother about Cort Palmerton and his odd but intriguing offer, sharing the details he'd learned about the man's personal life. She listened intently, and when her son finished, she spoke just a single word.

"Well…"

There was a long pause, and Thad waited patiently as she processed everything he'd outlined. Finally, his patience thinned.

"Yeah, Mom?" Thad prompted as he eagerly awaited his mother's approval of the plan.

"I'm going to pray on it, Thaddy, but I think it's a good plan. This guy sounds like maybe he needs some help, and I can't think of a better way to help him find peace than on an eight-day sail aboard Sea Sleigh."

"But?" Thad asked, knowing from her tone there was more coming.

"But we probably need to be careful. I mean, if this guy really wants to buy the boat and become a yachty, then it'll probably all be fine. That said, first we should double check to make sure his money is coming from a legitimate source. And son, well… I just wonder about the mental stability of the guy. We need him to be a reliable sailor, sharing a third of the watches and being able to do it safely. I know if push came to shove, you and I could make it to Florida alone, but you know how important the third person is if the water gets rough."

"Yes, I do Mom, and I agree with both of your points. They crossed my mind once or twice before I called you. Don't fret about his money and mental state. I can do some more research, and make sure we don't have to worry about either one. I just wanted to see if you'd be on board with it." He waited as the other end of the line remained silent. "Mom?"

"Yes, sorry, Thad. That sounds good. Let me know what you find out. And give my granddaughter and that sweet wife of yours a kiss and hug, please."

"Will do. Thanks, Mom. Love ya."

"Love you too Thaddy, bye."

Thad ended the call with a tap to his phone screen and stared up at the wall behind his office desk again. Both medals a stark reminder that his mom's guidance had always brought him success in life. As much as he wanted to dismiss her concerns, he knew she was right. He'd felt the same sense of disquiet too, and while he wasn't worried quite as much, he thought back to the property purchase gone bad back in 2018. He and his mother had lost nearly $100,000 in a fraudulent real estate scheme. He should have trusted mom's instincts then, but instead pushed her hard to make the extremely lucrative transaction happen. She'd relented, and an hour later their funds had vanished into cyberspace without a trace. Not even Amelia's brothers' position with the FBI was of any use. The case went ice-cold immediately after the transfer, and it wasn't long before they accepted that the $100K was gone forever, simply to be written off as bad debt. But his FBI brother-in-law, Bernie, would surely be able to help him here. As much as he hated to cash in the favor, he punched the name into his contacts and was about to send a text. Remembering that this kind of request could not be in writing, Thad walked to his office door and locked it before moving to the bay window on the opposite wall. Taking a long gander at Sea Sleigh, he watched her sleek form shift slightly in the breeze, then looked back at his phone, tapped the call button, and waited.

"Hey, Thad, how are ya buddy?"

Bernie's attempt to sound cheery was mostly drowned out by the FBI-all-business cadence of his voice.

"Good, Bernie, I'm good, I guess. Hey, sorry to bother you bro, but I need to cash in that favor."

There was a pause and a sigh from the other end of the phone before Bernie replied.

His voice was subdued, and the slight bit of cheer was now totally gone. The favor was immediately understood, and the less words that were spoken, the better.

"Name and address?"

"It's Cortland Palmerton." Thad continued with the address slowly and could hear the scribbling of a pen from Bernie's end of the call.

"Thanks, I'll get back to you soon."

"Thanks Bern, I appreci…"

Click.

Chapter 29 – Feedback

A full day hadn't even gone by when Bernie's name and number populated the screen on Thad's cell. He wasn't surprised by it, as Bernie had proven very fast and resourceful on a past inquiry. Thad was, however, caught off guard by the timing. It was dinner time, and he, Amelia, and Gracie were doing just that. Chewing a chunk of fish as he pulled the phone from his pocket, he stood up immediately and backed away from his chair.

"Honey, I'm sorry. Work call, I need to take this."

"Go ahead, it's okay. I'll heat your plate up if it takes a while."

Thad simply nodded as he walked briskly towards the rear hallway. Amelia had been more sympathetic than usual. He knew it was because of their situation, and she didn't want to cause either of them any more stress than they were already under. It was appreciated, and he made a mental note to thank her for understanding when he returned to the table. Not wanting to miss the call, but also not wanting his wife to know who was on the other end, he answered it with a generic greeting.

"Hello, this is Thad St. Marie." As the words left his mouth, he pulled his office door closed behind him, and headed toward the bay window at the other end of the room.

"What?" Bernie sounded confused. "I know who the hell I'm calling here, Thad, and I know you have my number in your phone?"

"Sorry, Bernie. I was eating dinner, and uh… never mind, I'll explain later. Wha-da-ya got for me brother." He stood next to his desk and listened.

Bernie proceeded to give Thad detailed information about Cortland Palmerton. His words were clear and concise, and spoken in a tone that screamed government official. Thad briefly pictured Bernie stroking his mustache as his brother-in-law spoke. He'd teased him about it in the past, suggesting he looked like one of the guys in the Beastie Boys' video for "Sabotage." Normally, he'd affectionately bust Bernie's chops about the mustache, but this was a different kind of conversation. The matter at hand was nothing to joke about, and neither man's sense-of-humor would be part of this phone call.

The majority of the information was not earth-shattering. It was mostly what Thad had already uncovered, highlighted by the accident in February making Mr. Palmerton a widower. Bernie dwelled on a couple of those particulars, including the multi-million-dollar settlement by the trucking company, but Thad could tell by his inflection that more was coming, and it wasn't good. Sitting down in his desk chair, Thad picked up a hand-carved wooden statue from his desk. He put the 10-inch-tall piece of fragrant Sandalwood to his nose and inhaled, trying to remember the man in Samoa who'd traded it to him for a Boston Red Sox hat. The memory was pushed away and Thad listened intently as Bernie began furnishing details that could only be obtained by systems within the highest levels of government security. Bernie highlighted some of Cortland Palmerton's activities, or more importantly, lack there-of. He slowly established that the man in question was emotionally unstable. There were the visits to a psychiatrist, which Thad and Bernie both decided wasn't altogether troubling. It also looked like Palmerton's job was in jeopardy, evidenced by corporate emails outlining an action plan with warnings of consequential termination. Bernie went on, describing a disturbing video he'd found on social media. The video showed Mr. Palmerton in a verbal confrontation with another man, surrounded by a group of children and adults. From what could be gathered in the seventy-two-second clip, the conflict appeared to occur shortly after a girls' soccer game. Thad was a bit more concerned, but still not to the point of bailing. Finally, his FBI brother-in-law told him about some activity on one of Palmerton's credit cards. Namely, there was a purchase at a liquor store and a pharmacy less than an hour apart.

"Getting the credit card purchase details wasn't too difficult, except for the pharmacy prescription. You know, HIPAA laws? Had to cash in a favor of my own to get the name of the script."

Bernie sounded especially pleased with himself on that particular piece of his findings. The information was detailed down to the exact brand of whiskey, and the specific sleep-assistance pharmaceutical.

Thad considered all the information, pondering everything carefully. Even after Bernie finished, Thad dwelled a second on the last bit of information before speaking.

"What exactly are you inferring there with the alcohol and sleeping pills Bern?"

"Not sure, maybe nothing. Could just be a coincidence, Thad. I'm just letting you know that a lot of this points to someone who is depressed and unstable. But then again, it could just be a guy who can't sleep. I'm not even sure I want to know, but who is this guy from Pennsylvania - how do you even know him?"

"Uhhh, alright, fair question. Listen man, he's just a potential buyer, interested in Sea Sleigh."

Bernie responded in disbelief before Thad could continue, "Wait, you're selling your sailboat!?"

"Yeah, we are, Bern. But hey, I'm not getting into it right now. Amelia and I will talk to you about that soon. For now, we're selling the boat, and this Cort Palmerton guy wants to buy it, but he also wants me to teach him how to sail it. I had an idea which would put him on the boat with me and my mom for a week or so, and it's why I'm asking about him. Understand?"

"Yeah, I think so. I'd proceed with caution here bro."

Thad was relieved that Bernie didn't push for details. Plus, Thad understood his brother-in-law was already breaking protocol by divulging confidential information about one private citizen to another private citizen. The less Bernie knew, the less culpable he'd be if his research of Cortland Palmerton ever came to light with a higher authority.

"I agree. Thanks man, I appreciate it, really." Thad scratched his chin and paused a half-second before continuing, "Listen, Bern, one more favor, okay?"

"Maybe, depends."

"Just don't say anything to Amelia, okay? She'll just worry, and right now, I can't afford to have her worry. That's all I can say."

"Man, don't ask me to lie to my sister. But hey, if she doesn't ask about this Palmerton guy specifically, then technically I'm not lying if I don't volunteer anything. Does that sound logical."

"You're the most logical guy I know brother. Thanks, I do appreciate it."

"Sure thing. And hey, we're even now."

"Even Steven. Talk to you later, I gotta go."

Thad hung up and put his phone in his pocket, went back to the dinner table, and kissed Gracie and Amelia on the top of their heads before sitting back down.

"All good?" Amelia asked.

She wouldn't suspect anything other than a work call, and typically stayed out of the real estate transactions her husband managed.

"All good," Thad responded with a smile, "Potential deal on a condo... had to answer it. Thanks for understanding."

Taking a bite of the barely lukewarm Salmon, Thad pondered what he'd just learned about the buyer.

Nothing I can't handle. It probably won't work out anyway, but if he goes for it, I'll do my due diligence to make sure Mom and I are safe. I'd just need a back-up plan, some kind of insurance policy in case things go bad.

The thought stuck in his head as he swallowed back the fish. Offering a brief smile to his wife and daughter, he cursed to himself.

Fucking insurance!

Chapter 30 – Renegotiated

This time when the number popped up on Cort's phone, he knew who it was. After the initial conversation with Thad, Cort had created the contact in his phone, and his pulse went up a few beats-per-minute when he read the name on his screen. It was good timing too, just one day prior to the deadline that Cort had set to begin searching again. One way or the other, he and Lucie would move on after this call.

"This is Cort." He answered the phone with a cautiously optimistic pep in his voice.

"Hey, Cort, this is Thad St. Marie. We talked a few days ago about the sailboat."

"Yes, of course. I was hoping you'd call back."

"Yeah, well, me too. I've had some time to mull over your offer, and I like it for the most part. Like I said last time, it's really just the timeline that's not doable for me, so I wanted to make you a counteroffer that I think you might be good with - kind of ticks all of your boxes." Thad went into salesman mode, pausing to raise anticipation.

"Alright, I'm all ears Mr. St. Marie." Cort tried to hide his enthusiasm.

"First of all, Cort, please call me Thad. If this deal goes the way I'd like it to, you and I are going to spending quite a bit of time together on Sea Sleigh. So, let's get on a first name basis, okay?"

"Absolutely, Thad, that sounds good."

"Good. So, this is what I'm proposing to you."

Thad laid out the alternative procurement plan, and Cort listened without interrupting. The revised proposal had Cort meeting Thad and his mother in Rhode Island in mid-November, where Sea Sleigh was presently moored. From there, all three of them would sail the boat south.

"We move the boat to Florida every November for the winter. The past three year's my cousin Katie was our third crew member. Katie won't be available for this November's sail, and you have the opportunity to take her place. You'd be learning hands on Cort, for over a week straight. It would equate to several months of sailing lessons. You'd probably know Sea Sleigh inside and out by the time we pull into Port St. Lucie."

Cort finally interrupted at the sound of the destination.

"St. Lucie, really?"

"Yes sir. Ever been there?"

"Not actually in St. Lucie, but not too far from there - right on the St. Lucie River. Really nice area from what I remember. Wow, it was like 27 years ago though. I'd like to see the area again." An image of the sharks on the reef flashed in his mind.

"Well then, Cort, this may very well be the opportunity to do that."

Continuing with the proposal, Thad outlined an alternative payment plan, which stipulated a $100,000 non-refundable deposit be paid by September 1st. After their sail to Florida, assuming Cort was still moving forward, he'd pay Thad a balance of $650,000. That would make the total purchase $750,000, including the sailing lessons.

"Cort, I'm sure you've already done the math, but this alternative plan shaves $45,000 off of your initial offer... a nice chunk of change in your favor."

"I appreciate that," Cort offered.

"Now, Cort, if you decide Sea Sleigh isn't for you after the sail to Florida, I keep the $100K and will have only lost 3 ½ months of selling time."

It was a compromise for each of them, but it benefited both parties too. Thad would gain time, and Cort would gain money and an extremely thorough understanding of Sea Sleigh. Thad made a few additional positive points about his alternate game plan, further convincing Cort that this plan could work. He was aware the economy and boat market would likely preclude another full offer anytime soon, and he figured Thad must realize it too.

"You still there, Cort?"

Cort sensed his patience was waning.

"Sorry, yes, I'm still here, Thad." Another silence, but this time much shorter. "I have to say I'm liking the counter-offer Thad. It does sound like most of my interests, and yours, are covered here. My only question is the month. November. Why not make the sail when it's a little warmer in Rhode Island? I think I'd be okay leaving sooner."

"Good question, and the answer is simply that hurricane season goes all the way through November. So, if we leave in mid-November, it's not terribly cold, and we miss all of the peak hurricane months."

"Ah ha, that makes total sense. Yeah, I forgot about the hurricanes." Cort agreed.

"I've sailed through some nasty thunderstorms Cort, and to say the least, it's miserable. But a tropical depression or even a low-category hurricane is a whole different level of misery, and danger."

"Yeah, for sure. No further explanation needed." Cort agreed again and decided he didn't have any other questions for now. "Well, if it's alright with you, I'd like to take a day or two to think about it… talk to a couple people and make sure it'll work. But Thad, I like the idea, and am inclined to accept your offer."

"I can give you a couple days for sure. Think about it and let me know as soon you can. I can't promise you I won't entertain other offers in the meantime, but I would let you know before I accept one."

"Fair enough Thad. I'll get back to you a.s.a.p. with an answer either way." Cort Palmerton's tone was positively confident.

"Sounds good, and feel free to call me on this number if you have any questions." Thad finalized his pitch with an optimistic tone.

"Thanks, I'll call you soon." Cort returned the cheery tone.

"For sure. And thank you."

Click.

Chapter 31 – Less Than Transparent

He hung up the phone, and at first, a small wave of guilt washed through his thoughts. He'd come across so upbeat on the phone, which wasn't exactly the way he was feeling. Within a few minutes, the guilt had manifested into an uncomfortable sensation in his gut. The information he had not disclosed could have altered the decision to proceed, but it was a shrouding of the truth he could live with for now. A word came to mind that he'd just recently looked up the meaning for, and he recalled the definition now.

ir-i-des-cent – *adjective* – showing luminous colors that seem to change when seen from different angles.

There was no denying that some colors were being concealed here. Eventually, when he knew the man better and the timing was right, when there was no turning back, maybe he'd disclose his whole story. In the present, he could justify keeping some facts to himself, knowing their well-being and futures were at stake. Before removing his ear pods, his mind went to a song that he hadn't heard in a while. Listening to it would surely lower his spirits, but an odd urge to feel the pain dictated the decision. With trepidation, he typed "iridescent" into the YouTube search engine, tapped the play button, closed his eyes, and tolerated the grief that came with his interpretation of the lyrics.

When you were standing in the wake of devastation
When you were waiting on the edge of the unknown
With the cataclysm raining down

Life Boat

Insides crying save me now......

Four minutes later he scrolled out of the app and turned off his phone, telling himself his planned course of action was the correct one. *Desperate times call for desperate measures.*

Chapter 32 – Deal Seal

Every single person involved agreed, making it a unanimous decision to accept Mr. St. Marie's offer. Of course, those persons were nobody other than Cort and Lucie, but two out of two was still 100%. They'd concluded just after 10:00 A.M. the next morning, following a 1.5-mile run. While walking an additional half mile, he laid out the plan to his daughter. Lucie was visibly apprehensive about being left in Texas with Pappy and Grammy for over a week, but she told him that she understood the need to do so. Cort promised her that as soon as the sail to Florida was finished, he'd fly straight to Austin, and they'd all have Thanksgiving dinner together at her grandparent's house.

Following a quick shower, he dressed, grabbed his phone, and stepped eagerly into his office. Lucie was sitting on the floor next to the window, hair in a neat ponytail, waiting for him to arrive. Cort knew why she was there without her having to tell him. He simply shook his head and smiled, signaling that she could remain.

Tapping the number in Thad's contact record, he gave Lucie a thumb's up. With her hair pulled up and skin donning a deep summer tan, he could see the resemblance to Celeste more than usual. The phone rang only twice before he heard the masculine yet friendly voice on the other end.

"Hey, Cort, how are you?"

"I'm good, Thad, thanks. And you?" Cort kept his voice upbeat and hoped his nervousness couldn't be detected on the other end.

"Well sir, that depends on what you're about to tell me, I guess."

Cort offered an understanding laugh, "Ah yes, that makes sense. Well, Thad, I won't beat around the bush then. I accept your terms. Let's seal the deal and make this happen."

"Excellent, that's great to hear. Thank you, Cort."

"Thank you! I can't tell you how excited I...," Cort glanced at Lucie, "how excited my daughter Lucie and I am for all of this." He winked at his daughter, who was already beaming. "We'll take great care of Sea Sleigh, and hopefully show her some places in this world she hasn't seen before."

"Awesome, I expect nothing less."

"So, what's next?" Cort was hiding his anxiety, knowing there was so much to do before he could even begin to sail their soon-to-be-new-home.

"Uh, well, in the short term, not too much. I'll contact the broker and have an agreement of sale drawn up. It might take a few more days than usual, given the out-of-the-ordinary stipulations. But once that's ready, I'll have it emailed over to you to review, sign, and return. And I'd say by mid to late-August, I'll be asking you to transfer the $100,000 deposit, if that works?"

"Sure, no problem. That all sounds good." Cort answered and simultaneously gave Lucie a more pronounced thumbs-up. She mimicked a clapping motion without making noise. Every tooth in her mouth was visible behind an ear-to-ear grin. "Anything else for now, Thad? You can call, email, or text me if you think of anything."

The pause on Thad's end gave Cort a second of disquiet.

"Thad? You there?" Cort hadn't heard the call end, but he wasn't certain.

"I'm here, sorry, Cort. No, nothing else really. But, uh."

More hesitation.

"What is it? What can I do?" Cort's heard the hint of concern in his own voice now.

"It's all good, Cort. What I was going to say is that between now and November when we set sail, it would be good to brush up on your boating terminology. Try to know the basics of the boat parts, equipment, sailing lingo, and that kind of thing."

"Yeah sure, of course. No problem." Cort was relieved - that would be easy.

"And one other thing Cort, and please don't take this the wrong way... make an effort to get in your best shape, okay?"

"Okay." Cort paused a few seconds. He wasn't overly insulted, but he also wasn't quite sure how to respond. "Yeah, sure, I can do that. You want your crew in good physical condition, right?"

"Yes, that's exactly right Cort. You'll want to have your strength, your stamina, and be well rested for this sail. I can't exactly promise you it'll be easy. Know what I mean?"

"Uh yeah, I do. I think you said seven or eight days. And we always have the chance of hitting some weather."

"That's correct," Thad confirmed, "you just never know."

"Yes, absolutely, I understand. Me and Lucie... my daughter and I just started a running program. By November, I should be able to do a few laps around the deck with no problem." Cort tried to cover the uneasy subject matter with a little humor, and it worked. Thad laughed, albeit nervously, and then uttered what was apparently really on his mind

"And Cort, again, please don't take any offense to this," more pause, "but you want to be in your best mental shape too."

Cort detected a deep inhale from Thad's end of the line could almost picture him cringing as the words were spoken. Four seconds passed as Cort made sense of the request. It seemed that Mr. St. Marie had done his research and was now concerned about how the aftermath of Celeste's death might negatively affect this deal.

"Don't worry about me, Thad." A bit more offended, Cort swiveled in his office chair, putting his back to his daughter. While the latest part of Thad's request felt much more personal, Cort felt a sense of relief that no disparaging reply zipped through his mind. A few weeks ago, the ITS would have beckoned his response to contain a few four-letter words. Instead, he responded politely and positively. "I'm doing well, dealing with things fine. I'll be ship-shape in every aspect when we pull up anchor in November."

It didn't need to be stated. Cort inherently knew Thad had probably searched his name and read all about the accident. He decided it was a little unusual for the mental health request by this man he barely knew, but also understood Thad's concern to some degree. In fact, if he was honest with himself, Cort agreed with the concern. While he himself wasn't sure he'd be completely stable in three months, there was no turning back now.

"Ship-shape," Cort repeated the vote of self-confidence.

"Alright then, that's what I like to hear," Thad's voice lightened, "we'll keep in touch over the next couple months, and I'll see you in November."

"For sure!" He stated it confidently, confirming Thad's statement. "I'll talk to you soon."

"Bye now, Cort, take care."

"Thanks, you too, bye."

Cort spun back around in his chair, and returned the big smile that Lucie flashed him. Pushing the mental health issue deep, he focused on the fact an agreement was in place. Neither spoke as he and Lucie simultaneously stood and moved toward each other, meeting at the edge of his desk. As they shared a long hug, he contemplated what had just transpired, feeling a little bit of shock at what it meant. He kissed the top of her head, and with his hands still on her shoulders, he stepped back. He looked down and she tilted her head upward until their eyes met.

"You ready for an adventure, little girl?"

Lucie simply nodded in confirmation, not quite able to speak. Cort saw the excitement in her eyes but detected the hint of apprehension too. He felt the same way, as he returned her nod. They hugged again, and while he showed external enthusiasm, Cort wasn't totally comfortable himself. Understanding that this was not the time to express his concerns, he offered her a simple affirmation instead.

"Me too, Luce. Me too."

***

She received his hug eagerly and squeezed her arms around his torso with a sense of excitement. This was happening, and she knew it was in large part because of her. Her mom would be very proud, and Lucie decided she'd go right to her bedside from here, kneel down, and tell her mother right away. Something held her in place though, and she was reluctant to let go of her father. In a couple months, he'd be leaving her for more than a week, and the thought was both sad and scary simultaneously.

Relax, Lucie, it's just a little more rough water before we find the calm area again.

She told herself everything would be fine, took a deep breath, and imagined herself exhaling out the deep nagging fear that had popped into her brain just after their run this morning – the fear that her father would not return from his sailing trip with Mr. St. Marie.

Chapter 33 – Loose Ends

His mind had been racing ever since hanging up with Thad yesterday evening, a myriad of responsibilities peppering his brain throughout the day. Some things needed to be handled sooner than later. He could now, with certainty, answer the Austin real estate agent's relentless inquiries over the past couple weeks. There'd been several texts from his in-laws about the same subject, which he'd skillfully danced around as well. He'd need to discuss everything with them too; the call was a dreaded one. Nevertheless, it was time to get focused and begin addressing the many loose ends.

Celeste had been instrumental in teaching him the value of making lists. After a few months of dating her and seeing the effectiveness of writing out his to-do's, he was sold. It began with post-it notes back in those early years, migrated to a small notebook he carried around in his car, and eventually moved into the "NOTES" app on his phone. In addition to the lists being effective, they gave him a real sense of satisfaction each time he crossed an item off. With the melee of thoughts spinning in his head the past few days, there may have never been a more appropriate time for a list than right now. One added benefit would be the mental connection to Celeste - he gravitated toward any activity reminding him of her.

After kissing Lucie good night, he propped himself up in bed and took his book out of the mahogany nightstand. Pushing the drawer shut, he recalled the day he and Celeste had picked out the bedroom furniture. She'd liked the set more than he did, and he was reluctant to buy it. Very deliberately, right there in the showroom and not caring who might see, Celeste laid back on the bed and teased her hair into a playful disarray then ogled him sensuously. The bedroom set was delivered the following week.

He set the book on his lap and opened his phone. Tapping the virtual keyboard with purpose, he listed the items to be resolved before setting sail in November. When he drew a blank, he set the phone down and read from the book he'd started just after Christmas last year. The novel, a gift from Celeste, was written and published independently, making it his first read in that category. She'd read it herself and highly recommended he do the same. As described by her, it was a story about personal faith, wrapped into an adventure set deep in the wild outdoors. While the first ten chapters had been a bit slow, it had not disappointed. He'd gotten halfway through it by late January, but this was the first time he'd picked it up since then. Tonight, he felt it was appropriate; tonight marked the start of a new chapter in more than one sense. And the personal-faith subject matter was something he could relate to now more than ever. Thinking about Celeste as he read each chapter, he related the only female character to her. Each time the woman was mentioned, he looked to the empty side of the bed. At least twice, he rubbed the sheet in the spot where her shoulders would have rested, wondering silently if she'd conversely related the main male character to him. They'd both been looking forward to comparing notes after he finished.

As he read, other random thoughts would be triggered, reminding him of an item that would need to be taken care of before he boarded Sea Sleigh in November. He typed it into his notes and continued reading. Five chapters and two hours later, his eyelids became increasingly heavy. He read the same two sentences three times before finally giving in. Sliding the page-marker in place, he set the book on top of his nightstand, and vowed to have it finished before he set sail. Looking once more at his phone notes, he realized there was much to do over the next three and a half months. While the items weren't necessarily listed in order of importance,

Life Boat

he decided it was a comprehensive list, and he looked forward to getting started. His lids drooped further and further as he read each item again:

1. Run with Lucie (physical shape)
2. Group therapy session/s and one more visit with Dr. Galley (mental shape)
3. Google Thad St. Marie
4. Call Manny and Gabby about Thanksgiving, etc.
5. Finalize UPMC Deal
6. Book flights to Texas and Providence
7. Transfer $100,000 into checking account
8. Meet with school principal
9. Learn boat and sailing terms
10. Contact real estate agent (here and in Austin)
11. Meet with attorney (amend will and testament)
12. Visit crash site with Lucie... z
13. Schedule physical... zzz
14. Visit siblin... zzzzz
15. Prac... zzzzzzz
16. zzzzzzzzzz

Zzzzzzzzzzz.

Chapter 34 – Tying Ends

The next morning started with coffee and another run with Lucie, two miles this time, with a pledge to hit the four-mile mark by October. After showers, they reconvened and made a batch of pancakes before Cort hit the office. For the first time in a long time, he didn't totally dread settling into his office chair. Staying busy was providing some mental health benefits. The past couple of weeks had carried a sense of relief, and he thanked Lucie silently as he pulled up the list of loose ends on his phone. She'd catalyzed all of this, and he felt mostly positive about their future and the relationship he was building with her. The feelings of loss and guilt were still front and center every day, but the incremental improvements were further motivating him to get better. A good portion of his brain activity was centered on Lucie, with another significant part of his head wrapped around Thad St. Marie and Sea Sleigh. Plopping down in his office, he nonetheless resolved to focus on work and began the process of finalizing the UPMC deal. For due diligence purposes, he called both Richey and John, left messages, and followed up his calls with immediate emails. By 10:30 he'd heard back from both, and they had a lunch date set for September 7th, the Wednesday after Labor Day.

After sending and answering a couple dozen emails, Cort called Dr. Galley's office. As expected, Trina answered the phone with her usual pleasant voice. He detected some surprise in her tone, but framed with positivity. After offering some brief small talk, he asked for an appointment.

"Joe has an opening next week, Cort. Can you do Thursday at 3:00?"

He agreed to the date and time, marking it on his paper calendar. Next, in the same vein, he pulled up the Group Therapy website, registered himself as a member, and signed up for a first session in mid-August. Setting the appointments gave him a sense of achievement, and some satisfaction that he'd responded to Thad's request. The man, he decided, was absolutely warranted in wanting Cort to be well. Conversely, Cort was curious to find out more about his two shipmates. While he already inherently trusted Thad and his mother Marilyn, he wanted his own reassurance too. Knowing absolutely nothing about them gave him just a bit of angst, and he'd certainly carry out a bit of due diligence research himself. Cort hoped a bit of digging could reveal the reason Thad had sped up the transaction timeline.

Over the course of the morning, Cort set up several other appointments and intermittently attended to work calls and emails. The job was not something he intended to keep much longer, but he decided to end his time at ComStart respectfully and on good terms.

Around noon he reconvened with his daughter, who'd been going through her clothes all morning. Lucie was taking inventory and figuring out what she'd need for the start of the upcoming school year. Celeste had always taken her shopping in early August, and Cort decided to keep with tradition, at least for the outset of her 5th grade year. Beyond that, her school wardrobe held the promise of being much different.

They ate tuna salad and crackers together for lunch, and Cort remarked that after this year, they might never have to eat fish out of a can again. He told Lucie he'd make her sushi, ceviche, and other fresh fish dishes from their catches right off the rear of the boat. She smiled and told him that they sounded good, but he sensed her hesitation at the idea of killing a fish.

After lunch, Cort made a call to Manny and Gabby, asking them to be on speaker phone so he could talk to them together. Lucie was allowed to sit next to him during the conversation, but Cort asked her to stay quiet for now. He explained to his in-laws that no house would be purchased in Austin this year, and that he and Lucie had adjusted their plans. Those plans, he explained, included the purchase of a boat which they'd sail into the Gulf, just off the Texas coast, early next year. Beyond that, and despite several questions from both of Celeste's parents, Cort was very vague with the details. While he and Lucie were quite certain they wouldn't be putting roots down in Texas or anywhere else anytime soon, Cort decided not to discuss their future with any degree of certainty. Despite Manny and Gabby's heartfelt disappointment in the news, the conversation went relatively well. Cort ended the call on a positive note, tossing them the prospect of Lucie coming to visit in early November, with Cort joining her there in time to spend Thanksgiving in Austin. Lucie's grandparents warmed up to the idea immediately, and tentative dates were set.

Back in his office with a full belly, Cort was anxious to check off one of the more anticipated items on his list. He turned on his PC, went to the Google site, and typed in the name *Thad St. Marie*. As he expected, there weren't an overly abundant number of people with the name, and Cort was quite sure the first few links in the list were about the man he was targeting. He read several articles about Thad before switching over to social media, finding public accounts for the man on both Facebook and Instagram. What he learned was nothing short of impressive. Thad St. Marie made his home in a small coastal town in Rhode Island called Narragansett, which was about 30 miles south of Providence. He was 38 years old, married, and had a daughter who appeared to be 7 or 8 years old. Based on the photos Cort had perused, the St. Marie's were a happy, wealthy, and a most attractive family. Several photos included Thad's mother, Marilyn, who was evidently an especially prominent person in his life. Her appearance gave the impression of a woman in her late 60's with a kind but tough soul. He decided there was no need to do research on Marilyn. Even though she'd be his only other shipmate, he put her in the *no-concern-whatsoever* category and looked forward to learning more about her through direct conversation.

Earlier photos, going back more than a year, showed ocean backgrounds aboard Sea Sleigh. In one photo, date marked eight years ago, Thad and his wife were toasting champagne glasses, holding a SOLD sign, with the catamaran in the backdrop. Cort surmised they'd just purchased the catamaran, which would have been when the boat was only two years old. Other photos evidenced that Sea Sleigh had been sailed across oceans, and the St. Marie's had seen numerous countries and several continents aboard her.

Most of Cort's focus was on Thad himself, which he gathered to be no less than 6 feet 3 inches tall, and quite possibly an inch or two beyond. Even before he read about Thad's history in sports, Cort assumed the man was athletically inclined. His physique wasn't overly imposing, but there was definition everywhere. For a man in his late thirties, St. Marie could have easily passed for a decade younger. He sported a thick wavy rug of light brown hair, reminiscent of a surfer dude. His overall look was that of a man who worked with a full-time athletic trainer by day and became a pot-smoking stoner by evening. Cort pondered the last name St. Marie, which was presumably French or Canadian, but facetiously theorized the guy was a descendent of the Vikings.

Three other links profiled Thad St. Marie's business; a real estate company based out of Killington, Vermont. Apparently, the company, owned jointly by Thad and his mother, had done very well over the past couple of decades. They specialized in vacation properties, buying and selling homes and condos in and around the well-known ski resort named after the town. From what information Cort was able to find, the partnership was worth conservatively somewhere between ten and fifteen million. Maybe that was speculative, but based on the corporate website, St. Marie Holdings LLC was doing very, very, well.

While Cort was not all that surprised to learn Thad was a world-class snowboarder in his late teens and early twenties, he was awed by the fact the man possessed two Olympic medals in the sport. One gold, one silver. Very curious about the details, Cort scoured several articles to learn Thad had gone head-to-head with the very well-known, Shaun White, in the 06 Winter Games. He'd earned the silver behind White in the Halfpipe event, then went on to beat White in those same games in the Big Air competition.

"Wow!" Cort spoke out loud to himself as he closed out the various pages on his laptop.

So much for me being the dominant male on this boat. Damn, I only had one guy to beat.

Cort was not an overly competitive human, but he'd been a successful athlete in his day, and had made a concerted effort to stay in good shape into his adulthood. The past half-year had taken its toll, but he resolved to work even harder over the next month and a half. While he wasn't at all threatened by his soon-to-be shipmate, a twinge of jealousy couldn't quite be denied. Not just for the obvious athletic prowess that this man possessed, but by his apparent life-situation in general. Then again, he'd felt general disdain for just about everyone these days and was envious of men with healthy and happy families. Overall, however, Cort ended his research of Thad with a confident feeling of security. The man was a clean-cut family man, ran a successful business, and was apparently an experienced boatsman with a long history of sailing. Cort assured himself he'd be in good hands (and strong ones) during their sail, and as the image of Lucie entered his mind, he knew his own well-being was the most important aspect of the upcoming journey.

Leaning back in his office chair, Cort rubbed his chin and thought deeper about the St. Marie family. While his general impression was a good one, there remained a nagging question about the transaction at hand. In his negotiations with Thad, he'd failed to ask something he always did during the purchase of any used item he'd ever bought. *Why are you selling?* Based on everything he'd read, this was a happy, healthy, and well-to-do family. And yet, Thad was anxious to make this sale happen, stating that time was of the essence. Cort knew it was none of his business, really, and the reason certainly wouldn't change his objective to buy Sea Sleigh.

Or would it?

He'd waived the inspection in his purchase offer. Maybe that was a mistake. Was Sea Sleigh the boat-equivalent of a "lemon?" Or was there maybe some other reason that could affect Cort's satisfaction with the sailboat. He pushed the bit of anxiety away from his thoughts and refocused on the positive aspects of the seller.

It'll be fine. I'll keep getting stronger. I'll take care of everything, and Lucie will be happy. We'll both be happy.

As an added measure of confidence, he got up from his chair, moved to the side of his desk and dropped onto the carpet. Forty-five seconds later, he rolled over on his back, satisfied that he'd been able to knock out 40 solid push-ups.

I'm good. I'll be fine.

Chapter 35 – Insurance Policy

Thad stayed very busy over the next six weeks, working on a list of his own. Many of his hours were being spent in the car, driving between Narragansett and Killington. Roughly 90% of the real estate holdings were in and around the ski resort, and he'd been traveling more than usual to keep the office in Killington under tight management. The staff had topped out at twenty-two employees five years ago, when the market had peaked, and St. Marie Holdings had done a record $19 million in revenue. The employee count was down to thirteen presently. The year was already two thirds gone, and revenue had only just recently reached the $5 million mark. The business was treading water, and in the past four months, there'd barely been enough to cover payroll. While much of the downturn was due to the market, and part of an economic cycle they'd planned for, there was no real recovery from the uninsured fire. Nearly all the company's surplus had been eaten by the loss, and Thad had even cashed in a few favors with the lenders to increase lines of credit.

While the financial issues were festering, nothing compared to the challenge he'd be addressing in the very near future. The money was an important step, however, so ensuring the funds were available was paramount to success. He reminded himself that it was his burden, and his burden alone. As much as he wanted to tell Amelia and his mother about the insurance, or lack thereof, his pride kept the information silently internalized.

When he'd find himself home with a free evening, Thad busied himself on Sea Sleigh, diligently doing odds and ends to get it ready to sail and ready to sell. He was a fair businessman and wouldn't think of turning his boat over to a new owner without it being in tip-top condition. The buyer, after all, had waived the inspection, and generously offered over and above asking price. He could take no chances of the deal going south because of some avoidable mechanical issue.

While his ever-so-understanding wife desperately wanted him to be with her and Gracie more than ever, she did not push back on his choice of time expenditures. Thad fibbed and told her working on Sea Sleigh took his mind away from the disease – that it was a necessary distraction from the inevitable. How could Amelia argue that reasoning? While the half-truth held some water, the larger part of his reason was the money. In the past, they'd hired skilled mechanics and cleaning services to maintain the catamaran. Those were expenses they'd hardly blinked at before; now those thousands of dollars for the services could simply not be spared. Thad had the knowledge and physical ability to maintain her, and for now, he was necessarily adamant about doing so himself.

He'd worked most of the Labor Day Weekend, taking only one day off to spend with Amelia and Gracie. The following Thursday afternoon, he was aboard Sea Sleigh again, changing the engine oil and thinking about their future. The doctors had done the initial tests months ago, and appointments were made accordingly. It had been agreed that they could wait until after the holidays, and the first surgery would take place on January 5th. From there, it would be a series of treatments and surgeries over the course of a year and a half. No guaranties were made, but the doctors were cautiously optimistic. Thad and Amelia decided they'd wait until the end of December to tell Gracie, not wanting to taint their 8-year old's Christmas. She still spoke of magic and Santa Claus, but they wondered if this Christmas would be the last of that innocence. Either way, they could see no gain in prematurely discussing the harsh reality they'd all face in the new year.

As he tightened a nut and breathed the petroleum musk-laden air, his phone buzzed from above him. Climbing out of the engine compartment, he set the wrench on a towel and glanced at the screen before picking it up. It was the insurance broker's office, sending a twinge of anxiety through his veins.

"This is Thad."

"Hi, Mr. St. Marie, this is Amy at the Yung Agency. How are you?"

"I'm fine, Amy, how are you?"

"Very good, thanks. Mr. St. Marie, I'm just calling to let you know the policy shouldn't be an issue. I emailed you over the information a short while ago."

Thad breathed a sigh of relief. "Great, that's good to hear. Thank you."

"You're most welcome. There are instructions in the email, but basically the questions on the short application will need to be completed, and there will be a health screening. Fairly easy though - just some basic vitals to be looked at, and they'll take a couple vials of blood to make sure there aren't any red flags."

"Good, that sounds easy. And the limit? We're able to get $750,000?"

"Yes sir, that limit is available. It's all detailed in the email."

Thad thanked the office manager at his long-time insurance agency again and ended the call. Keeping his phone out, he sat next to the open engine compartment for a few minutes and read the bulk of the email. After closing the app, he sat for another minute or two and gave himself an internal pep talk for the call that would be made next. Scanning the bay water, now sparkling like golden tinsel in the last sunlight of the day, he tried to take a mental snapshot of its beauty. While the pending sale of Sea Sleigh offered a huge relief to their financial situation, he was simultaneously saddened by the thought of it. Moving his gaze to the gray wooden dock, he followed it towards the shore and up the back yard to his home of nine years. He could picture Amelia and Gracie, sitting at the kitchen island… maybe doing homework, or maybe just playing cards or building a puzzle. He smiled. It was more than enough incentive for him to slide the phone open again and pull up the contact information for Cortland Palmerton.

Chapter 36 – Lucie

Lucie had finished her homework and was drawing again, an activity she'd started to enjoy after finishing her 4th grade art class. She'd put more time into it this summer, as both a way to practice and improve what she'd learned, and to keep her thoughts occupied and pass the time. She thought about her mother a hundred times every day. Her doctor was aware, as she shared just about everything with him in her therapy sessions. Her father, however, was not. Despite the deep sadness she'd been consumed by since February, Lucie used all her mental strength to appear even on the outside. The façade was put on for her dad's sake, knowing he was in deep sadness already. If he had to deal with her mental struggles too, she feared it would put him over the edge.

Returning to school had become a positive distraction, and visits to the psychiatrist had also been beneficial. Talking about her sadness and fears with the doctor and close friends helped her emotional state grow better as the weeks passed. This approaching adventure, however, had easily become the most useful diversion. The fantasy of traveling the world on a sailboat had cast a positive net of optimism over her, and these past few weeks had been good for her and Dad. Up until last week, when Dad and Mr. St. Marie had come to an agreement, she couldn't imagine anything negative about the awaiting adventure. Now that the fantasy was becoming a reality, there were less positive aspects of what was coming. Those negative thoughts were nagging at her now, and as she moved her pencil back and forth, Lucie fought back the tears that wanted to fall.

She'd been drawing boats the past couple of weeks. More specifically, she sketched catamaran sailboats, based on the online photos she'd seen of Sea Sleigh.

Now that this highly unlikely course they were going to embark on approached, her feelings about it grew more and more intense. They ranged on the high end from pure excitement as she considered the beautiful places they'd venture to, down to a gripping anxiety about dying somewhere at sea. The greatest fear centered around harsh weather. Her mind tended to play the scene from Frozen, in which the parents perish when their ship goes down in a violent storm. When the scene played in her brain, she'd fight the fear, reminding herself that cartoons weren't real. Despite the self-council, her 10-year-old brain was not yet developed enough to overcome the dread. The notion of being on the boat with her father in a gale was nowhere as daunting as the prospect of him being caught in a bad storm with two strangers. She worried deeply about not being there to save him if a dire situation arose.

At her usual spot in the kitchen, she had her drawing supplies spread out on the smooth quartz countertop of the oversized island. This evening her dad had returned to his office after dinner, but promised they'd watch something on TV together after he took care of a few pressing items. Lucie had just finished drawing the mast and sails when she heard the pocket door in his office slide open; seconds later his footsteps approached from behind and she replaced the negative thoughts in her mind with images of him.

I hope he's done working.

Fighting the urge to turn around, she waited patiently and hoped he was headed in her direction. The light sound of his socks on the hardwood stopped behind her, and she smiled to herself when she felt the light kiss pecked on top of her head.

"That's good, Lucie. Your drawing skills are getting better and better. It looks just like a real horse." He teased and smiled large, knowing she'd turn to correct him.

"Dad!" She spun around and punched his arm. "Seriously, what do you think?"

"You know I'm joking Luce. It's very good – I'm impressed. And I love that you're drawing boats. You know, at some point when we're anchored somewhere, maybe in a small cove just off some tropical island," her father paused, made eye contact with her, and they exchanged smiles, "I'd like you to draw our boat. Then I can frame it and hang it in the cabin somewhere. Maybe right above the captain's desk."

His request brought warmth to her heart, both because she wanted his acknowledgement and praise, and because he was talking more and more about the future, and less about the past.

"I'll do that, Dad. First, I'll get a little better at drawing though."

"I'm sure you will, Luce. It doesn't matter, I still want you to draw our boat."

Lucie nodded and pondered the thought as her dad set his phone down next to her on the countertop. He seemed to be better lately, and she hadn't seen him shed a tear during a meal in at least a week. His uptick in positivity was helping her own mental health, and she felt especially satisfied because it seemed her sailboat idea had started his mood shift. As he went to the other side of the island and began unloading the dishwasher, she thought about their plans after the holidays.

"When are we leaving here?" They'd discussed it just last week, but she wanted to hear it again.

"Well, I'm thinking we'll put the house up for sale next February or March. If that goes well, we can have it sold and be out when the school year finishes in early June. From there we can move onto the boat, and sail around the Gulf of Mexico and learn everything we need to know over the course of the summer and fall. Once hurricane season ends, maybe next December, we'll start sailing south through the Caribbean. And then go from there, wherever the hell we want to."

She considered the plan for a second. It sounded so wonderful, and aside from the fact that it wouldn't be complete without her mom, she was looking forward to it more and more each day. As she considered asking a follow up question, she heard the phone next to her vibrate against the quartz. Glancing at the screen, her heart skipped a beat as she read the name "Thad St. Marie."

"Dad, your phone. I think it's the guy with the sailboat!"

Chapter 37 – Minor Detail

Cort raced around the island and grabbed the phone on the fifth ring. Not wanting to miss the call, he slid the icon to the right to answer it and tapped the circular button for the *speaker* option.

"Hey, Thad, how are you?" Cort slid the pocket door shut as he re-entered his office, placed his phone on his desk, and kept his volume an octave lower than usual.

"I'm good, Cort, you?"

"Doing fine, thanks. Just fine." Cort made sure his voice was extra confident and cheery.

"Good to hear, Cort. And thanks again for the down payment. Those funds cleared a week ago, so no issue there."

"Right, good."

Cort was aware the funds had cleared, as evidenced by his online bank statement he'd checked the day after, not to mention the *thank you* email Thad had sent him confirming the transaction. He suddenly felt tense, sensing a reluctance in Thad's voice. Leaning forward, Cort swiveled his chair to the left and hovered over the phone. His eyes stared straight ahead out the window and he left the audio on *speaker*.

"So, Cort, I don't want to stress you out with what I'm about to tell you, because I want everything to work out with you and Sea Sleigh. And there's no reason that it shouldn't, really."

"But?" Cort grew a bit more tense, despite Thad's attempt to dispel any concern.

"But, well, I need you to agree to one more condition. Simple really, and no cost to you. I need you to take out a life insurance policy. I'm buying it and paying the premium. You just need to sign up for it."

Cort pondered the request, not willing to think too deeply about it yet.

"Thad, I have life insurance already. My daughter and I are protected well. I'm not sure..."

"Right, of course, I'm sure you are," Thad interjected, "but this policy would be for my protection more than anything. It would make me the primary beneficiary. Understand?"

"No, not really. Not at all." Cort's mind was racing, a bit of fear setting in that the deal was about to go sour.

"Sorry, let me explain. So, I'll email you an application for a term life-insurance policy. Like any life insurance, you complete the application, do a simple health screening, and then assuming it's approved, the policy will be bound. It's just until we get through the sail in November, and then I'll cancel it. In the meantime, I'm paying the premium, nearly $500, so it won't cost you a dime."

Cort listened, still unsure, replying with a single word.

"Ooooh-kaaay?"

"I know what's going through your mind right now Cort, and I'm sorry if I'm causing you any concern. You don't need to be at all. Our trip will be extremely safe, even in bad weather. I've ramped up the safety features 10-fold from just a few years ago. Okay?"

Cort pondered the words for a couple seconds. A soft thud just outside his office door caught his attention, but Thad's voice brought him back to the call.

"Okay, Cort?"

"Sorry, yes, okay. But if it's so safe, why the need for a life insurance policy Thad?" Cort's tone was no longer cheery.

"Ah, yes. Fair question Cort. I need it to be in place in the event, well, for the slight chance that something does happen. Even though it won't, it's just a safeguard."

"Safeguard for what? I'm still not sure I'm getting it." Cort's tone held more confusion.

"Cort, listen, I'm not going to get into my personal situation right now with you, but you just need to understand that the sale of Sea Sleigh is critically important to me." Thad hesitated, but Cort remained silent, signifying that he was waiting for more. "In short," Thad continued, "if something did happen to you while we're on this sail, I need to be assured I'm still going to have the money. That's it, it's as simple as that."

Cort was tempted to accept the vague reasoning he'd just been given. He understood there was a slim chance of something tragic occurring, and life insurance would be beneficial if it did. But it seemed more than that, and Cort wondered if St. Marie's concern had more to do with Cort's mental health. Maybe Thad was worried about Cort using the sail as an opportunity to leap overboard, covering up a suicide with what would be assumed to be a terrible mishap. He reluctantly reminded himself the thought had crossed his mind a couple months ago. But those suicidal thoughts were no longer, and Cort felt the need to reassure Thad that his mental health was much stronger.

"But, Thad..." Cort began his protest.

Apparently, Thad was already prepared to divert and cut him short, "Cort, listen, five years ago, a good friend of mine was our second mate. We were making this same sail from Rhode Island to Florida. He was on watch by himself one night and we got into some rough weather. Long story short, he went overboard because he didn't follow the safety rules - went to go pee without securing his tether."

Cort drew his own drastic conclusion to the story before Thad told it.

"By the time we'd realized he was gone, turned around, and found him, the guy spent over two and a half hours in the water. It was half a miracle, really, but we got to him in time. He was in bad shape, nearly hypothermic, but he lived."

Relieved to be wrong, Cort sighed loudly before speaking.

"Jesus, that must have been horrible. I mean, good that he lived, but holy shit man."

"Yeah, holy shit is right." Thad continued as Cort pondered the terror of the situation. "I'm not suggesting you'd do something that stupid, Cort, but my point is, shit *can* happen. This insurance policy is just a formality, but it's necessary for me."

Both men remained silent for four long seconds.

"Thad, this sounds like the beginning of one of those 20/20 episodes."

There was a brief chuckle on Thad's end before he responded.

"That's funny. But yeah, I get what you're saying. You don't need to worry about that. My mom and I aren't going to try to kill you, I promise. Right hand up to God." Thad laughed again and Cort joined him, but Thad's tone got serious again. "Bottom line is, Cort, the insurance policy isn't an option. Either we get the policy in place, or, well, I mean…"

Cort interrupted the negative notion, "It's okay, Thad, I get it. Send me the application and give me a week or so."

"I'll send it today. And listen, even though I'm the primary beneficiary, you can put your daughter down as the secondary. If by some chance something happens to both of us, the $750,000 would go to her."

The dollar amount caught Cort of guard, and he couldn't help but ask.

"It's for $750,000?"

"Yes, I know, it's a hundred thousand more than the balance you owe," Thad downplayed, "but the difference in premium to go from $650,000 up to $750,000 was only like $42. I figured a little cushion wouldn't hurt, and I'm sure there'd be some unforeseen expenses if you, well… you know. Anyway, don't think into it. If something happens to you, I'll take the six hundred and seventy-five thousand for my part of the deal, pay any miscellaneous costs associated with your death, and give your daughter the remainder. You have my word."

Cort didn't answer right away, but eventually gave Thad a bit of the reassurance he was waiting for.

"Not that I don't trust you, but I'll have my attorney look it over."

"Take your time, Cort. It's really your standard term-life insurance policy but do what you need to do. It might be a week or two before you can get the blood screening and that sort of thing anyway. Just keep in touch and let me know, alright?"

"Yes, okay, I'll do that, Thad."

"Thanks Cort, I appreciate it. And don't worry, this policy will be the worst $500 I've ever spent. I'm sure of it."

Cort chuckled again, which helped relieve the tension, and concurred, "Yeah, I hope so. Talk to you soon."

"Thanks for understanding, Cort. Bye."

"Bye."

Click.

Chapter 38 – Lifeboat

Cort was left to ponder the conversation, staring out the window blankly as he let it sink in. A few seconds later, he heard the muted sound of a floorboard creak, followed by what he presumed to be footsteps scuttling away from his office door. He purposely waited a minute before leaving the office. It gave him some time to digest Thad's request, and it would give Lucie time to get settled back in her spot at the kitchen island.

If she'd been listening long enough, Lucie was likely able to get the gist of his and Thad's conversation, which was simply that the sail could be dangerous and even life-threatening.

Damn it!

He walked out of his office and approached Lucie. She was sitting at the island again with her back turned, so he purposely cleared his throat to avoid startling her. She turned hesitantly when he coughed, and Cort could see she was struggling to maintain a calm and collected expression.

"Was that the sailboat guy?"

Despite her cover-up effort, he knew she was asking a question for which the answer was already known.

"Yes, it was." Cort smiled to himself. "That was Mr. St. Marie. Everything is fine, Luce. He was just checking in and making sure everything is on schedule."

"That's good."

Cort watched as she looked down at her drawing. Her hand hovered over the paper, but it seemed she couldn't move her pencil.

"Yes, it's good." Cort filled a glass of water from the refrigerator dispenser, watching her struggle from the corner of his eye. "Hey, what do you say we watch a movie?"

"That sounds good,"

She hesitated, her mind obviously elsewhere. Finally, his daughter finished her thought.

"I'll put my stuff away."

Cort drank two large gulps of his water as he waited for her to return to the family room. They convened on the sofa and got comfortable. Cort sat quietly and didn't turn the TV on. He waited until Lucie was settled in her spot, then shuffled closer to her feet and looked her in the eyes.

"Everything alright, Luce?"

Her eyelids fluttered a bit as she gathered her voice.

"What if something happens when you're out on that boat?"

He'd expected the question, presuming she'd probably heard a good chunk of his conversation with Thad. He silently cursed at himself again for not being more careful.

"Nothing is gonna happen, Lucie. I promise." He spoke softly but confidently, easily hiding the twinge of anxiety he himself was feeling.

"Well, what if there's a bad storm or something? What if the boat sinks?"

"It won't sink Luce. Even if one of the hulls gets a hole in it, there's still another hull to keep it floating. That's what's nice about a catamaran."

"But, Dad..."

Before she could counter his defense, he added more assurance.

"And even if for some reason both hulls got damaged, and the boat sinks, there's a lifeboat, Lucie. It's nice, I saw pictures of it. And it has a motor. We'd simply get in the lifeboat and motor to shore. No big deal."

"Really? Can I see it? The lifeboat?"

"Of course," Cort replied confidently.

He remembered there being a picture or two in the online ad showing the military-grade rubber raft, secured to the rear deck of Sea Sleigh. In fact, he recalled one photo solely devoted to the lifeboat. He tapped his phone attempting to pull it up, finally reaching the set of photos and scrolling until he found it. He and Lucie looked at it together, blowing up the photo on his phone and going over the details. He pointed out how durable and solid the raft appeared. He also projected there would be survival supplies within what appeared to be compartment under the front seat. She nodded, seemingly satisfied at the concept of a boat within a boat, just in case of emergency.

"Dad?"

"Yeah."

"When you get on Sea Sleigh, can you text me so I know the lifeboat is definitely still there?"

"Absolutely, Luce. That's actually a great idea, I'll do that for sure."

"Can I come with you?"

Cort hesitated, the lump in his throat temporarily disabling his vocal cords. Instead, he slid over and hugged her in her seated position, buying time to come up with the right words.

"I'm afraid you can't, Lucie." He paused ever so briefly, not allowing her to ask the obvious follow-up question, *why?* "The owner is only allowing me on this trip. Well, me and his own mother. I'm sorry, but he just doesn't want anyone else aboard... he has his reasons."

Lucie didn't protest.

"Maybe he's afraid it's a little dangerous? Or maybe he just doesn't like kids?"

Cort laughed and assured her that Mr. St. Marie liked kids.

"This sail is just more about business, Lucie. You wouldn't have fun anyway."

After a few seconds passed, he released his long hug but kept his hands on her shoulders and leaned back. Their eyes met.

"But, Luce, once the boat is ours, we'll have anyone we want on it, okay?"

"That's fine. Just promise me you won't do anything stupid during the sail, please?"

Cort laughed out loud again, harder this time, connecting her request to something Thad had said a few minutes ago, now knowing without a doubt that she'd eavesdropped on their conversation.

"I'll try not to, Luce."

Lucie giggled back, and hugged him again, but not before having the last word.

"Try hard, Dad."

Chapter 39 – Ends Tied

Time was unwilling to slow down for even a minute as Cort and Lucie's lives pushed on towards November. The next seven weeks slipped by as fast as any others. Lucie started school in late August, and her inaugural cross-country season had passed in a blur. She moved up from placing nearly last in the first meet, to finishing in the middle of the pack by the final invitational. Both Cort and Lucie were impressed by her progress. Even if there wouldn't be an official team in her future schooling, father and daughter agreed to keep running together as a squad of two.

Cort made time to meet with the Vice Principal about what would likely be his daughter's last year of traditional classroom learning. While the school administrator couldn't hide her expression of concern about Mr. Palmerton's plans, she was very helpful and said the district would do all they could to help set up a cyber-program.

Similar questions and concerns were posed from Cort's older brother and sister, who he and Lucie visited over an early October weekend. In a suburb outside of Baltimore, Lucie explored the woods adjacent to her uncle's house with her 14-year-old cousin, while Cort drank coffee and explained their upcoming plans to his siblings. Many questions were asked. Most of their inquiries held a tone of worry, and some a hint of jealousy. Cort answered all of them politely and was successful at stifling the mini flares of anger and anxiety evoked by a couple of the questions. Cort acknowledged to himself that the ITS had been under control more lately, proud that he'd been dispelling the thoughts before they got anywhere near his tongue. After an abbreviated day-and-a-half visit, Cort promised they'd come again before sailing south in the Spring, and everyone amicably hugged good-bye.

His meeting with John and Richey occurred as scheduled, and after a two-hour lunch, the UPMC/ComStart contract was signed in ink. Most of his time with the two men was business talk, but there was some heartfelt discussion about Celeste. The men reminded Cort how much they'd both liked her, and Cort thanked them for coming to the funeral that was somehow already eight months in the past. It felt more like eight days ago in his head, and he had to excuse himself from lunch at one point to gather his composure.

Emails and phone calls from the higher-ups at ComStart ceased completely. His supervisors were satisfied, and convinced Cortland Palmerton was back in the saddle. He felt relieved that management and HR were off his back, and because he knew he'd leave the company on a positive note. The UPMC deal, he decided, would essentially be the last contract he'd ever pursue as an employee of ComStart.

Over the next month, Cort barely spent two hours a day in his office - just enough time to answer any pressing inquiries and give the appearance he was working. He put as much time into his physical fitness as he did his job, incrementally reconditioning his body back to where it belonged. The hard work was paying off, and the physical and mental improvements were apparent.

Flights were booked, real estate agents and attorneys were met with, financial obligations were paid, and Cort studied up on his sailing terminology. He and Lucie visited Celeste's cemetery plot twice before building up enough courage to go to the crash site. After making numerous excuses for not being able to return to the ominous exit ramp, Cort finally agreed, it was time.

On a bright, cloudless Saturday in early October, the pair dressed in their hiking gear and headed north out of town. A quick stop was made at a roadside market, where they purchased a brilliant yellow chrysanthemum and placed it next to the shovel and bag of topsoil in the rear cargo area. Both father and daughter agreed that Celeste would like the yellow-colored mum the best. He parked at the bottom of the exit ramp in a graveled area off the shoulder, and the two walked together along the berm until they reached the spot. Finally, Cort stopped and placed Lucie's hand in his opposite palm, then covered it with his free hand. The gesture was as much for his own support as it was for hers.

"It was here, Lucie. This is where she was parked when the truck hit her."

Lucie didn't respond other than a curt nod, and Cort knew she was fighting her emotions. The emotions would not be defeated. He hugged his teary-eyed daughter then guided her down from the road's edge and 30 feet into the grass. It had recently been mowed, evidenced by the ripples of clippings that formed a pattern of waves. Between two of the ripples, Cort dug a hole a foot wide and a foot deep. Instructing Lucie to take the mum out of the plastic pot, Cort ripped off the top of the soil bag. Before putting a bed of dirt in the bottom of the hole, he pulled the small container from his pocket. He placed the white cardboard box in the bottom of the hole and poured half the bag on top of it.

"What was that?" Lucie asked the question, then sniffled as she wiped a tear from her cheek.

"Just a present your mom was going to give me. She never got the chance to, so I want it to stay with her. You understand?"

She offered another nod through another sniffle. The two placed the mum into the hole together and pushed the remaining soil around the sides of the flower, patting it firmly into the ground.

"It's perfect, Lucie. Beautiful, just like your mom."

She turned into the side of him and hugged his torso. They watched the tiny petals of the chrysanthemum being pushed by a soft breeze, fluttering in unison.

"I miss you so much, Mom." Her voice was muffled through the fabric of his shirt, but Cort understood the words. He stroked the side of his daughter's head, pushing the hair away from her eyes.

"I miss her too, Luce." Cort knelt and hugged her, then met her glossy eyes. "We still have each other though, you and me. And we need to keep it that way, right? We need to be healthy and happy. That's what your mom would want."

Lucie nodded and turned to the yellow flower that symbolized Celeste's brilliant life, then nodded again in agreement. They stared at their memorial for a few seconds together before she turned back and met his waiting eyes.

"You're right, Dad. That is what she would want."

***

Lucie felt muted satisfaction as she buckled her seatbelt and their car pulled onto the road. Since her mom's funeral, she'd overheard the term 'closure' used a few times in conversations among adults. As the car drove away from the crash site, she felt an odd peace about her mother's death, and she wondered if *closure* was that feeling. Being at the spot had given her an unexpected connection with her mom, and as she watched the yellow petals of the flowers move in the breeze, she'd heard her mother's voice on the warm wind. She glanced at her father's eyes in the rearview mirror, then gazed out the window in silent reflection.

I hope you felt it too, Dad.

Chapter 40 – Shrunk

As days turned into weeks, Cort checked off most of the remaining items on his to-do list. November crept closer and closer. He'd managed to procrastinate two of the more difficult items on the list until mid-October. The appointment with Dr. Galley was cancelled by Cort, but he'd rescheduled it out of guilt. It was a brisk Fall afternoon when Cort walked into the historic Victorian house and was greeted by Trina. After some brief pleasantries, he entered the doctor's office and sat back on the couch, determined to address one of his largest demons. He started by telling the doctor about some miscellaneous issues, describing how the ITS had subsided, but how he was still suffering from the inability to listen to music.

"I've been feeling a little better, doc, or at least I've been distracted away from the deepest depression. To be honest with you, doctor, I owe a lot of my progress to Lucie, my daughter. She's been my rock, which is odd, because it should be the other way around. I want to keep getting better too, but I still just can't shake all the anger and guilt."

Dr. Galley listened, then inquired, "What are the primary seeds of this anger and guilt, Cort. Who are you angry with?"

"I hate the truck driver. I have fantasies of hurting him doc, imagining I see him on the street and beat the living shit out of him. I dreamed that I stabbed him with a meat fork at a cookout, and it felt right. It's stupid, because he's in prison, and seeing him isn't even a realistic possibility. And of course, even if I did see him on the street, or God forbid, at a barbecue, I wouldn't hurt him. But I still have the fantasies." Cort jerked his head nervously to see if the doctor had written anything down in lieu of his last statement. "And I'm extremely angry at myself too.

Sometimes the guilt is so intense that I hate myself for what happened. Why I didn't do more… why I didn't tell my wife," He paused to take a deep breath and gather his composure, sitting up and moving his feet to the floor, "I could have prevented the whole thing, Dr. Galley. She'd still be here if…"

"Hold that thought, Cort," the doctor mercifully interrupted him, "The feelings of anger at the truck driver are normal. Of course you're angry at that man. I'd be shocked if you weren't. But Cort, try to focus on the fact it was an accident. That driver didn't purposely wreck into your wife. It wasn't pre-meditated. And I realize that fact doesn't change the result but harboring all this anger and hate is going to prevent you from experiencing forgiveness and peace. I want to help you get to that point, it's maybe the most important goal in this whole process."

Cort nodded but didn't reply. He tried to imagine the concept of forgiving the truck driver. While it seemed like an impossibility, he remained quiet and waited for Dr. Galley to continue.

"Now, Mr. Palmerton, Cort, I'm not sure I understand the guilt you're feeling. What could you possibly have done to prevent that accident? There's nothing…"

"There was!" Cort cut the doctor off, determined to tell him a truth he hadn't been able to voice to anyone. He softened his tone and started again. "There *was* something I could have done."

He proceeded to tell the doctor the events of that fateful day, including the part about the last conversation he'd had with Celeste. Cort explained that if he'd just directed her to drive further down the ramp and off the roadway, she'd have never been hit by the truck. He wiped tears with his sleeve, ignoring the tissue box on the end table. Finally, he finished talking, and awaited what he assumed would be some awkward response from the doctor.

"Cort?"

"What?" Cort stared at the rug under his feet.

"Look at me, Cort." Dr. Galley waited as his patient slowly lifted his gaze from the floor. Their eyes met, and Galley spoke again. "That's bullshit!"

There had been a few rare occasions when Dr. Joseph Galley dropped the psycho-babble technical terminology and spoke to Cort from the heart. Apparently, Galley decided this was an occasion warranting a painfully honest directive. Cort hesitated at the doctor's words. A bit confused by the tone and language, he asked for clarification.

"What's bullshit?"

"The idea you could have prevented that accident, Cort. That's total bullshit." Galley paused and let it sink in, then continued. "You did what any normal clear-headed person would have done in that situation. You correctly advised your wife to stay put until help arrived. That was the correct suggestion. Period! There's no way in hell you or anyone else could have predicted that some out-of-control truck would be coming down the ramp at that very point in time. You told me the driver was off his route and the truck wasn't even supposed to take that exit. You realize how unlikely that scenario was, Cort? The nearly impossible coincidence of that situation?"

Cort opted for a tissue to wipe his eyes and nose this time. "I don't know."

"Yes, you do know." The doctor retorted abrasively. "You're an intelligent man, and you know the odds were one in a million... maybe one in ten million. These feelings are normal, Cort, so I do get it. You're grieving, and grieving is a process. There are stages, and I'm sure you'll experience them; denial, anger, depression, bargaining, and eventually acceptance. Unfortunately, grief is also a breeding ground for guilt. So again, I get it, but this whole notion that you could have prevented it. It's total bullshit!"

Cort and Dr. Galley delved deeper into the stages, and it all made so much sense to Cort. Fourteen minutes later, their session ended. Cort stood and walked to the door, feeling much lighter as he stopped and shook Dr. Galley's hand.

"Thanks, doc. Thanks for the sessions. This one was by far the best, and quite frankly, the only one that I'd pay $217 for again."

Dr. Galley returned Cort's sarcastic grin and reciprocated his vigorous handshake.

"I won't be returning, Dr. Galley, but I'd recommend you to anyone needing psychiatric help." It was the best compliment Cort could think of on the spot.

"Thank you, Cort, and please do. Seems I'll have an open spot on my schedule going forward." The two men exchanged nods and smiles, and Cort began to walk out. "Wait, Cort, you mentioned earlier about the music. I'll send you a link to a song later. Something you said today reminded me of it. I know it won't be easy, but try to listen to it."

While Cort thought it very odd that a doctor would recommend music to one of his patients, he politely agreed.

"I'll give it a shot, doc, thanks."

He left and closed the door, deciding he'd come a long way since that first session. He'd always heard the cliché advice, that talking out one's feelings and emotions was therapeutic, but he'd never believed it. Today he was a believer. After genuinely thanking Trina too, he explained it was his last session. She looked disappointed but smiled after Cort hugged her.

"I want to wish you and Joe the best. Hope everything works out and you two are happy together."

Trina's eyes got glassy. Cort chose not to watch her shed a happy tear, and instead waved one final time before walking out the door.

Chapter 41 — Lyrics

Cort peeked at the text from Dr. Galley several times. It contained a link below a graphic of a man gazing out to the rolling waves of the ocean. The image itself was comforting, and the water, as it always had, brought him a sense of peace and tranquility. But that's where the confidence in tapping the link ended. He was familiar enough with the music of Imagine Dragons, recalling a few of the popular groups' songs that got plenty of play on the radio. Cort was somewhat surprised, however, that a man Dr. Galley's age would be into the relatively young group.

Trina probably turned him onto their music.

The YouTube link beckoned him to listen, but Cort was still hesitant. A large part of his apprehension was the song title, shown next to the graphic. "Wrecked," seemed insensitive at best, given the way Celeste had died. Dr. Galley was fully aware of the accident, and yet he'd recommended this song anyway.

More than a day had passed since the text showed up on his phone. Cort took a deep breath and decided it was time. Sitting up a little straighter in bed, he set his book beside him, and picked up his phone. Staring at the text again, recalling the last time he'd listened to music hadn't exactly gone well, he convinced himself he was better than that now. The curiosity finally won the battle over anxiety, and he braced himself for what would surely be an emotional listen.

It began with a catchy instrumental riff, highlighted by guitar strums, and Cort liked the rhythms. As the singer's voice began, however, the song took on a somber tone. The first few lines described a despondent man, struggling to hold back tears as he reflected on the loss of a woman in his life.

"Christ, here we go."

Cort muttered to himself, but let the song continue. The man in the song continued describing his pain, and the "wreck" his life had become. Anticipating the second verse to be equally difficult, Cort swallowed hard.

They say that the time will heal it, the pain will go away
But everything, it reminds me of you, and it comes in waves

Another lump formed in Cort's throat as he digested the lyrics. The two lines hit his psyche directly, likely just as Dr. Galley had intended. He placed his thumb over the screen, ready to hit the pause button if need be.

These days I'm becoming everything that I hate
Wishing you were around but now it's too late
My mind is a place that I can't escape your ghost

Astounded at how much he related to the words, Cort assumed the song writer must have lost a woman he loved in his real life. While the lyrics were somewhat general, they seemed to tap into his own feelings of loss and guilt. The song continued, growing in power at each refrain. Holding back tears, Cort listened until the final verse was simply too much for him to contain his emotion.

These days when I'm on the brink of the edge
Remember the words that you said
Remember the life you led
You'd say, "Oh suck it all up, don't get stuck in the mud
Thinkin' of things that you should have done"
I'll see you again my loved one

As the song ended, Cort wiped his face with his hand and smiled, now understanding Dr. Galley's full intent. His psychiatrist had listened and connected his feelings of guilt with those of the man in the song. Cort played "Wrecked" four more times and decided that while the song was heart-breaking, it was somehow encouraging. He hadn't been able to totally shake the guilt of the "wreck" that ended Celeste's life, but the last session with Galley and this song had dampened the remorse connected to his decisions that fateful evening. The feeling of total peace was still on the distant horizon, but not nearly as far out of reach as before. He was beginning to believe that the accident could not have been prevented, no less undone, no matter how hard he "got stuck in the mud."

Despite the urge to write a thank-you letter to the Imagine Dragons, he turned his phone off along with the lamp on his nightstand. Lying there in the dark, some of the lyrics echoed in his head. The last line replayed in his brain, and he imagined it being sung in Celeste's soothing voice. He wondered whether he would ever *see again his loved one.*

Chapter 42 – Group Session

Nearly another week passed before Cort found himself sitting nervously in a circle of twelve other people. Josh and Shay were the only two familiar faces, but they brought him a degree of comfort. He'd been anxious for the entire 19-minute drive to the Pine Township Community Center, where the group met twice a month. Despite his anxiety, the session with Dr. Galley had given him incentive to "open up." While the remaining guilt was attached to a different issue than what he'd voiced to the doctor, Cort convinced himself that tonight he'd vocalize what remained of the morbid thoughts in his head. He decided the group, including Josh and Shay, could think whatever they wanted to. If this first group session also became his last, Cort could live with it. For a chance to alleviate more of the weight of remorse on his chest, it was worth the risk.

After a brief handshake and hug with Josh and Shay, he found his seat and took in his surroundings. The meeting room was bright and comfortable, with a muted paint scheme of light greens and yellows. The faint scent of a baked item was intertwined with the smell of fresh coffee, both of which settled Cort's nerves a bit. Debbie, the group monitor, was a woman appearing to be in her mid-50's. Her sullen expression was somewhat masked by the smile on her face and upbeat cadence in her voice, but neither concealed the pain of her past. Cort listened and studied her face as she made some brief introductory comments. He was sure that the heavy lines in her forehead were a result of more than just age. She finished up her spiel with some words that gave Cort an uptick in confidence.

"As always, we encourage our members to be as open and honest as they can be. And please remember what is discussed in this room stays in this room."

Starting with the woman sitting to Debbie's left, group members took turns speaking, airing out their feelings and sometimes asking for feedback from the other members. Some were brief, stating what they wanted to say in the span of under a minute. Others spoke at length. One man who introduced himself as E.J. verbalized his pain for thirteen minutes, stopping when a particular memory sparked an emotion so strong, he could no longer talk. The man pointed to the woman next to him and lowered his head. The speaking order moved in a clockwise rotation, and Cort listened to everyone. Another woman had Cort especially choked up as she spoke of her nine-year-old daughter. The girl had drowned in the neighbor's pool just this past June. As she described how much she missed her little girl, it was impossible for Cort not to think of Lucie.

Forty minutes passed before the progression reached Shay. Josh sat to Shay's left, and Cort was after him. Shay raised her hand and gave an abbreviated wave to the group before speaking.

"I'm Shay and this is my husband Josh." She mentioned their own names for the benefit of a few unfamiliar faces in the circle. "Neither of us are going to say much tonight. We're here in support of a friend, who is attending today for the first time. Please welcome, Cort Palmerton."

Several of the group members said, "hello Cort" or "hi Cort," but the room quickly grew silent again. Cort took a small sip from his water bottle and swallowed back his nerves.

"Hey everyone, thanks... thank you for welcoming me. My name is Cort." He paused and turned the water bottle in his hands, attempting to settle himself. "This will be tough for a few reasons, so bear with me please."

He inhaled a deep breath before continuing. "My wife of sixteen years was killed in an accident back in early February. It's just me and Lucie, my 10-year... well almost 11-year-old daughter." Raising his head, Cort looked around the circle of people, but avoided eye contact with the woman whose daughter had drowned.

A couple of the others offered him a solemn nod. Cort took another breath and spoke again.

"It's been tough on both of us, to say the least. I've had some dark thoughts. They were very dark a few months ago, and lately it's been a little better, but I'm still struggling with some feelings of guilt." Cort stopped speaking and gulped down the lump in his throat. He paused and contemplated ending his turn until the group monitor interjected.

"Would you like to talk about the guilt, Mr. Palmerton?" Her voice was deliberate yet compassionate, beckoning Cort to go on.

"Yes, I think I would. Thank you. I think I'm struggling with the fact that something good has resulted from the tragedy. I've been bonding more with my daughter, and it's been so positive for me. I feel like I'm getting to know her better than ever, and, well… so, I don't know." Cort looked to the ceiling, squinting into the illumination from the canned lights. "So, I have guilt about feeling good about it, because this bond between Lucie and I has grown as a result of…," glancing around the room again, there were more nods confirming they understood without him being more descriptive. He couldn't quite say the next words, but the silence was nonetheless broken.

"Yes, it makes total sense," Shay interjected and reached over Josh's lap to pat Cort's knee in a gesture of console, confirming Cort's intended sentiment.

The group monitor spoke again, as the room became silent. "Mr. Palmerton, did you want to continue, or just pass the baton?"

After another deep breath and a prolonged hesitation, Cort shook his head up and down then spoke again.

"I know that must sound terrible to all of you. I feel so much shame right now. I'm so sorry, believe me I am. I'd do anything to have my wife back. Anything. I would. But this conflicting sense of satisfaction over the better relationship with my daughter, well… I don't know how to escape the guilt. The pain of losing my wife was so bad at one point that I considered ending... ending my life." Cort paused at the feeling of Josh's hand upon his shoulder, fighting to hold his emotions. He continued with a crack in his voice, "The irony is that, if it weren't for Lucie, I'm pretty sure I'd already be dead."

Cort sunk lower in shame, and he contemplated jumping up and running out of the room. None of the other members in the circle knew quite what to say, and more than a couple dabbed at their eyes.

"I get it, Cort." Josh's steady voice came from his right side. "All of it makes sense to me. Shay and I found each other through our tragedies. We found strength and love in each other, but we both dealt with those feelings of guilt and regret as we thought about the separate tragedies... the circumstances that brought us together."

Cort cleared his throat, wiped his eyes, and turned to Josh and Shay. The couple nodded in affirmation, as did several of the other members in the group.

"Thank you, Josh, I appreciate that. And thanks to the rest of you. Thank you for listening to me. Sorry for taking up so much time. That's it. That's everything I wanted to get out tonight." Cort raised his left hand briefly, almost in a gesture of surrender.

The group monitor put her hands together mimicking a praying gesture and stood up in her spot.

"That was good, Mr. Palmerton. Very good. Thanks so much for being open and sharing that. It's that kind of courage we need to heal and move past our pain."

Debbie sat down, and with several of the other members, offered Cort a curt nod of approval. After a quick introduction, the woman sitting to Cort's left began speaking, thereby ending his time in the hot seat.

As he sat and reflected on what he'd divulged, a wave of relief and accomplishment washed over him. The fact his guilt was affirmed had not been an expectation, and Josh's comments served as an added bonus to the therapeutic session. As Cort inhaled full lungs of air then released them slowly and silently, a notable sense of well-being replaced the guilt and anxiety that he'd arrived with.

***

Thad set his fork on the plate, reached across the table and took Amelia's hand in his.

Just tell her already.

Chewing the last remains of the bite, he sipped his water and smiled at his wife, who was beaming back at him expectantly. She spoke before he could get the words out.

"How are you holding up? Everything okay?"

"Yeah, it's fine. I'm just nervous about, you know, telling Gracie."

He made the excuse, avoiding the opportunity to tell her what was really eating at him. Now was the perfect time to do it. Gracie was with her grandmother, Marilyn. She'd taken her only granddaughter to dinner at her favorite seafood restaurant, leaving Thad and Amelia with some rare time to themselves.

"Me too. But it'll be okay, Thad, you need to stay strong and have faith."

He squeezed Amelia's hand a little tighter, bit his tongue, and swallowed back his guilt.

Faith is going to be very expensive.

She had enough to worry about already, and while Thad knew his wife would understand the reason he'd cancelled the insurance, it wouldn't change the fact that they were on the verge of financial ruin. He'd get the money from the sale of Sea Sleigh, which would pay for the upcoming treatments, and everything would be fine. Once they got through it all, he'd tell her all about it, and in hindsight it would all be relatively unimportant.

Chapter 43 – Apprehension

Thirty minutes after he spilled his guts to Josh, Shay, and ten total strangers, Cort stood near the coffee thermos with his newest friends, making small talk and chewing on a freshly baked chocolate chip cookie.

"I hope this was a positive experience for you, Cort. Shay and I are glad you came."

"It was Josh, thanks. And thank you both for getting me here. I'm glad I came too, and I'll come back for another one."

"Good. That's good. Let us know when, and one of us will try to be here for the session."

Cort hesitated as he pondered his response. "Okay, I'll do that. It won't be until early December now though. Lucie and I have some traveling to do the next few weeks."

"Is that right," Shay flashed a smile of excitement, "anywhere fun?"

"Well...."

He hesitated for a second before making the decision to tell the couple what he and Lucie were up to. After the information he'd divulged to the group, Cort decided his travel plans should be easy to discuss. Plus, he was interested to hear their reaction. Other than Manny, Gabby, and his siblings, who were only in the loop for phase one of Cort and Lucie's agenda, nobody else was aware of their intentions. Cort decided it might be good to get some feedback from two rational and impartial people. Eight minutes passed as Cort unveiled the details of the upcoming sail and his and Lucie's intentions thereafter. While the couple listened, Cort tried to read their expressions. He assumed they were forming opinions, and figured Josh especially, given his nature of being a cop, would be a bit suspicious and paranoid. Cort was sure the part about being on a boat with two total strangers would send a red flag up in the Leonards' minds.

"So that's the plan, whadaya think?" Cort posed the question as he finished outlining their agenda.

Shay nodded at Cort then turned to her husband.

"Well," Josh began carefully, "that all sounds, um… exciting. I'm guessing you have boating experience then?"

"Yes sir, lots of it over the past 25 years or so. I haven't been behind the helm in quite a while, but sailing is like riding a bike. You know?" Cort didn't want either of them to worry, nor was he up for answering a lot of specific questions.

"I guess so," Josh hesitated, "I've never sailed, so I don't know. Shay did some sailing back in the day, right honey?"

Shay nodded, "Yes, I did, back when I was a little girl. I made the sail between Trinidad and Tabago twice on an uncle's sailboat. I don't remember much though - that was nearly three decades ago."

"Well then, how about we get you both on the water soon? Once Lucie and I are settled in, we'll make some plans for you two and your boys to come visit us on *Sea Sleigh*. That's the name of the sailboat we're buying."

The couple glanced at each other before smiling and nodding back at Cort. He sensed they were hiding a bit of anxiety at his offer. Shay spoke and addressed the bigger concern she'd apparently been considering.

"Cort, I don't want to sound like your mother, but, uh, how much do you know about these two people that you'll be alone with for over a week? Thad and Marilyn, I think it was?"

The question didn't exactly surprise him. He understood the concern, and realized it was not an unnatural one. He himself had been a little hesitant at the prospect of being alone at sea with two strangers, but he'd done his homework and was satisfied with his findings.

"Not to worry, Shay. These two are stand-up people. I did a little google search and was impressed. How about this - Thad St. Marie has two Olympic medals... a gold and a silver. For snowboarding!" Cort's question and answer held a tone of enthusiasm, and he raised an eyebrow to highlight his admiration.

"Oh wow, that's interesting," Josh offered his sentiment with a nod, and then got straight to his primary objective, "how about I just run Mr. St. Marie through my database at work? No harm no foul, right Cort? Probably just confirm what your impressions are?"

Despite a smidgen of hesitation at the proposed privacy invasion, Cort was quite appreciative of the offer. Josh was right, *no harm no foul*. And maybe the officer's affirmation that the man had a squeaky-clean past would set him at total ease. If, on the other hand, something not-so-positive came to light, that would be just as important to know.

"Thanks, Josh. Why not, right? If this guy is an axe murderer, it's best I know before I fall asleep in my bunk quarters."

Cort grinned large and the three of them shared a cursory laugh. They exchanged quick hugs, said good-byes, and departed on a promise to get back together after the Thanksgiving holiday.

As Cort navigated the twenty-minute drive back home, he thought about Josh's offer and hoped nothing too alarming would be uncovered about his future shipmates. Departure was less than two weeks away, and he'd checked off just about everything on his to-do list. He couldn't imagine anything more disappointing than learning the kind of information that would debunk his and Lucie's plan. There was another part of his psyche, albeit a smaller one, that wondered if he'd proceeded in haste. His gut told him the decision was both a good one and a necessary one, and their road away from gloom was not a traditional road at all. Their route to a life of adventure and contentment was in fact a waterway; the seas and oceans between faraway lands were beckoning them. Cort admitted to himself he and Lucie had taken somewhat of an unconventional approach thus far, but everything was nonetheless coming together successfully.

Celeste, you would be on board with all of this, right?

***

Lucie's eyes were focused on the TV, as if she were totally into the movie, but with more than an hour of the flick over, she didn't even know what it was about. Her mind was somewhere else, thoughts floating through her brain aimlessly, like pieces of driftwood. She glanced over to Lilly at the other end of the couch and felt just a little bummed that their friendship would come to an end soon.

Not a big deal. Lilly's afraid of her own shadow. We probably wouldn't be friends too much longer anyway.

She pushed the thought away and let the others return. They weren't altogether better. The images of the sailboat itself were exciting, flipping through her brain just like the pictures they'd scrolled through on website for Sea Sleigh. The positive images were balanced by negative ones. Scenes of a rubber raft like the one her dad had called the lifeboat. She saw the clips in her mind of her father, hunkered down in the floor of the raft as it was battered by a massive storm. He was alone, and helpless, and she couldn't get to him.

Stop it, Lucie.

Every few minutes she'd mutter the words to herself, as the animated characters on the television screen she was watching danced and sang happy songs.

They'd be leaving for Austin soon, and from there he'd take off for Rhode Island. She'd looked it up on google maps using the school computer earlier this week. It was far away from Pennsylvania, and even further away from Texas. She wouldn't see him again for almost a week and a half. It seemed so long when she did the math and broke it down. *240 hours.* If each one lasted as long as the first half of this movie had, it would feel like forever.

Mom, I can't be there with dad on that boat, so you'll have to watch over him for a while.

Chapter 44 – Separation

After a quick thank you and good-bye to his in-laws, Cort grabbed his duffel bag from the rear cargo area and shut the hatch. The impulse to cancel the whole plan was nearly overwhelming, but he fought the urge, took Lucie's hand as she exited the rear-passenger side door, and walked with her under the Departing Flights sign. The last few weeks had progressed so fast, and now that November 10th was here, he felt rushed. A bead of sweat hung above his eyebrow, and while the Texas air was a bit sticky, Cort had no doubt the perspiration was a result of anxiety.

Relax, it's okay.

Everything had been taken care of, and the excitement had built as each preparation had been checked off. Passing through the sliding doors, the cooler inside air slapped him in the face, jolting his senses like a wake-up call. Despite the reassurance from his inner voice, he was second-guessing everything. The thought of saying good-bye to Lucie felt like jumping through the surf and swimming out into the open ocean. As he pushed his feet through the doors and into the lobby area, a wave of separation anxiety threatened to wash him back to shore. A glance backwards was made to confirm Manny and Gabby were still parked in the drop off area. The red hazard lights blinked on their SUV like a warning signal, seeming to relay the subtle message to his brain. *Think this over, it's not too late to change your mind.*

This sudden hesitation was unexpected, even confusing, and Cort was conflicted by his thoughts. As he'd told himself and Lucie numerous times over the last couple of months, there was nothing to worry about. Attempting to shift his brain back into logical gear, Cort replayed the phone call with Josh Leonard in his head. The trooper had run Thad St. Marie through the database and confirmed all was secure. "His last name may as well be Thad St. Teresa," Josh had joked. According to police records, the man had no priors. In fact, there'd only been one ticket on Thad's motor vehicle record in the past 10-year period; a measly stop sign citation. *Whoop-dee-doo.* If anything, Cort should be more concerned about Thad's mother, Marilyn. Her motor vehicle record contained a DUI, the occurrence transpiring eight years ago. Not a huge concern, although the premise of Marilyn steering the boat under the influence did cross Cort's mind.

"Are you okay?"

Lucie's voice snapped him back to reality as he shifted his eyes from the escalator, turning to see her watching him closely.

"Sorry, Lucie, just trying to get my bearings." He lied, hoping not to set off any alarms in his daughter's head. "There it is. Down that way to security."

Putting his duffel bag on the ground, he squatted to Lucie's eye-level.

"You be good for Grammy and Pappy, okay, Luce?"

"Yeah. I'll be good."

He could see in her face that she was fighting the urge to cry.

"Listen Lucie, I hate to be away from you right now, but we both knew this was coming, and we both know it's necessary if we're gonna sail around the world. Right?" Cort stated it matter-of-factly, as much to convince himself as he did for his daughter's sake.

"I know."

Her lip quivered, sending a shot of contrition through Cort's gut.

"Everything is going to be fine. You have nothing to worry about. I have nothing to worry about." Cort brushed a strand of hair away from her eye and kissed her forehead, the prickle of his beard invoking a muted smile across her lips. "You know I love you more than anything, right?"

Nodding, Lucie squeaked, "I love you too Daddy," then hugged him tight.

He held her for an extended embrace, kissed her head again, then directed her back to the waiting car. As she composed herself and let him go, his chest compressed, forcing out a long breath, and it took all the strength he could muster to keep from running after her. Before she walked back out the auto-sliding glass door, she turned to wave, and called out over the dull hum of the Austin-Bergstrom airport chatter.

"Don't forget when you get there, text me a picture of the lifeboat."

Cort smiled, waved, and yelled back to her, "I will. See you soon, Lucie."

As she disappeared behind a group of would-be travelers entering the airport, he snagged his duffle bag, then watched through the wall of glass as their car pulled away. Urging himself to keep it together, he turned around and walked towards the signs directing patrons to Security. *Security*. He silently wished security was available for purchase, as his psyche could certainly use a boost of it right now. Convincing himself that the path he was embarking on was the correct one, Cort mumbled the four words again under his breath.

"See you soon, Lucie."

***

As he brushed the strand of hair away from her eye, Lucie watched her dad intently, burning his features into her memory. She wanted to be able to pull up his image in her brain at any point while he was gone. His kiss on her forehead sent a wave of reassurance through her young mind. There was something about the scruffy facial hair that brought her comfort. Maybe it was because her mother always liked it too. Mom once told him it made him look stronger. His strength had always made Lucie feel protected, and his toughness was more important to her now than ever. She was glad that he'd chosen not to shave for this trip. Watching as he pulled the phone from his pocket, holding it just above his waist, she was confused at his need to check the time. Again. She glanced at his screen - 10:17 A.M. She knew from a conversation in the car five minutes ago that he had plenty of time to get through security and to his gate. The troubled look on his face confused her, but it wasn't an altogether unwelcomed feeling. Part of her hoped that something had gone wrong, and he'd have to reschedule his flight for a later date.

After a long hug and a brief pep talk, she knew he wouldn't be turning back now. Reluctantly, she did as he told her and started her walk back to Grammy and Pappy's car. Before going through the sliding glass doors, she turned and reminded him one more time about the lifeboat. Holding back her tears just long enough for him to answer her, she turned away and sobbed, then prayed during the entire drive home for his safe return.

Chapter 45 – Connection

For the first ninety minutes of the northeast bound flight, he kept his mind occupied with reading. With more than an hour left before landing in Providence, he closed the back cover, pondering the story and the fate of the main character. Telepathically, he sent the message to Celeste - *I think he made it.* Cort desperately wanted her to be sitting beside him now. They'd talk about the best parts of the book and discuss the ending in depth. Instead, he stared out the small window and hoped she'd interpreted it the same way he had.

For the remainder of the flight, snippets of Celeste traded turns with images of Lucie, playing through Cort's brain like he was flipping through a photo album. Despite the effort to stay focused on the happier times they'd all shared, he couldn't seem to control the programming - clips from the day of the accident featured prominently on the screen inside his head. It wasn't until the wheels touched down at T.F. Green International, that he was able to transition his thoughts from the past to what was coming in the very near future.

As instructed, he texted the number Thad had provided, letting the driver know he was off the plane. The driver shot a thumb's up emoji back for confirmation. He pulled up to the curb just as Cort walked out the set of double doors. Perfect timing.

Cort noted the difference in air temperature. It was mild, much more than he'd expected for Rhode Island in November. Inhaling a deep breath of the 62-degree New England air, he watched the black Ford Expedition pull up to an open spot. A well-dressed man in his mid-40's stepped out to greet him.

"Mr. Palmerton?" The man with salt-and-pepper hair and beard reached his fist outward for a bump.

"Yes sir, that's me." Cort bumped the man's fist with his free hand and smiled. He recalled the email with Thad's description of the driver who would pick him up. Now, as Cort watched the man with lentil-brown colored skin and friendly eyes, he made the connection to Thad's message and nodded a silent confirmation. The driver introduced himself with a name that Cort couldn't quite repeat correctly. After taking Cort's duffel bag and setting it in the rear cargo area, the driver turned to Cort again.

"Everyone calls me Kal. It's much easier to pronounce. Is that your only bag?"

"Nice to meet you, Kal. Everyone calls me Cort. Yep, that's it, one duffel bag for the next week or so." Cort shrugged, signifying he understood the question. It didn't seem like much, given the probability of cold weather and duration of time that he'd be away. Ironically, the driver had no idea that Cort was carrying enough mental baggage to fill an oil tanker ship.

Despite an earlier text warning from Thad that his driver was a talker, Cort sat in the front passenger seat of the SUV. Eager for a distraction, Cort buckled his seatbelt, scanned the vehicle's interior, searching for something quick and simple to initiate a conversation. Moving his eyes over the dashboard, Cort was taken back to another Ford Expedition he'd been in – Officer Josh Leonard's police cruiser. He pushed away the thought. A glance at Kal's dash-mounted name-placard triggered Cort's next question.

"So, Kal, where you from?"

"I was born in Boston, but I've lived outside of Providence for almost twenty years now. My father is from India, in case you were wondering about my last name."

Cort cleared his throat, caught off guard the driver had picked up on his observation.

"Oh yeah? I've never been to India, but I'd like to check out the country someday."

A half minute later, Kal was delving into his family history, describing the way his father and mother (a Peace Corp volunteer at the time) met in Calcutta back in the early 70's before moving to the United States. Cort listened and grinned for the most part, but his mind drifted to Lucie off and on as the driver synopsized the past two generations of his lineage.

After Kal's background, the topic of their discussion switched to Thad's family. For the remaining 14 minutes of their drive, Kal described his relationship with the St. Marie family, complimenting the way they'd treated him over the eleven years he'd been driving for them. By the time they reached their destination, Cort felt an even greater degree of comfort about the people he was about to meet in person. The car eased off the road into the parking lot of Belmont Market, a high-end grocery store where Thad had set up their rendezvous.

The plan was to stock up on a week's plus worth of food and beverages, drive straight out to the St. Marie's house where Sea Sleigh was moored, then pack up the boat and pull anchor. If they were efficient, there'd be a solid two hours of daylight left to navigate through the bay and the first few miles of open Atlantic waters.

Parked for less than three minutes, Kal pointed to another car pulling into the lot.

"That's them." He smiled and waved through the windshield.

The vehicle that parked next to them was a small Honda SUV that appeared to have some miles on it. Cort had been expecting something much larger and much newer to serve as transportation for a wealthy real-estate mogul. *Interesting.* They waited until Thad and his mother, Marilyn, climbed out of their vehicle, before exiting the Ford.

Mother and son exchanged genuine hugs with Kal before turning to their guest. Cort extended his hand as the pair approached. Thad took it in his right hand, cupped his left hand over Cort's and his own, and squeezed firmly as he gave two curt shakes. The power in the man's hands and confidence in his smile was not lost on Cort as he studied the features of the Olympic athlete. There was no less than a 4-inch vertical differential in Thad's favor, but his height was only part of what intimidated Cort. The abundance of raw good looks and ruggedness in the man's posture was impressive, and Cort did his best to reciprocate a confident strength in his own grip.

Marilyn stepped forward and offered Cort a hug he sensed held a degree of compassion.

"So nice to meet you, Marilyn." He offered the pleasantry while returning her hug.

Cort was impressed by her appearance too. She was an attractive woman, maybe mid-60's, and in good shape. A bit shorter than Cort was expecting, given the height of her son. Her white hair still had plenty of body, settling an inch or two above her cream-colored cable-knit sweater. Cort was reminded of the mother of Jason Vorhees from the 80's horror film, Friday the 13th. Marilyn's features, however, were kind and soft, and Cort was certain he wouldn't need to cut her head off with a machete at the end of this excursion.

After some brief inquiries about Cort's flight, the trio said 'bye' to Kal, and mother and son slowly began moving towards the front entrance of Belmont Market. Cort lingered behind with the driver.

"Take care of yourself, Kal. Thanks for the ride and the company." Cort shook his hand then put two $100 bills in it.

"Peace to you, my friend." Kal shot him a wink before climbing back into his Ford, flashing Cort a smile through the car's window before pulling away.

Trotting, Cort caught up to his new companions and they all went through the automatic doors together. Thad pulled three separate shopping carts from their docking station, wheeling one to his mother first, then to Cort, keeping the last one for himself.

"Cort, keep in mind we'll be out there for at least seven or eight days, maybe more depending on the weather. We've got two oversized coolers on the boat that should keep things cold for four to five days, and a working refrigerator that'll be on for the duration. So, there's only one rule as you pick out what you want to eat this week," he paused and put his finger in the air for a bit of effect, "get whatever the hell you want."

Marilyn giggled nervously and shot her son a glare, "Watch that mouth, Thaddy."

"I mean *heck*. Get whatever the heck you want. Sorry, Mom." He smiled and patted his mother on the back.

Smiling at their banter, Cort offered a thumbs up to the idea of having no-limits on food choices. He thought about his own mother, imagining how much she would have loved to be making this sail with him. Thad's voice interrupted his daydream.

"Also keep in mind that pre-prepared foods are gonna be a lot easier to make than cooking something from scratch," he turned to Cort and continued, "a boat moving up and down isn't the ideal chef's kitchen. Anyway, get whatever you like."

Cort simply nodded, still unsure what to make of this most unusual shopping excursion. He stayed behind Thad and Marilyn, watching them put item after item in their carts. Everything they were choosing looked very appetizing, and he contemplated just putting his cart back. Twenty-six minutes later, Thad and Marilyn had each amassed a heaping cart full of food. Cort had accrued a couple dozen items himself, including a prepared meal that was highlighted by sesame noodles and water chestnuts. Holding it up for them to see the package, Cort asked if they were okay with the Asian dish. Both agreed it sounded great. The three rolled to the checkout line and spent another ten minutes having everything scanned and bagged. When the cashier mentioned the $579 total, Cort stopped loading the bags into the carts for a brief second. It was the highest food bill he'd ever witnessed. Despite his mixed feelings about what was to come, one thing was for sure this week – the three of them would be eating like royalty.

Chapter 46 — Say Cheers

"Hey, hon, we're just pulling up the drive now."

Thad answered his phone and spoke to someone Cort could only assume was his wife. He smiled as he signed off.

"Okay, see you in a little bit."

Thad put his phone down as they rumbled over the cobblestone driveway, bringing the car to a stop at the end of a seven-foot-high Holly hedge. Beyond the wall of shiny green leaves on one side and the house on the other, Cort's eyes were treated to a most spectacular view.

"Amelia and Gracie will be back in about twenty minutes," Thad spoke to Marilyn first, but then looked to the back seat, "we'll get all the food and our bags loaded Cort, then you'll meet my wife, daughter, and cousin before we shove off. With any luck, we'll be pulling anchor in less than an hour."

Cort kept eye-contact with Thad, but his peripheral vision was elsewhere. From his vantagepoint in the back seat, he could see a portion of the dock jutting out into a section of magnificent blue water. The sparkling bay spanned nearly a mile before land was reached on the far side. Though the water view to the left side was blocked by the side of the house, Cort predicted that the sailboat was anchored just beyond his line of sight.

"Sounds good," Cort acknowledged Thad's words, but his mind remained focused on what he couldn't see. After exiting the car, Cort couldn't resist ignoring the luggage and walking around the front end to gain the full view of the bay. She came into view immediately, reminding him of one of the pictures he'd seen on the St. Marie's Facebook page. There she was, the 2016 Leopard 46 catamaran, in all her glory. Built by Robertson and Caine out of South Africa, Sea Sleigh was one of the most sought after makes and models on the market. Her sleek lines and masterful craftsmanship exuded quality, sparking a shot of adrenaline into Cort's bloodstream. Bobbing serenely, in a setting that would make most postcards jealous, the beauty of what Sea Sleigh represented was overwhelming. For Cort, it was like that exhilaration of getting the first glimpse of your brand-new house, multiplied times ten. Nearly at a loss for words, Cort managed a short sentence that brought a smile to the faces of his new friends.

"Oh wow, look at that."

"She's a beautiful lady for sure," Marilyn concurred his sentiment as she opened the rear hatch.

"I'll grab the wagons," Thad's words seemed to carry a forced enthusiasm, as he disappeared through a door in the side of the garage.

Within a couple minutes, both men were pulling two large wagons full of groceries down the gently sloping backyard towards the dock. With Thad leading, the men navigated their loads easily down to an opening in a two-foot-high stone wall that bordered the far end of the property. Thirty feet beyond the wall, the edge of the grass met a metal ramp attached to the dock. The first portion of the dock was an incline, making for a moderately difficult pull, but it transitioned into a run spanning seventy-five feet of level boardwalk. The final section was a short decline, ending on a small 10' X 10' landing area that had railings almost all the way around the perimeter. The exception was a 3-foot-wide opening in the far-right corner, where a safety chain was anchored to the top of one side and clasped to an eyehook on the other. At the floor level, an affixed metal ladder extended a few inches above the deck boards and led down nine feet to the water. As they were approaching, Cort had seen a part of the rubber raft floating near the bottom of the ladder. Now on the end of the dock, he could look over the edge and see it completely. After a quick inspection of the raft, his attention shifted elsewhere as Thad descended the ladder. While the captain pulled the lead rope attached to the dock and guided the raft under his feet, Cort's eyes were glued to the sailboat that floated in the deeper water just 100 feet away. He was daydreaming about being behind the wheel when Thad's voice interrupted his musing.

"Cort, you and Mom can start handing bags down. I'll fill the raft and take it all out to Sleigh while you two make another trip to the car."

Cort turned around, startled to see Marilyn; he hadn't even noticed that she'd followed them to the end of the dock. As Captain Thad instructed, Marilyn and Cort took turns handing bags of food and ice down until both wagons were empty. On the way back to the car, Cort led the way and Marilyn towed her wagon behind him. After a couple glances back at the boat, his eyes began to focus on the house and property in front of him. The home was a sprawling Cape-Cod-style estate, clad with a gray shake and outlined in white trim. Black shutters and an oversized red brick chimney gave it additional depth and texture, and high-end brushed-bronze light fixtures added to its richness. A small semi-private courtyard opened into ½ acre of lawn that was peppered with mature trees and shrubs. Edged flower beds of dark mulch lined the perimeter, and despite the lack of color in November, the manicured landscaping framed the picturesque home perfectly. Cort felt a slight sense of envy, but for the most part, the view brought a feeling of comfort and happiness.

Getting their food, clothes, and miscellaneous supplies from shore to boat turned out to be a more tedious endeavor than Cort had expected. After loading the wagons a second time, there were still several bags of food in the car, not to mention his personal belongings. His patience waned as his eagerness to board Sea Sleigh continued to build by the minute. Cort made a mental effort to curb his anticipation, knowing they still had to meet Thad's family. The super-hero-like captain would want to say his good-byes, and there would surely be some last-minute loose ends for him to tie up. It wasn't until after they'd completed the third and final trip from the Honda to the dock, that Thad's wife and daughter appeared in the yard.

She was attractive, a trait that Cort had expected well before he saw her. Even if he hadn't seen the pictures on the social media sites, he'd have been shocked if the wife of "Thor" was anything less than visually appealing. As the three of them approached the woman and child, Cort took note of a warmth in the wife's appearance that he hadn't picked up on in the photos. Maybe it was the shape of her lips, or the meandering auburn hair, or simply the earthy hue of her cashmere sweater.

Moving his eyes to the little girl, Cort took note of certain features - obvious tells that she was the St. Marie's daughter. Bringing his gaze back up to the woman, Cort focused more on her eyes as Thad introduced her, noting something else. It was possible he was misreading her face, but beyond the welcoming smile, he sensed a disquiet in her expression.

"Cort, this is my wife, Amelia." Thad's tone was business-like but pleasant enough.

"Hi, nice to meet you." Cort offered the generic greeting and unsure if he should shake her hand, he kept both to his side.

"Hi, Cort," Stepping twice in his direction, Amelia embraced him in a soft and brief hug. She released him quickly, but her right hand slid down his left arm and grasped his wrist.

"We really appreciate your help, thank you so much." Her head tilted slightly as a gesture of sincerity.

Cort didn't respond. As he tried to analyze the remark, Amelia let go and stepped backwards next to her daughter. Despite his confusion, Cort refrained from crinkling his brow, instead masking his uncertainty with a muted smile. He wanted to thank Thad and Amelia profusely and tell them that it was *he* who was receiving the favor. Instead, he studied Amelia's face as much as one could in the span of two seconds, pondering her behavior and perceiving it to be odd. There was something beyond the pretty, but he couldn't quite place it. A concern in her brow, maybe a sadness of sorts, possibly even a sickness. His eyes lingered ever-so-briefly as he studied her features. Stepping to his right, he moved in front of the daughter, who he guessed to be about seven or eight years old.

"And you must be Gracie?" Cort stooped and extended his hand. With an abbreviated smile, the little girl shook it in haste before turning her head coyly into her mother's leg.

Gracie had the same pronounced beauty as Amelia, muted by her cherub-like baby fat. Her eyes were bright and large, and she'd picked up the brilliant blue color in her irises from Thad. Oddly, like her mother, the little girl carried the same hint of woe in her eyes. As she shyly reciprocated Cort's greeting, he gave a warm hello and an exaggerated wave that was much too long. Gracie finally returned the gesture, waving her small hand before clinging tighter to her mom's side.

"Honey," Thad's voice cut the awkwardness, "can you take a picture of Cort, Mom, and I?"

His wife nodded and pulled out her phone while Thad stepped towards the knee-high stone wall that bordered the back edge of the yard. Cort followed Thad, and Marilyn joined them as she moved into position between her son and their very-soon-to-be second mate. Amelia shuffled a few steps to her left, putting the catamaran in the immediate background; the boat floating 100 meters behind them, appearing just an inch above Marilyn's head in the frame.

"Say cheers." She giggled to herself and watched the three people on her screen smile big.

Amelia clicked three shots, reviewed each one on her screen, then approached her subjects to share the best one with them. The vivid blue hues of the sky and water made a perfect backdrop for Sea Sleigh and her forthcoming passengers.

The four of them looked at the phone together for a second, quite content with the still-frame image of optimism. While none of them could know it then, there would be many times in the future when the photo would serve as a reference; a visual footnote to a story that would awe their children, their grandchildren, and generations beyond.

Chapter 47 – Lifeboat?

He was relieved the meeting with Katie was short and sweet, but the exchange of information they'd had wasn't exactly sitting well. Thad's cousin was pleasant enough and she wore a smile for most of their five-minute exchange of pleasantries. Explaining her new job training, and why she wouldn't be joining them, Katie said she was sincerely bummed about the situation. Cort remembered that it was her unavailability that catalyzed Thad's second purchase option, substituting Cort for Katie as the third mate on this sail. The brief guilt he felt was replaced by the feeling of serendipity, and he silently thanked Katie and her new employer.

The real unsettling information, however, came a few minutes into the conversation. Thad started by telling Cort that despite Katie's new job, she'd still be their eyes and ears back on the mainland - essentially their primary source of all weather-related information. The two cousins explained in tandem that she'd be utilizing professional grade weather tracking software, a program similar to what actual meteorologists use. Katie also made a point to say she was a huge "weather-geek," attempting to convey a sense of confidence and comfort to the man she'd just met.

Thad explained further, "I have the program app on my phone, Cort, but it'll be useless once we get more than six or seven miles offshore."

With a slight crinkle in his brow, Cort spoke, "Oh, I see, because we won't have any internet signal after that?"

"Correct. No internet or cell signal. Once we get out that far, our phones are useless except for taking pictures and videos."

Cort paused in consideration before continuing his thoughts, "So, how do you even get the weather reports from Katie?"

Thad nodded to his cousin, signifying Katie to answer the question.

"No worries, Cort, my cousin here has everything, including a SAT Phone. He checks in with me at least daily, more often if there's activity that calls for it."

Cort listened and made the quick assumption "SAT" was short for Satellite. He knew little about the technology, other than one could be used to make a call from a desolate area where there was an absence of cell towers. That tidbit of intel was only known because he'd seen Jurassic Park 3 at least ten times. After divulging the availability of the SAT phone, Katie turned to ask Thad a question, tempering her tone as to hide any hint of real concern.

"I assume you saw the two systems, Thad?"

"There was a brief mention on the weather channel this morning. Doesn't look like much," Thad shrugged.

Up and scurrying since 6:30 A.M., Cort hadn't caught any news all day. The weather channel would have been off his radar anyway.

WTH! Two systems?

As if he'd read Cort's thoughts, Thad turned to him with a slacken expression in his brow.

"I'm not worried, Cort. I think the first system is south of Jamaica and they said it's headed West… probably die out as it crosses over the edge of Cuba. The other one is just a small cell closer to Puerto Rico. It would have a long way to go north before we'd need to adjust for it. Katie will keep us in the loop either way."

Taking Thad's words as a prompt, Katie nodded at Cort and smiled, making him feel a bit better. A minute later, Katie was hugging the St. Marie family good-bye, then took off in a flash.

More hugs and kisses were exchanged between Thad, Marilyn, Amelia, and Gracie. The departure was heavy on smiles and optimism, overshadowing the apparent woe that Cort assumed was due to their temporary separation. He watched with a mixed sense of appreciation, anticipation, and sadness – excited to get underway, but already missing Lucie's presence.

Ten minutes later, the crew of three stood on the aft deck of Sea Sleigh. Marilyn began organizing items below, as Cort watched Thad push the thick-plastic-enclosed red button. It sent power to a small motor, which turned the gears hoisting their lifeboat out of the water. The raft rose until it hung suspended between two metal posts. Cort watched patiently as Thad ran line from small cleats on each post, through metal rings attached to the front and the rear of the raft, then back around the cleats. After securing everything, the captain pushed on the rubber hull, testing to ensure there was no front-to-back, or side-to-side swing. Confirming as much, Thad shot Cort a thumbs up, put his hands on his hips, and asked Cort the question he'd been waiting for.

"How about a quick tour before we pull anchor?"

A wide grin formed across Cort's mouth, "Absolutely!" As they turned towards the cockpit, Cort stopped abruptly. "Sorry, hang on a second, Captain. I need to get a picture for my daughter, Lucie."

Thad grinned, which Cort assumed was in reaction to being addressed as captain. Pulling his phone from his pocket and aiming it at the suspended raft, Cort took a shot from two angles, tapped some buttons, and sent his in-laws the photos via text message.

"Hey, Cort," Thad clarified, "you'll want to send any other texts or make any phone calls within the next hour. After that it's a dead signal just about all the way to Florida. I'm okay with you making maybe one or two quick calls from the SAT phone this week, but they're expensive. Katie and I will only use it for weather updates, and we keep the calls extremely brief."

"No problem, I think that was about it. Just a promise I made to Lucie… she wanted a picture of the lifeboat. Let me send another quick message and I'll join you in a second."

Cort opened the text he'd just sent to Gabby, instructing her to share the pictures with Lucie. A little embarrassed that he hadn't known about the cell signal until now, he added the following: *Also, we won't have cell signal out at sea, so I can't text/call you from my phone until we reach Florida. I may be able to call from a satellite phone later this week, but I'm not sure when. Hi to Manny and give Lucie a kiss from her dad. Thanks!*

Seeing the word "delivered" under the text box, Cort was satisfied he'd kept his promise, and turned to join Thad for a dime tour.

"You know that's not the lifeboat, it's just the dinghy."

"Huh?" Cort knew the term *dinghy,* which was slang for the tender, or the small craft that sailboat passengers used to get to and from shore. He was confused, however, at Thad's correction, not quite understanding the difference. In his experience aboard boats, the dinghy and the lifeboat were one in the same.

"Yeah, that raft is the dinghy, not a lifeboat." Thad put both hands in the air, raising his pointer and middle fingers on each one to signify quotation marks when he said "lifeboat."

"Oh, really?" Cort crinkled his brow, a bit embarrassed.

"Yes, but the good news is, Sea Sleigh comes equipped with a real lifeboat too. And on that note, how about we start our tour right here?"

Posing the rhetorical question, Thad stepped twice in Cort's direction, pulled up one of the seat hatch panels located just behind the cockpit. He pointed to an instructional placard that was affixed to a compacted 2' x 2' cube of thick rubber. The placard showed how to deploy the raft, which Thad proceeded to explain out loud.

"This is a Plastimo 6-person TransOcean offshore life raft, Cort. Top of the line. If you need it, you just pull this whole thing out and toss it overboard. It's tethered to the boat via a lanyard, which also activates the inflation. Very easy, and very critical in an emergency." Thad looked up and met Cort's eyes before continuing. "Under the seat inside the cabin, I also have a ditch-bag. It goes together with this life boat, so I'll show you that in a minute. The ditch bag contains extra medical supplies, water, food, flares, a vhf radio, and an extra epirb." Cort listened and didn't bother to ask about the meaning of 'epirb,' likely some acronym that he'd learn about soon enough. "In case the raft needs to be deployed, the only other thing you need to worry about is the ditch bag and getting the satellite phone in its waterproof pelican device, which by the way is buoyant."

Cort nodded, not ready to ask any questions yet, but very interested and a little bit anxious in this first segment of the tour. "Got it," was all that he managed to utter.

"Good, that's important. Not that our dinghy isn't important, Cort. In an emergency, and given time, I'd also want to release the dinghy too," he pointed at it, "that compartment in the front section has a gallon of fresh water, a lantern, some fishing gear, and a few other survival items. Plus, the motor would be helpful for sure. The gas is only gonna get you 20-25 miles, so if you're offshore further than that, then the real lifeboat will be much more useful. It's very probable you'd have plenty of time to get both, and whatever else you need. God forbid Sea Sleigh is ever damaged to the point where she can't be sailed, but if that happens, it'll likely progress slowly. Even when boats completely sink, which is difficult for a catamaran to do, they sink over the course of 30-60 minutes, a lot of times much longer. You might be in a bit of a panic, but you shouldn't be in a rush."

"Good to know, thanks, Thad." Cort's gesture of appreciation was genuine, and he nodded more than a few times to convey his gratitude to the captain. While he felt a little silly for not knowing the difference, the embarrassment was overshadowed by the sense that this vessel was going to be a whole lot safer than he'd bargained for.

"No problem. Now, all that said, don't worry about it. Chances you'll ever have to use either one in an emergency is slim-to-none. I have so many other safety features on Sea Sleigh… probably a good $40,000 in aftermarket safety equipment on this baby, and they're just overkill for that one in a million chance of something going terribly wrong. We'll get to the other stuff later."

Thad swiveled and was about to open the sliding glass door into the main cabin but paused and turned back to Cort again. He pointed at a key hanging on a small hook affixed to the door frame.

"This key is to lock the sliding door here. I recommend locking it anytime you leave the boat. In some countries that's more important than others, but I'd just make it a habit." He started to grab the door handle but paused again. "I just remembered; there was a copy we kept inside the drawer of the captain's desk, but it's missing." Thad shook his head and pursed his lips. "Damn it, I forgot to get one made. See, Cort, if you lock this and somebody is inside, they can't get out without a key. Oh well, remind me we need to make a copy when we get to Florida. In the meantime, do not lock this door if someone's inside. Understand?"

"I do," Cort nodded, "makes total sense."

"Good, back to the tour. Just relax now and enjoy this episode of Cribs."

Cort laughed, letting Thad know he got the reference. Cort recalled snippets from the MTV program that ran in the early 2000s, giving viewers a tour of celebrity homes via the camera crew's vantage point.

"Wow, Cribs, now there's a throw-back."

"Yeah, remember that, back when Shaq still played basketball, and didn't make cheap auto-insurance commercials."

Cort laughed again, and pointed in the direction of the hatch leading into the cabin, "Lead the way, Cap."

Chapter 48 – Come Sail Away

The seven-minute exploration of Sea Sleigh's quarters did not disappoint. Cort remembered most of it from the photos, but it was so much more special seeing it in person. From the well-appointed main cabin, complete with full kitchen, large dining table, and a beautiful teak captain's desk, they moved onto each of the three bedrooms. There were two sets of steps, one on each of the port and starboard sides of the main cabin, leading down into the sleeping quarters. Each of the bedrooms had its own full bathroom attached. Upholstery, bedding, and wall décor were all tasteful, with the right touch of nautical, but not overly so. Though he assumed Lucie might want to change some of the details in her own room, Cort was pleased there would be very little to do otherwise. The scent that tickled his nose was pleasant. Despite the tiniest hint of diesel, which he recalled was common and unavoidable, the primary smell was of something resembling fresh linens - probably from an air freshener or scented candle he hadn't seen.

They ended the tour in Cort's quarters. Dropping his duffel bag on the bed assigned to him, he looked around the cozy space. His eyes stopped on a painted black rectangular piece of wood affixed to the wall, just to the right of the port-hole window. The paint on the wood was purposely rubbed away in spots to give it an aged effect, serving as the background for a four-line poem, printed in stark white letters using an old-style font. When Thad turned and walked into the bathroom through an adjacent door, Cort paused and read the poem to himself.

Here's to tall ships, Here's to small ships,

Here's to all the ships on the sea.
But the best ships are friendships so,
Here's to you and me!

"Sea Sleigh is beautiful, Thad, better than in the pictures. This might be my favorite touch though." Cort pointed at the wall as Thad emerged from the bathroom holding a white plastic container with a red first-aid cross on the lid.

"Oh yeah, thanks. My wife picked it. Amelia pretty much decorated the whole boat." Thad grinned at the thought and changed subjects. "Hey, we'll be pulling anchor here in a minute and I'll fill you in on some more safety features as we motor out of the bay." As Thad spoke, he opened the lid of the white box, and showed Cort the contents. "This is just about every product on the market for seasickness. These are patches you put behind your ear," he pointed to a small band-aid-sized box, "and here's some cream you can rub into your skin too. The cream is supposed to do the same thing as the patch, but I don't think it's especially effective. Then we have Dramamine in this box. Pretty good stuff. But the best, strongest medicine is this Scopolamine. My personal recommendation." Thad picked the pill bottle out of the kit and held it up to highlight his not-so-subtle suggestion.

Cort scanned over the options, including a couple Thad hadn't mentioned, reading the labels as the captain patiently held the open box.

"You have your own little pharmacy here, Thad."

"Yeah, well, you can never be too prepared when it comes to this thing. Being sick can ruin the experience for sure."

"Do these patches work?" Cort was apprehensive about taking the pills, especially given the fact he hadn't eaten anything in six hours.

"I've never tried them, but Amelia seems to think they work. Then again, anytime we go out beyond the shelf, she takes Scopolamine. I think that's your best bet, Cort." Thad was doing his best to sway Cort without sounding pushy. Less than two hours away from being out in the chop, Cort decided to take the pill, but only after eating.

"How about I'll put a patch on each ear for now? Then after we eat, I'll take the Dramamine or Scopolamine. I'm just not a huge fan of pills, especially on an empty stomach."

Thad's face changed, and he wore an expression of muted concern. Without responding verbally, he opened two of the patches and stuck one behind each of Cort's ears. The silence was a bit awkward, but Cort stayed quiet. Next, Thad opened the lid to the prescription bottle, and tapped out two Scopolamine tablets.

"Here, put these in your pocket. We'll have dinner as we navigate out of the bay, and as soon as you're done eating, I'd like you to take both. Deal?"

Cort got the impression the offer was less of a suggestion and more like a rhetorical directive. He took the two pills from Thad's hand and shoved them deep into his pants pocket.

"Yeah, sounds like a good plan. Thanks."

"Alright then," Thad replied with notable satisfaction, "whadaya say we pull anchor and blow this popsicle stand?"

"Hell yes!" He fist bumped the former Olympian and followed him back up the steps and through the main cabin.

The two men walked to the front of the boat as Marilyn made her way behind the helm and control panel. He watched the captain detach the line from the mooring buoy before pulling anchor, which simply required flicking a switch sending power to an automatic winching system. With Thad's back turned, Cort stole a couple glances towards the shore, beyond Amelia and Gracie who were standing at the end of the dock, and up to the spectacular property and home.

That's one hell of a popsicle stand.

The captain shouted instructions to his mother as the anchor flukes separated from the bay's bottom. With the push of a button, Marilyn brought the engine to life and Sea Sleigh shifted directions. The sleek catamaran rotated eagerly until the bow reached a southbound alignment, at which point Marilyn straightened out the helm and pushed the throttle lever upward. With another button, Marilyn locked in the rudder and maintained course, then joined her son who'd already made his way to the aft deck. The two exchanged waves with Amelia and Gracie, who were standing at the end of the dock. Marilyn returned to the wheel while Thad lingered and blew kisses to his wife and daughter. After catching his projected smooches, they playfully returned his gesture and waved good-bye one more time. With a swift turn, Thad stepped toward the cockpit and as he passed, mumbled a few words to Cort. Something about a tradition, and he hoped Cort liked 'sticks.' Thirteen seconds later the speakers in the cockpit came to life. Grunting to himself at the sound of music, Cort knew there was nothing he could do except grin and bear it. *Think big picture.* Psyching himself into a positive frame of mind, he focused on the fact that after months of toiling and negotiating with both Thad, and himself, this voyage was finally underway.

As the vaguely familiar sound of soft piano keys overtook the low hum of the engine, Cort listened and tried to place the song.

I'm sailing away
Set an open course for the virgin seas
Cause I've got to be free
Free to face the life that's ahead of me

The lyrics and melody connected somewhere in his memories as Cort processed what Thad had said a few minutes earlier. *Oh, Styx, not sticks.* He made a brief attempt to block out thoughts of Celeste, trying to connect the words of the song to anything other than her. The attempt lasted a full 23 seconds - the next lyrics sending a shot of heartache through his veins.

Life Boat

And I'll try, oh Lord I'll try
To carry on.

Chapter 49 - Sesame Noodles

The waves grew as they passed Castle Hill Lighthouse, rolling into some two-foot swells as they traded the shelter of the land for the open waters of the Atlantic Ocean. Even as the catamaran began to move up and down, he'd confidently feasted on a hearty bowl of the sesame noodle dinner Marilyn had prepared. Still feeling great after the meal, his two shipmates had decided it was a good time to cover safety and the various emergency protocols. They'd be beyond the shelf and into deep open water within twenty minutes, and the seas would not be this calm again during the majority of their eight-day sail. Cort followed Thad around the deck; Marilyn went below offering to clean up the dishes. With the light so beautifully fading over the edge of the earth, the men reviewed several pieces of equipment including the harness and life vests, followed by a half dozen man-overboard instructions.

"These life jackets are the best on the market," Thad stated it confidently as he handed Cort one of them. "It's a West Marine offshore automatic inflatable life jacket with a harness. We have a bunch of the old-fashioned coast guard orange ones too, but they're shit compared to these. Wear this anytime you come outside."

"Okay, will do." Cort nodded, needing no convincing at all.

"These jackets are outfitted with an AIS man-overboard beacon, which would help aid in retrieval from local ships. Sorry, that stands for **A**utomatic **I**dentification **S**ystem. We also have two PLB's - **P**ersonal **L**ocator **B**eacons. One is normally just on mine and my Mom's harness. But I attached an extra one we had to yours for this trip. The general idea is that if I ever went in the water, whoever was left on board might not be able to operate Sea Sleigh well enough to find me, so having the PLB was an extra safeguard. My mom could probably get to me, but I'm not so sure Amelia could. Now, if Amelia went in, I'd likely be able to recover her as long as the AIS functioned. You get me?"

"I understand, yeah. Seems like a smart failsafe."

"Yes, for sure. And then in the off chance we both went overboard, the PLB's on our jackets would be critical. In my family, we have enough offshore miles and have seen enough rough weather to know the risks of going overboard are real."

Cort looked out to the horizon and the trillions of gallons of endless water and shuddered at the thought of floating out there alone.

"Did your mate that went overboard a few years ago have the PLB on his vest?"

"No, he didn't. We didn't have them yet, but that accident was an eye-opener. We bought them a few weeks after that sail." Thad paused and reflected. "It was really half a miracle we found him as soon as we did. And by *soon*, I mean two and a half hours after he went overboard. Not to scare you Cort, but the guy went in about 50 miles off Cape Hatteras. The water down there was probably 10-15 degrees warmer than the ocean you're looking at now. If he'd fallen in up in these northern waters, he maybe would've lasted an hour."

Cort pondered the scenario a second and responded, "Thanks, I think I'll be down in my bunk for the rest of the trip Thad." He smiled and pulled a laugh from the larger man next to him.

"Sorry, no more scary stories for now. Moving on. So, the harness on the jacket there," he grabbed the o-ring on the end of Cort's jacket harness and tugged it, "you'll clip one end of your nylon tether onto this ring, and when you're on deck walking around, I want the other end clipped onto the jacklines. Night or day. No exceptions."

Thad pointed to one of the jacklines, which had the appearance of a paracord. The line ran from stern to bow, and Thad pointed out there was one on both the port and starboard side. He also explained they were made from Dyneema, a material he claimed was both stronger and lighter than stainless steel.

"You can walk up and down this boat in the roughest weather imaginable, and as long as you're clipped into the jackline, you aren't going overboard. Got it?"

"Aye aye, Captain." Cort joked at first but adjusted his tone upon seeing the serious expression on Thad's face. "Yes, I understand."

Everything made sense, and Cort stayed focused while committing the most important items to memory. He had no reason to think this would be anything other than a safe and event-free sail, but still paid close attention to every detail. He perceived the additional safety measures as the icing on what was already a delicious cake. Presently, his hope was at its peak. This sail, he predicted, would open a window of clarity, and highlight the silver lining around the storm clouds in his head.

They'd almost walked the whole perimeter of the forty six-foot long sailboat and were back to the enclosed cockpit where the tour began. It was then Thad turned and posed the question.

"Hey, did you take the Scopolamine?"

"Oh, damn, no, not yet. The patches seem to be working fine, but I'll take the pills."

Thad handed Cort an unopened bottle of water he'd been carrying, "here, go ahead and take them now."

Obediently, and through slight embarrassment, Cort swallowed back both pills with a chug of water as Thad watched. Both men turned toward the operator's perch and continued the final piece of the tour. Cort was pleasantly surprised by the amount of cover it offered. The wheel, instruments, and captain's seat were protected by a roof and windshield. It would be cold; just as cold as the outside air temperature, but regardless of the weather, the person on watch would stay dry and out of the direct wind.

Thad scanned the darkening skies and decided to turn on the cockpit light before showing Cort the instrumentation. It was the instant that proved to be the point of no return. As the light brightened the inside of the cockpit, the glare on the interior of the windshield cloaked the outside from view. With the flick of the light switch, Cort's visual connection with the horizon disappeared, disconnecting his brain and inner ear. The queasy sensation pinged his gut a couple minutes later, mild at first, but it grew with each passing wave as he listened to Thad describe the symbols on the navigation screen.

"Thad, can we hold on a minute? I just need to step to the side of the boat for a second, just in case."

"Yeah sure, you okay?"

Unable to attempt an answer, Cort spun around towards the open side of the cockpit. As he stepped down and reached for the rigid cable railing, his stomach contents shot up through his throat. It was everything he could do to keep his mouth closed until his head was over the railing and clear of the starboard hull. A mix of sesame flavored noodles, water chestnuts, bile, and two small white pills sprayed out three feet horizontally before dropping down to the waves below. After a second solid hurl, he gathered himself, cleared his sinuses, and turned around. Thad was standing there with his hand extended, offering a damp paper towel.

Chapter 50 – All In The Legs (Day 282)

Twenty-six hours had passed since they'd left the calm water of Narragansett Bay, and Cort was still puking up anything that passed beyond his tonsils. He took a succinct bit of pleasure in nature's light show below him, pondering the chemistry of the bioluminescent algae as Sea Sleigh glided south at five knots. The pleasure was fleeting as another wave of nausea forced his stomach muscles to spasm - a purge of little more than an ounce of bile and water being the result. He'd been forcing tiny sips from the bottle, but even the smallest quantities refused to stay down. A heavy breath released after he cleared his throat and thought for the twentieth time about the Scopolamine.

Stupid ass!

Startled by the now familiar voice behind him, he flinched. Staying wrapped in a blanket and sprawled out across the aft deck, Cort cocked his head to see the captain standing there again with yet another paper towel.

"You alright?" Thad offered the towel and his sympathy.

"Yeah, I'm fantastic," a sarcastic smirk formed across Cort's lips before morphing into a pained smile. "Thanks, Thad."

They'd long since passed the point of land being visible. It was 250 miles back to the nearest coast, and the undulating swells had reached six to eight feet. The sway of the boat was relentless; up and down, to starboard and up, down and to port, rolling, rolling, rolling. Until yesterday, Cort was convinced there was no way to feel greater misery than what he'd been suffering since the beginning of February. He was wrong. It was difficult to fathom another seven days of this, but it was indeed the approximated sail time. That estimate didn't include the impending storm, which could extend their trip another two or three days and make for extremely rough seas. According to Katie's first weather report a few hours ago, the system had taken a turn north and gathered strength. Wind speeds had reached 40 mph, which was just over the threshold to qualify for a name. Both Thad and Marilyn agreed that "Dolores" was still hardly a threat, but her trajectory did create some muted discussion between the two.

"Hey Cort, I'm taking watch now. If you feel up to it, you can join me, and I'll show you some of the instrumentation?" Thad cordially made the offer, but Cort sensed his mood was growing increasingly unpleasant. He wondered if Thad's question was posed as more of an attempt to gauge his second-mate's current mental state.

"Why not, I'll give it a shot." Cort forced a chipper reply, covering up his hesitation to move into a vertical position. So far, the only modest degree of relief from the seasick symptoms came when he was lying down.

He pulled himself up and followed Thad through the cockpit, waving and forcing a smile to Marilyn as they passed the slider. She was sitting inside at the table, both hands around a mug, sipping something hot. Bringing the cup down from her lips, she returned the wave and the smile. Cort's grin disappeared as he thought about the liquid in her mug. While he couldn't see or smell it, just the image of it in his brain felt like a punch in the gut, and the nausea was instantly turned up a notch. He pushed through the feeling and stepped up to the captain's perch positioned just off the starboard side of the cockpit, where Thad was already tapping a few buttons on the nav screen. The space was roughly six feet by four feet, an area large enough for two people to stand in, but small enough that the men's shoulders weren't separated by more than a foot. The faint scent of Thad's deodorant caught in the wind and moved up through Cort's nostrils. Normally it would have been a pleasant smell, but normally Cort wasn't severely seasick.

"Cort," the captain pointed at the screen mounted on a small dashboard-like area in front of the helm, "this is a Raymarine A70 Charplotter, which is tied into the autopilot system and AIS. It's a great system and it's always running when the boat is in motion. This is the view you'll want to have up most of the time. Right here you can see your heading, along with…"

"Thad, sorry, hold that thought." Cort ducked back down a step and dashed through the cockpit to the aft deck again. A few minutes of hurling passed before he returned to the cockpit.

"Okay, I'm back, sorry."

He watched Thad turn in a jerk towards his voice, apparently startled that Cort had recovered so fast and maybe more because Cort was making another attempt.

"How about I just lie in the cockpit, and I'll listen and watch as much as I can from here. I just can't seem to be on my feet without getting sick." The cockpit was flanked on three sides by built in benches, each clad with large flat rectangular shaped cushions. Cort chose the one closest to Thad and sprawled out.

"I get it, buddy. That's not uncommon. How much sleep have you gotten?"

Cort shook his head solemnly, "Maybe two or three solid hours, tops."

"Oh boy," Thad pursed his lips, "that's no good. How about water? Have you been drinking?"

"I'm trying but it's not going to well. Seems like even the slightest bit of water is triggering intense nausea."

"I understand. Go ahead and get horizontal and relax. Try not to think about anything right now. You'll have plenty of time to learn this stuff once your inner ear recovers."

"Thanks, Thad. I'm sincerely sorry about this and feel like such an ass. I should be taking watches and giving you and Marilyn a break. I appreciate your patience."

"It's all good, bud, don't worry about it. You'll recover. Takes time." Thad focused on the electronic chart a few seconds before repeating himself. "Just takes time."

Five minutes passed in silence before Cort's voice broke the cool salty air.

"I'd be so scared of a shark."

"Sorry, what's that?" Thad cocked his head and made eye contact with Cort.

"Your friend who went overboard. I can't imagine how freak'n scared he must have been. Was it daytime or at night?"

"Day. Very early morning, but the sun was up. I'm not sure we'd have found him if it was dark."

"Jesus." Cort mustered the single word response as he pictured himself afloat, alone, in the vast expanse of the ocean. "He's so damn lucky a shark didn't find him before you did." As the images of that scenario popped into Cort's head, a strong twinge of nausea almost forced him to the aft deck again. Taking two deep breaths, the sensation subsided just enough for him to remain in his position on the cushioned bench.

"Sharks were the least of his worries, Cort." Thad spoke but his eyes remained focused on the screen in front of him.

"Really?"

"Yes, I'm serious. The chances of encountering a shark out in the middle of the ocean are rare. And even if one happened by, an attack would be very unlikely."

Cort wasn't convinced, and his expression must have said as much.

"I'm not making that up," Thad continued, "that's not the way sharks behave, despite all the bullshit reputation they have because of movies and sensationalized press."

"Wow, okay, I believe you, man, and agree." Cort assured Thad, who seemed to be very passionate on the subject of defending sharks, "I actually had a close encounter with some sharks many years ago, and you know what, in that situation your theory proved to be correct."

"There you go," Thad snapped, "but I promise you, it's not a theory. It's scientific fact. People's fear of sharks is so unwarranted. I mean, I get the fear, but statistically speaking, your chance of being killed by a shark is basically zero."

As he spoke, Thad pulled his phone from his pocket and tapped on his Photos app. Cort watched as he moved his thumb across the screen several times, scrolling through what Cort imagined were beautiful shots from all over the world.

"Here, look at this," he handed Cort his phone, "this is one of my favorites."

Cort recognized the subject of the photo as an enormous Great White Shark. The photo of the mammoth fish, which filled three quarters of the screen, had been taken from underwater. To the shark's left, in very close proximity, a man in full scuba gear was suspended in the dark blue ocean, aiming a camera at the behemoth. Cort studied the image before reading the caption below it:

> This Is The Most Dangerous
> Animal In The World
> Responsible For Countless
> Deaths Every Year.
> By His Side,
> We See A Great White Shark
> Swimming Peacefully.

Cort scanned the picture a second time and read the caption again. As the meaning registered, a grin formed across his lips.

"I like that," Cort offered a brief laugh through his tender throat and handed the phone back to Thad, "and I do like sharks. Let me tell you though, Lucie, my daughter, would really appreciate that. She loooves sharks. Maybe you could text that to me when we're back on land? She'd love it."

"Sure, absolutely. Hopefully I'll get to meet Lucie someday." Thad returned a smile before his face morphed into a serious guise. He put his pointer finger up, signifying the number one, and continued. "Your number one concern if you go in the water is body temperature. Ninety-nine times out of a hundred, hypothermia is what'll kill you."

"Yeah, I'm sure," Cort concurred, "that doesn't sound too bad right about now." He laughed at himself in jest, but Thad didn't appear to be humored.

"At first, you're just cold." Thad's voice took on a more consequential tone, and he glanced back to Cort to ensure he had his full attention. "When your core drops below 95, you start to shiver uncontrollably. It's very uncomfortable, but you're still in a normal conscious state. Doesn't take long before the sensation in your fingers and toes starts to fade though."

Cort nodded, choosing not to interrupt as he realized Thad was about to continue with the somber description of hypothermia.

"Below 90 degrees, the shivering intensifies. You fade into this different level of consciousness." He paused to check something on the nav screen, then glanced back to Cort and continued. "You're still there mentally for the most part, but your speech will start to slur. You might do irrational things, like take your clothes off, not even realizing you're cold anymore. Odd right?" He waited for Cort's reply.

"Yeah, that's very odd."

With a brief nod, Thad continued. "Now once that core temp gets down to around 83 degrees, you're in some big trouble. The shivering only comes in waves - no shivering at all for a stint, then violent shivering. And then the shivering will stop altogether. That's because the heat output from burning glycogen in your muscles isn't enough to counteract the dropping core temp. Your body shuts down to conserve glucose. Arms and legs start to get stiff because the blood flow is slowed, and the lactic acid and CO2 builds up in the muscles. Skin starts to get pale, pupils dilate, and the pulse rate falls."

Cort listened, quite impressed with Thad's technical terminology and biological knowledge. His overwhelming sense was still the nausea, but feelings of cold and anxiety were now close seconds.

"Below 80 degrees," Thad paused for effect, "your body goes into hibernation mode. Peripheral blood flow shuts down, which reduces your breathing and heart rate. That helps retain heat in most of your body, but it doesn't control the heat loss from your head. The body goes into what's referred to as a 'metabolic icebox.' You look dead, but technically you're still alive." Thad pursed his lips and glanced at Cort before finishing. "If you don't get treatment at that point, your breathing just gets so shallow that you lose consciousness, and at 75 degrees, the hypothermia is pretty much irreversible. After that, um, well… you know, that's it."

A few seconds passed as both men considered the prospect of death by freezing. Cort broke the silence.

"How about we talk about something more positive?"

"Okay," Thad chuckled a bit at the remark, "whatdaya wanna to talk about?"

Cort hesitated as he considered the question, sitting up some as he shifted his posture toward Thad a bit more.

"Tell me what it's like to stand on a podium and have an Olympic medal draped around your neck."

Despite the captain's position above and in front of him, Cort could see the wide grin form across Thad's side profile. Thad didn't seem entirely surprised by the question. Cort was sure he'd assumed that his buyer had done some due diligence research. After all, he'd obviously done his own homework to learn about Cort.

"Yeah, it's something. That silver was nice, but the gold was so much more special. Such a huge sense of pride, and confirmation - maybe even vindication of sorts, for all of those years of time and hard work that went into it. You know what I mean?"

"No, I don't know. I can imagine it's like nothing else though?"

Thad proceeded to tell a brief history of his life leading up to the 2006 Winter Olympics. Cort listened, impressed with Thad's accomplishments, but even more impressed with the humble nature in which Thad told them. He kept the descriptions of his achievements brief, even the most pivotal ones, and glossed over the highlights modestly. Cort peppered in a 'wow' or a 'sweet' here in there, letting Thad know how awed he was. When Thad finished his tale by describing the medal ceremony, Cort allowed a respectful silence to hang in the air as he pondered the man's victorious moment. Finally, his curiosity of the technical aspect drove him to his follow up question.

"So, Thad, what's the secret to becoming a world class snowboarder?"

Thad smiled again, a signal that both his pride and ego were swelling. Still, he chose an answer that muted both. He didn't boast about the fact that a high degree of strength and coordination were required, fostered by good genetics and countless hours of intense training. He also kept the fact that performing at that level, in that particular sport, required an edge of fearlessness and competitiveness that most humans never reach. Instead, Thad summed up his athletic prowess in a simple and somewhat sarcastic response, bringing a reflective grin to both of their profiles.

"It's all in the legs, my friend. It's all in the legs."

***

Thad was conflicted in his feelings for Cort Palmerton. While he really liked the man and future owner of his beloved sailboat, there was a growing concern about his condition. Despite the prediction that they'd bond and become good friends on this sail, Thad simultaneously wondered how long it would take the man to regain balance in his inner ear. When Cort dashed to the aft deck, Thad didn't watch, instead focusing on the bow and steering the ship. Through the muted sounds of dry heaving behind him, he struggled with emotions of sympathy and annoyance. This sail was not going as planned, and as much as he wanted to like his second mate, the fear of the man not being able to recover was plaguing his psyche.

He finished telling Palmerton about his Olympic experience, then thought back about what he'd told Cort earlier.

You'll recover. Takes time. Just takes time.

The words echoed in his own head as he and Cort stopped conversing. *Time* was the one commodity that Thad lacked, and as the hours ticked away, the pit of concern in his gut grew larger. Despite his best efforts to push them away, dark thoughts about his family's future were pecking at his brain.

We're running out of time.

Chapter 51 – Water

As the sun sunk down and the second day was left in their wake, Cort's health and hope continued to decay. He clipped into the jackline and made his way to Sea Sleigh's bow, settling against the front of the cabin where he could suffer in private. Staring down at his pale hands, he watched them shudder, and wondered about the cause. The temperature of the evening air, which he guessed to be around 50 degrees, wasn't uncomfortably cold. They were probably as far south as Virginia. The shaking could also be due to the chills – a symptom of the fever he could feel coming on. He'd ingested maybe two ounces of water, in total, since they'd left Rhode Island more than two days ago. The effects of dehydration were certainly a candidate for causing the shivers. Ignoring the irregular flutter of his heart, he thought back about his first four decades of life, and his absolute love of all things water related. As he gazed upon the Atlantic Ocean and reminisced with himself, Cort tried to make sense of how he'd physically and mentally reached this point in time… how something that had brought so much joy to his life was suddenly the catalyst for so much misery….

"Of course I cried when the doctor pulled me out, Mom - you know how much I hate when it's time to come out of the water." He'd joked to his mother one Thanksgiving, years ago, after she told the story of his birth during the holiday dinner.

Even before his earliest memories, Cort had always felt a strong connection to it. His mom affirmed baths were his favorite activity as a baby, describing how he'd lay there in the lukewarm water, smiling up at her as she sponged him clean.

He'd heard the many recollections of the infant years too. His parents would sit him on a blanket at the edge of the Allegheny River. While his mom, dad, and older siblings swam and fished, little Cortland was more than content to sit and toss small stones into the shallows. The splashing, the pattern of wind-induced ripples, the run of the current; the way the water interacted with its surroundings was enough to keep him entertained for hours.

The love of water grew as he did, and by the time Cort was a pre-teen, he wanted to be in or on the water whenever possible. Swimming, snorkeling, floating, boating; whatever activity enabled him to be surrounded by water became an instant interest. He'd naturally become a strong swimmer at an early age, both an expected development as well as a necessity, given his tendency to stay in the water for hours at time. Despite the shark encounter as a teen, he'd never developed a fear of the water, or for any of the creatures that called it home. If anything, the experience only increased his affection for the most plentiful substance on earth and further fostered his curiosity about the species that lived within it.

The fascination with H_2O became stronger as his knowledge of it grew. Its importance in the history of civilization and evolution of life in general escalated his obsession. The people closest to him were aware of his infatuation too. Shortly after the 1998 Adam Sandler film was released, his closest friends affectionately began referring to him as "Waterboy."

One day in tenth grade chemistry class, the teacher, Mr. Bryan, announced they'd be learning the symbols for all known elements on earth. He unveiled the periodic table, pulled down on a spring-loaded roller attached to the front wall of the classroom. Mr. Bryan started his lesson by apologizing for the large water-stain marring nearly a quarter of the chart. He said it had happened over the Summer, and the cause was a bit of a mystery given the fact that maintenance was unable to find any leaks in the ceiling. Without raising his hand, Cort blurted out a theory loud enough for the whole classroom to hear.

"Mr. Bryan, maybe one night the symbols had a little get-together, and a couple of the H's got too close to an O?"

It took a few seconds for his classmates to comprehend the wise crack, but the result was an entire room of students laughing out loud. As for Mr. Bryan, a huge grin formed across his face, and then he clapped. Years later, Cort had heard that Mr. Bryan kept the stained periodic table, using the quip with every ensuing class up until he retired.

In each of his college years, Cort left campus in May as soon as finals were over and bee-lined to the Maryland shore. For five straight summers, he worked at a variety of positions, including waiting tables, bartending, and checking I.D.'s at the nightclubs. His favorite job by far was at a small bayside marina, where he guided vacationers who came to rent wave-runners and pontoon boats. All the various positions offered good opportunities to make tax-free tips, hang out and party with friends, and take relief from the pressures of school. The real draw to the beach town, however, was much more basic than all those benefits combined. Living a couple blocks from the Atlantic Ocean was the only enticement Cort needed, and he spent his days off intermittently trading the sun and sand for the saltwater.

He was sitting in a fishing boat in his early twenties the first time he heard the song "Water" by Brad Paisley. It became an instant favorite. Over the past couple of decades, he'd listened to it a few hundred times. They never got old – the lyrics he facetiously imagined Paisley had written just for him.

The inexplainable draw to the water continued into adulthood, and if he wasn't immersed in it, he longed to be sitting somewhere in proximity to the water, staring upon it. Whether it was the ocean or a lake, a stream, or even a puddle, Cort could not help but be sucked in and hypnotized by its movement. The Gulf of California, on the Mexico side, had become a favorite body of water, not only for its beauty and warmth, but for its affiliation with the woman he'd fallen deeply in love with. One of his most cherished memories occurred in the waters just a stone's throw off the beach in Cabo San Lucas. He and Celeste, barely two years into their relationship, stood together in the waist-high water sharing both their gaze and their lips. As the tiny waves tickled their warm skin, he remembered thinking that no other place and no other person could be more perfect. He paused for a couple seconds, right after an especially sensual kiss.

"Ouch! Damn it, something just bit my foot!"

"Cort? Are you okay?" There was just enough concern in her voice to hide the hint of amusement.

"I don't know. Hang on a sec."

He put his left hand on her shoulder for balance, and lifted his right foot up to his thigh, as high as he could without falling over. With an expression of exaggerated pain, he reached into the water with his right hand, groping his own foot and seemingly searching it for an injury.

His fingers moved slyly to the bottom of his bathing suit, where the ring was secured to the inside fabric with a safety pin.

"Oh, wow." Cort looked up at Celeste as he clutched the diamond studded jewelry.

"What is it, are you hurt?" She seemed genuinely concerned now.

"No, I'm not hurt, but I know what bit me."

"What, Cort? What was it?"

"I was bit by true love Celeste." As the words came out, he stood up straight, took her hand in his, and kissed it softly before sliding the ring on her finger. "Will you marry me?"

A few weeks ago, despite the painful absence of his true love, he'd told Lucie the Gulf would be one of their planned sailing destinations. He wanted to show his daughter the beauty of the Mexico Coast, and more importantly, the place where he'd made some of his favorite memories with her mother. He'd been looking very forward to sitting on the deck of the boat, where he and Lucie could gaze at the setting sun's reflection atop the aqua-blue waters.

Now, as he leaned up against the exterior wall of Sea Sleigh's cabin and stared out upon the never-ending expanse of rolling waves, Cort winced a little as the confusion entered his seasick brain. This substance had brought him so much comfort, intrigue, and enjoyment throughout his life. Now it was doing just the opposite. The notion itself made him even more nauseous. He clenched his hands together in angry fists, but the trembling continued. An agonizing thought entered his brain. It was both unexpected and unwanted, yet it needled through his mind woefully. Despite his unwillingness to accept the premise, and against every fiber of his being, he theorized that it would be perfectly fine if he never saw water again.

Chapter 52 – Weather Report

Halfway through day three, the crew was tired and on edge. Cort's lack of energy was due to the inability to digest any food or water for more than 60 hours, and Thad and Marilyn were dragging because they'd each been forced to add 50% more watch time to their schedules.

Cort lay in his bunk with the stainless-steel salad bowl resting on the built-in shelf next to him. Thad had gifted the bowl to him yesterday morning, explaining there was no reason he should have to go up and out to the aft deck every time the urge to hurl beckoned. And while Cort still felt the need to get fresh air from time to time, the salad bowl had saved him several trips to his now infamous spot at the rear of the boat. Cort promised to buy Thad a new bowl as soon as they reached their destination, and Thad accepted the offer without hesitation.

Among the list of disappointments he'd logged, the inability to get to know Thad and Marilyn was near the top. He'd probably spent thirty minutes conversing with the two of them in total, and twenty-five of those were in a single conversation with Thad yesterday. Close behind in his mental catalog of setbacks was the knowledge, or lack thereof, he'd gained thus far. They were a third of the way into the sail, and he'd learned almost nothing about the operation of Sea Sleigh. Time was being wasted, and he only had himself to blame. At the very top of the list was the notion that he and Lucie's dream was in serious limbo. There was no longer a confidence their plan was going to work. With each passing hour of nausea, he got closer to pulling out the white flag and surrendering. As much as the thought of giving up pained him, he knew this sickened condition was not one he could sustain much longer.

"Cort." Thad's voice crept through the open door to his bedroom where he lay half-awake.

"Hey, Thad, what's up?" Cort managed to prop his head up a few inches, enabling himself to see the captain standing at the bottom of the steps, peeking around the wall into his room.

"I'm about to call Katie on the SAT phone to get a weather update. Just thought you might want to make a call to home?"

Despite the eagerness to hear his daughter's voice, Cort was tentative. He knew his own voice was weak, and she might pick up on it. If not her, Manny and Gabby would surely be right there listening. They might know something was wrong, and he didn't need any of them worrying.

"Sure, thanks."

He climbed out of the bed, deciding it was a gamble he'd have to take. Desperate for something positive, he followed Thad up the stairs and into the main cabin. He couldn't help but notice that Thad was wearing shorts, and as Cort climbed the steps behind him, it was impossible not to stare at the man's legs - the definition in the calf muscles was impressive.

Wow!

He thought back to Thad's "all in the legs" remark, recalling their earlier conversation about Olympic greatness.

He wasn't exaggerating.

Walking past the open slider, Cort noted the mildness of the outside air, pausing to let the warm breeze wash over his stagnant presence.

"It must be sixty degrees out there."

"Sixty-four. Very nice." Thad's response was pleasant enough but sounded somewhat forced. "Tomorrow could be in the low 70's."

"Oh good, that'll be really nice." Cort's excitement was muted, but the temperature would allow him to be outside as opposed to in the stale air in his quarters. It was something positive. Even if the misery-level in his gut was the same in either spot, he theorized that being able to focus on the horizon would help his condition more than anything.

"Yeah, we'll see. Depending on what Katie tells us, it could also be very wet and very rough." Thad placed a bottle of water in front of Cort and nodded once, the gesture compelling his second mate to drink it.

Cort didn't respond as he pondered the system named Dolores, hoping it'd made landfall and dissipated somewhere much further south. He twisted the cap off and sipped a half ounce back.

"Where are we now?" Cort asked the question just as Marilyn stepped into the cabin, having left the steering system on auto-pilot. She heard the question and answered before her son could.

"Middle of North Carolina. How're you feeling?" She reached and placed her hand on Cort's shoulder, adding an extra sense of comfort and concern to her question.

He looked into her kind eyes before dropping his head, "I'm, um, well... I've been better."

"You poor thing," she patted his back, "maybe get a shower later and get out on deck this afternoon. The fresh air should help you."

Cort reluctantly took another sip of water and nodded, assuming he was starting to get ripe. Her suggestion was probably as much for her and Thad's benefit as his own, and more evidence they were becoming aggravated at the situation.

Thad handed Cort the SAT phone, which looked more like a walkie-talkie.

"This will be like making an international call, so you'll dial 001, then your area code and phone number. Just keep it as brief as you can."

"Got it, thanks." Cort nodded and pulled out his own phone, searching his contacts until he had Manny and Gabby's numbered pulled up. Dialing, he nervously smiled at his shipmates and punched each number with growing anxiety. After the third ring, he heard Manny's voice.

"Hello."

"Manny, hey, it's Cort. How are you?" Cort forced energy through his vocal cords, trying to mask his true state of mind and body.

"Oh, hey there. No wonder I didn't recognize the number. How are you, Cort, and where are you guys?"

Cort clenched his jaw through an uptick of nausea, glanced at Marilyn, and responded. Three seconds later, he heard Gabby's voice. The three talked briefly before Cort introduced Marilyn and Thad to his in-laws. After a few pleasantries were exchanged between the five of them, Manny broke in with the question.

"Hey, uh, Cort, I assume you three are aware of this storm system making its way north? Dolores?"

Cort hesitated, wondering if maybe he should let the captain answer the question, and Thad took the que.

"Manny, this is Thad. Yes, we're aware of the system, and are about to get a detailed report from my cousin. Depending on what she says, we may need to alter our course. I can assure you we'll be very careful and avoid any potential danger."

There was a pause from the Austin end of the call. Cort imagined Manny and Gabby with puzzled expressions on their faces, unsure how to respond.

"You still there?" Cort spoke into the phone more directly.

"Yes, sorry, we're here Cort." Gabby chimed in apologetically. "Thank you, Thad."

Another three-second silence passed before Gabby spoke again, "Hey, Cort, I'm assuming there's a certain little girl you'd like to speak to?"

"Now who might that be?" Cort was able to muster a brief laugh with his sarcastic response, despite his churning stomach.

"Hang on, she'll be right here."

Cort waited anxiously as more seconds passed, recalling Thad's remark about SAT calls being expensive. Finally, he heard the voice that pumped joy and sadness into his heart simultaneously.

"Daddy?"

"Hi, Lucie, I'm here." He swallowed the ball of emotion, "how are you?"

"I'm good, Dad. Are you okay?"

"Sure, I'm fine, Luce - looking forward to seeing you in a few days and making some pancakes."

She giggled at the thought. "Me too, that sounds good."

Cort glanced at his shipmates to see Marilyn smiling, but Thad's expression held concern. The captain immediately posted a grin in response to Cort's eye-contact, but the signal Thad had given was a reminder the call needed to be short.

"Hey, Lucie, Thad and Marilyn are sitting here. You want to say hi?"

His shipmates offered a simultaneous "Hi Lucie" and she returned the greeting.

"Hopefully you'll get to meet them soon. You know I think Captain Thad here might just like sharks more than you do Luce."

"That's cool," her voice held a bit more excitement now, "have you seen any yet?"

"No, we haven't yet, but we'll keep looking." Cort inhaled a breath to stave off the urge to barf. He mentioned a few more details about Sea Sleigh, forcing himself to remain positive despite the growing sensation in his gut. Thad and Marilyn watched his expression battle between nausea and optimism.

"Lucie, I'm sorry we can't talk long. I just wanted to let you know everything is good here and tell you I can't wait to see you."

There was another pause, and he thought he heard Lucie inhale before she replied.

"Call again as soon as you can and be careful, Dad. I love you."

"Love you too, Lucie. I'll talk to you soon. Bye."

"Bye, Dad."

Cort handed the phone to Thad as he stood and moved from his seat to the slider.

"I'll be back in a few minutes."

He spent the next eight minutes in an all too familiar horizontal position, clipped into his harness with his head extended over the rear deck. When he returned to the cabin, Thad was placing the phone on the table, and he and his mother both wore troubled expressions. They looked at him as he entered, their faces sagging further.

"You okay?"

Thad tried to sound polite, but his expression was an indication that Cort closely resembled death-warmed-over.

"What'd you find out?" Ignoring the question, Cort kept his words to a minimum.

"Nothing good," Marilyn responded, and Thad followed.

"Mom and I will talk it over, but we'll need to, uh, alter our course. Dolores is still moving north, just now starting to veer in towards the coast. They predict her to make landfall a hundred miles or so north of Charleston. Problem is, if we continue this heading, we'll run smack dab into her first."

"Okay," Cort's voice was laden with hesitancy, "so we turn around, right?"

Thad snuck a glance at his mother before answering, "Maybe, yes. We could also skirt around her to the east. If we get far enough out, we'd miss most of the winds and rain, and we'd only lose about a half a day. But if we turn around, or even just hang out here and wait, we'll lose at least a day or two, maybe more."

Cort pondered the possible scenarios. The thought of rougher seas was daunting to his mind and his gut. But the thought of being on the water for an added day or more was equally upsetting.

"Hmph." It was the only response he could come up with on the spot.

Marilyn and her son watched Cort as he shuffled towards the steps to his bedroom. He paused before making the slow descent, turning towards them before speaking.

"I need to lay down. I know my vote doesn't count, but I think, whatever choice gets us to land the soonest sounds best to me."

***

Lucie had been composed until he said they couldn't talk long. Even though his voice sounded different, maybe weaker, it was still so comforting to hear it. Her grandparents hadn't mentioned that it would need to be a short call, and she'd never expected there to be a time limit. She had a lot of questions and much more to tell him, so when he said the call was going to be over soon, Lucie gulped and held back a sudden rush of sadness. She took a deep breath before answering to make sure her voice wouldn't crack.

"Call again as soon as you can and be careful, dad. I love you."

"Love you too, Lucie. I'll talk to you soon. Bye."

"Bye, Dad."

She'd managed to hold it together and say good-bye to him with a strong voice, but now, almost two hours later, she knelt beside the bed unable to speak her prayer out loud. Instead, she silently asked for help.

I'm worried about Dad, and I hate that I'm not there with him. I need your help now. Please Mom, keep him safe and make sure he comes home.

Chapter 53 – No Mas

As the third day painstakingly undulated into the fourth, Cort Palmerton appeared to be in trouble. Thad was well aware that his sickened shipmate hadn't eaten anything since before the initial vomit 75 hours ago - he'd probably lost six or seven pounds already. From his position behind the wheel, Thad watched the sickly pale man wrapped in the same blanket, enter the cockpit and turn right to the port side, step up onto the hull, and clip into the jackline before shuffling towards the bow. Before he was out of earshot, Thad made an offer.

"Hey, Cort, can I get you some water or broth, or something?"

"No, but thanks." Cort turned and shook his head. "I just came out to watch the horizon for a while. Gonna get my balance re-calibrated soon, right?"

"Yeah, definitely." Thad raised his voice over a small gust of wind, the volume somewhat masking the uncertainty in his tone. "Just keep trying to drink, buddy. I know you might not feel like it, but you need to hydrate."

Cort moved forward and put his hand up in weak wave of acknowledgement, but before returning to the front of the boat, he turned back to Thad again.

"Which direction are we going?"

"Southeast. We decided to side-step Dolores."

As his second mate continued his shuffle towards the bow, he offered Thad a thumbs-up without looking back. He watched as Cort grabbed a cable just to the left of the mast and used it for balance. Pushing a few buttons on the navigation screen, Thad adjusted the course by two degrees and turned his gaze back to the bow. Cort's form, framed by the day's last light, shifted west across the horizon.

He wondered about the man standing at the front of the port side hull, staring out across the open sea, apparently contemplating his future. How dark were his thoughts? Thad sucked in a deep breath as he considered his own situation and the fear growing inside himself. He knew there must be strong doubts metastasizing in Cort's head. Doubts that could have devastating effects on both of their futures. Maybe, he thought, the man on his bow was considering taking a swan dive, disappearing forever into the vast ocean. The terrible notion brought an unexpected sense of relief to Thad's troubled psyche. He tried to extinguish the small flame of ill-will, but it remained and festered.

In a sudden jerk of his head, Cort turned and glanced back at him, but Thad abruptly looked down and avoided eye contact. A second later he was watching the back of Cort's head again, rhythmically moving up and down, sinking into the backdrop of the dark ocean and rising again into the brightly contrasted smoke-gray sky.

Cort turned around again and began moving, shuffling back down the port-side hull, through the cockpit and to a position next to the captain's lair.

"Will you and Marilyn be switching soon?"

"Yeah," Thad answered with interest, "she's due up here in about twenty minutes or so. You want to take her shift?"

"I wish I could, Thad, really, I do. No, that's not why I came back here. I just wanted to talk to you for a minute."

The shame and embarrassment in Cort's eyes was grossly apparent. Thad nodded in confirmation and braced himself for what he sensed was coming.

"Listen, Thad, I'm sorry," Cort paused and swallowed, "it's just that, uh, I'm pretty sure this isn't going to work for me."

"What's not gonna work, the boat?" Thad knew exactly what Cort meant, but he feigned confusion anyway.

"Yeah, the boat."

Thad saw the disappointment and loss in Cort's eyes and could see that he was doing his best not to cry. Swallowing another large gulp of air, Cort continued.

"I just can't contemplate feeling this way again. It's too much for me, Thad. The misery is indescribable."

"I understand," Despite a growing disdain for the man in front of him, Thad kept his voice compassionate, "but don't give up yet. It could pass any minute now, and you'll feel like a new man. Really." As he spoke the words, Thad sensed Cort wasn't buying it. It seemed the man's decision was all but made, and his own heart sunk at the premise of the purchase-deal falling apart.

Cort nodded as a sign of appeasement. He pulled the blanket around himself tighter, covering up the same blue hoodie he'd put on just after boarding Sea Sleigh three days ago, and pushed the slider open.

"I'm gonna try to get some sleep. Maybe when I wake up, I'll feel better."

Thad didn't respond, remaining silent in his brooding as the glass door slid shut and the man disappeared below. Scanning a horizon that wasn't exactly welcoming, Thad knew those same skies would become much darker and threatening in the coming hours. He imagined Cort's thoughts would do the same. As he contemplated Cort's departure from the plans that had been set forth, an even darker thought materialized in his own brain.

***

Spreading his feet apart, Cort anchored his position and remained standing, focusing many miles into the distance on the line separating the water from the sky. As if the weakness and weariness weren't heavy enough, a sense of shame added weight to both. The embarrassment of getting sick and a harassing frustration in the inability to cure it was pulling him down. Despite the desperate attempts to will away the queasiness in his gut, it remained as strong as that initial wave more than three days ago.

Barely able to come to grips with what he was about to admit, he walked back to the cockpit where Thad was taking his watch. It was time to let him know the hard truth, which was that the purchase of Sea Sleigh wasn't a viable option anymore.

"But don't give up yet."

Thad's plea of encouragement sounded like a formality, and while Cort appreciated the gesture, he wasn't certain Thad had his well-being at the forefront. Nodding at the notion, Cort was willing to offer the weak gesture of hope for both Thad and him. He could feel the captain's eyes on the back of his head as he pulled the blanket around himself and opened the slider. Thad's growing frustration with him was evident, likely a result of being exhausted, but more so now because the purchase deal had just about been kiboshed.

Descending the stairs to his bedroom, he wondered if he and Lucie's future was about to change drastically. He hadn't completely given up, but something positive needed to happen soon to salvage their dream. He laid on the bed, stared up at the ceiling, and made a plea.

If you're listening Celeste, please help me.

Chapter 54 – Shooting Star

The sun had long since sunk below the horizon, leaving clear skies and no sign of an approaching storm. Cort exited the cabin, clad in his same clothes and same blanket, and noted the air felt a bit warmer. He offered a sad hello to Marilyn, then turned toward the opposite side of the boat. Despite the growing dizziness and decline in strength, he managed to clip in and find his way to the spot on the front port side. Maybe it was the fever playing tricks on his cognitive function, but the stars seemed to be bigger tonight.

He assumed the dehydration would materialize into a more severe medical condition soon. They were less than a day away from the half-way point of the sail, and despite lying in bed for the best part of the 78 hours, he was physically and mentally exhausted. The sliver of hope he'd taken away from his talk with Thad a couple hours ago was on the verge of disappearing, a sense of desperation creeping into his psyche.

A haze of lightheadedness materialized as he sat and leaned back against the slanted exterior of the cabin just left of the mast. He noted the calmness of the sea and wondered how long it would last as they approached Dolores, and she approached them.

What had Thad's cousin said? Two hundred miles south?

With decent wind, they'd reach it by mid-day tomorrow. Sooner if the storm continued to move north in their direction. He tried to put the intersection of danger out of his mind and tilted his head backwards. The white glow of the stars burned brighter than he'd expected, each one appearing fuzzier than it should. Rubbing his eyes, he attempted to regain focus as the lack of hydration altered his perception of the heavenly bodies. While his eyes adjusted, a sensation of levitation lifted him several inches above the deck. Moving one hand to his forehead, the heat he felt was a sure indication of a fever and the cause of the delusion. His hand reached back and grabbed a rope attached to the mast. The security of the rope was comforting, but he released it without fear a few seconds later. While he inherently understood the hallucination wasn't reality, part of his brain welcomed the notion of floating off into space.

The sensation of his body returning to the deck came over him just as a glowing ball flashed across the sky. It appeared to be large enough and bright enough to be a meteor, but Cort was aware that his brain wasn't operating on full cylinders. Despite his compromised cerebral function, the logical assumption was made - the instance of passing light was a shooting star, crossing space in a diagonal trajectory from heaven to earth. The rare celestial display triggered images of his wife, and his brain formed a consequential theory that made him smile.

"It was you, Celeste. You were the shooting star, not me. I get it now."

As he spoke aloud to the illuminated sky, Cort felt a wave of comfort wash over him. He thought back to the song he'd heard months ago in his car, presuming she'd sent him a sign through the lyrics. Now he was convinced she had, conveying the message it was her life, not his, that had burned bright and died quick.

Wow, I almost really blew it with my first interpretation.

He smiled to himself as the thought crossed his weary mind and the feeling of dizziness returned. He spoke into the night air.

"I wish I could talk to you just one more time, Celeste. Just one more time."

He closed his eyes as a warm gust of wind washed over him, and the sound of it passing was perceived as words through a most familiar voice.

Celeste's voice: "You *can* talk to me, Cort."

The auditory perception in his left ear startled him, but it comforted him too. Turning his head, Cort felt a soothing peace as the image of Celeste sitting next to him materialized.

Cort: "Is it really you?"

Voice of Celeste: "Do you know another woman who looks and sounds like me?" Her mouth remained still as the words were spoken, but she managed to giggle at her own sarcasm. Cort grinned back, not caring if she was real or not. His hallucinogenic brain made the decision to respond as if it were her in the flesh.

Cort: "God, I miss you so much, Celeste."

Voice of Celeste: "I miss you too, Cort."

Cort turned his head straight again, fighting back a tear that could scarcely be shed from his dehydrated ducts. Afraid to look back, he was sure she'd be gone. Instead, he reached his left hand out, and felt the sensation of soft fingers on his. He turned, relieved to see her still there, wearing a most beautiful smile. He thought back to the last day he'd seen it, just before she left the house for yoga.

Cort: "I got your gift, Celeste. It made me sad beyond belief."

Voice of Celeste: "I know you did, Cort, and I'm sorry about the timing." Her lips remained still, and her smile was unphased.

Cort: "I finally understood what you went through when you lost the other pregnancies. The unshakable remorse. The guilt. The depression. I understand all of it now all too well." He wiped his eyes. The lines in the face of Celeste's image were not of sadness, but of empathy. She felt so real, and her emotions pulsed through Cort as if they were his own. Still, she did not respond.

Cort: "Celeste?"

Voice of Celeste: "Yes?"

Cort: "What if you hadn't died that night? And what if you'd lost the pregnancy like the other ones? Would we have…?"

Voice of Celeste: "What, Cort, what are you asking?"

Cort: "What would have happened to us Celeste? I'm worried we wouldn't have made it." Two tears struggled down his right cheek as the words came out. He was sure his question would drive her angelic image away, but it remained, hovering nearly transparent just above the deck's surface.

Voice of Celeste: "Oh Cort, love of my life, don't dwell on that. It's senseless to worry about something that can't be. Please, don't."

Cort: "But, Celeste, I just..."

Voice of Celeste: "But nothing, Cort. You need to let go of a fear for something that cannot happen. Besides, don't you remember what I told you after we lost the last pregnancy?"

He thought back to that evening as they lay in bed, when she'd said the three words to him that brought comfort and security back to their relationship, solidifying their bond for eternity.

Cort: "You said, that," another tear fell as he quoted her, "life goes on."

Voice of Celeste: "That's right, my love. Life would have gone on for us, no matter what. I promise you. And it must go on for you now. For you and Lucie."

Delirious and overwhelmed with emotion, Cort fought to stay in his present state of mind, struggling to come up with another question to delay her inevitable departure.

Cort: "I have something else to ask you."

Voice of Celeste: "Yes?"

Cort: "Is there a heaven? Will I see you again?"

Voice of Celeste: "That's a very good question now, isn't it? And you know I can't answer that, don't you?"

Cort did not speak, shaking his head from side to side without taking his eyes away from her spirit-like representation.

Voice of Celeste: "I *can* remind you of something you once told me, Cort. Something that you believe and that I do too." She paused and waited for his nod. "I can tell you that when we pass away, our energy never leaves the earth. It just reincarnates into another form within our surroundings. That means I'll never leave you completely, Cort, right?"

Cort: "I remember telling you that now, yes. I think we were hiking that day, right?"

Voice of Celeste: "That's right, and I was pregnant with Lucie, in the middle of the second term. Remember?"

Cort nodded and quietly wept at the joyful memory, barely able to catch his breath. He gathered his voice and answered the beautiful ghost sitting next to him.

Cort: "Yes, I do remember, Celeste."

Voice of Celeste: "You were right about that, Cort. My energy still exists, so when you and Lucie lay in the grass in our back yard, just know I am there. And I'm in the air around you too. You're breathing me in and out of your lungs as we speak. And, Cort?"

Cort: "Yes?"

Voice of Celeste: "There is one other place I'll always be for you, more so even than the earth and air. I don't have to tell you where that is because the answer is such a part of you already. You know where, don't you, Cort?"

"Water?"

The voice that uttered the word was not his own, and not Celeste's. Confused, Cort turned toward the rear of the boat to where the voice had seemingly originated. The image of Celeste dissipated in his peripheral vision as he was startled back to cognitive thought. His mind returned to reality and his body twitched in surprise when he saw Marilyn standing on top of the deck. There was a look of concerned compassion in her eyes. She leaned toward him with one hand grasping the boom for support, and the other hand holding a clear bottle of transparent liquid. She repeated her offer.

"Water, Cort? It looked like you were talking to yourself, and it worried me. You should drink this, otherwise you'll dehydrate completely." Marilyn made more of a plea than a suggestion.

Cort simply nodded and reached his hand back, taking the bottle of water, and offered a genuine thank you. With that, Marilyn turned and walked back to the aft deck and gingerly made her way into the cockpit. Unscrewing the cap and taking a long hard drink, Cort finished nearly half of the 24-ounce bottle in one long chug. Twisting the cap back on, he waited, expecting the intense feeling of nausea to return with force. But it didn't. To Cort's utter shock, the water in his belly caused quite the opposite effect. Thirty seconds after swallowing back twelve ounces, all sense of nausea in his gut was gone. He stared up to the speckled sky as the fog on his brain dissipated into the Milky Way, and a discernible feeling of wellness pulsed through his veins. Gulping back six more ounces, Cort was astonished at the miraculous effect. Cherishing what he assumed would be a short-lived feeling of well-being, he gazed into the heavens as the clarity in his vision returned. A few seconds before he left his spot to join Marilyn in the cockpit, Cort caught another streak of light tailing from the sky and vanishing into the horizon. As the second shooting star disappeared, Cort concluded that it was Celeste bidding farewell. He simply raised the water bottle in his left hand, acknowledging the woman he knew would always be a presence in his life. With his right hand, he blew a kiss into the trade winds and softly whispered three simple words of gratitude.

"Thank you, Celeste."

Chapter 55 – The Past and the Passed

"Thanks, Marilyn. The water was exactly what I needed." Cort nodded and held up the empty bottle for her to see, showing her he'd drank every ounce. "I didn't throw up any of it."

She smiled, relieved for both of them. "That's good, Cort. You seem much better already. There's some color in your face again."

Cort nodded in silence, contemplating what to do next. His eyes lingered on her for a second, noting the moss-green wool sweater and matching beanie. She looked comfortable behind the helm, and comfortable with life.

She must have some stories.

He began to turn away as Marilyn looked back to the navigation screen. His fingers wrapped around the handle on the slider, but he hesitated. Most of the last three days had been spent laying in his bunk, and there was no desire to return. He'd barely talked to Thad, and he'd conversed with Marilyn even less. Cort jerked his head back in her direction.

"Would you mind some company out here?"

Marilyn turned to him, the offer apparently surprising her.

"Sure, I'd love some." She pointed to the cushioned bench in the cockpit closest to her perch in front of the helm, inviting him to sit. "We can talk if you sit there, and you'll still be able to see the stars."

"Good deal, thanks."

Cort got comfortable, and the two sat in silence for fifteen seconds before Cort spoke again.

"Thad's sleeping?"

"Yes, he's probably out by now. His watch ended about a half hour ago, so I'm sure he's sound asleep. We're on 6-hour shifts now - I'll wake him up around 3:00 A.M."

"Oh, okay. Guess that's not how you'd normally break it up?" Cort asked, his question holding a tone of guilt.

"Well, no. Normally we'd each do 4-hour shifts at night. So, with three of us, it's on watch for four, then off for eight. But don't worry about it. Thaddy and I will be fine." She offered a reassuring smile, but Cort's frown remained.

"I'm really sorry about this," his head shook back and forth as if he were confessing to a crime, "it's just that, well, I never would have predicted this kind of reaction. I suck."

"Oh, now, Cort, c'mon, don't beat yourself up."

Marilyn touched the navigation screen a couple times and got up from the captain's chair, took another glance toward the moonlit horizon, then stepped down into the cockpit. She patted Cort on his back before sitting on the bench catty-corner from his.

"Is it safe for you to be down here?" Cort glanced back at the empty helm.

"Sure, it is, don't worry. I set it on auto pilot, and that's perfectly fine. Out of habit, I'll still go up and look every 5-10 minutes. Thad and I both do that. Despite the technology, he and I always worry about running into something that shouldn't be there. It's like having the back-up camera in my car - I still use the rearview mirrors every time."

Cort nodded in agreement, "Yeah, it would be bad to run into something out here. Like Dolores?" Cort posed the hypothetical in a question form and smiled sarcastically.

She laughed, "Yes, we don't want to run into her. Don't worry, we'll make sure we steer clear of the hurricane. I'm sure it'll still be rougher than normal, but this boat can handle it." Marilyn stated it confidently, before adding, "Plus, we have God on our side."

"That's good," his lips closed into a tight smile, "I'm not too worried about the boat. Me on the other hand, well, I'm not sure I can handle it."

"Hey, you're looking a lot better right now. Do you think you're over the hump?"

Cort pondered the question. "I think I might be. Drinking the water may have been the turning point - thank you for that. I was just considering taking a watch soon, if you think it would be a good idea?"

Marilyn smiled with excitement. "I think it would be a great idea. Can I show you some things about the nav-system, so you feel comfortable using it?"

"Yeah, I mean, sure, this is as good a time as any, right?"

Cort followed her back up to the captain's seat, and they stood next to it on either side. The navigation screen was positioned right in front of the wheel, and an easy reach from the sitting position at the helm. Marilyn showed him the various views that were available, touching a couple of the icons on a toolbar along the left side of the screen. She explained there were two views used routinely, so they focused on those for the tutorial. The information was plentiful, and Cort was surprised how much there was to know about a travel corridor that was nothing but open water. After a few minutes of reviewing different symbols and various tidbits of data, Marilyn turned to Cort.

"You must be hungry. Can I make you something to eat?"

"I am feeling hungry now that you mention it, which is so strange. I didn't think I'd ever be hungry again. But still, I'm not sure I want to chance eating anything. I feel so much better right now. I'd hate to go back to where I was."

In true motherly form, Marilyn pushed a bit, "How about just starting with some broth? Mostly water, but you'll get some salt and some calories in you too."

He couldn't deny that hot chicken broth sounded delicious. "Maybe if I just take it slow, one sip at a time?"

Nodding her approval, "Here, Cort, you take the helm for a few minutes," she pushed a button on the control panel, "it's on auto-pilot, just stay here and I'll make you some."

Cort sat in the captain's chair and gazed through the night. The horizon was barely discernable, but it was there, along with his hope for the future he and Lucie had planned. The sense of relief he had was overwhelming. The difference in his body and brain from just a half an hour ago was incredible. Putting the back of his hand against his forehead, he noted the fever was gone.

Unbelievable!

Despite the utopic change in well-being, the fear remained that the queasiness would return. The ocean was relatively calm right now, but from everything he'd gathered, it would not remain that way. He pushed the fear down, and smiled to himself, focused on the notion that the seasickness could very well be over. He watched the starlit water with a renewed sense of peace and focused on the rhythmic music of breaking waves all around him. Eleven minutes later, the swoosh of the slider broke his hypnotic state. Marilyn emerged holding a large mug with thin steam rising above it.

"Here you go, dear," her sweet calm voice reminding Cort of his childhood, "be careful now, okay, it's gonna be a little hot."

"Thank you, Marilyn, this looks fantastic." He took a slow sip and moved it around his mouth, both cooling and savoring the hot liquid before swallowing it. "Wow, that is so good."

"There's more in the pot, Cort, so don't be shy. Have as much as you want, and there's plenty of food in the fridge too. You must be famished."

"Thanks. I'll see how the broth goes first, but I might just eat a horse or two when I'm done."

They laughed together, both happy at his return to health. He watched the wind move a few locks of hair across her forehead, anxious to get to know her.

"I'm glad we have this chance to talk, Marilyn. I feel like we've barely spoken since we met at the grocery store four days ago."

"Yeah, I'll admit it's been a little odd. Thaddy and I weren't sure if you'd ever get out of your hole down there."

Cort laughed a little at the reference to his resting place, also at her son's pet-name.

"I can't wait to tell him I'm feeling better. He went to bed thinking, well, never mind, it doesn't matter. He'll be relieved. And you two can both catch up on some sleep. I plan to make up for all my missed watches."

"He'll be excited, Cort. I'll let him know when I switch with him."

"As long as I'm still feeling good, I'll take the next watch. What time will that be?"

She looked at her wrist. "I expect to see him again around 3:00 A.M. But, Cort, don't be too sure he'll let you take a watch. It'll depend on the weather. As we skirt around this hurricane, it won't be ideal sailing conditions, other than we'll have great wind."

"Right, that's true. How about this? Don't say anything to him when you two switch. I'll set my alarm for 3:00. If I wake up still feeling well, and the weather is decent, I'll come up myself and relieve him. I kind of want to surprise him anyway. Okay?"

"Yes, alright, that's a good idea. If you wake up and seas are high, don't feel like you need to take a watch. Thaddy wouldn't let you anyway if conditions aren't good. It shouldn't take us more than a day to get around Dolores though. Hopefully by the time we hit Charleston, it'll be smooth sailing the rest of the way."

Cort nodded and took a big gulp of broth, swallowing back a third of his mug.

"This is soooo good. You said there's more?"

Marilyn laughed, seemingly both amused and happy that his appetite had returned.

"Yes, there sure is, and there's some chicken penne pasta in the fridge too. It's in a yellow bowl with a lid on it if you're interested. Just put it in a pot and heat it up on the stove for 10 minutes."

"That sounds really good, but I'm nervous." Cort pondered the chicken and tomato sauce over the noodles, and his stomach growled in anticipation.

"I do think you're over the hump, Cort, but it's your call. Maybe just take a bite or two at first and see how it sits?"

Agreeing wholeheartedly, Cort disappeared below, filled his mug with the rest of the broth, then transferred the pasta into the empty pot. Thirteen minutes later, he emerged with the mug in one hand and a bowl of chicken penne in the other. Plopping down on the bench nearest Marilyn, he took small sips and small bites while the two chatted. An hour passed by easily with no sign of nausea as Cort and Marilyn talked. He told Marilyn about Celeste in as much detail as he could without getting too choked up. While he avoided a total break down, both his and Marilyn's eyes glossed over more than once as he described the love he'd shared with Celeste. He spoke at length about Lucie, and how much they'd learned about each other in the past nine months. Marilyn mostly listened, and nodded, and offered her own insight once or twice. She seemed somewhat guarded, and Cort sensed an apprehension in revealing too much detail about her own past. He'd unsuccessfully attempted to shift the focus from himself to her story several times before finally finding the question that triggered her to open up.

"So, Thad, is an only child too, like Lucie, or do you have other kids?"

She blinked twice and chewed on her lip for a second before answering.

"Thad *had* a brother." Her voice trailed as she looked away.

"Oh, I'm sorry, Marilyn, I didn't know. I'm so sorry." He immediately regretted his question.

"No, it's okay, you didn't know. It's, well, it took me a long time to come to grips with it, but I've found peace, just in the last few years."

Cort watched her expression shift as the soft light from the navigation panel illuminated the lines in her face. She wore a sad smile, and Cort assumed the events of past decades were flooding her mind. For several seconds, her gaze stayed locked upon the open sea off the bow of the starboard hull. Despite the tentative expression, Marilyn's voice remained strong as she unveiled her history. It started with a few happy memories of when her two sons, Thad and Logan, were just young boys. The mood of her story transitioned to one of a somber chronicle as she told of Logan's death. He was nine and Thad was ten when the diagnosis came. It hadn't been a total surprise, given the fact the disease was hereditary. Spinal Muscular Atrophy is what Cort thought he heard her call it, making a mental note to google it later.

From her description, he gathered the genetic disease typically afflicted every other generation. Her father's sister had also died from it at the age of seven, so Marilyn had always known she was at risk of passing the gene onto one or more of her children. She described it as a 'relentless monster' that'd slowly crippled her son before eventually killing him.

"SMA wasn't really treatable back in the early 90's. Medical science has come a long way since Logan died," she shook her head and shrugged, "if he'd been diagnosed today, the advances in treatment could have extended his life indefinitely."

There were a few seconds of awkward silence as Marilyn paused to adjust another setting on the navigation system. Cort sensed a slight shift in Sea Sleigh's direction but didn't ask if they'd changed course. Marilyn sat back, apparently satisfied with her adjustment, and continued.

"After Logan passed, our family spiraled. My husband and I started bickering, and the fighting just snowballed from there. We grew apart over the next four years, and in 99' he had an affair and left me and Thaddy. They were tough years for us, but we did okay."

Marilyn brushed over the trials and tribulations during the worst period, progressing her story into the early 2000's. According to her, that's when Thad rekindled his interest in snowboarding. She explained that her boys had tried it back when they were kids and were immediately hooked, always choosing it over skiing. But without Logan, Thad lost his desire. Then at the age of fifteen, he went with a friend's family up to Killington for a weekend, and just like that, he fell back in love with the sport. He begged his mom to take him any chance they could, and so they hit the slopes whenever there was an opportunity. At first, she'd ski, and he'd snowboard, but it wasn't long before his skills took him to slopes she couldn't follow.

"He got very good in a short amount of time."

Marilyn theorized the sport helped keep Thad connected with his brother's spirit. He began to enter competitions, and after a year or two, he was winning just about every event he competed in. She said it was such a great release for him, and his brother's memory always served as motivation to do his best. In one post-Olympic interview, he'd dedicated both of his medals to Logan.

"Now me on the other hand, well, my therapy after Logan died wasn't quite in the form of a sport. No sir. Instead, I chose a crutch in liquid form." She turned to Cort and smiled sarcastically.

Marilyn went on to describe her escalating addiction to alcohol over the ensuing decade or so. The alcoholism had created a whole different slew of problems, but she'd figured out a way to be under the influence and still manage to function. Despite several interventions by Thad and his wife Amelia, plus a few stints of rehab along the way, she just couldn't quite break off the relationship with the 'devil in a bottle.' After being arrested for DUI in 2017 and spending a night in jail, she said she'd let God back into her heart.

"That's what did it for me, Cort. It was my renewed faith that led me out of the darkness."

"That's wonderful," Cort offered, "I'm happy for you."

"Thanks. I don't know what your relationship is with God, and I won't ask. That's your business. But, if you ever want to talk about it, I'm here."

"That's kind of you, Marilyn, I appreciate it. Honestly, I have some soul searching to do with my faith. The relationship with the man upstairs has been, well, it's been a little strained lately. But let's save that talk for another night if that's okay? I think I'm going to go below and shower, then try to get some sleep. I want to be rested, and clean, when my alarm goes off at 3:00."

"Sure, Cort, I understand. But I'll take a raincheck on that conversation for sure." Marilyn reached for his hand.

Cort reached back and stood as he took her hand in his, moving into her space and embracing her in a hug. They held each other for several seconds, transferring empathy for each other in the process.

"Goodnight, Marilyn." Cort released her and turned for the slider.

"Goodnight, Cort. Get some rest young man."

He smiled to himself and slid the cabin door open. The 'young man' designation triggered a fond memory, reminding him of the reference his mother had often used.

Chapter 56 — Lifeboat

A shower was always rejuvenating, but the comfort and cleanse from the hot water had never quite reached this level before. Four days of sweat and sickness were washed down the drain as Cort did a final rinse. He'd kept it brief, as instructed, but the three minutes under the shower head were borderline ecstasy.

Pulling on a fresh pair of underwear, he hung the towel on the rack and went back to his duffel bag for some shorts to sleep in. Shuffling the folded items around, he realized this would be his first real change of clothes. *Ugh!* The color caught his eye just before he began pulling the zipper closed. Reaching back into the bag, he grabbed the light blue rectangular envelope and read the word "DAD" across the front. Recognizing the writing on the card as Lucie's, he ripped open the seal with a sense of elated excitement. It was apparent that the card was hand-made, evidenced by the cardstock paper folded in half — the edges not quite matching up perfectly. On the front, under the word 'DAD,' she'd drawn and colored yellow Chrysanthemum flowers, reminding him of the ones they'd planted for Celeste. The memory, surprisingly, made Cort happy, and he opened the card with a renewed sense of hope for his and Lucie's future. On the inside, she'd written a simple message in the top half of the space:

Be careful and have fun!
I love you so much!
PS – Don't forget about your lifeboat.
Love,
Lucie

Life Boat

Under the words, she'd drawn a picture of a yellow sun. At the bottom, there was blue water with her rendition of Sea Sleigh's lifeboat. She'd obviously drawn it from her memory of the photos on the website and done an impressive job. Cort grinned and read the message again, amused by both her drawing and the not-so-subtle reminder. Sliding the card back into the envelope, an ironic notion struck him as he processed the words she'd written, "Don't forget about your lifeboat." Something clicked in his brain, and a stark realization became evident. It wasn't the inflated rubber dinghy secured to the aft deck that made him feel safe. It wasn't even the 6-person TransOcean offshore life raft and ditch-bag that brought him a sense of security. Nothing in his life, not even God, had even come close to being the savior that his 10-year-old daughter had.

Lucie, you are my lifeboat.

A tear ran down his cheek as the epiphany was processed. She'd saved him from death once already, and her existence would serve as protection for his mind and body going forward. Lucie had been his saving grace since the second day of February, and the reason he was on this catamaran with a sense of hope for their future. He kissed the card and put it back in his bag carefully. After setting the alarm on his phone for 3:00 A.M., Cort climbed into bed and turned off the light. As he closed his eyes, a message to his daughter was relayed through silent thought.

I'll never forget about my lifeboat, Lucie. I love you.

Chapter 57 – Altered Course

"You don't look well, Thaddy, did you sleep alright?"

There was deep concern in her voice. He forced a weak smile to ease her mind.

"I slept fine, Mom, but I'm still tired. Don't worry about it though, I'll be okay." Thad proceeded to switch spots with his mother.

He watched her closely, trying to gauge her reaction to his claim. It seemed she wanted to tell him something important but remained silent as they traded positions behind the helm. She turned to him once but still held her tongue. It wasn't until she'd opened the slider and moved halfway into the cabin before she turned back to him and spoke.

"Thaddy, we're about to hit the roughest stretch here, so don't hesitate to come and get me if you need a hand. Will you be warm enough?"

He'd traded his shorts and long-sleeved t-shirt for pants, a thick sweatshirt, and a raincoat. Fully aware the winds alone had dropped the temperature nearly fifteen degrees since sunset, and that they'd most certainly see some intense rain before the night was over, Thad had prepared himself. He waved his hand from his chest down to his waist in a gesture to display his apparel, satisfying his mother's concern.

"Thanks, Mom, I'm ready for it." He smirked and tried to sound more upbeat as he asked her a question. "Any word on Cort?"

His mother hesitated.

"Yeah, we had a good talk. The guy's been through a lot Thad, so take it easy on him. He wants to talk to you."

"Oh yeah, about what?" His voice trailed, purposely veiling his knowledge of the probable subject matter and his utter contempt at the thought of it.

"I'm not sure. He just said he was anxious to talk to you. Maybe you'll see him soon." She seemed to be hiding an emotion, or maybe some bit of information. He already knew what it was, but kept the knowledge to himself, just in case she was referring to something different. Setting off any kind of alarm in Mom's head would be problematic.

"Yeah, I'm sure I'll see him soon enough." He couldn't quite hide the vexation he was feeling, and his mom picked up on his underlying tone.

"Thad, be nice. Seriously!" She climbed the two steps back up to him, kissed him on the cheek and turned back toward the cabin. "Good night."

"Good night, Mom."

As his mother pushed the slider closed behind her, Thad's thoughts about his predicament spun recklessly through his brain. He struggled with the new vision of the future, his mind wrestling with it for the next thirty minutes. Finally, as the image of Amelia and Gracie waving to him from the dock was firmly planted in his thoughts, he was able to make peace with the extremely difficult decision. Reaching up to the navigation screen, he tapped a button and nervously moved his finger to the directional adjustment arrows. A split-second later, the rudder moved, shifting their vessel ten degrees westward. Fear mixed with adrenaline pulsed through his veins as he considered their altered course - Sea Sleigh was now moving towards the edge of a category III hurricane.

***

More than 1,400 miles away, Lucie tiptoed past her grandparent's bedroom on her way to the finished basement. Passing through the kitchen, she checked the time displayed on the oven. 3:18 A.M. Restless with worry and unable to fall back to sleep, she half-filled her glass with water and walked down the stairs slowly. Grabbing a throw-blanket and settling on the sofa, she tapped the power button on the remote, then the guide button, and scrolled down until she found The Weather Channel.

After a short commercial, the weather lady appeared in front of a large screen, and Hurricane Dolores was immediately the primary focus. As the path of the storm stuttered across the screen, she shivered as it moved north along the Atlantic Coast. She knew her dad's boat would be just a speck in comparison to the rotating clouds that filled half of the television screen.

More silent prayers were made, both to her mother and to God, begging them both to bring her father home to her soon. Lucie had an odd feeling that her father, like herself, was not sleeping right now. More troubling was the idea that he was in danger, but she also had a strange sense the weather was not the greatest threat to his safety. She closed her eyes but couldn't shake the feeling of dread. This time she pleaded to him, hoping against hope that he was going to be fine.

Please Dad, you promised me you'd be careful and stay safe. Please keep your promise and come home.

Chapter 58 - Wake Up Call

The forceful whisper came from just outside his open door. It didn't wake him because he hadn't been sleeping. Well before his alarm had gone off, he'd been lying awake, listening anxiously to the waves beat against the hulls for the past hour. The pounding had become violent, and Cort was convinced a wrecking ball of water would burst through his bedroom wall any second. He'd been roused by muted screams as the fierce winds whipped through the rigging. Thunder rumbled in the distance, getting closer together with each sequence. The flashes of lightening through the small portal window served as a clear message that Dolores was approaching their piece of ocean. A section of steel cable collided intermittently against the aluminum mast. The rhythm wasn't perfect, but every few seconds, like some warped version of Morse code, the wind caught the cable just right and sent a ping into the night. Cort was wide awake now, quite sure sleep wouldn't find him until they'd found their way through the brutal weather system, but there was no way he'd be volunteering to take Thad's watch.

"Cort, hey, Cort."

His name hadn't completely left Thad's tongue the second time when Cort lifted his head from the pillow and replied.

"Yeah." Cort whispered back, assuming it was on behalf of a sleeping Marilyn.

Thad appeared startled by Cort's abrupt reply. He held his glare on Cort a split second too long, the hesitation and facial expression telling of anxiety. Cort returned eye-contact uneasily, assuming this seasoned sailor was also having major trepidation about the storm.

"Cort, I need your help."

Cort nodded back, both as an answer to the captain's command and as a confirmation of his own assumption. Another less positive thought developed - maybe Thad's hesitation was a second-guess at his request for assistance from a man who'd been useless up to this point. It was a fleeting thought, but Cort had undoubtedly caught the odd look in Thad's eyes. There was a fear; a darkness of sorts, and the result was a slip of confidence in Cort.

Cort dressed in a flash and peeked at his phone. 3:41 A.M. He sighed out of both fatigue and tension, as he considered going out into the harsh elements. The phone nearly dropped from his hand as another large wave rocked the boat and he stumbled back towards the bed. Standing upright, the rise and fall of the boat felt more dramatic, providing a better sense of the true elevation changes. Despite the turbulence, he didn't feel nauseous, and decided he'd give Thad the good news soon. He'd felt nothing short of fantastic when the nausea had subsided, and the renewed energy from the broth and pasta was remarkable. That feeling of well-being he'd gained a few hours ago was disappearing, and as he followed Thad up the stairs into the main cabin, all sense of comfort was replaced with intense consternation. Still, as soon as he was done helping Thad with whatever task was at hand, Cort planned to tell him the purchase deal for Sea Sleigh was back on.

Thad was standing by the door to the cockpit when the men locked eyes again. Cort gulped and swallowed. The uneven look was still there, and it was one Cort couldn't quite discern. Maybe, as he'd assumed, it was fear, but he couldn't shake the premise there was something deeper and darker in Thad's eyes. The captain raised his pointer finger to his lips, gesturing for quiet, and spoke in a focused whisper.

''Mom just came off more than a six-hour watch. She's only been sleeping for about twenty-five minutes.''

"I understand." Cort paused a second then pointed toward the rear slider. "Can you let me know why the hell you woke me, and please don't tell me we're going out there?"

Thad nodded back and gestured for Cort to move closer. Complying, he stepped forward until Thad laid his hand upon his shoulder. Their heads were less than two feet apart, and close enough that Cort could detect the scent of coffee on Thad's breath.

"We have a tear in the main sail, right above the clew. It's not good. If we don't get it down it'll keep ripping all the way across, understand?" He didn't wait for a response. "As I pull it down, I need you to feed it into the sail bag. Otherwise, the sail and ropes could catch and toss me overboard."

Amongst other thoughts racing through his mind, Cort tried to remember what the hell the clew was. His confusion with Thad's request materialized into a question that held a bit of challenge to it.

"You'll be harnessed in though, won't you?"

"Yeah," Thad hesitated, seeming to contemplate his response. "We both will be. It doesn't mean I can't get thrown over. I'd still be attached to the boat, but it could be a bitch to climb back on myself, especially if I'd been injured."

There was a detectable tone of annoyance in Thad's voice. The explanation seemed a little odd, maybe even contrived, but it made enough sense that Cort decided not to question it. Furthermore, he decided not to ask any more questions at all. He'd do what Thad told him to do, and hopefully be back in his bunk in a few minutes.

Handing Cort his life vest and a yellow raincoat from under the bench seat, Thad stated the obvious.

"Put the coat on first."

As they zippered and buckled in silence, drops of rain began to pelt the window. Thad vocalized his immediate thought but kept it to a whisper.

"We're right at the edge of it, and it's gonna get nasty."

"*Get* nasty? What do you call it now?" Cort replied sarcastically and raised an eyebrow, gesturing out the back slider.

Thad didn't respond to the rhetorical question, instead issuing a quick shush and pointing toward the bunkroom where his mother lay resting. He slid open the glass door and waved Cort through first. Reluctantly stepping into the wicked elements, they remained semi-sheltered in the cockpit as the winds and water swirled around the enclosure. It wasn't as cold as Cort had expected, but the windchill outside the cockpit would be significant. Thad turned and locked the latch on the slider behind them, then hung the key back on the hook.

"Whoa! I thought you said not to lock that unless we were all on deck?" Cort regurgitated the captain's instructions from a few days ago, breaking the self-instructed vow of silence Cort had just made to himself.

"Relax. It's only for a couple minutes. We're rocking too much. If I don't lock it, the door could slide open hard and wake Mom, or break the glass."

"Fine. Let's just do what we need to do and get the hell back inside."

Thad nodded dismissively, half-pretending he hadn't heard the comment. Lifting one of the cockpit benches, the captain pulled out a neatly folded vinyl sail bag before stepping up onto the starboard side deck. Cort followed close behind, and they both paused just outside the cockpit to survey the sea. Cort could not recall ever being more intimidated by Mother Nature than at that moment. The sea and night were nearly devoid of light, illuminated dimly by the mast and deck lights from the boat. In every direction, there was nothing visible beyond a hundred and fifty feet, but what could be seen was daunting. The small circle of ocean around the boat was alive, churning as if it intended to swallow the craft whole. Twenty-five-foot swells rose on every side, climbing close to the height of the mast itself. At the crest, the water boiled and broke for long durations before regaining height and strength. The swells took the catamaran to their peaks before surfing it back into the dark valleys. Cort couldn't tell if the feeling in the pit of his gut was nausea or anxiety. As he scanned to the eastern sky searching for a sunrise that wasn't there, he wondered if this storm would take his life - take all their lives.

With one hand still clenching the stainless railing, Thad grabbed his own nylon tether and clipped his carabiner onto the jackline. He waved Cort forward, and in one swift motion, grabbed Cort's dangling carabiner and attached it to the jackline too. While the move was made in a flash, it wasn't the speed of the act that surprised Cort the most. It was the fact Thad had clipped Cort's line in front of his own.

"Hey!" As the word pierced the wind, rain, and churn of the ocean, Cort's tone and volume surprised even himself.

Thad stood from his crouching position at the challenging word, still holding tight to the railing, and with his free hand he put his finger to his lips then pointed toward the deck. Cort shrugged, dumbfounded, but Thad spoke with indifference to the gesture.

"I've decided you should go first. Safer that way. And keep it down."

Crouching and clinging tight to the railing post, Cort semi-ignored the shushing gesture. *We're in a fucking hurricane and his biggest concern is waking his mother.*

"Now what?"

Thad stepped back over Cort's harness line, handed him the sail bag, and pointed toward the front of the boat. He cupped one hand around the side of his mouth to filter his voice directly at Cort.

"Turn around and walk to the front and hold on tight to that bag."

Mother Nature reacted to the men, the storm taking their presence as a challenge. The sky unleashed larger pellets of water and battered their slick vinyl coats. As the wind speed intensified in tandem with the rain, the whistling and whipping sounds through the rigging increased several decibels, sending an audible warning to the mortal beings.

Cort nodded at Thad's rather abrasive demand. The tone in his voice had changed, carrying something closer to a harsh ultimatum than a protective command. Cort reluctantly accepted that the situation called for it and did not challenge the order. It was neither the time nor place to ask for an explanation. Turning slowly and crouching, Cort followed the railing one hand over the other. An aggressive fear grew within him as he shuffled forward across the drenched deck. He placed each foot carefully, planting the front one firmly before picking up the back one. There was nothing more to do or say; the task at hand was laid out in no uncertain terms, and he would simply execute it as quickly and safely as possible.

Chapter 59 - Storm of the Eye

At first the muffled knocking sound coming from the cockpit area didn't register. Cort had heard the muted thumping but dismissed it as part of the surrounding orchestra of the hurricane. It was likely just one component of the boat pounding against another, disturbing for sure, but not at all shocking. A quick glance behind showed that Thad wasn't acknowledging the noise, confirming for Cort that his focus needed to be elsewhere. Both men continued to progress toward the front of the boat as it rose high on another crest and surfed back into a deep valley of dark water.

The second succession of knocks was louder; Cort half-cocked his head and caught Thad glancing to the rear of the boat. Thad abruptly pivoted his head to the front again, but the men's eyes met for a brief second. It was an instant Cort interpreted as awkward - the captain seemingly trying to gauge his reaction to the sound without drawing more attention to it. Pausing to listen through the howling wind and rain, Cort could no longer ignore the current series of more persistent knocks. They were rapid, but random and unsteady, and likely being produced by a person.

"Hey?"

Cort shouted through the weather this time, ignoring the earlier warning about his volume. *If this storm didn't wake up Marilyn, then yelling sure as hell wouldn't.* Thad's expression was troubled, but he didn't respond. Cort persisted.

"You hear that knocking, right?" Shouting again, Cort ignored the subtle vexation in Thad's face.

"No." Thad shook his head dismissively, spraying large drops of water from his hood. "C'mon, were almost there."

Cort paused in his stance, disbelieving his own ears. He hadn't imagined the sound, but as he listened now, there was only the noise of crashing waves, whistles of wind, and the popping of drops against their coats. Accepting again the knocking was of no concern, he moved another step forward. A mere second later the unmistakable sound of a fist pounding against glass penetrated the fury of the night. This time the sound reverberated from close proximity, near his feet, followed by the glow of light from the cabin window he'd just passed.

Cort turned around and crouched lower to the small window, shocked to see Marilyn's face through the glass. She looked scared, and Cort was perplexed. Focused on Marilyn, Cort realized it was her pounding a minute ago, likely thumping against the rear glass slider, and probably very concerned that it was locked. But as he read her lips and watched her desperate hand gesture towards her son, he realized that she was not frightened for herself. She was shouting "LOOK OUT!" from the other side of the glass and pointing towards the real danger. Cort cocked his head to the left, just in time to see Thad unclip Cort's carabiner from the jackline.

Standing in a flash of unbalanced motion, Cort took a wobbly step backwards, completely confused by what was transpiring. The look in Thad's eyes had grown darker and even more sullen, reflecting some sort of premeditated pain.

"I'M SORRY!"

Thad's volume was elevated to ensure audibility, but the words held a distinct lack of emotion - robotically delivered as if he were apologizing for a future that could not be altered. Interpreting the words as a warning, Cort instinctively knew something awful was about to happen, and all senses became sharpened with fear. The motion of Thad's right hand did not go without notice. Cort saw the captain's elbow cock backwards before it plunged forward. Fortuitously in that micro-second, the boat hit a wave and changed direction just enough to throw the men's balance off - the shift altering the trajectory of Thad's arm as he stumbled forward. Cort caught a glimpse of the silvery metal flash, and he knew the knife was coming before it pierced his skin. Managing to side-step a direct blow, the cold blade sliced his raincoat, undershirt, and skin at a 45-degree angle. Two inches of the razor-sharp steel cut through his skin and oblique muscle, sending the sensation of a horrible sting to Cort's brain. Neurons were firing but Cort simply couldn't process the events that had just transpired. He only knew he was in critical danger, and the realization his life was in jeopardy helped him maintain focus. The storm, the ocean, and everything that lie beneath the water's surface - none of it posed as much of a threat as the man in front of him.

A rush of adrenaline helped mask the pronounced discomfort a couple inches below Cort's rib cage. He let go of the sail bag and gathered his balance in expectation of another rush. The bag flew off wildly and slapped Thad's head as it whipped by, wrapping around a cable at the rear of the boat. The brief distraction gave Cort an extra second. This time he was prepared for the wild swing of Thad's knife wielding arm, and he dodged the second attempt by an inch. As the hand of his assailant passed by his body, Cort lunged forward and tackled him to the deck. Thad went down awkwardly underneath Cort's weight, landing hard on his left side. The knife remained in Thad's right hand as he tried to wriggle into a position where he could use the weapon again. Wrapping both hands around Thad's wrist, Cort attempted to control the hand holding the deadly blade. Maneuvering his knees up under his body, he managed to shift all his weight onto Thad's abdomen, temporarily subduing the attack.

"THAD! STOP! DON'T!"

The words pierced the howling storm and struck Thad's eardrum, rendering him still for a second as he stared up into Cort's face. There was a helplessness in Thad's eyes now, giving Cort the impression for a split-second that the assault was over. The impression was fleet, like in the eye of a hurricane, when everything becomes temporarily calm. Thad's left fist came up and around, landing on Cort just below the knife wound. The blow stung, like he'd been stabbed again, but despite the intense pain, Cort maintained his grip on Thad's wrist and rolled sideways. The men grappled as the waves rocked the boat to starboard, shifting their weights into the cabin window. Both glanced at Marilyn's face, now ridden with dread and tears, her mouth moving wildly. Her voice through the glass was muffled beyond comprehension, yet the panic contained within it was unquestionable.

From their knees to their feet, the pair continued in an awkward and unbalanced battle. Mother Nature mimicked a raucous audience as the rain drove harder and the waves grew larger, intensifying the dramatic death match within her arena. In his desperate effort to retain control of the hand holding the knife, Cort gave up leverage, and Thad used that leverage to push his opponent backwards. Cort's foot hydroplaned on the deck, forcing him to give up more ground, and a split-second later he felt the back of his thighs against the top cable of the deck railing. It was too late to change his momentum as the weight of his upper body toppled him further backwards. His legs remained pinned against the railing, while the rest of him was sent into an upended summersault. Finally letting go of Thad's wrist, he was able to flail his arms around in a last-ditch effort to grab something… anything. An upside-down view of the boiling ocean flashed while his hands reached back toward the railing. Both legs came around simultaneously and slammed against the outer hull. A wave of disorientation passed, and Cort found himself right side up again. By some miracle his left hand had managed to find the stainless-steel rail post, holding on just long enough to reach his right hand up to the lower cable of the railing. Moving his left hand to another piece of the cable, he clung tight and attempted to regain control of his view. A large wave pounded the side of the boat, almost pushing him up and over the deck's edge, but it fell just as fast and pulled Cort back down along the outside of the hull. The sight in front of him was terrifying; Thad on the deck, holding tight to a mast cable with one hand and gripping the knife securely in the other. He knew what was coming next as Thad inched forward and lowered the knife towards Cort's left hand. Desperation came out in Cort's shrill cry.

"PLEASE, THAD, NO!"

Thad hesitated but for a second, holding the knife in front of him and shifting his weight to keep balanced. Helpless and clinging to the cable rail, Cort watched Thad's eyes, blank of expression, as he yelled back.

"I'M SORRY! IT'S EITHER YOU OR HER!"

There was an instant of confusion and fear as Cort tried to process what he'd heard,*"you or her?"* It didn't make sense, but there was no time to ask questions. Thad swung the knife wildly towards Cort's left hand. Cort released the railing in expectation, but not before the blade caught the thickest part of his index finger, cutting a deep slice between the two knuckles down to the bone. Clutching tight with his right hand, another wave slammed him against the hull and submerged him from head to toe; the pressure of the water pinning him against the hull and enabling him to maintain his hold. His grip was weakening, but he squeezed hard and opened his eyes again; his vision returning after the salt-water washed away from his face. Thad had been knocked back by the wave but was now shuffling on his knees towards the last remaining contact point between Cort and Sea Sleigh.

The notion of letting go and being swept into the open sea was worse than the thought of being knifed to death. The morbid question raced through his head, whether exposure and hypothermia would take him before something else did. Maybe he could just drown himself immediately upon entering the water. The thought was terrifying, but likely the best-case scenario. He assumed the fade to black would be inconceivably scary, but rather painless, and much less petrifying than the prospect of floating in open water with blood discharging from multiple wounds.

Cort's eyes locked onto Thad's for what he presumed to be the last time. He searched deep for a glimmer of humanity, something he might find to change the course of his pending demise. Creeping closer, Thad raised the knife in preparation to strike the other hand. He hesitated, and his eyes became glossy just before he jerked his head away toward the cabin. Eight feet away, the image of his mother's pained face in the window injected him with a shot of sanity. When he returned his gaze, Cort saw the glimmer that he was seeking; a softening that told him his fate had not quite been decided. With his grip slipping, Cort clutched the rail cable with one hand and groped the edge of the deck with his other. Thad pushed the knife tip into the deck, pressed the lock release button and folded the blade back into the handle, then shoved it into his pocket before reaching out to Cort.

Despite an absence of trust, there was no hesitation as Cort thrust his bloody hand upward with the last remaining strength, his bicep and forearm muscles burning in pain. Seconds away from falling into the churning black water, he could come up with no better choice than to reach out to his would-be murderer. Thad latched onto Cort's wrist with both hands and shifted his lower body into a sitting position, thrusting his legs against the rail post as he began pulling Cort upward.

As Cort's chest and torso came up over the edge, Thad abruptly halted his pull. Cort lifted his head, expecting to see the knife in Thad's hand again, poised high and ready to send a final plunge into his back. Maybe he planned to kill Cort completely before tossing him overboard, not willing to risk the ever-so-slim chance of Cort surviving the ocean, being rescued, and telling his harrowing tale of Thad's attempted murder. Instead of a psychotic premeditative glare, he saw a combination of shock, fear, and confusion fill Thad's eyes. His mouth hung open and his gaze focused just above Cort's head; eyes steadily raising to follow the object of his horror. Turning in a jerk, Cort immediately understood what had rendered Thad frozen with terror. The titanic wall of water that was bearing down on their existence was beyond petrifying. Both men watched in horror, staring aghast for a half-second, in disbelief that a wave of such magnitude could exist. Cort scrambled forward pulling his legs up and over, releasing Thad's hand and grabbing the first solid object he could reach. He knew the deck rail would offer no protection from the two million gallons of water about to violently crash over their world, but instinct told him to hang on and hold his breath.

Chapter 60 – Air

The starboard side hull rose into the wave as the port side followed and tucked below it. The mountain of seawater pushed the catamaran into a vertical position with both hulls parallel to the top of the wave, the massive breaker now cresting white, forty feet above them. In a swift motion, Thad unclipped his carabiner and clung tight to a cleat just above the cabin window, bracing his feet on the bottom of the boom. Cort wrapped both hands around the rail post with his feet searching the cabin wall for support. Finally finding solid ground on the window, the sliver of security was brief as the glass shattered under his weight sending one leg through the open hole. The wave continued to curl, taking the boat in a sideways roll and sending both men into an inverted dangle. Cort watched Thad let go and push away from the aluminum boom, his body narrowly missing the hard metal and tangle of ropes. Thad's feet hit the sail and slid down it, toward the top of the mast, which was disappearing into the boiling sea. Just before reaching the water, his left foot wedged between a mast tang and the connecting cable, ripping his shoe off and slicing a gash through the bottom of his foot. His body spun around, hitting the ocean in a sideways position, and disappearing into the dark water.

Cort's right leg remained stuck inside the cabin while the craft turned upside down and whipped him under the ocean's surface like a rag doll. He managed to gulp one last breath just before being submerged, but it was expelled from his lungs as the impact with the water pushed it back out. Dizzy and panicked, his hands searched for a hold; any kind of leverage to pull his leg out of the open porthole. A shard of glass from the window frame pierced his upper thigh, triggering an underwater scream and stealing the last breath in his lungs. Reaching back with both hands, he grabbed the edge of the window and was able to break off the sliver of glass and push his leg away, but he could not pull it free. The pressure of the water rushing into the cabin sucked him with it, and the thought flashed in his brain that these were his final seconds of life. Before his lungs exploded, he felt force on the bottom of his foot; a hand that untangled something from around his ankle then thrust his leg outward and free from the small rectangular hole. Released, he swung around and reached into the hole, groping wildly expecting to find a hand, but there was nothing. Fading from consciousness and about to pass out, he pushed away with both feet and found the surface a few feet above him.

Breaching the air with a gasp, Cort coughed out seawater before inhaling several deep breaths. The period of relief was fleeting, barely allowing recovery before he was pummeled by another crashing wave. The massive pressure of the water hit him like a bus; the fathoms below him giving way to the force, sending him deep down into the churning sea. All sense of direction was lost while his body was twisted and spun in a tornado of water. Only seconds passed before the water surrounding him became still again; the brunt of the wave passing by. Eyes opened to blackness and the sting of salt, with no sense of which way was up or down, and scarce enough air left to wait and see which way his life vest took him. Feeling the slight pull of buoyancy, he swam hard towards the perceived surface. Seconds ticked past as he pulled against the water in the direction presumed to be up, but there was no end to it. Sensing for the second time his lungs were about to explode, the belief that his heart was beating its last beats zipped through his oxygen-starved brain. The image of Celeste passed between his lobes, and he assumed he was with her in the afterlife.

Her image disappeared as his skin felt the element of air engulf his head again. He coughed and regurgitated salt water, sucking in oxygen and returning to consciousness. Disoriented in the dark churn, Cort spun around in the water searching for anything to hold onto. The outline of the two hulls was still prominent, illuminated from below the surface by the cabin lights. He swam hard against another large wave that forced him further from the capsized vessel.

The lifeboat!

If he could get back to Sea Sleigh, it would be possible to swim down to the hatch and release it. Two more attempts, and two more crashing waves moved him further from the darkening object. As the fourth wave washed over him, he returned to the surface unable to find any sign of the catamaran.

Spinning 360 degrees twice, Cort searched the darkness for anything that wasn't ocean, but there was nothing but dark sky and even darker water. The sting had intensified as soon as he'd entered the ocean, but his brain had been focused on immediate survival. Only now, as the salt bonded with the pain nerves within his fleshy wounds, did he become consciously aware of the discomfort. The reality crept into his psyche, that he would die alone and in the tight grip of fear. The question needled at him again; would hypothermia take him before anything else did? The spike of adrenaline he'd just had was trying to convince his body the water wasn't so cold, but his brain knew the false sense of warmth would only last so long. He thought of Thad's earlier conversation, and wondered when the first stage would creep in.

Please come soon.

He thought about Marilyn and Thad, wondering if they would survive. As a salty wave washed over him, the images of his boat mates were replaced with those of Lucie. Cort closed his eyes, and kept them shut. There was nothing to see anyway, and the salt sting was uncomfortable. The image of his daughter's face brought him comfort, and he could almost hear her calling out to him. Her voice grew louder, and deeper, and Cort realized it wasn't her voice in his head at all. Eyes opened as he turned from side to side, focusing on the howling. The wind, he was sure, was playing tricks on his auditory system.

"Cooooooort!" The faint call across the wind and water was convincing.

"Mooooooom!"

Was that real?

Cort searched desperately through the driving rain and salty spray.

"Mooooooooooooom! Cooooooooooorrrrrrt!"

He was certain now - the muffled call was Thad's. Squinting and straining his burning eyes, he could see nothing in any direction and no longer heard any sound resembling his name being called. Swimming hard across the breaking waves in the direction he'd perceived the voice from, Cort desperately hoped his ears hadn't deceived him. Two waves broke over his head in succession, and as the saltwater from the second one cleared from his vision, a dim light materialized in the distance. Gasping for air and exhausted already, Cort stopped swimming and squinted into the abyss. He picked up the gleam again in his peripheral vision, just as the call came again. It was louder and clearer this time, inspiring Cort to yell back in the direction of the light with all the voice he could muster.

"THAAAAAAD! His shout was stifled by a wave that rose from under his chin and slapped the front of his face. Coughing the ocean back out of his mouth, he heard the voice penetrate the darkness again.

"HEEEEERE!"

Swimming harder now, he fought the fatigue and pushed in the direction of the voice and the light.

"THAAAAAAAAAD!" His yell was absorbed by the wind, but Cort spotted the partial silhouette against the blackness. The dark shadow was bobbing erratically, raised well above the water line, and Cort's adrenaline kicked in again when he realized Thad was kneeling in the dinghy. The men drew closer to each other, Cort swimming across the current and Thad using his hands to paddle towards him. Thirty seconds later, Cort appeared out of the black ocean and Thad hoisted him up and over the inflated rubber hull. Each man lay back into the raft, drenched and depleted and sucking air.

"Tha… thanks." Cort managed to yell the stuttered gratitude between breaths. Thad responded with nothing more than a quick nod of acknowledgement. After several seconds of heavy inhaling and exhaling, Thad shouted the question through the driving rain.

"My mom? Did you see her?"

"No, she was still below. I'm not sure if she got out. Sorry."

Despite the rain and saltwater dripping down Thad's face, Cort could see the deep pain in his eyes. He wanted to tell Thad how she'd saved him from drowning, but those details could wait. Cort had questions. For starters, he wanted to know why Thad had tried to knife him to death, why he'd changed his mind, and why he'd saved him from a watery grave just seconds ago. Instead, he stayed silent, thankful to be out of the ocean, but still in fear of the man sitting six feet away from him. Cort understood that "saved" was a temporary condition at best, as the wind across his wet skin chilled his body and blood. His relief of being out of the water was replaced by the realization that his present situation was only moderately better, and in some facets, maybe worse. Turning his head, Cort eyed his unwanted raftmate who was huddled in the space beyond the front seat of the small craft. Thad had his knees in his chest, arms around them, seemingly trying to retain a bit of body heat. The man's face was grim, carrying an expression of being completely beaten.

The waves continued to break all around them, sending large quantities of spray up and over the men, as if partnering with the pounding rain to keep them soaked. Cort hollered through the wind, from the rear of the raft to the front.

"We're gonna die in this raft, aren't we?"

Thad turned his head and gathered his air for a response but decided not to speak. Instead, he simply shook his head from side to side, then reached under his butt. Both hands emerged, clinging tightly to a large white piece of polyester material that Cort recognized immediately.

Chapter 61 — Warmer Air

The howling wind muddled the words, but Thad's instructions were nonetheless clear.

"Take off your clothes."

"Take off my clothes?" Cort couldn't help but repeat the instructions in the form of a question, despite there being no other interpretation he could come up with.

"Yes, now. Take them off and put your life vest back on. That material doesn't hold water, so it will dry as soon as your skin does."

Cort hesitated, but as Thad began to remove his own life vest, Cort accepted the unorthodox directive must be for his own good. Thirty seconds later, both men had disrobed down to their sport-short briefs, wet skin reflecting the dim light of the lantern. Cort followed suit as Thad put the life vest back on over his bare torso. As he zipped it up, Cort noticed Thad was still wearing the one shoe he'd retained through the rogue-wave event. The other foot was bare and bleeding from a 2-inch-long laceration. Cort assumed the shoe had been ripped off by something sharp as they were flipping upside down with Sea Sleigh.

"You're keeping one shoe on?" Cort shouted over the driving rain, now pelting their bare skin.

Thad simply shook his head, moved to the center of the raft, gripping the sail bag, and removed the single shoe carefully. He tucked it deep into the side of the raft, where the inflated hull squeezed it between the solid floor and held it in place. Cort watched in confusion but was too cold and exhausted to question any of Thad's actions at this point.

Must be some sentimental pair of shoes.

"Get in, feet first." Thad gestured towards the sail bag, which he'd stretched out in length along the floor of the middle section of the raft, holding it down close to the floor so that the wind didn't catch and rip it away.

Cort complied without question, understanding the sail bag would act as a potential life-saving cocoon. Pushing himself in and along the bottom of the bag, he curled a little to fit into what was roughly a six-foot long space. He watched out the end hole as Thad took his drenched t-shirt and wrung it, forcing most of the water out before handing it through the hole.

"Wipe your skin off. Get it as dry as you can. Hurry."

After removing ninety percent of the moisture from his rain-soaked body, Cort handed the t-shirt back out the hole.

"Move over!"

Thad barked the order then backed into the hole, wriggling his way past Cort's body until his feet reached the end of the bag. He grabbed the battery-operated lantern, which Cort assumed would give off a small degree of heat. The tight space made it difficult for Thad to reach his hands out the opening and wring out the t-shirt. Bringing it back in and wiping himself as dry as possible, he tossed the t-shirt back into the rain and pulled the drawstring sewed into the end of the sail bag. No further instructions were given. None were needed. Both men turned their bodies, rotating until their backs lined up, and then stopped moving. Raindrops pelted against the bag, reminding Cort of the sound of hail hitting a windshield. The impact of the drops could be felt through the bag, as a significant portion of the men's skin was pressed against the interior of the material. Both were shivering, but Cort took some comfort in Thad's next words.

"Be patient, it'll warm up. Just try to calm down and rest, maybe even sleep."

"I would if I trusted you." Cort uttered the jab, caring little about its potential effect.

Thad didn't respond, but the air got a bit thicker as the remark circulated through the confined space. Minutes later, the skin on their backs began to lose the chill, and before the rain stopped ten minutes later, their shivering had ceased altogether. Cort was surprised, even shocked - the bag was performing the duties of a makeshift Dutch oven. Despite Thad being the absolute last person on earth he wanted to be next to, Cort was thankful their body heat was being shared and retained. Ironically, he understood that without his would-be-murderer and the sail bag, he'd have died of hypothermia within a couple hours. Instead, while still in a state of discomfort, their bodies stayed warm enough to function properly. As minutes passed, the chill disappeared, and warm skin became steadily warmer. Cort's thoughts became more random, and he could feel himself drifting into an unwanted state of sub-consciousness. Between the sound of the waves, wind, and random droplets of ocean hitting the sail bag, he struggled to focus. Before he realized it had happened, the exhaustion had overtaken him, and his brain slipped into a deep state of sleep.

Chapter 62 – Aired Out

The feeling of heat and the sound of deep breathing pulled Cort out of his slumber. When he opened his eyes, there was momentary panic as an unexpected light and the perception of suffocation struck him. The alarm was brief as the recollection of his present situation flooded his thoughts, and his brain interpreted the light shining through the sail bag as the sun. It had risen above the horizon high enough to crest the hull of the raft and illuminate the top portion of their cocoon. As he reached his hand out the small hole, Cort's arm brushed against Thad's thick hair, which was partially blocking the bag's opening. Cort didn't care, and the rustling of the man next to him was neither welcomed nor unwelcomed. Loosening the drawstring, Cort separated from the sappy blood sticking him to the inside of the sail cover and clambered through the hole, glancing back inward as he exited. A line of the thick crimson liquid had filled the valley at the bottom of the bag, but the half pint of coagulating blood wasn't just his. Looking deeper within the chamber, he noted that another small puddle had collected at the far end of the bag, next to Thad's lacerated foot.

Taking note of the sun's position, Cort estimated it to be around 8:00 A.M. He'd slept four hours. A deep thirst overcame him as he emerged from the open end of their makeshift shelter. The smell of the cool sea air coupled with the sight of the sun rising above the horizon was sublime - not even a hint of the previous night's furious weather. A hesitant smile crossed Cort's lips, like the protagonist at the end of a horror movie who'd escaped the reaper and found refuge. But not quite. Thad followed behind him. They emerged like two caterpillars leaving the cocoon before their metamorphosis was complete. For a brief minute, Cort's feelings of vexation for his raft-mate evaporated into the humid air that followed him out of the bag. The relief, however, was brief, as a visual wave of the events that had taken place just hours ago washed through his thoughts.

Unlike his mind, the sea was calm. Had Cort not known better, he'd swear they were adrift on a large lake. Clambering his way to the rear seat of the raft, he began examining the outboard motor hanging loosely to the back end. It appeared damaged at best - the motor housing was gone, and the throttle handle was cracked and bent at a sixty-degree angle to the left.

"It won't work, I tried last night."

Thad spoke and extended his hand, holding a jug of water he'd pulled from the front compartment of their tiny vessel. The voice from behind him erased any sense of serenity Cort was clinging to and he turned to make sure Thad was not approaching him. Cautiously, he took the jug from Thad, who like himself, was clad in thigh-length underwear and a life vest. Chugging back a long drink of the water, he watched over the bottom of the jug as Thad moved to the front seat. Even at opposite ends of the inflated rubber craft, there were barely seven feet separating them. Eye contact was made between the disheveled and weary looking raftmates, just before Thad followed up his analysis of the motor with an optimistic thought.

"Doesn't matter anyway, Cort, we won't need it. We're only hours away from rescue. Not days, just hours."

"Yeah well, I guess that's only if you don't kill me first, right?" Cort's reply was sarcastic, and he didn't try to hide the anger in his words. He glanced across at Thad, who like himself, looked like he'd been dragged in by the cat. Thad didn't respond, seemingly stifled by shame. Seconds of tense silence passed before Cort added a question.

"You think if I was still floating out there alone, they'd locate me by the signal coming from my vest. I mean if hypothermia or something else didn't get me first?"

"Well actually, no. I disengaged the signal in your vest before I came down to wake you last night. If you hadn't found me in this raft when you did, I doubt…" Thad trailed off, then offered, "I'm sorry about that, Cort. What can I say?"

The nonchalant tone in Thad's explanation triggered a burst of outrage in Cort.

"What can you say?!" Cort's words carried a sharp incredulous tone now. "How about maybe you say what the FUCK was going through your head when you tried to cut me in half!"

"Calm down, Cort. It doesn't matter now, does it? I mean, I didn't kill you. In fact, I saved your life." Thad calmly turned away from Cort in the most non-threatening manner possible. He positioned himself sideways, straddling each side of his seat. Cort's blood temperature rose as he stared at the side of Thad's head from the back of the raft, but Thad refused to return eye-contact.

"It does matter! It fucking matters a lot!" Cort was shouting now, "I'd appreciate knowing what the hell your reason was. Or is it that you're just goddamned bat-shit crazy?"

Thad turned his head away further, despondent, and stayed silent. Cort calmed his tone, realizing that his anger was creating the opposite effect that he was wanting.

"Thad," his voice a bit tempered now, "you said 'it was either me or her'. You remember last night? You yelled it at me right before cutting my hand. What did you mean? Tell me what you meant by that, tell me right now!"

Abruptly, Thad turned and erupted at Cort.

"MY DAUGHTER!" His eyes shifted and he lowered his voice. "It's Gracie!"

"Your daughter? I don't understand?" Cort's anger hadn't subsided, but he softened his tone as Thad's words struck their target.

"She's dying, Cort." Thad confessed and lowered his head. "My daughter is dying, and I'm trying to save her. That's all. Is that a good enough reason for you?"

Cort's mind went to Lucie as he tried to comprehend the gravity of Thad's reply. He looked down to the floor of the raft, which had taken water overnight and was filled with a two-inch-deep mix of sea water and rain. Cort stayed silent and waited. After a long pause, Thad continued. He explained that his daughter Gracie had a rare disease, the same one that had taken his brother from him when he was only nine years old. Thad described the genetic disorder and the way it attacked the motor neurons controlling muscle movement. Cort already knew about the disease from Marilyn's story last night, but he listened without interrupting. Thad finished by saying that he and Amelia had gambled on having a child, believing they were relatively safe because the disease normally skips a generation. They lost the gamble, and now, as Gracie was approaching her eighth birthday, the atrophy was beginning.

"She needs surgery, multiple surgeries… and a boatload of other treatments." Thad paused, his annoyance with having to explain himself now evident. Finally, he spoke again, his voice more tempered and less sullen. "Medical science has come a long way, just within the past ten years, and the doctors feel the condition can be controlled and maybe even stopped. But…"

"But what?" Cort pushed, still angry, but concealing it with a tone of compassion.

"But it's extremely expensive. The treatment program will take place over 15 months, and the cost is going to be somewhere north of a million dollars."

Cort contemplated the financial issue, still not satisfied and still certainly angry.

"Thad, listen, I'm sorry, really, but I'm not understanding. Don't you have health insurance? And even if it wasn't completely covered, you obviously have assets you could liquidate. Are you that f'ing greedy that you'd kill a guy before selling a few?" The irritation increased Cort's octave again as he finished.

Thad shook his head dismissively from left to right and pointed into the bottom of the raft.

"We need to bail this water out. Here, help me."

Cort watched Thad take the bottom lip of the sail bag's opening and submerge it in the water on the raft's floor. Taking the other side of the sail bag, Cort put his anger on brief pause, not wanting to compromise their small vessel and only separation from the ocean. It worked perfectly, as the men held the bag down until it filled up with a gallon-or-so of water. Each man simultaneously lifted the side of the bag's opening over the edge of the raft, picked up the rear of the bag, and emptied the water. They repeated this a half-dozen more times emptying each of the three sections of the raft. While they worked, Thad explained.

"Financially, I'm in dire straits. My real estate business is under water. It's a long story, but a couple years ago when the market turned, late in 2023… you remember?" Cort nodded in acknowledgement and Thad continued. "I needed to cut overhead costs to stop the bleeding profits. I gambled by self-insuring a lot of our properties. It wasn't supposed to be for long - just a year or so until interest rates went back down and the market, well, never mind." Thad paused, seemingly reflecting on what Cort assumed to be a poor decision. Continuing, Thad confirmed the assumption.

"Anyway, we had a fire. A big fire. It was a total loss, to the tune of $4.1 million in property damage. Uninsured. All of it."

"Christ," Cort absorbed the gravity of the loss, but it didn't prevent him from pressing further. "Well, that's terrible. I get it. But still, between the rest of the business assets, and again, the health insurance?"

With most of the water emptied from the raft, the men sat back down.

"We lost our health insurance policy too, Cort. Technically, I guess I let it lapse. I never intended to have the coverage cancelled. Whatever. I know, stupid right? But you don't understand how bad the situation was. And my mom… she didn't know about any of it. I mean, she knew about the fire, but not the insurance…" His voice trailed off some and a few words were mumbled before Cort understood again, "…so caught up in the damn ministry the past couple of years. I couldn't bring myself to tell her how bad it was. God, I hope she's ok." He paused as thoughts of his mother distracted his train of thought. A few seconds passed before he continued. "And my wife, Amelia, doesn't know the half of it either. She thinks that us selling the boat will just be a cushion fund. She knew we wouldn't be sailing again any time soon and didn't question my plan to sell Sea Sleigh."

Cort interjected, "So, your mom and wife had no idea about your plan to kill me and collect the life insurance? And you just figured nobody would ever know?" Cort asked the question but didn't wait for an answer. "The insurance company would've investigated. They'd figure it out?" His anger grew as he sensed Thad had thought through these dilemmas already.

"There'd be no investigation, Cort. Your body would never be found anyway. Even if it did wash up on the beach weeks from now, there wouldn't be much left of it. I'd have suggested it was suicide, and the information they'd dig up would support that." He paused, sensing he'd triggered another level of anger in Cort, then offered more. "And, Cort, please understand, I never planned to kill you. I decided that last night, as a last-gasp chance to save my daughter. Everything was working out so well before we left Rhode Island. But then, damn it man, you got sick and fucked up everything!"

Cort's blood was beginning to heat. Despite his conflicting compassion for Thad's daughter, Gracie, and the guilt he felt about forgetting to take the Scopolamine, he could scarcely believe what he was hearing. His next words were nearly spat out.

"Jesus Christ, man, what the fuck is wrong with you! I hope it was worth it you prick, because if we do get rescued, you're going to prison!"

Thad snapped back, "Hey, don't judge me! It's my little girl. I'd do anything for her." He paused at the thought of Gracie then aimed his retort back at the man sitting two arm's lengths away from him. "Wouldn't you kill for someone you loved?"

Cort shook his head and answered without hesitation, "No! No way!"

"Really, Cort? Are you telling me, if you were given the opportunity to go back in time and kill that truck driver before he set out on his delivery back on February 2nd… are you saying you wouldn't?"

"Holy shit, Thad!" Cort fired back, but paused as he thought about the question briefly, the memory of the murderous dream he'd had filling his head, "No, I wouldn't kill…" He hesitated again and pointed his finger at Thad before continuing, "That's not even the same thing anyway, not even close, you psychopath!"

"It's kind of the same thing, Cort," Thad's voice was steady, but elevated a few decibels too, "and I bet if you were honest, you'd consider killing that guy. Aaron, I think his name was?" Thad kept his tone even but was getting more heated himself as he stared back into Cort's eyes. "And you? I believed I was helping you. You were a fucking basket case. Are you gonna sit there and tell me you never considered offing yourself?"

Both men had stopped emptying the sail bag, glaring at each other on the verge of eruption. Too angry to speak, Cort remained still and silent while he waited for further explanation into Thad's deep knowledge of his recent past.

"Yeah, I know all about you." Thad's voice took on a demeaning tone. "My brother-in-law works for the FBI. He gave me everything I needed to know about you. That's right, I know about what you've been up to since your wife died. And for what it's worth, I'm sorry about that. Truly I am. But I know stuff. I know you bought a bottle of whiskey the same day you filled a prescription for Dayvir… Dayvirgo… or whatever the fuck that sleeping pill was." Cort glared at Thad but did not respond before Thad added on more. "Something tells me you were planning to take them both together."

"HEY!" Cort snapped back at the accusation. Despite knowing it was the truth, his blood was in pre-boiling stage, like when the tiny bubbles appear on the bottom of the pot of water. "That was months ago. That's not me anymore. I came on this fucking trip as part of my road back. Mine and Lucie's road back! How dare you think you could take my life and leave my daughter without her father! You're Goddamn lucky I don't just kill your mother-fucking-ass right now!"

"Oh really," Thad snapped in a shout, "you're gonna kill my ass, huh, you sure about that?" Thad challenged back and let the sail bag drop from his hands.

Cort retorted, rather calmly now.

"What Thad, you think I'm scared of you? You think your fucking snowboarding skills are gonna protect you against me?" Cort clenched his fists tight and looked hard into Thad's pupils.

Thad raised from his seat in the front of the raft, thrusting a threat downward.

"Maybe you should think about what you're saying, Palmerton. Maybe you should realize that it's just me and you out here, and it's not too late for me to finish the job."

Cort lowered his head and shook it slowly, feigning fear and defeat at Thad's standing warning. He lowered his hands to his side, just long enough for Thad to feel unthreatened. In a burst, Cort lunged at the Olympic athlete, wrapping his arms around Thad's lower back while pressing his face into his abdomen. In one swift take down move, he lifted Thad off the floor of the raft and slammed him down with a wet thud. Before Thad could gather his wits and his balance, Cort reached his right hand back and pushed a solid straight jab, connecting in the corner of Thad's left eye. The shot stunned the larger male, so much so that Cort sensed he'd knocked Thad out. Opening his eyes, Thad lifted his head and reached his hand up to block any other potential punches, but he was a split second late. Cort was already sending his right fist down again forcefully, landing it on the bridge of Thad's perfect Roman nose. Thad's head shot backwards into the rubber hull of the raft; the lifeboat shifting so much that Cort paused in disbelief. Thad's hands lowered in defeat, as blood began dripping from the split at the top of his nose just between the eyebrows.

Positioned on top of his opponent with his knees straddling each side of Thad's torso, Cort paused to assess the damage. His own hand was broken, which he knew from the pain and cracking sound when he'd connected the second punch. Thad's body lay limp, sunken down to the raft's floor, his back flat and his legs forced further over the raft's side. Despite the apparent victory, Cort was not completely satisfied and pondered dropping another punch to Thad's face. He stared down at the man, and for a second, felt remorse. Like himself, Thad was a father, desperately attempting to save his daughter and himself from devastation.

As his body slumped further into the raft, the shift in position enabled Thad to reach the opposite side hull. His left hand was now within grasp of his single shoe, still wedged between the hull and floor. Cort interpreted Thad's hands-down posture as a gesture of retreat, but his brief compassion for his foe dissipated. The urge to strike him again returned in an impulse of rage. Images flashed in his mind; the goalie's father from the soccer game, the salesman at the car lot, and most of all, the truck driver who'd killed Celeste. All of Cort's suffering and anger came to a head, mere seconds away from erupting - it would take an act of God to keep him from knocking Thad unconscious. Catching his breath, Cort watched the eyes of the man beneath him try to regain focus. As Thad's pupils straightened into a stare of defensive fury, Cort lifted his hand, poising it ready for another devastating plunge downward.

The punch did not fall, but it had nothing to do with God. In the seconds Cort had contemplated which hand to strike with, he'd failed to notice Thad reach for the shoe. Frozen in place, Cort felt the sharp metal against his throat, and it paralyzed him. In one swift motion, Thad had grasped the knife he'd hidden inside the shoe, flipped open the blade with two fingers, and thrust it upward against Cort's jugular vein. The pressure was felt across the whole length of the blade, which Thad was applying firmly enough to lacerate several layers of skin. With his head positioned twenty-six inches directly above Thad's, Cort stared down into the eyes that had seemingly lost all sense of solicitude. Cort's own eyes widened in anticipation of the knife being pulled across his throat, and the expectation of his blood waterfalling onto his killer's face.

"Thad," Cort's eyes softened in desperation, his voice now feigning compassion, "I'm sorry. Please, I'm begging you not to."

Cort gulped - the movement in his neck enabling the razor-sharp blade to deepen a hair closer to his carotid artery. Cort closed his eyes, no longer willing to look into the hollow dark stare of the man who would once more determine his fate.

***

Thad kept his eyes focused and stern, unwilling to let his stare offer an iota of sympathy as he considered his options. He could pull the blade across, and the man above him would bleed out inside of a minute. From there he could puncture both lungs of the dead body, attach it to the busted motor with a rope, and heave both over the side. There would be a mess to clean up in the raft, but he had an ocean full of water at his disposal. Seconds passed and Thad watched a droplet of blood fall from the knife blade down to his cheek. Barely flinching, he held the knife firmly against the throat of the man whose death would help end his worst nightmare.

As the man above him closed his eyes, Thad absorbed the emotion in Cort's face. He understood the pain and fear of a man who was also sacrificing everything for his daughter. Remaining stoic, more seconds passed as he contemplated his next action.

Maybe there's another way? Maybe God has a different plan?

Staring intensely at the man whose blood was slowly dripping down next to his ear, Thad wondered if another solution was within reach.

Both men remained still, and Thad watched Cort open his eyes, quite possibly about to make one final plea. No words were spoken, but their stalemate was resolved abruptly. Unexpected and in the blink of an eye, the resolution to their dilemma transpired in a way neither of them could have ever predicted, catalyzed several minutes earlier as they'd bailed water from the raft. During their efforts, they hadn't given a second thought to the fact the water they were emptying into the ocean contained nearly six ounces of blood.

Chapter 63 - Carcharodon Carcharias
(several minutes earlier)

For a 19-year-old, she was large. At 17 ½ feet long and just under 4,300 pounds, it was rare for her to encounter another creature with greater dimensions. Even within her own species, one of the largest amongst the shark genus, she dwarfed every other member of her shiver. Despite the common name designated to her by humans, only the lower half of her body reflected a white hue. Furthermore, the "great" tag was somewhat of an understated description for the largest predatory fish on earth. While she had no conscious awareness of those statistics, her age and size provided important instinctive direction. There was an automatic knowledge that she was within her prime reproductive years, and her physical dimensions provided the ability to be more aggressive around competitors, even when other white sharks were included among them.

Those factors also equated to the inherent cognition that food was as important now as it would ever be in her life. A soon-to-be-mother, her two primary priorities were the safety and nourishment of her unborn. Eating was a forgone reaction to an available food source, with no conscious thought required. Whether she'd eaten three months ago, or three days ago, she would not pass up the opportunity to consume calories. In nearly every one of those opportunities, the result was the painful and violent death of her targeted prey.

Her first litter of four pups were born two years earlier and she was presently eleven months into her second pregnancy. Birth wouldn't take place for another month or so, but she'd begun her migration into these warmer waters several weeks ago. Swimming at an average speed of five miles per hour, she'd make her way south over the next three to four weeks and give birth somewhere far off the coast of northern Georgia. Shortly after birth, her pups would swim away and take care of themselves. The swim of some nine hundred miles would then be made back to the cooler waters of the North Atlantic. There she'd find refuge off the coast of Massachusetts, one of the areas where other Great White sharks were beginning to grow in population again.

The large portion of her brain devoted to smell would provide her ample opportunity to detect prey, and that was precisely the signal that she was receiving now. Tiny particles of blood had just collided with the olfactory lamellae; the sensory cell covered skin folds just inside the two nares on either side of her snout. The particle concentrations were low, indicating the source wasn't within her immediate range, but that indication changed nothing. Her brain computed she could reach whatever was bleeding within a short period of time and possibly be the first predator to its location. Even if she wasn't first, there was a very high probability she would be the largest and most dominant predator on the scene. That conclusion came unconsciously, the preprogrammed result of hundreds of millions of years of evolution. Her decision to pursue the food was without malice; no feeling or emotion forced her to swim faster or slower, and no consideration was made for the animal about to suffer and die to provide her and her babies the necessary sustenance for survival. Her direction changed automatically with the jerk of the muscles in her tail, and she abruptly pointed her large frame towards the promise of fresh protein and fat.

Visual contact was made less than one hundred seconds later. Her approach to the object floating on the surface was careful and concise. There was extra caution taken given the objective to protect her unborn, and because the potential prey wasn't submerged and completely visible like most of her food sources were. Keeping a wide berth, she came around the narrow end of the dark colored object of her focus. A depth of fifteen feet and a total diagonal distance of thirty feet was maintained as she circled it. The scent was most definitely blood, but the visual features of the prey were not exactly familiar to her. Mixed signals were being sent to the optic lobes and olfactory receptors. After making two revolutions and perceiving no threat, she moved in and tightened her counterclockwise perimeter inspection.

The blood concentrations were higher as she got closer, confirming the object was indeed the source. Unsure of what to expect, but showing little fear, she moved in with the intent of contact. The free nerve endings beneath the surface of her skin could give a better indication of palatability. Keeping her belly faced away and protected, she moved in and brushed the side of her prey with the top of her snout. At contact, the floating animal jerked forward with an apparent attempt at escape, but immediately settled back into a non-responsive stillness, bobbing on the tiny waves like it had no reason to be alarmed. Uncommon, but not overly concerning, the response was perceived positively in her brain. The loss of blood coupled with the unnatural motion signified a disabling injury, and what would most likely be a safe and easy target. While her brush-test was less conclusive than she'd expected, the second test would be much more decisive.

With her unborn pups always at the instinctive forefront, the automatic decision was made to attack from below and take the first bite with an element of surprise. Diving down 45 feet in a matter of seconds, the magnificent shark turned to pinpoint her final ascent. Pause was taken as she scanned her target again from the depths. Something had changed. There was more to the shape than just seconds ago. Another piece had become visible - likely a fin, or tentacle, or wing. Dangling from one side, a piece of the injured animal hung just above the surface, dipping in and out of the water, baiting her to indulge. The new section was also the part of the animal that was bleeding, which she could see and smell better as she rose. Slowly at first, until there were just twenty-five feet between her and her next meal, and then with a quick burst of adrenaline-fueled speed, she rose like an ascending torpedo and opened her enormous jaws. Eyes rolled back as she broke the surface in an explosion of salty spray.

Chapter 64 - Horror Movie

A silver-white cloud framed by a heavenly-blue sky was the first image to come into focus. As his brain regained cognitive thought, Cort realized he was floating in the water, but his memory of how he got there was unclear. He'd been on top of Thad, who was holding a knife to his throat. That he was sure of, but... *how long ago was that?* The pain from his rib area and finger jarred his memory, as the salt water swished around the open wounds again. Now it was coming back to him. He been thrown out of the boat, just as Thad's face pushed up and forward and smacked him in the chin. It was a head butt and knock-out blow. His senses now sharpened by the brisk ocean water, he questioned the timeline again.

How long have I been in the water?

Buoyant in his vest, he treaded water and pivoted his body in search of anything other than the ocean, desperately hoping to spy the dinghy. There was no sign of Thad.

Did he float away in the raft, or is he bobbing somewhere in the water too?

Pushing the water with his legs and arms, Cort spun around almost 360 degrees. A sense of hope entered his psyche as the raft was spotted.

Maybe 100 yards away?

He could swim to it in a couple minutes, assuming Thad wasn't inside and paddling away from him. More confusion. There was no sign of another person, not in the raft or in the water. Considering his previous thought, Thad's absence did offer a very slight and brief sense of relief. The fact he was now alone, however, was becoming more concerning by the second. Before beginning his swim toward the raft, Cort scanned in all directions and yelled out into the vast expanse.

"THAAAAAD"

No response, and no visual of anything other than the gray rubber craft atop the calm water.

"THAAAAAAAAAAAAD"

More quiet, more concern.

Stay calm. Don't think, just swim.

Defying his own will, thoughts began spinning in his head as he pushed the water behind him. The events that occurred just before being rendered unconscious were coming back to him, and the most logical explanation for why those events happened as they did, materialized into a stark realization.

We were knocked out of that raft by something below.

"Oh, Christ."

He mumbled the words as the images entered his head. He tried to will them away. There was an eerie calm as the water seemed to become more still and quiet - a chill ran up his spine as he considered the predicament of his immediate situation. Just as the dreadful image of a shark dragging him below flashed in his brain, his eyes picked up the horrifying form as it surfaced less than sixty feet in front of him. Directly in the sight line between Cort and the raft, the dark triangular tip breached the surface. For a brief second, he tried to tell himself that it was a dolphin, but there was no mistaking what he was witnessing. As the fin moved in a horizontal line across twenty-five feet of surface before submarining below, Cort knew those were not the actions of a dolphin. This was the second time in his life he'd made the same revelation - déjà vu of the day on the reef with his mother, 27 years ago, struck him like a lightning bolt.

Frozen in shock and an all-consuming terror, Cort's arms and legs stopped pushing and he grabbed the sides of his life jacket in an effort to make himself smaller. Wide-eyed and in a state of pre-panic, he scanned the surface and peered into the water below him. The raft loomed in the distance, still another 250 feet away, but something deadly swam between him and his only chance at salvation. Attempting to fight the debilitating fear, Cort switched to an optimistic thought.

It could be a small shark, just curiously sizing me up. A small shark wouldn't attack something as big as me.

The notion was enough to generate movement again, and he swam in the direction of the dinghy, consequentially in the direction of the fin. Four seconds later he felt the water move along his right side. A definitive push of pressure in the ocean materialized around his foot, and he knew the shark was swimming in extremely near proximity.

Shit, oh shit!

Turning his back to the raft, he pivoted his body and pushed the water behind him with his arms and legs, loosely mimicking a backstroke, but keeping his head and eyes level with the surface around him.

Nothing. No sign of anything for ten, thirteen, fifteen seconds. Just as Cort began to believe he was alone again, the fin popped up and cut the flat water like a knife, thirty feet away and on the opposite side of where it originally appeared. Several feet behind the dorsal there was another breach of the surface. Most certainly its tail fin. The distance between the two black triangles sent another rush of adrenaline and panic through his veins, as he calculated the fish to be very large.

Pushing harder, he moved away from the shark and in the direction of the raft. Desperately trying to remain calm, he knew the shark could overcome him at any second. There was no chance to outswim it. He glanced toward the raft again, and it seemed a bit closer, but still much too far away for a chance at reaching it first. Shifting his head back again, he searched the surface for movement, all the while bracing himself for impact. His body began to shiver, and he couldn't decide if it was due to low temperature or the intense and all-consuming fear he was suffering. A hypothermic sleep would be so welcomed right now, but that degree of mercy was not an option for him.

Keep swimming, don't stop!

As tears filled his wide eyes, contact was made on his left leg. The feeling of a massive body passing next to him was unmistakable, and the only thing more shocking than the rough sandpapery texture of the shark's skin, was the fact that it didn't bite him. The shark passed by slowly and deliberately, seemingly sizing up its meal and deciding which portion to consume first. Cort surmised the shark was doing just that - examining its prey before striking. It was impossible to know the shark's thoughts, but no other explanation could be formed in his panicked brain. One fact was confirmed without doubt, however, as its mass passed by him methodically. This shark, circling him in the open ocean, was nothing shy of enormous.

Several seconds passed before he felt the current shift underneath him again, the shark passing directly beneath his legs this time. This was it. Cort could sense it; somehow, he knew the shark would attack from below. That's what sharks did. Just like the first victim in Jaws, the skinny-dipping woman - he wouldn't see it coming. He wouldn't know he was being eaten until the teeth closed upon him. He knew it was why a shark attack was one of the most intense terrors a human could fathom, and the fear was crippling him now. Cort took another deep breath, and that's when the image of Celeste entered his brain. She was whispering something to him, so softly that he couldn't make out the words. But when she mouthed it for the third time, he was able to read her lips.

Be still.

In that instant, he decided he would not die in the grips of the paralyzing fear circulating through his body. He closed his eyes, flipped a switch, and accepted what was going to happen. This was his fate, and quite possibly God's plan. He decided it was better to be at peace with it than fight it in terror. This was a battle that simply could not be won. He would listen to Celeste. His arms and legs stopped moving, almost involuntarily, as Cort spoke out loud and made his final offerings.

"Mom and Dad, I didn't think it would be this soon, but I'm looking forward to seeing you. Hey Mom, how ironic is this? Of all the ways to go, right? I could really use that piggy-back right about now, but it'll be okay. I can't wait to go snorkeling with you again."

Pausing for a brief second, he felt the tears leave his cheeks and enter the salty water surrounding him; he smiled, knowing the cycle had been completed and they were returning to the waters from where they originated. The smile disappeared as he spoke to his daughter next.

"Luce," he choked on her name and swallowed a gulp of remorse, "I love you so much, Lucie… more than you'll ever know. Be brave, and be happy. I'm so sorry I'm not there with you now, but I promise someday - I promise I'll be with you again."

He muttered the apology in a low voice with his mouth hovering just above the water. As the words left his lips, a bitter irony struck him. He was floating helplessly in the ocean, about to be engulfed by an extremely large mouth of razor-sharp teeth, all as a result of a Shark Week episode he'd watched with his daughter.

What was it called, Great White Bite? Christ.

Sensing a lack of time to offer much else, he spoke to Celeste, ironically echoing the words he'd uttered to her the very last time they'd talked.

"Celeste, stay where you are. I'll be there soon."

He was certain now the words would also be the last ones to ever leave his lips. Relief pulsed through his veins as he let a large breath of air escape, then laid back into the water. Raising his legs as high as he could without completely submerging his head, he put his arms out to his side. Floating peacefully in the shape of a small letter "t," he closed his eyes, tried to clear his mind of all thoughts, and waited for the strike. A silent prayer was made to a God he wasn't quite sure existed, but solemnly pleaded to anyway in case one just might be listening.

Please God, give me the strength to endure the pain, and take me home. Amen.

***

Seconds passed as she dove to a comfortable depth and the involuntary decision to attack the animal from below was confirmed. Again. There was no longer movement from this smaller, and much more submerged target. A forceful strike would not be necessary. She could bite and eat with less concern for her own safety and the welfare of her unborn. Redirecting her massive form, she made a decisive turn upward and swam directly towards her prey.

Chapter 65 - The Jaws of Death

Cort's mind was almost clear, but the anxiety of the attack could not be totally removed. Violent images of the attack transpiring raced through his mind, and yet the fear of it was mostly subdued. His acceptance had brought an overall feeling of peace and serenity. He waited, almost impatiently now, in an odd sense of anticipation for the contact.

It came.

The sound and feeling that he'd been expecting; a muted swoosh of water followed by the force. Thoughts passed through his brain at lightning-fast speed, as the world conversely decelerated into slow motion. As he'd predicted, there was equal pressure from opposite sides. In that micro-second, his brain processed a myriad of thoughts. The feeling wasn't exactly shocking, but the location of the pressure caught him by surprise. It came along the sides of his torso, just near the top of his rib cage; not on an arm or leg like he'd expected. He closed his eyes tighter, anticipating the excruciating suffering to follow. The fact that there was no pain, however, was not a major revelation. The assumption was made - his prayer was being mercifully answered.

Next, the sensation of being elevated.

I'm being pushed out of the water by the shark's snout, the actual bite hasn't happened yet?

Another split-second passed, and more unexpected sensations. Synapsis fired at light-speed, processing that the pressure he felt was not from a shark. What he presumed to be hands now gripped the sides of his chest, and what felt like wrists lifted from under his armpits.

Eyes opened wide to see a blurry upside-down image of Thad's head against the bright blue sky. This was not a dream, or some after-death experience. It was Thad, in the flesh, with a pained expression of panic on his face. The man who'd threatened his life just minutes ago for the second time, was heaving Cort over the side of the raft. As Cort's body slid upwards and inwards, his legs followed in a frantic flurry of kicks, and not a split-second too soon. The terrorizing image filled his peripheral vision. Cort tilted his head to his chin just in time to see the enormous head of the shark knock into the side of the raft. Her eye rolled back in sync with a flash of the endless white triangular blades against the soft pink of her protruding gums. A frantic scream escaped from Cort's lungs as his lower extremities landed in the raft with a thud. Sitting up in a flash to inspect them, Cort half-expected to see a foot missing. The exasperated relief that washed over him materialized into several heavy breaths followed by uncontrollable sobbing.

"You alright?" The voice from behind him was shaky, but calm.

Cort moved his lips, but he couldn't speak. Ten more seconds passed before he turned his head and wiped his face, trying to gather his voice.

"Yeah. I think…" His voice cracked and he tried again. "I think so. You?"

"Sure." Thad's response was but a loud whisper. "I'm just tired."

"Yeah, me too, just a little bit." Cort forced a sarcastic smile through a sob, and propped himself up a little, eyes on the water and scanning the ocean around the raft.

He paused, gained his composure, then spoke to Thad again.

"Hey man, thank you. That shark was about to eat me."

"Don't mention it, Cort. It wasn't gonna eat you anyway. Just take a bite or two." Thad winced a bit and forced a teethy grin.

"Ha ha ha." Cort's chuckle was slow and forced, carrying relieved exhaustion. "Those would've been some big fucking bites!"

The men laid their heads back and laughed together harmoniously. Cort exhaled a few deep breaths and gathered his thoughts. He was piecing it together now, realizing how the shark had attacked the raft from below, striking the bottom like a rogue submarine, knocking the men upward and outward. Thad had apparently made it back into the raft, spotted Cort, and managed to propel the raft to a last-second rescue. Cort turned his head to the front of the dinghy, locking eyes with his savior. Thad remained silent, partially blanketed by the sail cover, and breathed heavily through his nose. Thad spoke first.

"What do you think, Cort? I saved your life, so maybe we can call it even?"

"Well, you actually tried to kill me twice today," Cort paused, "but technically you saved my life twice too." Another pause as he shook his head incredulously, "Christ, I guess that does mean we're even?"

They laughed again, as Cort turned away to the horizon and pondered how absolutely insane the past few hours of his life had been. The series of events were nearly preposterous, and yet they'd happened, part of both of their histories now.

"Thad," Cort tilted his head and waited for Thad's eye contact. "How the hell did you lift me out of the water like that? I mean, it felt like I was being ripped out of the ocean by some machine!"

Thad gave a little appreciative laugh before answering, "It's all in the legs Cort. It's all in the legs."

Thad's voice trailed off a bit, with some strain in his effort to speak. Cort initially smiled at Thad's answer, but took closer notice of him now, taken aback at how pale his face was. As he processed Thad's sickly appearance, a notion struck Cort's brain, causing him to look down to the floor of the raft. The sail bag that concealed Thad's legs was turning pink and floating in a half inch of crimson-tinted water.

"Oh God, no." Cort knew what he was about to see before he grabbed the sail bag and threw it to the side.

The utter carnage remaining of Thad's lower legs was nothing less than grotesquely nauseating. Where sizable muscles once were, mangled chunks of flesh and skin flailed back and forth in the dark salt water. Both extremities below the knee were shredded, and the remnants of a shattered bone among the bloody meat triggered Cort's gag reflex. Jerking his head to the side, he hurled several ounces of thick liquid down the rounded curve of the rubber hull.

There was brief confusion as Cort processed the butchery. He realized the shark had not crashed into the bottom of their raft. Instead, the shark's target had been the legs protruding over the side. The serrated teeth had penetrated deep into skin, muscle, and bone, pulling Thad down as it violently jerked its two-ton frame back into the water. As Thad's legs were yanked downward, his body became the lever and the side of the raft acted as the fulcrum, combining to make a human catapult. His head was forced skyward into Cort's chin, knocking Cort out in a micro-second and launching his unconscious body eleven feet through the air. At the sight of Thad's legs now, Cort felt faint and nearly lost consciousness again. He breathed deeply and spoke slowly.

"Oh... Jesus... Thad."

Without looking back to the mangled flesh, he wiped the puke away from his mouth and scrambled up the inside of the raft's hull to Thad's head, which had slumped down and was resting against the seat. Cort cradled him under the neck and head, pulling him into his lap to support his upper body.

"It's bad, huh?" Thad's voice was weak now, and his eyes were fading.

A quick head shake was all Cort could manage. No words, just an adjustment to his position while Thad searched upward in the direction of Cort's face. Situating his body with his back to the bloody mess, Cort put the exhibition of violence out of his view, enabling him to see down into Thad's eyes directly.

"Listen, you hear that, Thad?"

It was faint, but distinctive. The distant droning of a helicopter propeller. Cort scanned the sky in the direction of the noise, but there was nothing visible yet. Thad managed a slight nod, and his lips parted for a second, but no words came out. Cort attempted to comfort him.

"It's okay, friend. Everything will be okay. Don't speak, just hold on now. Just hold on."

Staring into Thad's soul for a final time, Cort searched for the right words. He could see his own reflection in Thad's eyes, a reflection of the extreme physical and emotional pain they'd both endured. The past year had changed both of their lives in ways that could not be prepared for - ways that no man should ever have to prepare for. Their separate suffering now oddly bonding them together, and in this moment of closing, Cort felt an unforeseen empathy for Thad St. Marie. While Thad remained silent, Cort sensed the empathy was being returned. No words were found by either of them. Little sound at all could be heard - the world suspended in quiet calm. Cort accepted that nothing he could do or say would change the man's fate, yet his mind searched for a final plea, some offering of peace. He pictured Thad's wife and daughter standing on the dock and waving good-bye.

"Amelia and Gracie - they're waiting for you, Thad. You can go to them now. You can go home."

Thad's mouth shifted slightly into a soft grin, then the light in his eyes faded to a lifeless stare. Cort raised his head and searched the horizon, unable to hold back tears. He let them fall freely and pondered how he'd manage to move forward from here. An unexpected wave of remorse washed over him as he said a silent good-bye to the deceased man in his lap. The static hum of a helicopter grew stronger, scattering thoughts through Cort's brain, filling it with uncertainty about what the future held. Pushing the negativity away, he focused on his own daughter and planted an image of Lucie firmly in his mind. It was only in that instant of Thad's passing that Cort fully accepted his future – that his and Lucie's life would move forward.

***

She'd reluctantly fallen asleep, waking hours later to the bright sunlight on her face. Shifting her head to avoid the direct beam passing through the basement window, Lucie looked back at the television. The satellite image now showed the circling clouds breaking apart as they made landfall in South Carolina. She smiled, not so much because the hurricane was fading, but because an intense feeling washed through her brain like a wave, leaving a calm trail of peaceful foam behind it. In her mind, she could see her dad, standing on a large boat, safe and warm. She pushed the power button on the remote, leaving her in the silence of the morning. Sliding a couple feet to her left, she repositioned herself on the sofa allowing the beam of sun to shine on her face again. Lucie closed her eyes and heard a soft familiar voice whisper in her ear, saying the only three words she needed to hear.

"*He's coming home.*"

Chapter 66 - Solace

Two men in Coast Guard uniforms assisted Cort as he stepped up a metal ladder and crested the side of the 130 foot-long-ship, a stark-white cutter sporting dark orange diagonal stripes. The blanket around his shoulders offered a degree of comfort as the men escorted him through a door, down some steps, and into a corridor leading to the medical bay. One of the men explained that they'd x-ray his mid-section first. Assuming the scan didn't show any internal bleeding, he could forgo the chopper and stay aboard until they reach Charleston. They'd stitch up his finger and torso, and maybe put a few in his neck too. After that, the man instructed, Cort would be interviewed by one of the officers. They'd need his statement as soon as possible. Cort nodded at their instructions but was still in a state of disbelief, his brain fogged by shock as he silently recounted the events of the past day. The facts were still extremely troubling to him, and yet a mixed sense of compassion clouded his feelings about his ex-companions.

As they led him down the corridor, Cort noted a painted sign on the door to his left labeled Fitness Room. The next door had a window in it, and he read the word 'Lounge' as he glanced beyond the letters and through the glass. His peripheral vision caught her form, a lady sitting in a heap at the end of a sofa. She was wrapped in a blanket like the one around his own shoulders, and she was holding a cup of steaming liquid. Her face was pointed at the floor and hard to see, but the hair was immediately recognizable.

"Marilyn!"

Cort shouted and knocked hard on the glass. The man in front turned around and hesitated a second before speaking.

"Sir?"

Cort had already started opening the door as his eyes met Marilyn's, her face showing a sign of life; the cloud of despair momentarily dissipating from her expression.

"Sir, Mr. Palmerton, I have instructions to get you immediate medical attention, then hold you in solitude until we're able to conduct an interview. Please follow me."

"Jesus Christ, man," Cort glared back at the uniformed man, "I thought she was dead! Let me just see her for a second."

The two men turned to each other and made eye-contact without speaking. The one in front nodded at Cort with a hint of apology.

"Make it fast, you have one minute."

Cort rushed through the door to her as Marilyn stood up and reached out both arms. They embraced in a firm hug, her head buried into his chest and shoulder. The relief was brief, as the final events aboard Sea Sleigh passed through his mind. He was certain her thoughts were of those same events. Three short seconds passed before Marilyn let go and took a step backwards, her sullen eyes connecting with his again.

"My son? Where's Thad?"

He swallowed hard, looking away as his eyes became glossy with compassionate sorrow. The last scene from Jaws raced through his mind; Hooper emerging from the depths and asking Chief Brody about their companion's fate.

"Quint?"

Shaking his head slowly to the left, then back to the right, Cort lowered his eyes and searched his mind for a way to explain what had happened; a way to tell her that despite what she witnessed in those final minutes before their boat capsized, her son had saved his life and died nobly. He glanced behind, to the Coast Guard officer who was glaring impatiently through the window. The man made a hand gesture, waving Cort out of the room. Cort nodded and raised a finger, indicating that he'd be out very soon.

Turning back to the woman whose son had passed away in his arms less than thirty minutes ago, Cort met her gaze and fought back another wave of sadness. The shadow in her eyes and the lines surrounding them were reflections of her life, reflections of this moment; the suffering they held was deep. Cort held her more firmly, sensing she might collapse to the floor. Before he could speak, her eyes dropped as the realization hit her. She knew by his expression her son was no longer alive, and she could not watch his lips say the words. Mercifully, Cort knew he did not have to utter them.

"Marilyn. Look at me, Marilyn."

She reluctantly raised her head, the shame and regret in her eyes nearly overshadowing her sorrow.

"I can't tell you everything right now, but Thad saved my life, and I'm going to save his legacy. When they question you," Cort continued, "the only thing you remember from last night is going down below to sleep after your watch, then waking up as the boat was flipping. You scrambled, did whatever you did to escape, but you never saw any sign of us until I walked in here a few minutes ago. You got it?"

She hesitated at first, confused for a second as she processed his instructions. Her eyes widened as the intentions became clear; she nodded in confirmation then glanced to the man in uniform who was pushing through the lounge door.

Cort hugged Marilyn again. Somehow through all the horrifying events, and nearly perishing three times in the past 12 hours, he was alive. The sheer irony that his life was saved twice by Thad and once by Marilyn hit him now. That reality would not change regardless of any ill-will he harbored, and Cort accepted that he could not alter what had transpired. Thad had died, and that was punishment enough for him and his family. It was impossible to undo the fatalistic experience they'd all been through, but Cort now held the power to help affect a positive future. There were but a few seconds for Cort to confirm what he planned to do. Holding Marilyn's shoulders, he pushed away just enough so he could look into her eyes, and Cort offered one last consulate measure of solace.

"Marilyn. I'm sorry your son didn't make it, but I promise you that Gracie will."

Epilogue (Day 851)

The light patter of raindrops on the umbrella were inconsistent, as if the clouds couldn't make up their minds about how much water to release. He leaned forward and stooped down. She pecked a kiss onto his scruffy cheek, and he watched her walk to the bus with no regard for the falling droplets. He grinned to himself, relieved she didn't care about the effect of the water on her hair, and he wondered how much longer it would be the case. She turned and offered an abbreviated wave before moving to help the girl in front of her. The assistance wasn't necessary anymore, but out of habit, Lucie kept her hand just below the shoulders of the smaller girl as the first two steps upward were taken.

A slight breeze chilled the skin on his arm, combatted by a tepid sense of anticipation in his veins; his body and mind were warmed by the energy of what this last day of school symbolized. The breeze moved the tree limb high above, pushing extra drops from the leaves into a freefall dive to the green nylon fabric below. The sound of the increased patter frequency took his thoughts to the past, and he was reminded of the sound that small waves make against inflated rubber.

So much had happened since that day, nearly two years ago. His medical needs had been minor, consisting of little more than some stitching and antibiotics; those injuries now only afterthoughts with scarcely noticeable scars as reminders. Her doctor visits, on the other hand, had been frequent and invasive, involving multiple surgeries and various other treatment regiments. They were most certainly working, and he was reminded of their success as she climbed the bus steps with little issue. Her progress was an echo of the music in his head, one song in particular playing as she climbed each step. Cort heard the piano and violins in the background of his thoughts, the volume and tempo elevating as she reached the top step and turned towards the back of the bus. Ironically, the song playing in his mind was called *Gracie's Theme*, and it was one of his new favorites. He smiled at the thought and was thankful the music - that all music - had returned to his life.

For the mental scars, there'd been several more trips to group therapy, which he'd attended once a month for nearly a year. Josh and Shay were often part of those sessions, and they proved to be healthy for more reasons than one. A friendship had evolved like none Cort had ever had, and promises were made to remain in touch with the Leonards. Plans were set for Josh, Shay, and their three boys to visit them in the Southern Caribbean islands – their rendezvous point would be Trinidad.

In those first few months after Cort's rescue, there'd been nightmares. Each one replayed clips from his encounter with the shark he'd undoubtedly determined was a Great White. The horrific dreams included the garish carnage that had ended Thad's existence, and they haunted his sleep regularly. Cort talked about the dreams in therapy but voicing the disturbing night terrors only offered a marginal degree of comfort. Unfortunately, and not surprisingly, the other members couldn't relate. One morning, after an especially disturbing night of bad dreams, Cort recalled something Lucie had mentioned months earlier, and decided to approach his fear more scientifically. He began researching Carcharodon Carcharias, with the hope of finding some rational answers. Something interesting was uncovered in his investigation; facts that offered an explanation as to why a cold-water species of shark had been hunting in the warmer currents off the Carolina coast. The most likely reason was that the shark was pregnant and had migrated south to give birth. While Cort could never be completely sure, he decided to accept the logical rationale, and it gave him comfort. From that point forward, he methodically pushed away the notion of the shark being a blood thirsty killer, enabling his nightmares to transition.

Over time, his perception morphed, and he saw the Great White in his dreams as a beautiful fish and mother-to-be, acting instinctively to ensure the health of her unborn.

Equipped with his newfound knowledge and even greater compassion for sharks, Cort searched and made contact with the South-African couple from the Shark Week episode. The owners of the sailboat, "Bite Me," were thrilled to learn of the American man's interest in their research, and grateful for the very generous donation Mr. Palmerton had made to further their efforts. They agreed to stay in touch, and loose plans were made for a visit. When the time came, they'd meet in person and spend time sailing the waters along the South African coast together. While the meeting wouldn't likely happen for a couple years, Cort and Lucie were already anticipating some White shark sightings. Lucie also had a different sense about the future encounter, which she shared with her father. There was something oddly exciting about the prospect of meeting the couple's son, who she'd remembered from when they'd watched *Great White Bite* on TV. She admitted to Cort that the boy was most definitely cute.

Forgiveness. One of the residual benefits of those group therapy sessions was coming to terms with his own guilt, accepting he was not at fault for Celeste's death. Furthermore, Cort had searched deep within his soul and ultimately forgiven Aaron, the Bravo Transport truck driver who most certainly was at fault. In a move Cort struggled with for months, he decided to let Aaron know it directly. On a sunny afternoon in late-April, as the tree buds forged a final push through their scales, Cort made the ninety-five-minute drive north on I-79 to the Erie County Prison. After completing two forms and satisfying all security measures, he was guided to a small, non-descript cubicle. Sitting in a hard plastic chair, he waited on one side of a glass wall, noting the faint smell of bleach and laundry detergent that added to the sterility of the room. When the prisoner arrived in his beige jumpsuit, the recognition in his eyes was apparent. Aaron had looked at Cort several times during the trial - the expression of despair and hate he'd seen in Cort's eyes was simply unforgettable. Accepting that the man whose wife he'd involuntarily killed was indeed sitting across from him, Aaron's expression turned to confusion. Cort picked up the phone receiver on the wall. Reluctantly, Aaron did the same and brought it to his ear.

"Aaron?"

"Y-Y-Yeah. I'm... Aaron." The prisoner's reply was hesitantly slow.

Cort offered a brief but genuine smile before speaking,

"I just came here to say, um, to tell you... I forgive you."

Cort hung up the phone promptly, leaving the prisoner sitting on the other side of the window even more perplexed. That was the end of the visit, and Cort walked out of the room. Within the chain-link and barbed wire fencing, Cort left behind a wrath that had been plaguing his heart for much too long.

A few weeks after visiting the prison, Cort and Lucie packed up and left the bubble of the Pittsburgh suburb. Cort had ended his career amicably with ComStart, just twenty days after the Coast Guard's rescue, and his company even threw a small retirement dinner honoring his sixteen years of dedicated service. The 12" x 8" plaque of dark stained wood and a metallic engraved plate was nice; he looked at it exactly twice before placing it neatly in a storage container.

They'd settled into the seaside community after a few months. Because the move was mostly Lucie's idea, it was much easier to pick up and relocate. Their new home was only meant to be temporary shelter anyway, and now, thirteen months later, the house was under contract with a new buyer. After closing, they'd put the bulk of their belongings into storage, and move onto the boat. Lucie adapted to the new school and made friends easily, like he'd known she would. Her traditional education gradually shifted to a hybrid of in-class and cyber, providing a convenient opportunity to complete much of her work online. Going forward, she'd take classes entirely via the cyber-program for at least the next couple of years, maybe longer; their travel plans were open-ended.

The boat purchase had been a relatively smooth transaction. She was a catamaran very similar to *Sea Sleigh*, and there was barely any negotiation in the purchase. Cort offered full asking price and waived an inspection. The seller agreed within twenty minutes of the offer. The only change the Palmerton's decided to make was the boat's name, and the decision was easy. The suggestion was made by Lucie and they both agreed it was perfect. The chosen name reflected both an important page from their past *and* their outlook on the future. A local artist was hired to paint it across the stern, and Cort smiled every time he read the words 'Life Boat.'

Sailing lessons were much more fun and productive this time. His inner ear adapted fast, and Lucie's own nausea subsided steadily through each of the first three outings. By their fifth time out in the sound, she was no longer getting queasy. Most days school finished by 1:00, and they'd spent many a weekday afternoon motoring around the bay and hoisting sails when the wind beckoned. Guided by an excellent teacher, their yachting skills were acquired over several weeks of practice. The best part for Cort was that the instructor hadn't attempted to kill him, not even once, during any of the lessons.

Writing had also become *a thing*. Cort never imagined that penning a novel was in the realm, and yet he'd loosely inked more than 150 pages. It started with recording his thoughts and emotions about all that had happened since Celeste's accident, randomly scribbled into a spiral notebook. Eventually, those thoughts turned into tangible sentences and paragraphs. A year later they'd evolved into pages in a word document, and even a few organized chapters. He kept a short list of possible titles in the Notes app on his phone. The favorite so far was the same name they'd given to the new catamaran. Despite the inability to consider himself an author, which he'd learned was known as *imposter syndrome*, he believed there was a book waiting to be shared in his future. Regardless, he found the writing to be therapeutic and continued to do it more for the catharsis than anything else. There was much left to write, including an ending that was still coming together.

His relationship with Marilyn continued to get stronger with each passing month. Their bond developed unexpectedly, but quite organically. She helped fill a missing role in Cort's life that had been empty since his mother passed away. Conversely, Cortland Palmerton became a welcomed surrogate for the sons she'd lost.

As Cort watched the bus pull away, he reflected on the past couple of years. Tilting the umbrella back slightly to get a view of the sky, he could see a beam of sunlight in the distance, breaking through the dark clouds - the bad weather was dissipating. Smiling upwards, he said a silent thank you. Just then, a fleeting gust of wind caught the underside of his umbrella. His hand tightened around the J-shaped handle, tugging back against the brief bluster. The soft fingers that held his other hand squeezed a little tighter and pulled in the opposite direction of the wind. The additional bracing was hardly needed, but Cort appreciated the gesture.

"Thanks for hanging on to me." He turned and grinned at the owner of the supportive hand.

"Get used to it." She turned to meet his eyes and returned a smile so radiant that he could nearly feel its warmth on his face.

They laughed together, and he kept his stare affixed on her eyes. They were beautiful, and full of energy. The lines around them were still present, but they'd changed somehow. The tiny marks of pain and loss were suppressed, replaced with new lines of hope and happiness. They told of a renewed soul, filled with wonder and excitement for what the future held. And above all, they told a story of a newly found love. One that could not have been predicted by her, and certainly not one he'd ever imagined would be possible.

As he smiled and turned away, Cort wondered if she might be able to detect that same deep sentiment in his eyes. Whether she could or not, the emotions were there, and he silently vowed to love her without hesitation. He undoubtedly knew Celeste would want it that way, both for him and for Lucie. She'd have told him with a gentle touch and a soft comfort in her voice... *life goes on.*

Acknowledgments

This book is the result of so many efforts besides my own, and I'm eternally grateful for the assistance from so many people.

To all my friends and family members, who've influenced my mind over the past 50 years, thank you for your inspiration. Your personalities are embedded into the characters that I create. If you caught your name in this book, or a glimpse of your own traits in one of these characters, it's probably not by accident.

Special thanks to friend and fellow author, Andrea Couture, who was an integral and instrumental part of the editing process. This story is undoubtedly better because of her valuable insights and recommendations, and her contributions are greatly appreciated.

To A.Vogel, another major contributor to the editing of the initial drafts. Your professional expertise was an invaluable resource, and an influential component in this book's final version. I'm grateful for all your help.

Much thanks, Mom, for always supporting my writing, and for your editing efforts. Your proficiency in grammar and spelling, overall grasp of the English language, and general knowledge of what makes a book better, were most beneficial to me in my toils.

Appreciation to Micah Campbell, and Anatolian Press. I'm excited to be part of this publishing company, and an extremely grateful new member of the AP Family.

To my ARC readers, who donated their time, resources, and recommendations to me - thank you E.J., Valerie, Andrea, Kristina, Debbie, Marcy, and everyone else, for your feedback. Your input was greatly valued and most helpful.

Gratitude to Alix Klingenberg, for the use of your beautiful poem. Such fitting words to introduce this story. Thank you, Alix, for writing them.

To Sadie Butterworth-Jones, your cover design work is fantastic, and I appreciate your work in bringing the story to life with an image. Thank you.

To former PA State Trooper, Corporal O. Leonard, and Cranberry Township police officer, Josh S. - your contributions in police work provided authenticity to a subject that was critical to the storyline. Thank you both so much for your time and knowledge sharing. Sincerely, I appreciate it, and acknowledge the critically important work performed by officers of the law.

A note of gratitude to FBI agent, Mike, thank you for letting me pick your brain.

Thank you to John, the Butler County Deputy Coroner. I found our conversation about autopsies most interesting and very helpful.

Sincere and heartfelt thanks to Chad and Sarah, my shipmates aboard the real Sea Sleigh. I cannot overstate how much your patience and compassion meant to me during our four days at sea. Cheers, my friends! I know I apologized a hundred times for my unfortunate condition on board, but I'll mention it one more time for the record - I'm sorry to both of you, and to your salad bowl.

Last, but not least, I want to acknowledge you, my reader. I'm grateful that you've spent some of your 41,785,200 (on average) minutes of life to check out my work. I hope you enjoyed it, but even if you didn't, I sincerely appreciate you reading Life Boat. Thank you!

Author's Notes:

In the year before I published this book, there were 72 unprovoked shark attacks on humans, with 9 of them being fatal. Conversely, humans kill roughly 10,000,000 sharks each year. As much as authors hate typos, I so wish that number was an error. Unfortunately, the number is indeed a one with seven zeros after it. I hope that sentence is a profoundly sad one to read, and those statistics are equally as upsetting to you as they are to me. If I could speak directly to the sharks of the world, I'd tell them something like this:

While I understand the reasons why many of us humans are afraid of you, I simply cannot grasp why some of us treat you the way we do. Please understand that we're flawed in our mindset, brainwashed over the decades by movies and media. I do like to believe, however, that we're coming around as a species, getting educated by dedicated professionals who are teaching us how truly amazing you all are, and what an integral part in our ecosystem you play. On behalf of some of the human population, I want to sincerely apologize to all of you. I'd also like you sharks to know that a portion of the sales of this book will be donated to an organization dedicated to saving the oceans and sea-life through conservation and education.

Much of the story line in Life Boat relates to feelings of fear, grief, loss, and suicidal thoughts - all extremely sensitive and important emotions, born from causes that are numerous and complicated. I'm certainly not a mental healthcare professional and would never dare delve into the causes and cures for those feelings. I will, however, attempt to add a tiny bit of perspective to life with some basic math. At the time this book was being written, the average life expectancy of a male was 78 years, and for a female it was 81 years. For arguments sake, let's take the average of both, and say the life expectancy of a human is 79 ½ years old. That means on average, a human will live for 41,785,200 minutes. To be fair, let's eliminate 1,576,800 of those minutes, because most of us don't remember much from those first three years of life. That still leaves 40,208,400 influential minutes of life - quite a few. Now, consider that in each of those minutes, there is the potential for a human to experience greatness, joy, ecstasy, pure elation - something so positive that it changes a person's future for the better, and becomes a time in their life they'll remember until they take their last breath. Of course, there's a flip side to the math, because each of those 40,208,400 minutes holds the potential for something devastating. An event so traumatic, so damaging and hurtful, that it's engrained in a person's mind and soul forever.

Something I can state with extremely high statistical confidence – if we live for even half of the average life expectancy, we'll experience both ends of that spectrum, multiple times. My hope, for everyone, is to be able to focus on and build upon those positive experiences while minimizing the effect of those negative ones. I also hope, no matter what, the conclusion is made that the highs are worth the lows. I say this realizing it's much easier said than done, and admittedly, the negative moments can be consuming at times. I understand how the cumulative effect of such negative events might create a sense of despair, or even cause someone to question whether life is worth the struggle. I've been there, and I believe all people will experience deep sadness in their lifetime. Part of my goal in writing the storyline of this book was simply to serve as a reminder to us all that help is available for those dark times in our lives. That help comes in different forms. For some of us, it's a person, a friend or family member - somebody who loves us unconditionally and will always be there for support. Or maybe it's a mental health professional who can help guide our minds through the darkness and into the light. Sometimes it's not a person, but an animal providing that love and positive reinforcement. Others may find solace in their faith in a higher being. And for others still, it could be something as simple as music, a special place, or some inanimate object that brings one peace and healing.

Whatever that person or place or thing (let's call it a *lifeboat*) might be, I strongly recommend we hold on to it with both hands. Nurture that lifeboat, be kind to it, and never take it for granted. Furthermore, I recommend having more than one, a back-up so to speak, because our lifeboats may not always be available. They pass on, move away, or simply cease to exist. Redundancy is a good thing here, because when it comes to support, we can never have enough. I further hope the story of Life Boat might offer just a small slice of inspiration to a reader who might be struggling, or at the very least, put life into some relative context. 40,208,400 memorable minutes might seem like a lot, but trust me, they go by fast. Those minutes, both the good and bad ones, should be embraced and cherished - each one is part of who we are. Regardless of your belief in how we were created, it's a fact that no single person on this earth is exactly like us. Not now, not in the past, and not in the future. Each of us is a uniquely special human being, literally one of a kind, and this life that we're experiencing right now is the only chance we'll have to live it. I sincerely hope you'll hang on to yours tooth and nail, and never give up the fight, no matter how difficult it might get.

Many wonderful organizations exist that specialize in mental health, with 24-hour crisis lifelines. The dedicated people running and working for these organizations are trained to serve as lifeboats. They can help us navigate through the storm of troubled waters and guide us safely to shore. A portion of the sales from this book will be donated to one or more such organizations.

Thank you, for reading *Life Boat* by Luke Eckley.

I truly hope you enjoyed it and that it left you with the same sense of awe and satisfaction that it did me the first time I read it.

Sincerely,
Micah, Anatolian Press

If you did enjoy this book, please consider leaving a review on Amazon.

This is an exciting time for all of us here at Anatolian Press. We have an incredible team of authors, and I am made better every day by knowing them.

Here's what we have coming up!

The Life of Billy Blaine by RS Hamilton
The Summertime Circus by SL Dooley
The Psychotic Son by Deborah Dobbs

Please visit www.anatolianpressllc.com and follow Anatolian Press and Luke Eckley on Instagram @anatolian_press and @author.lreckley

Made in the USA
Middletown, DE
23 May 2023

30929883R00241